My Wingman

My Wingman
Tessa King

First Edition

ISBN:
9798998716812(hardcover)
9798998716805(paperback)
9798218648916(ebook)

Published by Tessa King
www.tessa-king.com

Dedication

To Kenny, my partner in crime – thank you for making me laugh and supporting me even on the tough days. Your love is the sunshine that chases away my clouds.

To my incredible family and friends who are always there for me. You are the greatest cheerleaders.

And to anyone out there battling an invisible war, know you are not alone. Keep fighting for every good day. May this book be a reminder that laughter, hope, and a good dose of sarcasm can conquer even the toughest battles.

Do not neglect to show
hospitality to strangers,
for thereby some have entertained
angels unawares.

Hebrews 13:2

Contents

PROLOGUE

NOW

Sitting on this bench next to me is my oldest companion, Grief. He has been with me for as long as I can remember, a constant presence throughout many phases of my life. Just as I change and mature, he ages and stiffens over time. During this visit, Grief has excelled into the grumpy old man version, crabby and downright rotten, quickly wearing out his welcome. Unfortunately, he is my only current travel companion. Perhaps this journey will find me more.

CHAPTER 1

THEN

IT WAS A BRISK fall morning, and the Spanish moss was blowing gently in the wind. I was just a child. I broke away from the small gathering and wandered off on my own. My grandmother, Lily, was still giving hugs to people at my grandfather's gravesite, but I needed to get away for a minute. I didn't like seeing her that way. I knew too well what it was like to feel that way, to feel that lonely. I couldn't let that darkness consume any more of me. I was already turning into a shell of a person.

I stopped in front of a monument of a young angel. She stared down at the reflection pool held in her arms in the form of a shell. I stood there thinking, what was she looking for? She seemed so sad. For a split second, I imagined, or at least I think I imagined, she looked up at me. Directly at me. First, I felt shock, and gradually a sense of peace overwhelmed me. The wind had stilled, and as she looked back down, the water calmed. Something changed in her expression; I knew she found her reflection, herself. She had been lost. When I think back, I wonder if I somehow helped her find herself. Or was it this sullen angel who was helping me?

I stood there in awe for several moments until my grandmother caught up to me. She grabbed my hand in hers, it was so soft, warm, and she squeezed lightly. "I see you found an angel, my dear Clover. " Isn't she a spectacular thing?" she whispered, gazing off at the angel and then back at me. "You will find many angels throughout

1

your life. Each one there to guide you."

Grandma Lily took her thumbs and gently brushed both of my cheeks. Her hands almost looked like the wings of an angel in her movement. "You know you have been visited by many…. why, look at all those angel kisses!" I thought of those words often through the years, when mean kids called me "freckle face," as I tried unsuccessfully to lighten them with lemon juice and attempted to find the perfect foundation to cover them. With time, I grew to embrace my freckles and her words. I also often thought back to when the angel found herself in the reflection of the calm water.

It had always been Grandma and me growing up, and for a few of my early years, my Aunt Ruby until she moved out. My mom died from complications of my delivery, and I had no siblings. No one knew who my father was, and he either had no idea of my existence or chose to act as such. I had experienced a lot of emotional turmoil all through my younger years, and my grandfather's passing just added to it.

Grandma and Ruby were always the strong ones. It seemed they had a superpower to help them deal with loss. Even through my teen years, I never felt strong like that. The only power I had to escape all the sadness was to leave. So when I made plans for college, I was grateful I would be moving from my home in Savannah to Chicago to start my studies. It was a chance for a new start, and hopefully a place I could finally heal.

★★★

When I first moved to Chicago, everything was new. I knew absolutely no one. But then I found Reese. She and I met at a local music festival. It was an extremely hot and humid August evening. I hadn't finished unpacking but heard the bass notes through my open window. I decided to go see what the music was all about and maybe find some breeze to cool me down. The block party was fairly empty, likely due to the heat index. There was only one individual brave enough to be dancing in that heat, Reese.

Everything about her screamed free spirit – her wild, spiky hair, bohemian style choices, even the shockingly bright blue scooter she drove around town (which matched her hair color at times).

She danced like she had no care in the world, arms waving all around her, and her tie-dye skirt moving in sync with her body. Wow, this woman had passion in the way she moved; energy just radiated from her. As the band took a well-deserved break, she walked to the bar tent and rested in a chair next to me.

She turned and held out her hand, "Hey, how's it going? I'm Reese."

"Hi, Reese." I shook her hand, noticing the lovely spoon ring wrapped around her index finger. "I'm Clover; it's nice to meet you."

"Clover, huh? That's a cool name. I have always hated mine; it's so fancy and formal-sounding. You dig the band? I've heard them a few times before and had to check them out again. Unfortunately, their hot guitar player isn't here tonight. This lame-o is filling in." She shook her thumb at the young man seated a few tables away. He seemed handsome enough to me. "What brings you out?"

"I just moved here from Savannah, been unpacking all day. I heard the music playing from my place up the street and convinced myself I had done enough for today, so I walked down."

Reese grinned. "Well, Clover from Savannah. I'm glad you ventured out this evening. I need another brave soul to dance with, and it sounds like you need to break loose."

It didn't matter what I said. She would take no raincheck on the adventure for the evening. Soon after, the two of us were enjoying the band's next set. We danced, flirted with a few guys (to buy us drinks), laughed, and by the end of the evening, I had officially made a new friend in my new city. I had also gained a hangover from hell.

Reese offered to show me around the neighborhood the next afternoon if I promised to join the yoga class she taught twice a week. Yoga would be a new experience and a chance to meet more people. I agreed.

Saying Reese's class was a challenge was an understatement, regardless of the hangover. Perhaps I imagined her saying it was a beginner's class. It was surely not for the yoga novice. She was so nimble and made it look easy.

As I attended that morning, my mind wandered, and I felt lost, tired, and frustrated; coincidentally, that accurately explained my transition from Savannah to my new life at school. Reese promised she would help me adjust, grow to appreciate yoga, and remind me to find my breath and enjoy what life handed me. Through these past few years, she has never let me down. Not once.

I never met anyone like her and never had the pleasure of having a bestie before. I had "friends" throughout my childhood, but no one I truly trusted or that I let in. I managed to lay low, kept my head in the books. It was easier that way, I didn't have to get too close. For some reason, though, I couldn't help but like Reese. A year after moving to the Windy City, she and I decided to be roomies and found a small place to rent together.

Reese's family was wealthy. Like *WEALTHY.* Although she and her mother did not see eye-to-eye on many things, they supported her financially as long as she continued working on her degree. Reese was not the studious type, choosing psych as her major so she could finish her bogus degree and get on with life, as she said. Although she had no idea what she wanted to do after graduating, she knew it had nothing to do with psychology. She did decent in her studies, taught a few yoga classes, and welcomed the substantial monthly check from her family.

I, on the other hand, did not have a stream of income from family. My Grandma Lily raised me. She worked so hard to barely get by. I always knew that if I was going to be successful in life, I would have to do the same and work even harder. Thus far my hard work paid off, as I was accepted into my program of choice, received a partial scholarship, and was studying pre-med. Once enrolled in classes, I also found a part-time job working nights as a lab assistant.

Reese would have loved a more spacious and modern apartment, but she respectfully agreed to find something that I could afford. I insisted on paying equal halves of our bills, even though her family could pay for the entirety. After some searching, we finally found a quaint two-bedroom near campus above a coffee house. That was the selling point for Reese. I remember her reasons to sign the rental agreement.

"Think about it," she encouraged. "We will save on coffee-scented candles because the building will always smell amazing. We will always be steps away from our next caffeine fix. Most importantly, we can totally watch all the hot guys going in and out from our window. It's absolutely perfect!"

I laughed. "I guess I was sold on the in-unit laundry, newer appliances, warm ambience, and the fact that it was well under budget. But, indeed, my friend, you make very vital points."

We signed the lease and moved in the following week.

***

Many months passed. Life was getting bigger quickly. I began to meet more people, and I did my best to open myself up a bit. Reese and I had a great time, and our friendship was more like sisterhood. Our apartment had started to earn that comfortable feeling of home.

It had been over a year since I felt that at ease. Actually, it had been that long since I made it back to Savannah. Between work, school, and having a limited budget, there was little chance for a visit to see Grandma Lily. I felt guilty about leaving her there alone. We spoke at least once a week; she failed to convince me she wasn't lonely.

One afternoon at the apartment I was daydreaming for a lengthy but unknown amount of time, thinking back to my childhood. I gave up studying, the words were all blending together.

Sitting upside down on the couch, feet up the back cushion, head hanging off the edge, I called my grandmother to check in. I bored her with my day-to-day mumbo jumbo, updates on school, the weather. I was hoping to avoid the love-life inquisition. It worked for a beat, but she interjected with her usual questioning. Without letting myself sound excited or hopeful, I spilled the beans and told her about a young man who recently asked me out.

She sighed as I explained my uncertainty in agreeing to the date. "Clover, you must put yourself out there at some point. It cannot hurt you to try. It will hurt more if you stay forever guarded. Just think about that, trust your judgment and be safe." Why couldn't she tell me to forget it, that it was useless, and to save myself the troubles.

I heeded her advice, agreeing to a coffee after a Friday night shift with my coworker Smith. I had Reese on speed dial for emergency purposes, but I made it through, surprisingly. I mean, it was just coffee. Smith and I had a lot in common. We were both in school studying the sciences, and he had also moved here from the South. We had similar taste in music – well he claimed to enjoy all music. Kind of sounded too agreeable, forced, if I'm honest. I did not let my guard down easily, but admit I was comfortable enough around him. The evening was pleasant. Smith seemed sweet, was very attentive, and did not hold back his charming demeanor which he had certainly learned growing up down south.

Even though the following weeks were extremely busy, I updated my grandmother on my studies, my new developing relationship with Smith, all which made her happy to hear.

In several conversations she called me Sloane, my mother's name, without catching herself. It was odd, as she had never done that before. Maybe the experiences I had described to her, about school and dating, especially at this age, had her thinking of my mother. I never thought about how difficult some of this could be for her. I took note to see if the trend continued.

A lot of time passed with Reese and I on different schedules, but we shared yoga time twice a week. Besides brief chats over morning coffee, weeks went by where yoga was the only guaranteed time we could count on. I never broke my promise to her and continued to attend routinely. It had started to become more natural to me, and I looked forward to that downtime each week, time to reflect and take care of myself.

Calm the waters, you could say.

It also helped that Reese and I always hung out for a while after class. We kept with tradition since the first weekend we met.

On a Saturday after yoga, I asked Smith to join us so that Reese could be formally introduced. She was starting to hassle me that I had a serious boyfriend for months, but still never allowed her a chance to properly screen him.

I did my best to convince him we could all go out together, to no avail. He said he was unable to attend, a friend from back home was in town so he was entertaining. Reese and I went ahead to a new, local music hotspot without him.

It was quite crowded but still had a relaxed vibe. High tables with dim overhead lights were scattered. Reese was inspired by the larger dancefloor directly in front of the corner stage. When we walked in, she quickly set our things down at a table up front. It was almost too close to the stage fog machine for my liking, but I was grateful the speakers were hanging overhead and were not in our faces.

Her older sister's ID enabled us to obtain a couple of beers from the retro looking bar. I had a fake but was always too scared to use it.

We intently watched as the band set up. As I glanced around, I was excited to see Smith walking through the crowd. His dirty blonde hair was still wet from a shower, his dark brown eyes scanning the packed house for a place to sit. Perfect! Maybe he and his friend could still hang out with us.

As his eyes peered over to a table up front, I grinned and waved at him. I truly had no idea Reese had this place in mind, and was unaware of his plans for the evening. I started to think this must be some kind of sign, us meeting up like this, but tucked the idea away.

Then as he turned toward me, I knew I had been discovered. He responded with a half-smile and immediately registered a look of ... disappointment? Damn, he probably wanted a night to hang out with his buddy.

I walked up to him, "Hey, crazy we all ended up here, huh? Do you and your friend want to join us? We have a great table."

He grabbed my arm and led me toward the table, "Yeah, crazy. Look, we nee-"

Just then, a gorgeous blonde with flawless waves in her hair and bright red lipstick stepped in. "Smithy, did you find us a seat?"

"Well, *Smithy*, who is this?" I said with my voice shaking, glaring at him.

"I'm Rachel, his girlfriend" she giggled. "I flew in this afternoon to see him." She pinched his cheek as if he were a young boy. I was immensely annoyed. "You must be his friend Clover. I can tell by your hair and freckles – he, um, mentioned those to me." Insert freaking obnoxious fake laugh. "He says you guys have a fun time at work."

"Uh, Clover.... This is Rachel," he added.

"This is perfect," I awkwardly looked around to find anything to stare at without looking like an emotional idiot. "I hope you have a great time visiting. You can have our table, my friend and I were just leaving."

"The fuck we are!" Reese barged in between us, her back to them. "We have a great table, are going to watch an awesome band and dance our gorgeous asses off. Nevermind this asshole. They can *leave* or find their own damn table. Emphasis on the former, if you can't take the hint." She glanced back at Smith and Barbie-girl. If looks could kill, he would've been on the floor.

Smith looked back and forth between Rachel and me for a minute, and eventually found his voice. "Look, Clover, I'm sorry about this. We'll leave. We can talk later, I'll explain."

"No need dickhead. I think you are all done here," Reese chimed in. "Come on girl, let's go dance." She grabbed my arm, pulled me the opposite direction toward the floor. Smith and his blonde made their way to the closest exit.

"I cannot believe this! What the hell just happened?"

"Clover, he wasn't that important...if he was, you would have introduced me sooner. Fun for a few months...but girl. Not. The. One." She shook her head back and forth at me.

"It was too soon to tell. What if he wa-----"

"Stop it right there! The band is starting, so let's dance. And check out their hottie guitar player. Best way to move on is to, well.... Move on."

"Is that fancy PSYCH 101 advice?"

"No clue, you think I pay attention to that crap? Seriously?" Then she pulled me into the dance floor, front and center.

Dance we did. All night.

And she was absolutely right about the guy on guitar. He was gorgeous. Jaw-dropping. He sat on a round wooden stool, only a dim blue stage light cast down on him. He played guitar left-handed and was talented. He was totally into the moment of the song, bobbed his head to the beat, eyes closed, tapping his foot in rhythm.

But when he opened his eyes, it was like the colors of the Caribbean. The most beautiful blue, with sparkling green centers. They were, um, angelic.

"Aren't they amazing?" Reese shouted over the music. "I told you this guy can play guitar! What a night! Stare at *him* a bit, and you'll forget about what's his face!"

"Who?"

"Exactly," she laughed and threw her head around, her wild arms claimed all the space in the vicinity. "Let's just have some fun, Clo! We can go back to being serious tomorrow. Deal?"

"Yes. Deal." I glanced back up to the stage. The man seriously could make me forget all the troubles of the world. His brown hair was all a mess, like my emotions that night. I no longer knew what to think or feel. I listened to the Reese version of the voice in my head and decided to let it all out on the dance floor.

After a few songs I sat down to get some air. Reese returned shortly, after making a stop at the bar to get us another round. I thanked her, promising to reimburse her when we got back to the apartment. She's so generous, and could care less about repayment, but I liked to keep things fair.

"No worries! Some really cute guy got them for us." She turned back over to the bar, promptly sending him a smile and a flirtatious wave. He nodded politely. He looked a bit out of place here, very refined in a tailored navy blazer over a crisp white t-shirt, with some ridiculously expensive looking designer jeans. He seriously looked like a cologne model in a magazine.

"Hot. No ring. Game on," she proclaimed, speaking to me while still looking his way.

"Oh no. You look smitten!" I chuckled. Isn't that how it goes? I got dumped and she gained the attention of a sexy-as-sin man in a matter of an hour. I reminded myself to breathe. Everything happens for a reason.

The evening turned from girls' night out dancing, to watching Reese flirt with new hottie from the bar. She invited him to join us. Architect Nick. The two of them had something going.

I politely replied anytime I was brought into the conversation but kept occupied with the music and watched the guitarist. I could not seem to keep my eyes off him. Hopefully the stage lights in his eyes prevented him from noticing my ludicrous staring.

The evening ended. Architect Nick and Reese exchanged numbers. We headed back to our place and crashed hard.

That night brought dreams of an angel from my past.

In the morning, I was out of sorts and Reese noticed.

"What's wrong with you, Clo. Are you still thinking about what's his face? He is not worth it, honey. Let me run down and grab us some coffee and streusel. It will help." She grabbed some cash from the cuss jar we recently started.

"That's not it exactly. I *am* upset, disappointed really. But I'm more in deep thought about this dream I had."

"Spill it," she demanded, sitting back down, money tossed back toward the jar, missing entirely.

"What about breakfast? Is that off the table now?"

"Have some cereal while we talk."

I begrudgingly agreed. Cereal, not my favorite.

I explained my dream.

I was sitting back in my high school classroom. It was so vivid. I was spacing out during everyone's speeches ahead of me. The boy I had been crushing on had asked my "friend" to the movies the previous day. She called me that evening to tell me about it. When I think back on it, she never actually asked me if it bothered me – not surprising. I remember sitting on my bed that night, crying. I didn't want to bother Grandma Lily with my silly troubles; she already had plenty on her plate, taking care of me and working two jobs. But I realized I didn't want to share the information with *her*. I needed my mom. But she wasn't there, she never had been. It wasn't fair that my friend not only was going on a date with the boy I liked, but she also planned on shopping with her mother for a new dress to wear to the movies.

In the classroom, I was feeling heartbroken, reliving the flood of emotions with another reminder of the loss of my mom. Then I felt a familiar current. On the screen in the front of class was an image of this amazing angel. The girl speaking said it was the Doge's Palace in Venice. Her speech on architecture was moderately interesting, but that particular picture took my breath away. I looked at the archangel Gabriel, and immediately felt that emptiness lessen.

His eyes seemed to peer out of the screen, directly at the hole in my heart and somehow dulled that ache. When the teacher repeated my name minutes later, I blinked my way back to reality. I was up next and somehow was able to look within myself for strength to move on with my day.

"That's deep girl," Reese explained. "My dream analysis is simple. The dickhead is going out with another girl, then I met an architect. There are some commonalities to the dream. Our evening definitely triggered the memory. Combined, I think you simply need a simple nudge that you are going to be fine. You are the most amazing, smart, and talented bitch I have ever met. And your kick-ass bestie is here to help you out. Call me Gabriel." She laughed. Then she squeezed my arm, tilted her head to the side, and shrugged, asking if her response was suitable.

"Wow, well that is one way of looking at it." I ran my fingers through my hair. "Thanks, Reese. You're the best."

"You bet I am. And I'll always be here for you."

Time just flew, weeks seemed like days. Reese and I both had a lot going on. I had finals to prepare for, she had Nick.

They seemed to hit it off exceptionally well and began spending a lot of time together. He was plenty nice and made her the happiest I had ever seen. I didn't mind that they were constantly together, and he spent many evenings at our place. They never made me feel like the third wheel, and they didn't have to make an effort to prevent it, we all just naturally got along.

I called my grandmother to catch up with her on several things. She asked about what's his face, as Reese and I now referred to Smith. "That was going nowhere, Grandma. I'm glad it ended before it had opportunity to become more brutal."

I heard a voice in the background, and asked who was visiting. "Oh, that's your Aunt Ruby. She stopped by to give me a hand with a few things." Ruby is my only aunt, seven years older than me. She was already married and resided only a few miles away from my grandmother at the time. I was grateful she could help out and keep an eye on things while I had been away. "Tell her hello for me," I asked.

"She says hi back. So, how are your studies going? Another year almost gone, can you believe it, my dear? You will be done in no time now. It is racing by. I remember when I moved you in. You were so excited to get there, you forgot to pack half of your things. Do you remember having to turn around?" she said.

"Grandma, are you okay? You never moved me in here," I questioned, concerned.

"Oh yes, oh my. I know. I was just thinking back to your mother's trip to school." She brushed it off. At the same time, my phone beeped. I received a text.

RUBY: We should talk sometime soon.

The dots appeared while she continued typing and I kept my grandmother on the phone.

RUBY: Mom seems to be getting confused a lot lately.

ME: Oh no. We'll catch up soon. Can you call me later?

RUBY: Yes, of course. Chat soon.

"Grandma, why don't you hang out with Ruby while she is there. I can call you tomorrow. Sound good?"

"Of course, my dear. We'll talk then."

That took an interesting turn. I started to panic; the room became smaller as I paced. Caged tiger mode had kicked in. Reese and Architect Nick were hanging out in the other room, and I didn't want to interrupt. I grabbed a light sweater and my purse. With no idea where I was headed, I said a quick goodbye, and bolted out of the apartment.

Life started to feel overwhelming. School, work, jerk-Smith, then Grandma Lily. I needed to sort out my thoughts, put some miles on my shoes, kill time before Ruby called me back later that day. I ended up down at the Pier.

The weather was dreary so luckily it was not very crowded. The sky was covered, the air was damp. You could see the low clouds swirling as they engulfed the skyscrapers.

It feels like rain, I thought. I started humming the John Hiatt tune in my head and ventured on, admiring the ripples on the water. Eventually the rain fell.

I never carried an umbrella in the city, it seemed so crazy to me since they always broke from the wind. Ever notice garbage cans filled with broken umbrellas? What a waste. Light sweater, light rain – no problem. Enter lightning. Super. I decided to head inside somewhere close.

I entered the first door I could find and walked into a gallery. It was filled with stained glass, what a wonderful find! It was warm, dry, and cozy. The colors from the surrounding glass cast a rainbow of light that could consume anyone's soul. Waiting out the rain, I walked around taking in all the beautiful pieces on display. I approached one gorgeous Tiffany glass and sat down on a bench to look at it more closely. It was as if it drew me there. Two angels holding torches that displayed bold colors of blue and red, the flames glowed realistically.

My breath slowed. These angels of peace and mercy brought on that sense of calm that I had craved. I sat there enjoying the moment.

I was abruptly startled when someone approached from behind and dropped something on the floor which made a loud thump. The noise could have vibrated every inch of glass in there. Seriously? Nothing like ruining a quiet, peaceful moment of reflection. I sat for another second, taking in the smell of a cologne. It had a citrus, woodsy scent to it. It soothed me. In that room of spectacular colors, warmth, and then that refreshing fragrance, I found myself comforted.

I turned to see who or what could have caused the obnoxious noise. I gazed for a moment and then recognized him. Oh my. Those eyes – that blue-green magic flickered toward me.

"I believe I am now in the presence of three angels," he spoke softly, in a slightly raspy voice.

"Huh? Not a chance." I replied. "Do you visit here often so you can use that pick-up line?"

"Is it not working?" He laughed. Wow, his smile was stunning. I glanced down and noticed his leather guitar case sitting on the floor next to him. He appeared to have been caught in the rain for a while; his clothes were soaked, brown hair had ringlets dripping down close to his eyes. I caught myself staring, and it took all my might to regain focus and reply. But what could I say to that? *Yes, that was the most amazing line ever, and you must be heaven-sent.* Nope. Couldn't say that. Cheesy as hell.

"Well, I'm not a pick-up line sort of gal."

"Well, why don't we grab a drink and you can explain to me what kind of a gal you are?"

"Um,- I'm thinking it is a little early in the day for a drink." Crap. I had to stall, to get my wits about me. What was I thinking? That beautiful man, *the* guitar player, asked *me* to have a drink.

"Oh, got it. You can just say you're not interested. No need for silly excuses," he said, his voice deep as he lowered slightly and glanced at the floor. He reached for the handle on the guitar case.

"Sorry.....um, not an excuse," I recovered quickly. His gaze turned back to me, and his head cocked to the side like a cute puppy waiting for the next instruction, brows lifted. "I could use a coffee to warm me up, but you cannot laugh when I order."

"Deal." He flashed the sweetest smile and we headed out the door. "I'm Elliot."

I smiled, elated to spend more time with Elliot. "I'm Clover, it is nice to meet you."

"The pleasure is all mine, Angel."

CHAPTER 2

ELLIOT AND I PLANNED to visit Franklin, Tennessee, together next year. He agreed to accompany me to celebrate my student loans being paid off in exchange for time devoted to visiting some of the historical Civil War sites here. I love how he is—*was*—such a history buff. Then suddenly, our plans, and my soul, came tumbling down just over a month ago.

Reese gave me the grief lecture before convincing me to take some time away in an attempt to find peace of mind. It was the first time she sounded so analytical to me.

Her degree in psychology made our conversation on grief quite intense, constructed of all the detailed stages, things I should expect to feel, and her thoughts on how I could persevere.

It was at that moment that my filter dissolved, and I let it all out. "That is all a bunch of bullshit. Nothing that you said makes any sense to me, Reese. Claiming there are stages suggests that there is movement through grief. Let me tell you, as someone who has been dealing with this my entire life, you sound like an ignorant fool. The clinical texts have taught you absolutely nothing! Grief is nothing but emptiness and despair! It never goes away! *This* will never go away, and I can never go back to who I was before!!"

Reese sat in front of me with a look of shock on her face. She grabbed the warm beer from my hand and placed it on the coffee table, pulling me into a fierce hug. "Finally, girl, you are letting something out. I know it has been a rough, difficult road. It does not matter what you say to me; I'm just glad you are letting down your walls. I am here for you, Clover. I will help you through this. Forget the stages, everything I said. Let me be here for you."

She eventually convinced me to take this trip, the exact one Elliot and I had planned.

★★★

My hands are cramping up. I have been squeezing the edge of this concrete bench so hard for God knows how long. I glance down at my palms, and the pebble pattern reminds me of the leather grain on his guitar case from that first day we met. Now I sit here, alone, with nothing but these memories. My best friend is gone, my Elliot. Here I am. I made it to Franklin. Now what? *Breathe. One breath at a time.*

I choke the tears down, dry my eyes and get myself as collected as possible. Reese encouraged me to take this trip, she even offered to join me if I wanted company. I feel bad I turned down her offer, but I know in my heart I should be alone for a while. The truth is, nothing has given me any sense of closure, and I do not expect to find any.

My life is every bit of a mess at the moment, and detaching, even temporarily, from my bestie is not the wisest thing I've done. But I made this trip to look for answers within myself. Reflect. Figure out what is next in my life.

I love Reese a lot, but she would annoy the hell out of me here, I'm sure of it. The town is cute, but there is a limit on things to do that would pique her interest. That would turn to extra time for her to psychoanalyze and preach to me. No. My heart is telling me to go through this on my own, for now.

But I do not feel alone. Empty yes, but not alone.

In my soul, I still think I am going to turn a corner and see Elliot here. Maybe I am losing my mind, maybe this desperation is what I need right now to help me heal. Maybe I am not strong enough to admit he's gone. That would break me. I am not sure what I'm going to do, but somehow know I am supposed to be here.

I know he is here with me. In spirit, in my heart; somehow, he is here. It's as if the metronome representing our time together hasn't stopped ticking yet.

The Reese voice inside my head speaks to me. *You will find your way through this. You always do.* I take a few deep breaths. As I stand, I accidentally bump into the shoulder of the cutest little girl.

She glances up at me, with the biggest and brightest eyes. "Oh, I'm so sorry," I tell her. "Please forgive me. I didn't see you there."

"That's okay. I'm little. People don't see me a lot," the sweet girl explains. I glance around and do not see anyone with her. She must have parents nearby. Still, no one approaches.

"Miss, do you have someone watching you?"

"Yes. My mom – that is her café right there. She can see me through the windows. I am supposed to be checking for garbage on the tables out front. It's my important job. We have to keep everything nice, so people come inside and we stay busy. That's what she tells me. All. The. Time. Over. And. Over." The girl, about eight years old, rolls her eyes and shakes her head back and forth, pigtails circling her head. What a spitfire, this one.

I chuckle. "Well, you are doing a fantastic job. You also convinced me to head in there and get a coffee. Thank you, Miss."

"My name isn't Miss, it's Penelope. But you can call me Poppy. Or Miss Poppy, if you want. That sounds fancier."

"I see. Hi Miss Poppy, I'm Clover. It has been lovely speaking to you."

I head toward the door of the café, and Poppy abruptly runs in front of me, shouting at the woman behind the counter. "Mom, I found us a customer! We both have names like flowers!" She giggles and then turns around to return outside.

"Well, hello! Is your name Rose? Daisy? Lily? Or I can just

draw a flower on the outside of your cup."

"No, Lily is my grandmother. I'm Clover." I giggle.

"Both beautiful names, but I have a better chance of drawing a clover, so that turned out well." She draws an adorable four-leaf clover on my cup, the leaves look like connected hearts. "Now what can I fill it with for you?"

"Please, don't laugh. I like those frothy, caramel, calorie-filled, whipped-cream topped kind of drinks. What would you recommend?"

"No need to be embarrassed. We all love those drinks! Some act like they don't and order *sophisticated* drinks. I say carpe diem. Order the caramel macchiato if that is your pleasure."

"Sounds perfect, thank you." I watch her prepare the delicious drink and notice this is the first time in days I feel lighter, encouraged. Who knew a friendly barista, an energetic young girl, and a eight hundred calorie beverage could improve my spirits. I look forward to seeing what else the day may bring and attempt a half-hearted smile.

I glance for a nametag on her shirt, but the lovely woman isn't wearing one. She has a sweet face, and an innocent quality to her that makes me feel she is too young to have a daughter of Poppy's age. "Your daughter is quite something," I mention as she hands me my macchiato.

"Yes, Poppy is one of a kind, that girl has a heart of gold. I adore her," she says as she watches her child closely through the window.

I take in the natural charm of the café. It is bright and cheery; a vibrant yellow is painted on the walls. If Elliot was with me here, we would sit, enjoy the drinks (after he teases me about the girly beverage choice), and discuss what we feel the paint color is called. It feels like a sugared lemon to me. He would most likely say it is banana taffy yellow.

"My name is Sadie," Poppy's mother addresses me, bringing me out of my daydream.

"Hello, Sadie. You have a lovely place here. It gives off a happy vibe, something I really need today."

"Oh, well I am glad we can help. Everything okay?" She senses the shift in my tone.

"Yes, I'll be fine. Here visiting, but had plans to be here with someone. It didn't turn out as planned." She flashes me a friendly smile, calming me for a bit. Not a sad smile of pity, like I've received over the previous weeks anytime I was approached. This was a genuine smile, that directed a true energy through me.

"I'm sorry about your plans. I say it is impossible to plan, as it never turns out as expected. Especially with a kid," she sighs, but then grins. "But everything happens for a reason." She peers out the window again, checking on Poppy.

"Yes, you are correct. Thank you. It was very nice meeting you today. And this macchiato is fantastic. I'll be back for more this week."

Sadie's smile widens. "That's great, let me know if you want to try anything different. Are you staying in town?"

"Yes, I have a room at that cute bed and breakfast up the street. I will be around for a week or so. Playing it a day at a time for now."

"I hear it is quite charming. But you'll be back, the coffee isn't the best there. They only serve the sophisticated kind." She chuckles. I still have no idea how old she is, even when she grins there is no trace of a line or wrinkle anywhere on her glowing face. Maybe that is how happy people age, or she had Poppy when she was fourteen.

"Good to know. I'll see you around."

I head out the door, giving Poppy a high five as I pass, telling her how tidy she has it looking. She seems quite satisfied with her achievement and continues with her chores, now sweeping the sidewalk. "Bye Miss Poppy, see ya later."

I walk down the street, glad to have met some friendly towns-people. Everyone here has been so jovial since I arrived earlier today. The owners at the bed and breakfast are the kindest, cutest couple. My check-in process took forever because I couldn't stop chatting with them.

Now Sadie and Poppy have shared their positive energy and smiles with me. This may be the right place for me to do my necessary soul searching. The caffeine kicks in, and I pick up my pace.

I make it back to the bed and breakfast in no time. Sadie knows how to make the perfect comfort drink. Game plan – read a bit, prepare for the crash after this afternoon high I've had, give Reese a call if I can catch her, maybe nap. I glance around my room and look at the mess I created earlier. I arrived and lazily tossed my stuff inside before immediately closing the door behind me. This would drive Elliot insane. He enjoyed carefully finding a place for each item packed, even if the stay was only overnight. It was a tad annoying, to say the least. He used the cliché home is where your heart is. Change of plans – unpack and organize. This is for Elliot.

I take my time, and question why I arrange and rearrange which drawer I am placing my belongings into. Seriously? What is wrong with me? I smile, shake my head and accept the fact I will forever unpack my crap when staying away from home. Now, the fatigue sweeps in and I feel a nap is overdue.

I fluff up my cozy pillow and lean back on the bed. The emptiness hits hard. My love is not here with me. I try to focus on something else. The room is decorated in white and teal. A lovely cardinal painting hangs on one wall, another is empty except for the large window peering out over the courtyard gardens. I note the sunbeams flickering through the pergola, cute adirondack-style chairs underneath. What a lovely, serene place. I can smell the fresh cookies baking, the sweet aroma helps me settle more comfortably into this feather bed.

My attempts to breathe deeply and meditate fail me as I miss him. I miss him so damn much. He could shelter me with his strong arms, sweep the hair from my face and gently kiss my forehead to take away the sorrows and struggles of any day. Tears well up in my eyes and I try to blink them away. I need to rest, I drove through the night and, honestly, I haven't slept well in days. Sheep counting is not my thing. Maybe the paint chip game will work. I glance around the room. *Peacock blue…. St. Bart's teal. ….Butterfly pea flower…..Curacao.*

I startle awake hours later, hearing my phone vibrate on the adjacent nightstand. Two missed calls, damn. I must have been out cold. I see Everett's name appear on the next screen. My heart sinks as I think back to the recent missed call from him, just over a month ago.

CHAPTER 3

THEN

THAT LIFE CHANGING EVENING, I had finished teaching a yoga class for Reese after pulling a double at the lab. She and Architect Nick only had the doors open on the new yoga studio, Arise, for a few weeks and had not completely figured out their schedules. I work all the hours I can get on night shift, but I won't turn away chances to earn extra moolah, so filling in yoga class is a no-brainer. Every bit helps when I need to travel more to see my grandmother, whose dementia has rapidly progressed in the last couple years.

When I finally arrived home, exhausted, I snuggled up on the couch and dozed off. I knew Elliot wouldn't be home for another hour or so from his gig. When I woke up, I had missed a call from Everett. Strange, I thought. Why would he call me and not his brother? Ah, Elliot probably had his phone off if he was on the road.

I hit the call button to dial Everett, three tries to get it to work. I desperately need a new case. I don't even know if it rang fully one time, and Everett picked up. "Hey, Everett. What's up?" I could tell I was on speaker phone, there was tons of road noise in the background, and he let out a heavy sigh.

"Clover.......eh, Elliot... There has been an accident."

Time stopped.

. . . . . "Please, Lord, no. Tell me he's alright. He's alright, right?" My heart beat so heavily in my chest, I was suffocating, hyperventilating.

"Hey, it's ok. I mean, he's hurt, but he's already at the hospital being treated. I don't have all the details yet. I'm on my way now, left an hour and a half ago...but you need to go be with him. I won't be there until 5AM or so. I'm driving like a bat outta hell, but it's still going to take some time. I'm sending you the info now."

"Mmhmm, yes...... Okay. I'm on my way." *Think. Breathe.* Oh my God. Keys. Purse. I was out to the lot and realized I was still wearing my yoga pants, bralette, and flip flops. Fuck it. I remembered I had a hoodie in the car. "Everett, you still there?" my phone switched over to my handsfree device.

"Yeah, I'm here. Clover, are you okay? Stay calm. You need to get there safely," he tried to sound calm, but I was not convinced. "Do you want me to stay on the line? I don't mind."

"Um, Sure. Can you keep talking? I don't want to be alone," I barely squeaked out, knuckles white from gripping the wheel so tightly.

"Absolutely. I have another six-ish hours to go, I can talk as long as you need."

"Everett, do you know what I'm walking into? Is it bad? I don't know if I can handle this. Why did they call you? You're all the fucking way in Nashville."

He quietly chuckled. "I see the cuss jar hasn't done a damn thing for you." The tradition I had with Reese carried over when I moved in with Elliot. We both had things to work on, that was one we did together. "From what they told me, Clo, I am still listed as his emergency contact. Surprised me too. After all your time dating, you would think--"

"Everett! For the last time, we are not a *thing*. He is my best friend, my soul mate, but not my lover. It is not like that." Damn, this man is frustrating. Each time I interact with him, I realize why he and Elliot were not the closest brothers in the world.

"Sure, sure. Blah, blah, blah. I get it," the sarcasm surpassed the fear in his voice for the first time on the call. "All I know, is they called me. Someone crossed a median and hit the van going pretty

24

fast. It hit the driver's side. They had a hard time getting him out, but he was alert. I know his leg is broken, and they are checking for other injuries. The other guys were in Austin's car, following behind the van."

"Did they call your mom?"

"Not sure. But she's still overseas in Morocco with Number Three, so it's possible they couldn't get through. I've tried several times, no luck yet."

Their parents divorced just before Everett was born, Elliot was almost three years old. They don't hear from their father often; he has a new family – wife and her kids. Claire, their mother, travels the world and recently met her third husband in Greece. She loves her boys dearly but does not make it home as often as I think she should.

"Okay. Well, would you keep trying to catch them both? I'm a block away from the hospital. I'll let you know as soon as I have more information." The shock was wearing off a bit, and reality was slamming into me with full force, and I stuttered. "Uh, E...Ev...Everett, thanks for staying on the phone. Talk soon."

"Clover, it is going to be okay. He's Elliot. He's Superman."

"I hope so. May his guardian angels be surrounding him now." Like me, Elliot had the markings of an angel. Behind his left earlobe was a small birthmark in the shape of a feather. I said he was my personal angel, in the flesh. He never accepted the title and proclaimed it to be the marking for the perfect wingman. My wingman. My Elliot.

I rushed into the emergency room and tackled the first person I saw in green scrubs. I'm not sure how I was even able to say his name, I was so fearful. My eyes betrayed me and allowed the tears to begin building again. It was unclear if the room looked fuzzy due to the crying, or if my body was preparing to drop. I warned the kind nurse of the latter.

She sat me down in a wheelchair, sped me around the corner into a small, private conference room. I was relieved to see the lightheadedness pass quickly with a few slow breaths; I was able to focus again. She sat in a chair in front of me. Oh, shit. It just got real.

"Your friend has sustained multiple injuries. There are several fractures on his right femur, a handful of broken ribs, a fracture in his left wrist, and lots of scrapes and bruises. *But* he will be okay. They are finishing a few more scans to check for any internal damage, nothing is suspicious currently. He is awake and talking, and stubborn." She finally took a breath. I reciprocated. Stubborn: that was music to my ears. He was going to be fine.

"Oh, thank God! Where is he, can I see him?" She was caught entirely off guard as my arms immediately wrapped around her into the tightest hug I may have ever given. I needed to look into those precious eyes of his. I was scared to see him, but that was the only way I knew he would be okay. I would feel something more if it was not true. A bond like ours creates an energy field that would most likely crash if something was severely wrong. That was all I could think that entire time, like a broken record. I would know. *I would know.*

"Miss, I can have someone take you upstairs to the room where he will be admitted. It may be a while before he is out of imaging. The surgeon has arrived, as that leg requires an extensive procedure. They will update you on when they will prep him for surgery. Do you have anyone else with you?"

I closed my eyes tightly for a moment, pushed away the pain in my head as tension set back in. That sounded like a lot. He'd have a long road ahead, but I would get him through it. Whatever it took.

"Oh, sorry. What did you say?"

She cleared her throat, sounding annoyed with my lack of attention. "Miss, I can take you and any other family members upstairs. Unless you have other questions I may answer first?"

"Yes, thank you. It's only me so far. His brother is en route." I glanced down, realizing I forgot my hoodie. Bimbo Clover made a striking entrance. Shit. "Also, is there a giftshop or somewhere I can get an actual shirt?" I begged of her as I tugged at the hem of my top and shrugged.

"Of course. I can get you a scrub top from the closet if you would rather head right up."

"That would be ah-mazing. Thank you so much."

Nurse Betsy, as I finally read her badge, quickly grabbed a shirt for me. While she ran to seek the volunteer who would escort me upstairs, I slipped it over my head. Extremely unflattering, five sizes too big, but offered more coverage than what I had. She also handed me a warm blanket to cozy up in when I reached his room. Bless her heart.

I sat in the recliner chair, now even more exhausted, wrapped in the warm blanket. My mind told me to get up and pace, but my body couldn't take it. The synchronized clock on the wall seemed to tick so loudly while I focused on the second hand. I no longer heard all the other alarms dinging in the background from up the hall. The chitchat at the nurse's station had quieted down, shift change brought with it a more relaxed feel here. But there would be no relaxing until we were together.

After another hour or so, they brought him in with a bang. Literally. The gurney bumped into the wall, leaving a decent scar in the paint. "Geesh, I already crashed once tonight, can you try to be careful?" Elliot said through a raspy voice, but with a big grin on his face.

I had not completely stood up before I did the full check over him. Those eyes, still sparkling sapphires with their stunning emerald centers. One was a little swollen, and there were stitches above his brow, but they emanated his love immediately. He had tubing to help him breathe which hung from his nose crookedly over one corner of his mouth, but the nurse getting him settled straightened it so I could see a full smile that he flashed at me.

I barged right over, excused myself to the young nurse, and kissed him. He smiled again, "Hello, Angel. You look like shit." I was covered up by the new scrub shirt but had messy-bun yoga hair and certainly no remnants of make-up left.

Right. "You should look in the mirror once in a while yourself, Elliot!" I was elated that he had his sense of humor. If he acted in any serious manner, I would have had an emotional breakdown. "I am so glad to see you, awake. Here." I was in need of more humor, the tears were going to pour otherwise.

"I'm good. Hopefully this wrist doesn't mess with my careers." Elliot *would* be worried about his professional well-being. He was working at an amazing pastry shop only a block away from our place in Old Town, taking culinary classes, and played in the band whenever time allowed. His manual dexterity was quite important for culinary techniques and guitar.

"Horse, then cart. Let's concentrate on getting you feeling better! You still have a surgery to endure."

"Piece of cake," he attempted to wink and then caved to the pain. "They'll give me some good stuff for that, isn't that right?"

The nurse wasn't into his humor. Elliot didn't care. That's how we got through serious moments in life. Laugh and snuggle. I wanted to snuggle him so badly at that moment, but I knew I wouldn't be able to control myself, and he was already broken. I settled on resting at the edge of the bed. I switched between holding his good hand and brushing my hands over his face. He had dirt or dried blood covering his wingman mark. The nurse retrieved a damp cloth so I could gently wipe that off.

Soon a short, heavier-set bald man entered the room. He was the surgeon. Finally, an official update. "Hello, I'm Dr. Helian."

"Oh no, doc. Did you say your name was hellion?" Elliot was clearly banking on his humor to get through the stress.

"Um, no. It is Heee-Leee-In," he spoke slowly, tracing the spelling on his starched lab coat like Vanna. He quickly added a grin. I'm sure he's dealt with all kinds. "I plan on having you back in surgery in a few minutes. The sooner we repair that femur, the better your recovery. This procedure can last several hours. We'll keep you here for a few days to monitor, and then won't wait long to get that physical therapy started. To confirm, have you had any previous surgeries?"

"No," Elliot and I said simultaneously.

"And any known medical conditions or other symptoms?" he prompted.

"No, I've been lucky so far, I guess."

"Okay, that's good. We did run some additional blood work on you to check on things. We noticed on some of your x-rays, in addition to the injuries from the accident, that you have a condition called situs inversus. You may never have experienced any symptoms, many do not."

"Situ Inversions, what? Can you explain in English for me?" Elliot was no longer joking.

"Situs inversus. It is extremely rare, but basically you were born with the organs in your chest and abdomen reversed. Your heart, liver, spleen, and stomach sit on the opposite side than where they should typically. They function normally, but develop in the altered location. We did the extra imaging studies and workup to be certain all will go smoothly in surgery."

"So, what you're telling me is that I'm ass-backwards, but going to be fine?"

Dr. Helian laughs, "Well that part of your body is okay. And, yes, it will have no impact on the procedure. Now, I am going to let the team in here to get you prepped, and I'll meet you in the OR," he looks at Elliot, then over to me. "And we'll chat once he's in recovery and I will see you for an update." He walked out into the hallway, and the team came in.

"Elliot, your brother is on his way, will get here when you're in surgery. I'm keeping him updated. Still haven't heard from your mom or dad, but we'll keep trying. Austin and the guys just got back – they stayed at the scene to save as much of the equipment from the van as possible. He said he'll call in the morning, but I will text him with updates too. Is there anyone else you want me to call?"

"Clover, my angel, take a breather. I'm going to be fine. It sounds like you already have things under control. Get some coffee or whatever syrupy concoction you can find." He chuckled, then stopped, clearly the ribs are sore. "In no time, surgery will be done, and I'll be back here with you."

The team unhooked a bunch of things, grabbed several IV poles and made a smoother exit with the gurney than their entrance. I sent a couple of texts to Everett and Austin, tried calling Claire again – no answer. I wrapped back in my blanket, dialed Reese.

"Shit girl, this better be good! Do you know what time it is?"

"Hey, I'm at the hospital. Elliot was in an accident." Even though I knew things were going to be okay, just saying those words had me a bit choked up.

Her voice immediately sounded more alert. "Wait, what? Is he okay, Clo? Do you need me there?" I hear a loud thump. "Crap, I fell over trying to get shorts on while holding the phone. I can be there in twenty minutes."

"Wait, wait. No need to. He's okay, in surgery now. He's pretty banged up, but he's going to be fine. His brother will be here soon. I needed to hear your voice, help me get grounded again. Stay home, rest. But, can you do me a ginormous favor and bring me some clothes here in the morning…..well, later today?"

"Sure, babe. No problem. Text me what you need, I'll be there by eight. Nick can open the studio on the way to his office. If I don't hear from you, I'll grab you the basics. Good?"

"More than good. You're the best. Thanks, Reese." I start to hang up.

"-Hey Clover…he's going to be okay. Hang in there." She did her smooch sound and hung up. The tears started to burn my eyes. I needed to stay strong.

I sat back in the chair, pulled my knees up to my chest, resting my chin on top of them. As I wrapped my arms around my legs, the tension across my shoulders felt worse than I've ever experienced.

My entire body was on edge. I wished I had more room to get up and stretch a bit. Maybe a walk would help the restlessness.

I walked the hall for an infinite number of laps until a nurse politely asked if I could find a place to sit. I didn't want to walk outside to pass the time, partly because I didn't want to be too far away from El, partly because it was the middle of the night, dark, and I would be alone. I rested for a while in a waiting area, staring at a television, unaware of what was actually on. I closed my eyes for a while. I must have slept, because I woke up and another hour and a half passed. I was trying to rest but stay alert. I ventured out to find the cafeteria gated off; eventually I found my way back to the fifth floor, the same nurse was prepared to prevent me from pacing the hall. I asked her if I could get some coffee; she pointed me in the direction of a small conference room area down the wing.

I located the vending machine, thankfully. Powdered cappuccino-ish liquid filled my cup at lava scorching temperature. Looked awful, but after a slightly burned tongue, the taste was tolerable. It had caffeine, so it was good enough. Hopefully not caffeine and Pseudomonas. I carefully turned with the hot cup in hand and headed toward Elliot's room.

At the desk ahead, I spotted Everett. He appeared upset. "I was told room 514, but it's..... empty. Can you doublecheck for me, please?"

I tried to hurry, careful not to spill, and finally caught his eye. He walked over to me, looked at my strange outfit up and down, and then gave me a smile. "Hey, Everett."

"Clover, how is he? How are you? Where'd he go?"

I ushered him to the room, still 514, and set down my crappo-shit-o. Immediately, I jumped into him, and he gave me the biggest hug. He squeezed me tightly, and then held me in his arms for a few minutes. "Sorry, I overreact with cuddling under stress," I confessed.

He glanced down at me, and I believe tears formed in his eyes. "I've heard that about you. It's okay. Everyone is a bit stressed out."

He still hadn't released me from his arms. Maybe he needed it more than I did?

"He's still in surgery, but things are going well. Maybe another hour they said? You should sit, it was a long drive, you must be exhausted," my speech muffled by being so scrunched into his chest. I attempted to create a casual exit and pulled away slightly. He kept me there, sighed, and rested his chin on top of my head.

"The last thing I need to do after a six-hour drive is sit back down."

"Six hours? How did you manage that?" I knew he liked to drive fast, and this was an emergency, but damn. Six hours, he had to be flying.

"Don't ask. I'll only admit there was little traffic this time of night which definitely helped speed things along. The Benz cooperated." There he was, the Everett who name-drops and brags about all his badass toys. Everett works in Nashville as one of those crazily overpaid music industry attorneys. He likes to party, jump from girl to girl, and will most likely never settle down. Elliot and Everett possessed very different personalities and clashed like crazy, but they still cared deeply about one another. Everett always looked up to his older brother. I think knowing Elliot was vulnerable that night truly affected him. I had never seen him so worked up.

He continued the hold on me. We both took several deep breaths. I could feel his heartbeat against the side of my face. Finally, he pulled away, grabbed my hand and led me to the chair. He stood behind me for a few moments. As we watched the city lights twinkling out the window, he placed his hands on my shoulders and dug his fingers in deeply – attempting to work out the knots. He must have been able to read my mind.

★★★

In Chicago a week later, a day after the services were held, Everett stopped by the loft to pick up a few of Elliot's things before his drive back to Nashville. I told him that he could grab whatever he wished. He was looking for a picture in Elliot's room, a family picture with El and his parents, while Claire was very pregnant with Everett. I believe days after it was taken, their father took off. Everett sat down on the desk chair in Elliot's room, slumped over, put his head in his hands and started weeping. I didn't see him cry at the service, and he only shed a few tears while we were at the hospital. This was his meltdown.

I sat next to him on the floor and started crying with him. I had no idea what to say, so why try to conjure up something that would end up sounding ridiculous or ingenuine. When Grief heads back into life, sometimes you have to embrace it, I should know.

After a few minutes, he rubbed his face, took a breath so big I thought his ribcage would explode, and stood up. "Want a beer?" Just like that, he flipped a switch and turned off the extreme emotions.

"Hmm, yes. Actually, that is a brilliant idea. Let me grab a couple. I'll meet you on the couch." I returned with a small bucket of beer on ice, and a pint of mint chip ice cream. "Can never go wrong with ice cream."

"Interesting combo, what the hell!" he laughed.

The following hours consisted of stories exchanged, his included childhood memories, mine were the recent years I spent with his brother. We laughed, cried some more, and finished off all of the ice cream and the beer and passed out.

Everett woke up slightly crabby, I assumed from the hangover. He never admitted to the hangover, and insisted it was because he planned on driving home the night before, and he hates spontaneous plan changes. The week had already brought plenty of abrupt changes. I worried this would only be the beginning of meltdowns.

As I walked him out, I asked him to please give me a call anytime. The following weeks continued with his drunken calls, where he exhibited major mood swings of highs and lows. He explained he had missed several days of work from the aftermath. He was simply out of sorts, and I vowed to keep in touch with him. He had acquaintances galore, but no true friends. His mom already flew back to her latest husband after the service, and his dad still never came around. We could help each other through this.

CHAPTER 4

RELIVING THOSE MOMENTS HAS my heart racing. I stretch out all my limbs on the bed, trying to release some tension and calm back down. I reposition the pillow so I can more easily rest my head while holding my phone. I really should call Everett back.

ME: Everett, saw I missed your call. Everything okay?

Everett usually had his shit together. Sometimes I don't know how he managed it. High-profile, stressful deals going down all the time, but it never seemed to faze him. Perhaps that is why he made sure to always have fun when there was downtime. Work hard, play hard. Elliot always worked hard and was on track to be a successful pastry chef, even talked about buying into the business with his boss who was not nearly retirement age but was not dead-set against getting a plan together. Play hard – not exactly what I would call El's use of downtime. He stayed in shape, was active enough, but never quarreled with the idea of kicking back and relaxing. Actually he was quite good at it, and he taught me to be much better at it as well.

Everett did everything as if he had something to prove. He loved to call Elliot and give all the details of the craziness he was up to. He'd go on and on about which entertainer he was working with next, how they invited him to their lavish parties. Elliot would roll his eyes whenever on the call. Everett...always in a hurry, on a mission. But losing his brother was taking its toll.

My phone finally shook awake.

EVERETT: Everything is fine. Just seeing how you are doing. Busy?

ME: Nope.

The phone rings. Another struggle to swipe to answer. I keep forgetting to pick up a new case. Turns to missed call. I battle the damn thing, but get the annoying case off the phone and I dial him back.

"I thought you decided not to talk. Glad you're there."

"Sorry – phone struggles. How are you?"

"Good today. I still cannot believe you don't want to stay at my place. I'm not that far away. How was the trip?"

"Drive seemed like forever! The ride was quiet, ya know? But I'm here, settled in and making the best of it. This place is really nice, and I've made a couple of friends already."

"So, you're there to come up with a new game plan? Figure your shit out? I can help, I am great at planning. I live for it. Seriously," he sounded strong, better.

"I'm not sure there will be major plans made here. Currently, I struggle to walk across the room without tripping on my own feet. Part exhaustion, part braindead," I admit.

"I was in the same funk, doing a bit better the last couple of days. So I am clearheaded and at your disposal if you need it?"

"Well, you will be busy when that truck arrives tomorrow. Sorry for throwing all of that your way." Knowing I couldn't afford the loft on my own, I had to break the lease. In a matter of two weeks, I will be homeless. I boxed most of Elliot's things, shipping them to Everett, he can keep/store/sell whatever he wants of that. My stuff is going to a storage unit. Reese has offered to let me stay with her and Nick until I get settled.

Since graduating a couple years ago, I still have not taken my MCATs. I really have only focused on getting a paycheck and helping with my grandmother. I did the back and forth thing – Chicago to Savannah - for a while; unfortunately, her mental state keeps worsening so a couple of months ago my aunt Ruby offered to move in to Grandma's house to help out.

That has lessened my concern and my need for constant traveling, but still I have felt lost. Not certain which direction my life is headed, not sure which career path to take. I am starting to realize med school may not happen. Time is slipping away. Reese always has my back and if I liked it enough, she welcomed me to join the business, maybe open a second studio location. I have been so confused and undecided. Elliot had been doing so well, was close to having his culinary certificate, and was working on the deal with his boss. He and I were comfortable, making ends meet, but didn't exactly push each other to move forward.

"Clover? You there?" I guess I had drifted off in search of a well needed game plan.

"Yep. Sorry, see…..braindead. So, I did get a call that the truck is confirmed to arrive at your place by 10 AM. You going to be okay with all of that?"

"Actually, I paid the company to unload it all at the storage unit. I am not ready to deal with it. Plus, I was thinking I would head over and see you? Up for a visit?" I could sense *he* really needed this. I, on the other hand, was still feeling the need for some alone time.

"Ev-, maybe in a few days? I have a few things planned here," I lied. "Once I tackle those on my own, I will get a hold of you. That okay?"

He cleared his throat, poorly disguising his disappointment. "Of course, of course. I understand. But if you need anything at all, please call."

"I will. You'll do the same, right?"

"Sure thing. I'm okay though, really. I know you have been worried about me, but I can deal." There's the tough guy act, trying to prove himself.

"I know you're strong. Me, not so much. But I have a good feeling about my visit here. I'm here for a reason. Everything happens for a reason, I was reminded today. I suppose some of the things happening have been fucking shitty, but we're still here for something. Now it's time to figure out what."

"Sounds like a woman on a mission. Go find it, Clover!"

"I'll get right on it. But first, I need to find some dinner. Chat soon, Everett?"

"Yes, soon," he stalls a second, and then hangs up.

Two things I know for certain. One, I must find a new phone case. Two, I am starved and need to eat. Time for another walk outside.

The winding hall of the bed and breakfast finally leads me to the blue front door, and onward outside. I follow the large cobblestones, through a crafty ivy-covered archway, which meet the sidewalk running along the main street. I look both directions checking to see which way I may find a diner and a cell phone store. It looks like the hustle and bustle is all to the left, I'll head that way.

A couple of blocks down, I spot a small diner on the corner. The blinking neon sign in the window alerts me it is open. While waiting to be seated by the host, I become immersed in the nostalgia of the space. Several tables and booths sport red and white checkered tablecloths. Each one has a vase with a daisy and red carnation adding a charming look. The L-shaped counter has a few patrons sipping coffee. Behind it, a small pass-through window gives a glimpse of an extremely busy cook working diligently over a griddle. Above is the chalkboard with mini-menu and list of today's specials. It smells delicious and clean in here at the same time. There is a small glass freezer with several flavors of ice cream ready for scooping, and a rotating countertop display of cut pies and cakes. Yum!

An elderly man is seating me at a booth near the center of the diner, but I ask if I can have the table up front. I prefer to look out the window to the sidewalk and downtown. He kindly changes locations, then fills my water glass, and hands me a menu. I settle on the turkey club and fries, but plan on ordering some lovely dessert after.

There is limited traffic on the sidewalk for people watching to occupy the time until my meal arrives. I suppose most individuals are also sitting down for dinner this time of night. There are a few out for an evening walk; some pass carrying small shopping bags. I have never been comfortable dining out alone. It has an alien feeling to me, as if others think I'm odd or stare at me while pondering my story.

Without Elliot, I will need to dine alone more often, or stick with carry-outs. He and I loved to try new places for dinner. For some time, we were selecting restaurants by the alphabet. Each month a new place, with the next letter of the alphabet. This month would have been the letter *P*. However, we never made the selection before the accident. Now, I'll be the weirdo girl eating alone. I may have to finish to Z on my own to say that we did it.

Finally, my dinner arrives. The sandwich is terrific, on a flavorful, soft marble rye that must have been baked fresh today. My stomach feels extremely better with some sustenance in it. I have not been eating well through all of this. Stress has always caused me nausea; comfort food like this should help increase my appetite.

I have almost finished my club and pick out a slice of cheesecake to go with a cup of hot tea. Waiting for it to arrive, I see Sadie and Poppy walking by outside. I tap on the glass and wave. They both return a smile, and Poppy gestures for me to come outside. I inform the waiter that I'm stepping out just for a moment, so he doesn't think I'm going to dine and ditch.

On the sidewalk, Poppy introduces me to her golden retriever. "Clover, this is my dog Chance. He's the best dog in the whole wide world!" She does not stop petting the top of his head during the introduction. I kneel to scratch his ears and greet the cute pup.

"How are the two of you this evening?"

"*Three,*" Poppy corrects me, nodding down to Chance.

"Of course, *three* of you?" I chuckle. Kids are so funny.

Sadie explains, "We are just out for a quick walk, the weather cooled off so nicely this evening, I couldn't sit inside. It also helps Chance stay calm through the night if he's spent some of this energy. As a matter of fact, it helps all of us sleep better."

"It has turned into a lovely night. After dinner, I need to stop at the store and then I plan on sitting outside at the bed and breakfast for some leisure reading. They have this super cute sitting area in the garden and hopefully have the fire pit going. I don't see spaces like that often at home, in Chicago."

"Is that far away?" Poppy asks.

"Not super far, but that would be a long drive, and you do not travel well in the car," her mother adds.

Poppy wraps her hand around her neck, closes her eyes, and sticks out her tongue. "I barf." She laughs. "And Mom hates driving into cities. Maybe Dad can take me sometime?"

Sadie nods her head. "Yeah, maybe. But don't get your hopes up too much, little one."

I sense frustration in her voice, there must be more to that.

"I knowwwww. He's always busy. But maybe if I ask him, he'll think about it."

"Sure, sweetie. You can always ask."

In order to change the subject, I ask them to join me for dessert, offering to move to the outdoor seating area to accommodate their dog.

"No, we really should get going, but it does sound lovely," Sadie declines, Poppy sticks out her bottom lip. "Plus, Chance is not one to sit calmly for too long."

"Gotcha. Maybe some other time. By the way, do you know where I may find a store with phone accessories nearby?"

"Sure, just another block this direction, only a few storefronts from my café," she points in the same direction I was planning on heading. Good, that sounds easy. "Well, enjoy your dessert!"

"Yes, thank you. It was nice running into you. See ya!" They take off down the street, Chance pulling them energetically. I go back inside to finish my cheesecake and tea. When there's only a bite or two left, I begin to daydream again, recalling my first date with Elliot.

***

After meeting at the stained glass exhibit on the Pier, we spent hours talking over coffee, ordered cheesecake. We shared stories about our lives, laughed until we were in tears. He sat next to me and took every chance he could to touch my hand or put his arm around my shoulders on the bench behind me. It was adorable, and comforting. It felt like we had known each other for years. Elliot and I communicated so well. He was so charming that evening, and I could not believe he wanted to hang out with me for so long. We walked along the lakefront after it stopped raining and he held my hand the entire time.

I received a text from Ruby saying she would call in an hour when I decided I should head home. That was going to be a conversation I should not miss. When I explained I had to end our visit, Elliot offered to escort me home. How could I object to that?

We passed the coffeehouse storefront, the butterflies were becoming quite active in my stomach. He opened the door and allowed me to walk up the stairs in front of him. At the door to my apartment, I placed my hand on the doorknob to open it, and he folded his hand over mine gently. He placed his other hand to my shoulder and spun me around.

It was surreal, we looked into each other's eyes for a moment; still no awkwardness. He brushed the hair from my face, tucking it behind my ear and smiled. Slowly he leaned in, tilted his head to the side and gently kissed me. It was soothing, comforting, and passio….well, it was soothing.

Elliot stood back and let out a deep breath. I wasn't sure how to take that? I decided to say something. Nervously I asked, "Weird, right? You're like so freaking hot, but....nothing."

He glanced at me with those gorgeous blue-green eyes, and then started laughing. "That good, huh?"

"It was very nice, do not take that the wrong way. But for the fantastic afternoon we had, hours of conversation, I was expecting these huge sparks to fly, lightning bolts to flash!"

"And then I would open the door, frantically pushing you into the apartment all the while kissing you and wildly running my hands all over your body?!?" He is still giggling.

"Yes. Exactly!" I replied, relieved he was finding some humor in this too.

"I didn't want to push my luck," he said. "And don't feel bad. Strangely, I get it. I was expecting the same. No offense, but it just didn't happen to turn out the way we both envisioned it."

"Thank God for that!" Reese opened the door, she must have been ear hustling from inside. "We wouldn't want to witness that kind of erotic behavior, especially with company over." She chuckled, "Come in lovebirds, no point in standing out there."

"Elliot, this is my best friend and roommate, Reese," I pause. "Reese, this is –"

"Um, the guitar guy! Holy shit!"

"Hello, Reese," Elliot shakes her hand, somewhat blushing. "Can you give us another minute out here, please?"

She took the hint and left us alone. We stood there facing each other, smiling, and still holding hands. He finally broke the silence. "So, if she is already your *best* friend, I will have to go as *just* your friend."

"For some reason, I feel it will need to be something stronger than that! I know the kiss wasn't what we expected, but this feels like more than a typical friends-thing."

"Soulmates? *Friendly* soulmates?"

"That is exactly what I would call it." How did he know that I was feeling that strong of a connection as well? I wouldn't argue with what he said, but it was altogether very odd. We were odd.

The odd couple. From that moment on, we were inseparable – but things never became physical. Always there for each other, helping one another through life. I still had Reese, but she was growing closer to Nick and had less time for me. Elliot filled that void.

***

My lovely daydream ends as the waiter approaches my table, "Miss here's your check. Do you need anything else this evening?"

"No, thank you. Everything was wonderful," I say. As he walks away, I put the cash for the bill and tip on the center of the table, tucked under the flower vase. I grab my purse and walk to the door. It is starting to get dark out already. I'll make the trip to the store quickly and hopefully have time to enjoy the firepit when I get back.

The town of Franklin really is lovely in the evening. At dusk, the lights of several businesses create a warm glow, they even have a retro theater sign that is lit up. The sidewalks have mature trees lining them where you can see the colorful store awnings through the leaves. I can see up ahead a tall monument in the center of a park. I would like to check it out, but I have my heart set on sitting near a fire this evening. I will have plenty of time in the coming days to take a longer stroll and investigate further ahead.

I see Sadie's café across the street, so I should be close to the cell store. The scenery is distracting me because I've already walked too far. I need to cross the street; hopefully they don't ticket for jaywalking here. There is a break in the traffic and I swiftly skip across the street to the store. The space is small, but they have a large inventory of items packed in here. It is more like a general store than a cell store. They carry phones and accessories, but also have a fair share of touristy apparel, snacks, and books closer to the counter. I love the feel of the space. It has an old, exposed brick wall behind the counter. The wall reminds me of the one in our living room of the loft. Elliot loved its rustic beauty.

After searching a while, I locate a new case that should work on my phone, and it comes in a variety of colors. I choose bright yellow; it will be easier to find in my purse at night.

While waiting in line to pay, I also grab a few snacks to take back to my room. A couple packs of cheddar popcorn, a gourmet watermelon lollipop, and shortbread cookies fill my hands. It appears my appetite is returning, along with a probable stomachache. I hope the person in front of me is almost done, I am not sure how long I can juggle all this crap.

In my peripheral vision, I see a shadow of a man walking out of a store across the street. I take a step closer to the window to get a clearer view. By now, the man is walking away from me, but I swear it is Elliot! He's tall, his gait and the way his arms sway by his side look just like him, even his hair is the same chestnut brown. I am not sure what I'm thinking as I throw all my items on the counter and tell the clerk I will be right back. I have felt all along that Elliot has been with me, somehow not truly gone. Could he be here – in some way? This is absurd, but here I am jogging across the street, dodging cars, to catch this man.

As soon as I get to the sidewalk, he is getting into the back of a car, the door starting to slam shut. "Elliot!" I yell. He doesn't look back, the door closes and the black sedan drives away. Well, he didn't recognize the name – I must be losing my mind. I can faintly smell the lingering scent of this man's cologne; a lavender, mandarin, and cedar musk still haunts the air as I stand here.

I see something sparkle on the sidewalk under my feet. I realize the light is reflecting from a beautiful display in the jewelry store behind me. Well, not a sign from above – no angels reaching out to me here. This was only my mind playing tricks on me. I better not mention this to Reese, she'll have me committed.

The clerk from the cell store opens the door and shouts at me. "Ma'am are you still wanting to make your purchase? We are closing in ten minutes if you still need your items." I nod yes in his direction and begin walking back, waiting first for a few cars to pass.

I enter the shop and pay, take my bag full of goodies and return outside. I cannot help but look around for the man or the car he left in. No sign. I better get walking back, before the slight bit of daylight decides to disappear too. I use the walk to clear my head, convincing myself that my fatigue and desire to see Elliot again just got the best of me. A momentary lapse of judgment. Nothing to fret over. I must let it go, let him go.

The return to the bed and breakfast is very enchanting. In the front yard, the ivy arbor is now lit up with twinkling fairy lights and the crickets are chirping loudly. There is a cute swing hanging on the porch that I may visit for a morning coffee ritual. I go inside and find no one at the entrance to greet me. Maybe they only stand post when expecting arrivals.

My room has the bed already turned down. How fancy...this is not the kind of place I typically stay in. Thankfully I put all my stuff away earlier so the staff did not see my mess when they came inside. Maybe that is why Elliot always took time to do that, so smart. I set my things down on the counter for later. The store clerk already put the new case on my phone, so I won't have to mess with that. Now what? I'm not quite tired yet; recent events brought me a second wind.

Outside the window I can see a flash of light. I pull the white eyelet curtains back to look closer. The fire is lit already. Perfect! I grab a light jacket, switch into my comfy ballet flats and head out back. There are several individuals already enjoying the space, sitting together, sharing a bottle of wine. I notice a s'mores station set up; it looks delicious but the cheesecake is still settling from earlier. I pass behind the row of chairs and now am facing the back of the house, it looks much larger from this view than the front.

The garden is elaborately designed, full of colorful flowers in bloom, winding paths, and a small koi pond with a stone waterfall trickling into it. They have managed to create a very enjoyable outdoor space here. I take a seat on an open chair near the fire. I love to listen to the crackling sounds the wood is generating. At home Elliot had a eucalyptus candle in his room that made the same sound. He said it would be romantic – even though he never took time to date.

He vowed to be my wingman and through the years made several attempts setting me up on dates that typically didn't make it to a second one. He always told me one day he would help me find the man of my dreams. I wasn't holding my breath. I hope that someday it just happens. Magically. Like our friendship happened.

I only tried to fix him up once and it was a complete disaster. He could not fathom how I thought the crazy woman would be his type. She was gorgeous, but he said she was nuts. I only knew her briefly from yoga class, and in all honesty, we never talked during class so I was going off my gut instinct. It clearly was wrong. Elliot was devoted on establishing his career and wanted to take time before settling down. We always talked that each of us would meet our Mr./Mrs. Right and someday start families. Maybe we would be neighbors and our kids could go to school together. How I'm going to miss doing that.

The fire popped loudly and several of us jump in surprise; we all look around and chuckle. Most are couples carrying on private conversations. One older gentleman sits alone reading his e-book. I lean back in my chair, close my eyes, and take in the sounds of the fire and waterfall. The warmth begins to lull me to sleep. After an hour or so, I wake up. Gosh, I hope no one heard me snoring or talking in my sleep! I glance around and only the man reading remains out here. The others already ventured inside.

I need to do the same. Bed is calling my name. I feel relaxed and hope I am capable of some decent sleep tonight. I walk back to my room and change into my huge comfy night shirt and climb into bed. The fire still glows dimly through the window. It doesn't take long for me to doze off.

CHAPTER 5

I WAKE TO VOICES outside, glance at the time on my phone. Wow. Nine-thirty. I slept well and through the night. I stand up to stretch and pick up the chocolate on the nightstand. "Mmmm, that's smooth milk chocolate," I say aloud, not sure who I expect to be listening.

Currently, I have no itinerary for the day. I take a nice, soothing shower with one of the complimentary citrus mint shower bombs left in the bathroom. I get dressed, energized, and ready for the day ahead. The moment I step in the hall, the smell of bacon consumes me. I walk down to the dining room for breakfast. The counter has a variety to choose from: muffins, fresh fruit, yogurts, scrambled eggs, and bacon. Wow, if I sample all of this, I'll need to go back to bed.

I make a small plate with a yogurt, some fruit, and a couple pieces of this thick applewood bacon. A glass of orange juice looks like the better beverage choice – only sophisticated coffee here. It appears everyone is dining outside. My solo dining fear kicks in and I choose to sit inside to avoid questions. The breakfast is really good, and I decide my first mission of the day. Real coffee from Sadie's. Then maybe a walk to see the monument in the city center. From there, I'll wing it.

As I glance at my phone, I see a text pop up.

EVERETT: Hope your morning is off to a good start! Call me if you want company.

Wow. He's really persistent. I still do not feel up for company.

The city has plenty to occupy my time, and I already feel a sense of peace here. I'm not going to mess with how well this is going.

ME: Hi! Things are good here, have a busy day planned. Did the moving truck arrive yet?

EVERETT: I'm glad you're good. I just heard from them, they are running two hours behind. Not a big deal.

ME: I hope it goes smoothly. I'm headed out now. Talk later?

EVERETT: Yes. Enjoy your day!

Enjoy my day. I'm going to give it my best shot. Back in my room I switch from my purse to a small backpack, put my phone, wallet, and camera in it. Sneakers seem more sensible today for walking. I exit to the main street again. The day is bright, sunny, and feels like it is going to get quite warm.

I take my time walking to the shopping area of town. I decide to check in with Aunt Ruby. I dial her number.

"Clover, how are you? It's been a few days."

"Yes, I was busy packing up things at home and then drove down here to Franklin for a while to get away. How's grandma doing today?"

She sighs. "It hasn't been the best of mornings. She's not herself today, just very quiet and wants to be alone."

"I'm sorry, Ruby. Thank you for being there for her. It has been more bad days lately, hasn't it?" I worry that my aunt is going to get worn out dealing with all of this. I know when I've been down to see my grandmother it is both physically and emotionally exhausting. It has been a couple of months now since I visited.

"Yes, definitely more bad days. I'm grateful she doesn't get mean or angry. Just lost."

"I know the feeling. The lost part."

"Clover, darling, how are *you* doing? I am worried about you." Ruby has the kindest heart. She is very similar to my grandma in that way, always worrying about everyone else. I imagine my mother was that way too, it probably runs in the genes.

"It hasn't been easy, but I'm doing alright. Taking time now to figure out my next move," I start to choke up a bit. "I need to get settled. Reese is letting me stay at their place for a bit, but I need to decide where I'm headed. Any ideas?"

"You can always move back here. You can spend time with your grandmother." She has been diligently trying to have me move back. Not so I can take over caring for Grandma, but to be home in general.

"I'm not certain that's where I'm supposed to land. I have a basic biology degree, not much for work experience. I really need to figure this all out." I am beginning to feel frustrated, not at Ruby but myself.

"I know. A lot is going on. We're fine here. You take some time to find yourself. We do miss you very much. Maybe you can visit soon?"

"Yes, of course. Maybe I will come down. I'm already halfway there. Let me think about it."

"That would be wonderful, Clover. I won't mention it to Lily until I hear from you. And, my darling, I understand if you can't right now. But you made my day by mentioning it!" Her voice brightens.

"Okay. I'm walking and need to pay attention to traffic and watch my step. I'll call you soon. Give grandma a big hug and kiss for me?"

"Of course I will. We love you, Clover. Stay safe and call if you need to talk."

"Thanks, Ruby. I will. Love you too." Perfect timing, I'm almost in front of Sadie's café.

Sadie's is very busy this time of day. Several people are in line to order, and the majority of tables are taken. She spots me as I walk in and smiles and then gets back to filling orders. When I approach the counter, she asks, "Same thing today? Or you feeling adventurous?"

"Surprise me, but nothing too sophisticated. And we can go iced today, it's getting warm outside. I could use something refreshing!"

"You got it! I know just the drink."

I sit down at a corner table while waiting for the coffee to be ready. I reach into my backpack to grab my phone, but accidentally grab the lollipop first. I spin it around in my hand debating if I should have it now or wait. It makes me think of the Dream Lady sculpture in Lincoln Park with the poem talking about the lollipop sea. On occasion, I would walk from the loft to the park to think. I'm not sure if she was a fairy or an angel, but the winged woman in bronze had also guided me and helped me find answers while I was lost.

***

Days before my aunt moved in with my grandmother, I went on one of my walks, and I sat down in front of the sculpture. The children shown sleeping beneath her seemed so peaceful. The best nights of sleep I had as a child were with my grandmother holding me, singing lullabies, until I drifted away. Most nights I never dreamed or at least never remembered them. But those evenings being held in her arms, often brought magical images to my slumber. I sat beneath the Dream Lady that day, wishing I could comfort my grandmother like she did me when I was young.

I knew I had to take care of her. My life could wait. I decided to go home and tell Elliot that I needed to move back and help her. I had my mind made up. It would be hard to leave, but also necessary. Just as I was leaving the park, Ruby phoned. On that call, she informed me of her plans to move into grandma's house, so someone was around her all the time. I would still visit often to give her breaks and check in with my grandmother. However, I didn't need to uproot and vacate the city I had grown to love or my friends that I loved even more. I was relieved and grateful.

***

I jump as Sadie announces, "Clover, your large hazelnut frappe is ready. Extra whipped topping, too!"

"Thanks, this looks amazing!" I retrieve it from her. This woman truly loves what she does. Each time she hands someone their order, she exudes happiness. You could not help but feel it and return the sentiment. But as I return to my table, that energy wanes, and I begin to worry about my grandmother. I decide that after a few days here, I will definitely go visit. I need to see her and Ruby. I sip on my frappe and feel overcome with emotion. The tears begin to well up.

I feel a tapping on my shoulder. "Hi!" Poppy smiles and sits down at the table across from me.

"Well, hello, Miss Poppy!" I try to collect myself.

"You look sad." This girl may be young, but she is observant beyond her years.

"I do? Well, I'm okay. I'm just missing some people."

"It's okay to be sad. I miss my Dad all the time, but Mommy tells me that it is normal to miss someone when they are away. He's not far, but it isn't the same. Nothing is the same since the divorce."

"I'm sorry, Poppy. A girl as sweet as you should never feel sad. Can I give you a lollipop to cheer you up?" Her eyes brighten, and my heartstrings tug a bit.

"May I?" she reaches for it. Southern manners are prominent here.

"Sadie, is it okay for Miss Poppy to have this lollipop?" I better check. These days you never know. Allergies, or just fear of sugar high may prevent it.

"Of course!" she glances over with her big smile. "What do you say, Penelope?"

"Moommmmm, you didn't give me a chance yet." She rolls

51

her eyes. "Thank you, Clover. It is my favorite color. Pink!" she emphasizes the "P" with her enthusiasm.

"You are welcome. I'm glad it's your favorite."

"What are you doing today? Something fun? I want to go to the splash park. My mom says maybe when her afternoon helper comes we can go." She crosses fingers on both her hands and waves them in front of her. "I wore my suit underneath today just in case. The tag is scratchy though. It's new. I got it for my birthday, and Dad was going to have a pool party for me with my friends. He had to leave for work though, and we couldn't have it."

"Well, it sounds like you may get to use it today! That sounds very exciting. I'm going to walk around town and check things out. Hopefully find a good spot to relax."

"You should go to the splash park. It is super fun!"

My phone vibrated. Everett's picture appeared on the front as his text arrived.

"Is that your boyfriend?" Poppy asks while swinging her legs back and forth, lollipop now frantically being unwrapped.

"Ha! No. Just my friend's brother. He's a friend too, I suppose."

"Whoever he is, he's cute!" she touches the edge of my phone with her sugar-coated sticky fingers.

"You think so, huh?" I laugh. Oh, Sadie is going to have her hands full with her!

"Yep. Very cute." She sat there staring at the phone for a moment. "Are you going to call him?"

"Not right now. Currently I'm hanging with my friend Poppy and having my morning coffee."

"That looks more like ice cream to me!" she giggles.

"Poppy, you need to leave her alone and come back here to give me a hand. Can you fill up the napkin holder over there, please?"

"Yes, mom." She hops down. "Thanks for the sucker. Call your boyfriend!" she winks my way, giggles some more, and walks back to the counter.

"Okay, silly. See you around!" I gather my things and walk outside, waving goodbye to Sadie as I exit. Wow. The sun is shining relentlessly now. It is definitely warming up today. I wonder if I can find something inside to do later when it becomes downright hot. I grab my phone to search, noticing the message from Everett I had forgotten about.

EVERETT: Hey, sorry to bug you. Do you have that number for the movers?

I look up the number in my phone contacts and forward it to him.

ME: Still no show?

EVERETT: Not yet. I'll figure out what the hell is going on.

ME: Back to grumpy Everett on a mission.

EVERETT: ;) You doing something exciting now? Life figured out?

ME: Just had coffee with a new friend. Off to site-see now.

EVERETT: Hot?

I decide to tease him.

ME: The coffee?

EVERETT: No, your friend?

ME: She's like eight. Weirdo! LOL But her mom is very pretty.

EVERETT: Oh, sorry. Ooops.

ME: Get ahold of the movers. Chat later, weirdo.

I continue on my walk through town. I pass several small boutiques with cute outfits on the window mannequins, art galleries, and antique shops. If I had a steadier income, I could do a major shopping spree here. So many cute things to see. I walk past the jewelry store from the previous evening's mistaken identity event. I see the large monument just another block up. It is getting blazing hot out here; I feel sweat beads forming on my skin. I'll check out this area and then ask at the tourist center for a list of interesting indoor activities for the day.

The monument I noticed yesterday stands tall in the center of the roundabout. Thankfully, I'm not driving here because those things confuse the heck out of me. I cross the street and walk up to the steps of the monument. It is a confederate monument here for well over a century. Nearby several cannons sit. What a wonderful center, full of history. It is lovely to stand here and look down the main street, the period lighting lines the streets. This is something Elliot would have loved to see. I am glad I am doing this, seeing it for him. I walk around the center a while, reading the historical plaques, seeking some shelter from the sun under the trees.

After a while, I look at the map in the guide I grabbed at the entrance of my bed and breakfast. It shows the tourist center is just a block away. I walk in that direction, hoping they have some much-needed air conditioning. I approach the entrance of the building, and see a "Back in 15 minutes" sign. Seriously? That is something I am not accustomed to seeing in Chicago. Well, I'll keep moving on.

My drink is now gone, and I turn to toss it into a close garbage can. I need to seek out somewhere close to step in and spend time and cool off. Maybe a museum or that art gallery I passed earlier. I see a church ahead. I am not certain if it is cooled, but it is quite beautiful, and I feel the need to check it out. There is a marker outside that has a summary of its history. It was used in the Civil War as a shelter and hospital, and suffered great damage. This should be part of my Elliot history tour. I decide to go inside now, if it is open.

As I enter, the floor squeaks beneath me. I am overcome by the beauty inside. It is a remarkable church, intricate woodwork and large beams above which contrasts the lighter color painted on the walls. I walk up the center aisle closer to the front and take a seat in a pew to the right. Most churches are comforting, though sitting here I feel especially peaceful and can only believe that Elliot would have loved it. Perhaps he's here with me in a way. I close my eyes and begin humming our song in my head. I open them and immediately become drawn to the stained-glass windows ahead of me. The Tiffany work is magnificent, in particular an angel who is seated with one arm stretched above her head. She is truly stunning, and it takes my breath away. As I am mesmerized by her beauty, a rainbow of light casts through one of the windows landing on my hand, flickering, almost dreamlike.

My mind jumps to the afternoon in the hospital.

CHAPTER 6

THEN

ELLIOT HAD BEEN IN surgery for what seemed like days. Everett was with me. In order to pass time, we walked the halls. We sat in the room silently until one of us would ask the other how long it had been. A couple of times I broke down; the waiting around made me stressed and emotional. Everett pulled me into a tight hug each time, telling me it would be okay.

After a while, the surgeon came in and said Elliot was stable, and headed to recovery, that everything in surgery went well. We would be able to see him soon. Thank heaven! A nurse ushered us to the recovery room. There was Elliot, sleeping soundly with all sorts of activity going on around him. Several nurses were in and out, checking his vitals, adjusting IV lines. At one point they ran a quick EKG. He still had not woken up yet. Everett and I sat waiting. He held my hand and occasionally gave it a squeeze.

After an hour or so, Elliot opened his eyes, blinking a few times and smiled over at me. Everett stood up, walked up to the bed and lightly touched his shoulder.

"Hey brother, it's me, Everett. I made it. You don't have to say anything. I know you are looped out of your mind. I just wanted you to know I'm here. Clover is here, too. It's good to see you, man."

Elliot just blinked a few times and smiled at him. He was awake enough to grasp some of that, but it was obvious it took all the effort he could muster up to keep his eyes open.

"Hi, Elliot. I'm here. You just rest," I assured him. He smiled again and dozed back off.

It wasn't much later that he opened his eyes again. You could see his mind working, but he was trying hard to get the words out. Then he said in a raspy voice, "Can you grab me a banana sandwich?"

"A what?" Everett looked to clarify.

"A banana sandwich. You know," he repeated, as if Everett and I were the weird ones in the room.

"Are you messing with us, Elliot?" I giggled. That did not sound like something he would want to eat after not having food for how many hours. I'm certain he didn't eat anything during the gig last night, so it had most likely been since lunchtime yesterday that he had a morsel in his stomach.

"Sure, do you want anything else on it?" Everett played along.

"Yep, some cheesy crackers." Again, the reply was spoken softly, but with the most serious of looks accompanying it. He was speaking whatever was on his mind, but the anesthesia was messing with him.

"That sounds disgusting, bro. Maybe we can ask the nurse for something lighter to start. When she's back, we'll ask."

"Yeah, okay."

"You feeling okay, Elliot? Do you need anything? Are you in pain?"

"I feel gah-reat! Just sleepy." That was over the top. He was trying to cover-up something. He seemed out of it still, which I hoped equated to no pain.

The nurse walked in, bringing some water and crackers. Plain crackers, no banana sandwich. "You can sip on the water, hold off on the crackers for a bit until you wake up some more." She pointed at me, "I'll put you in charge of that, alright? And if he starts to feel any pain as he wakes up, you can press this button here." She picked up the wand clipped to the bedrail to show me. I nodded back to show her I understood.

In an hour, they moved him back to Room 514, where he was to spend the next couple of days getting stronger before a plan would be made to go home. As he woke up and became more alert, Everett decided to mess with him.

"Hey, Elliot. Do you still want that banana and cracker sandwich?"

"What..are you crazy? That sounds disgusting!" he whispered out. I noticed he hit the button for pain meds.

"We thought so too, but that was what you requested." I chuckled.

"I do *not* remember saying that. Please tell me I didn't say anything else that odd or embarrassing."

Everett chimed in again. "You mean admitting your deep love to Clover and how you have a never-ending desire to jump her bones?"

I reached over to slap him, while he giggled.

"Now I know you are messing with me!" Elliot smiled but blushed a bit.

"What is *that* look about?" I had to ask.

"Nothing. No look. Thank you guys for staying with me."

"Nice try, brother. Why are you changing the subject?" Everett would not let that go. Part of the brotherly love was a constant desire to humiliate each other.

Elliot stalled a moment. He tried reaching up and scratching his head, a habit of his while in deep thought, but couldn't due to the IV in his arm. He switched to the other arm, realizing he had a cast on the other broken wrist. I quickly stood up and went to help him.

"Where?" I asked touching the top of his head, gently rubbing.

"Just a little higher and to the right....my right. Oh yes, right there – you got it, thanks. Now if you could make my leg feel better, that would be amazing."

Everett chuckled again. "So about that deep desire you were talking about earlier?"

"Oh shut up, Everett. You are so annoying." I stuck my tongue out at him like a toddler.

He was starting to focus and look around the room more, a sign he was truly waking up. For a moment, he stared up at the ceiling, in a daze, and his eyes widened like he just had a shocking epiphany. Maybe it was just a glimpse of the accident, like a horrible nightmare. He had not spoken about it earlier; I'm sure it was a terrifying experience. Elliot's eyes looked in mine, this time a very serious stare. Oh my, what is going on in that mind of his? Certainly, he was not finding truth in the previous jokes. I couldn't place the look though. He looked foggy again, slightly confused. Maybe just tired.

"Elliot, my wingman, you should rest." I encouraged him to sleep. Maybe that would give me time to figure out what the hell that look was all about. He dozed off. Everett sat back in the chair, trying to get some rest too. He had been up all night driving and then waited through the surgery. I had no clue how he could still be awake and thinking clearly. I suppose he was used to stressful, sleep-deprived situations.

El may not have spoken, but he was definitely saying something with those gorgeous Caribbean eyes before he fell asleep. I sat in the chair next to the bed, holding his right hand. There was no cast here, and I wanted him to feel my touch, to know I wasn't going anywhere. A flash of light in a rainbow of colors came through the beveled edge of the window, landing directly where our hands were resting. It felt warm as it danced there for a few moments.

I felt him squeeze my hand. He woke up and looked over at me. "My brother. I saw you with my brother." I am sure my face just scrunched up in confusion. He must have been half asleep or confused from the pain meds.

Everett woke up, "Did he say something? About me?"

"I'm not sure what he was mumbling about." I told him. Understatement of a lifetime right there.

He scooted his chair closer, "Hey, man. You need me? Need

something?"

Again, Elliot looked at me, and softly said, "I saw you *with* my brother."

Not even a second later, a monitor started beeping. His heart rate sky-rocketed, and his breathing sounded labored and fast. Two nurses ran into the room, moving us out of the way. They started looking at things, and then one asked us to leave. Elliot's eyes peered into mine without blinking, all the way until I was out in the hallway and they closed the door between us. I felt extraordinarily helpless. The fear in his eyes as I walked away saying his name, still reaching out my hand to him, had me hysterical.

There was confusion. Everything happened quickly. A team went in, the doctor. This did not look good. Soon after, overhead announcements were being made regarding his room number. What the fuck happened? I was pacing in the waiting area, Everett just sat staring at the wall as we waited for any news.

An eternity passed. Finally, we were approached by the physician. He walked into the room, glanced around noting no one else was nearby. The doctor, who looked like he was sixteen with a rounded face and extremely short crew cut, asked me to sit down. He pulled a chair from the other wall and sat in front of us, elbows on his knees, hands clasped, basketball coach style. Not. Good.

"I am very sorry to bring you this news." He hung his head for a brief second, then looked back up to us. "We are uncertain at this time as to what caused the cardiac arrest. We tried for quite some time but were unable to resuscitate him. I'm so sorry for your loss."

And that is when everything stopped like I had been sucked into a black hole where I would disappear forever. My heart. My mind. I could not think. I fell to my knees, completely undone. Everett knelt alongside me with his arms wrapped around me. I wept, shaking violently. Everett was just blank as he held me as tightly as he could, his face stone. How could this happen? They said he would recover from these injuries. It is not fair. He's too young. We didn't have enough time.

CHAPTER 7

Now

SUDDENLY I HEAR THE large, heavy wooden door close at the back of the church. I wasn't aware of any other visitors inside. I had been in my fog for a while. It startled me for a moment. I took a few minutes to slow my breathing, calm my nerves back down. Each time my mind revisits that afternoon I feel the immeasurable pain fill me again. New details unfold that I hadn't seen before. I look back up to the angel in the window and beg for some sort of peace. It feels like her arm reached out and hovered over me. I shiver. Perhaps she listened to my plea. I stand to look around, stretch my legs before I begin to navigate my way out.

I am both happy and sad as I walk toward the back of the church. This truly is a remarkable place, and I am glad I took the time to stop in. The sadness is in my grief and emptiness, but I feel a rainbow of hope – a need to look ahead. I glance back over my shoulder to the angel above one quick time and smile. I know I will get through this. Today just may be a little tough. I turn back to make my exit, a little more weight floats off my shoulders.

I walk into the vestibule, stopping momentarily to dig through my things to find my sunglasses. While standing there, I smell an aromatic lavender and mandarin musk, just as I did last night outside the jewelry store. How oddly familiar, and this time a hint of sandalwood is faintly there. This is not typical of a church smell or incense used. It's definitely someone's fragrance. I look around, still no sign of any, er – human, existence here in the church. I step outside the church desperately onto the steps and look all around… still no one to be seen. I feel woozy from rushing into the heat so frantically. I have to concentrate on slowing my movements and grab the railing to recenter. As I pause, there is only an elderly couple across the street. No one else nearby. Perhaps I'm losing my mind. I *know* someone was here.

As I turn the corner outside, driving away is a black sedan. Could it be possible? What on earth is going on? Can the cologne *and* car be entirely coincidence? I have no other reasonable explanation. I may need to seek advice from Reese on this one, and soon.

I walk aimlessly in the general direction of the bed and breakfast. I plan on speaking to Reese about this, but I need time to think it through, in peace and quiet.

I am now thoroughly sweating from the heat. It is difficult to take each step. My legs feel like I'm hiking uphill through quicksand. I pick up the pace, knowing I'll collapse soon if I do not make it back. The emotions are wiping me out, and I would rather not pass out in front of a bunch of strangers downtown. I study my tennis shoes on each step, reminding myself to glance up occasionally to avoid collisions with people or things. Eventually I make it to the entrance of the bed and breakfast. I rudely sneak by the hostess, Hayley, in the front room, avoiding small talk.

I enter my room and collapse forward on the bed. Oomph. The puffy feather bed is soft and soothing, enveloping my entire body. With my feet dangling off the edge, I use my toe of one shoe to pry on the heel of the other, kicking it to the floor, then repeat on the other. I scoot up, roll onto my back, and stretch out. The air in the room is cool, and a slight hint of the shower bomb scent I used in the morning is lingering in the air.

I reach over to my nightstand, pour a fresh glass of water and grab a pack of cheese crackers. I try to think through the events of the past twenty-four hours. Running out of the store into the street chasing a man who looks like Elliot last night. Smelling the same scent in the church and then finding a car of the exact make and model cruising away today. There has to be a logical reason, but my mind only allows me to think of Elliot. I need an intervention like I've seen on those reality television shows, or maybe a visit with Dr. Phil.

I grab my now yellow phone and text Reese.

ME: Hi friend. Just checking in. How are you doing?

The phone immediately rings. The picture of Reese with her tongue sticking out at me, eyes-crossed, appears on the screen. I smile every time I see it. I swipe to answer.

"Okay, what is going on? You never text just to say hi, or check in," she accurately accuses.

"Hey, are you busy? Do you have a class soon?" My thoughts translate to: This is going to take some time. I am borderline insane. Psychotic break just around the corner. Desperately seeking help.

"I have plenty of time. No class until three. What's going on, Clo?"

"I'm going to start with please do not think I'm insane. I just need to get this all out so I can talk through it logically."

"Intriguing, I'll bite. What happened?" She already has me worried. I begin to explain the events leading to my unsettled state of consciousness. I give her all the details, while snacking on my crackers. When I get through the entire explanation, she pauses for a few moments before replying.

"I may need you to repeat that again! You rambled on so quickly. Between the food chomping and what sounds like you running a marathon, I am not sure I caught everything you said. Were you pacing the entire time?"

"Sorry, I was stress eating, and then hanging upside down off the edge of the bed and kicking my legs in the air. Forgive me, I am feeling a bit restless here while all of this is processing."

"You are the strangest person I've ever met in my life. But I love you, dearly. So, just to get this straight. Girl sees guy. Girl risks life running across street. Guy gets in car. Girl shouts name of another guy. Car drives off. Girl smells his soap or cologne or something. Next day, girl smells more soap or cologne. Girl runs outside. Same car drives off. But, this time no guy spotted?"

"Are you writing a stick figure book right now? What was that?" I'm trying to be serious here, and she is mocking me?

"I am just trying to break it all down, reciting in simple terms so you remove all of the other emotions from the surroundings and thoughts."

"Oh, yes. Gotcha. I guess that is all of it."

"Clover, did you ever *actually* see his face?"

"Well….er…..no."

"So the back of this man's head and the way he walked reminded you of Elliot?"

"Please do not tell me I'm crazy or desperately concocting stories in my mind."

"Okay, I have to go then," she laughs. "Just kidding."

"Ha, ha! Not funny. I really called to get your advice. This has me really worked up."

"Well, look at me…still using my bogus degree! Mom will be freaking proud. All joking aside, Clo, you seem to be creating a lot of this based on the state of emotion you are in. I know that sounds harsh, but it is true. You want to see him soooo badly, you are imagining that you are. That brown haired man with a fairly normal walk , wearing a scent that can be purchased in any local drug store, could be one of millions. It is not uncommon to see, hear, feel someone you just lost, especially in a traumatic loss. You are not crazy. I think you are just trying to deal with it in your own way. Give yourself some time. Are you having other flashbacks too?"

"I am doing a lot of mental reminiscing if that is what you mean?"

"Yes, exactly. Clover, it is okay to feel like this. It will get easier with time. Allow yourself these moments, but call if you need to talk. Let it out. I'm worried that you are there alone and will just shell all of this inside."

"I know. Sometimes I need to have quiet, alone time. It's the only way I know how to let myself crash. I have to crash before I can crawl my way back out of it. Does that make sense?" I'm not sure if I explain it well enough. It is hard enough to go through, let alone put into words.

"Of course. But don't let yourself crash too hard. You sound like you have also taken some time to relax, have fun. Please allow yourself more of that. You are allowed to keep moving on. There is no harm or guilt in doing that."

I sigh deeply. "Easier said than done, but I will keep trying. Thank you, Reese. I knew you would help me sort through this. I am planning on hanging around here for a few more days, and then leave for Savannah for a visit. I hope to spend some time figuring things out. Where I am going in life."

"A visit with Lily will be good for you. But please don't put too much pressure on yourself to figure everything out, now. It is not a great idea to make big decisions when you are going through so much. You know you can stay with me and Nick for however long you need. The offer still stands on working on a new studio, too. We really are nearing that point to expand. I could use your brains to help. Just think about it."

"Ok, I will. I think I'm going to take a nap. Call you later, alright?"

"You got it, babe. I miss you. Talk to you soon. Hugs." She makes a smoochy sound.

"Bye, Reese." I hang up. I didn't realize how long I was sitting like that, but the blood has all rushed to my head, face flushed. I sit up and get a sudden headache. Oh, super. I will definitely rest a bit. I feel better after my talk with Reese, too. Not insane – that is great news. I'm not sure if any of what she says is based on her degree, but regardless she has a talent for it.

I faintly hear calming instrumental music playing outside on the patio. It is soothing, intermixed with a few chirping birds. I push down the duvet, and pull the sheet up to my chin. The fan is on, swirling a cool breeze about the room. I take in a few deep breaths to clear my thoughts. After years of practice, I am still not an expert at meditation. I tell myself to let the weight of my body float off, try to breathe evenly. Eventually I drift into a sleep.

In my sleep, my brain goes haywire, and I have the most bizarre images in a dream. I am here in this bed, snuggled up with Elliot. This itself would not be that odd, considering we did cuddle a lot and had plans to eventually visit this town together. In *this* dream, we are.....naked! The eyelet curtains are waving in the breeze from the fan. He is laying to my left, propped up on his right elbow with his cheek in his hand, facing me. The details I envision are incredible. His hair is a mess, face flushed, with the sexiest smile glowing. He reaches as he sits up a bit taller, hovering over me, and takes his hand to caress my face with the back of his fingers, so gently. It is endearing, the touch sends goosebumps all over my body. I reach out and meet his hand with mine, intertwining our fingers. I notice a scar on his pinky finger as he holds my hand, running our fingers back and forth in a sensual manner. I spend a second running my thumb over the scar, like I am taking the sting out of it.

He leans in, kissing my nose, and whispers, "I love you, Clover. I have been waiting for this for so long." I smile back replying, "I love you, too." His eyes seem more intense, darker blue, less green. It must be from how dilated they appear right now. The passion has us both overloaded on hormones that can do that. My eyes should be entirely black! The sheet gets pulled up over our heads, and we both start giggling.

I wake myself up. What. *Theee.* Fuck! This is the most insane dream I can recall ever having. Elliot and I never felt that way about each other. We never discussed even trying to create more out of our relationship. I will not admit that the dream did not shock me. This is just all crazy on steroids.

As Reese explained to me on the phone earlier, my mind is

dealing with his loss in many ways. I have been reminiscing a lot, remembering all of our times together. But this was very different. It created an image from the future that will never happen. My imagination generated changes in him. I never noticed that scar before, or maybe had never been close enough to see it? He was probably supposed to get that scar at the shop, burning it on a pan.

Am I more upset that he will never have the chance to fulfill his dreams, or that we will never take a chance on us....to be more? When we first met, it was obvious neither of us felt *that* kind of love for each other. It was a platonic rapport we shared, as strong as it was. Most of our friends and family questioned it constantly. Everett always teased us, thinking we were secret lovers – or at least friends with benefits. We learned to deal with his obnoxious remarks. My grandmother believed me, but for quite some time pushed me to find if there was more there than I would let myself see. Eventually she tired of encouraging it. Reese was the only one who genuinely accepted our relationship as it was. Of course, she spent the most time around us. If she ever doubted it, she would have asked me, right?

I wonder if deep in my heart I hoped he did have new feelings growing for me? He never pursued anyone, no dating. Elliot's excuse was his focus on his career. I always accepted it. Perhaps it was his way of showing me, that he never found anyone else, never wanted anyone else. Maybe I was his one. However, as my wingman, he continuously promised to find me the right man. If he meant it to be him, why go through all the trouble of introducing me to other guys, or setting up those blind dates? Wait. Stop. He clearly had no feelings for me or thoughts of changing *us*. If he did, he would have communicated it, somehow. We both loved what we shared. It was not supposed to change.

I can revisit this later with Reese, maybe she can continue her guidance. I need to forgive myself for dreaming of a future, of any kind, with Elliot. I am certain it is just part of my old pal Grief interfering. He needs to keep his nose out of my dreams and his mind out of the gutter.

I am now extremely restless; a dream like that would make anyone restless. I'm not interested in reading, television, solitaire. I change into my workout clothes in hope that some yoga asanas will assist with that. I slide the red and white paisley chair toward the bathroom to make some space. On my first sun salutation, I practically fall over going into warrior pose, kicking the footboard on the bed. That was not graceful. I clearly do not have enough room to do this in here. I walk out of the room, down the stairs, and head out to the garden. It is still rather warm late in the afternoon, but if I can handle hot yoga at home occasionally, I can do this here.

Luckily no one else is outside now. I locate a level, grassy area over by the koi pond and begin. It is actually quite comfortable here. My spot has some nice shade, the wind is picking up a bit, and I move smoothly through my short routine. It feels good to be out here, practicing, clearing my thoughts. I finish up in corpse pose, relaxing. Soaking in the energy around me, breathing deeply.

Suddenly, I feel a hot, wet tongue licking my face. Relaxation over. I sit up and realize this is Chance, Poppy's dog, who covered my face in slobber. He has no collar on, but I recognize him from my introduction yesterday. He sits down next to me, panting like crazy. I walk over to the outdoor grilling area and grab a bottle of water from the mini-fridge.

"Here you go, buddy. You look thirsty. Where are you coming from?" I ask the dog, clearly my brain is still in insanity mode for the day. Now I'm talking to dogs.

"CHHAAANNNNCEEE! Here, Chance!" I hear someone yelling from behind the beautifully blooming hydrangeas at the back of the property. Then I see Poppy crawling through the bushes on her hands and knees. "Chance, come here!"

I shout back, laughing. "Poppy, he's over here!"

She stands up, brushes off her knees and runs over. Dramatically she starts panting like she is out of wind, tongue hanging out, dropping her shoulders, hands at her side. "Gee whiz, Chance! You wear me out!"

"Hi! What is happening here?"

"Well, mom is cooking hamburgers outside. Chance and I were playing in the water, and then he saw a rabbit or squirrel and ran off. We live just two houses down, behind those bushes back there. Not far. Well, sort of far....if you're running!" She is in her suit still, purple with white polka-dots and a cute ruffle around the waist.

Within a minute, Sadie comes walking *around* the bushes, looking for Poppy and the dog. I spot her quickly and wave. "Hi, Sadie! We found him. All is well."

"Well, thank goodness. That lunatic dog! Did you see what he was after, Poppy?"

"I think a bunny, maybe."

"He's so silly – it could have been a bumblebee," she adds as she kneels down to put his collar on him. "They were playing in the sprinkler. I took his collar off so his mane wouldn't get all smashed down around it. Then, boom – he takes off. Never a dull moment with us!"

She looks around the garden a bit, admiring how pretty it is. "Wow, I always wondered what it looked like back here. The place is so charming from the front, but this is amazing!"

Poppy and Chance are looking at the fish in the koi pond. They are easily amused.

"It really is a nice, clean place. The atmosphere is just what I needed, and the prices were very reasonable. You were right, they could work on the coffee though. Maybe you could provide them coffee delivery?"

"You know, I could ask if they would be interested in serving our beans here. It would be good advertising for the café. Maybe I'll stop by sometime and talk it over. Great idea, thank you!"

"Sounds like a win-win to me! The owners are super friendly. I'm sure they would love to hear from you. Plus, you are sort-of neighbors, right?"

"I guess we are. Hey, not to cut this short....but my coals are going to burn out if I don't get the burgers on. Are you hungry? It isn't a huge spread for dinner, but it is closer than the diner, and it's on me for your great idea." She really is one of the sweetest people I have ever met.

"Are you sure? I do not want to impose." I refrain from appearing too eager, but it would definitely beat dining alone again.

"Absolutely, it will be fun. Come on." She leads the way. Poppy and Chance follow. Poppy is skipping, excited for dinner company. We make it back to their yard. It is a lot smaller than the garden at the bed and breakfast. Sadie has a few potted plants around a brick paver patio. Poppy has a swing set towards the back, with a bit of sand underneath it. The wooden dog-eared fence is painted on one side to look like a big row of gigantic flowers – daisies I think, and some dandelions. There are spots it is in need of repair – most likely how Chance made his way out. What a fun yard, though. Poppy and the dog go over to the swing to play.

Sadie sees me staring at the fence mural. "I see you are quite talented – now I know you could have drawn any flower on my coffee cup!" I admire her work some more.

"I don't have time for a lot of gardening, so we adapted. I don't have to water those or weed them and they bloom all year. Between running Poppy all over, and the shop, things get a bit hectic."

"Do you have any help?" I hope I am not prying.

"Not a lot. Poppy's dad does the bare minimum. It is very frustrating. He travels a lot for work. He maybe sees her twice a month, a weekend here and there. It's unfortunate." She shrugs her shoulders. "We are trying our best."

I walk closer to the grill, which now has the wonderful scent of cheeseburgers billowing from it. "It looks like the two of you are doing exceptionally well, considering the situation." We both sit down on the picnic table nearby. "I grew up without knowing my dad at all, my mom died having me, and my grandmother raised me. I turned out….er, I'm doing okay."

"That must have been very difficult. Must be, I mean. That is something you deal with your entire life. I'm sorry." Her sincerity is very touching.

"Thanks. It's a lot. I may not have it all figured out right now, but I know I will be fine. The two of you will find your way through this too. Poppy seems like an energetic, happy kid. I see how much you mean to her. You are lucky to have each other." I remember Poppy telling me about her mom consoling her when she is sad. She will be fine. They both will.

"Some days are harder than others, but each one is getting better. We've been divorced for three years now. Sometimes, I think about moving back home closer to my family. But this is home. Poppy is comfortable here. It makes it easier to see her dad, when he is home from the road. I am finally getting settled, the café is picking up. The community has been great to us. I just cannot risk moving and starting over again."

"That totally makes sense. If I lived here, I wouldn't move either. It really is a nice area. Everyone is kind. I'm glad I made the trip."

"Yes, may I ask why you ended up travelling alone? You mentioned you had other plans." She paused a moment, checked the grill, and sat back down. "I mean, if you want to talk about it."

"Sure. I recently lost my best friend. He and I had this trip planned for next year, together. I just needed to get out of the city and decided to make the trip myself. Maybe heal a little. Figure things out."

"Clover, I'm sorry. I didn't know. I will admit, I think you are doing amazing. I could never go away alone and keep my sanity."

"I wouldn't say I'm staying completely sane. But it has already led to discovery for me. I need to stick it out."

Sadie stands up to plate the food off the grill. She calls Poppy over to go wash her hands for dinner. I help her get everything else out of the kitchen. I adore the swinging saloon doors leading to the kitchen from their back mudroom. The kitchen is decorated subtly, in a soft lavender and grey. The counters and cabinets are a bright white. There are a few butterfly images hanging. It is homey and comfortable.

Sadie hands me a refreshing salad from the ice box. She carries a condiment and napkin caddy in one hand, and a bowl of southern style potato salad in the other. I am drooling, it all looks so wonderful.

As we approach the table, Poppy is already seated. She is pointing at my phone which I left outside. "Your boyfriend just called you!" She giggles.

"You came on this trip alone and left your boyfriend at home?" Sadie flashes me a look of confusion.

"Oh, no. Misunderstanding. No boyfriend. That's my friend's brother, Everett, calling to check on me. We've been trying to help each other through all of this."

"I see. That is lovely. He must be a gentleman, showing concern like that for you. It is good to have those kind of people surrounding you."

"Aaaaannnnd, he's cute mom!" Poppy just could not wait to add that.

"Poppy, it's not like that. He may be a looker, but not the guy for me. He's just a good friend." Did I just admit that Everett was my friend, and good looking? Oh boy. I am in need of a lobotomy.

"Let the cheese melt down a second on these. You need something to drink? Wine, beer, soda, water?"

Considering the way my brain is acting, I definitely need something. "A beer would be great, thank you so much."

"Oh, good. I would have felt strange drinking alone. Poppy, you want a lemonade or water?"

"Duh, mom. Lemonade." Poppy sarcastically responded.

"Is that how we talk to one another?" She gives a stern stare to her daughter.

"Sorry mom. I would absolutely love a lemonade, thank you." I have to chuckle as the girl adds a terrible British accent onto the end of her statement.

Sadie rolls her eyes. "Oh no, not that accent again," she whispers my way. "I'll grab the drinks; be right back."

My phone vibrates alive again.

1 missed call(s) – Everett

EVERETT: Hi. Wanted to let you know the truck made it okay, just late. Call me when you have a sec.

I am not going to call right now, that would be rude. I can reach out to him later this evening. I'll let him know real quick, before we start eating.

ME: Ev – just sitting down to eat. Call you later.

EVERETT: Can't you talk while you eat by yourself?

Ugh. There it is, the pity party for people like me who dine alone.

ME: FYI, I am dining with friends.

EVERETT: Oh, right the hot one! LOL

At least he got a laugh out of me on that one. He is such a guy. Sadie is back, everything looks delicious. I begin eating like I have been deprived of food for years. I am so hungry my stomach thinks my throat got cut.

"Everything okay, with your friend?" Sadie asks, while twisting open her beer.

"Yep, he's fine. Everett has been overly protective of me the past few days. He is nervous that I am travelling alone. What will he say when I drive the rest of the way to Savannah? Ha!"

"Well, I hope he stops you!" Sadie shocks me a bit with her remark. "What I mean to say, is you really shouldn't be travelling alone. It is a crazy world out there. I would worry about any woman driving a long distance on her own. I haven't known you but a couple of days, and I would worry about you too."

"That is very nice of you to be concerned, but I've made this trip to my grandmother's a hundred times. I'll be fine, honest."

"Just because you feel that way, does not make others worry less."

"Everett is just trying to act like his brother. I understand he is going through this too. But if you knew him, you would question his motives. It seems like he is still trying to prove something to Elliot. Maybe it is just being protective, but he has never been this interested in me in all the years I've known Elliot. It's just kind of weird."

"Even if he is trying to prove something to his brother, perhaps he's trying to prove something to himself, too. You never know how men are thinking. They have that caveman instinct to stick their chest out and carry-on like Tarzan."

We both laugh at her perceptive thought.

Poppy chimes in, "Boys are confusing."

"Yes they are," her mother and I say at the same time. "It is best to stay away from them altogether," I add in.

"Right?" Sadie adds, unconvincingly. I wonder if she gets lonely. I haven't dated anyone seriously since Smith. That only lasted a few months and was years ago, but I always had Elliot. He made it feel less lonely. Our connection was better than any other I could imagine (except maybe for my dream this afternoon).

"So you haven't dated at all in the last three years?" I pry.

"Not really. I have had a few guys ask me out. I went on one date when I clearly was not ready, so I didn't give the poor guy a chance. Right now, it is not my main priority."

"I get it, trust me. I always hope that when I meet the right one, I'll just know."

"Wouldn't that be nice!" She picks up her beer. "Here's to finding and realizing it is Mr. Right!" She tilts her beer at mine and we clink together and both take a sip. Poppy grabs her glass of lemonade and reaches over to clink into the beer bottles again.

Back in her British accent, "To Mr. Rights-es-sss..." I am cracking up.

"This really has been a wonderful night, thank you so much for inviting me. I haven't had this much fun for a while!"

"Neither have I. It is nice having a friend to talk with over a beer. Laughter is the best medicine."

"That's the only medicine I can prescribe right now. Maybe someday." I think about my dream of becoming a physician.

"Oh, medicine is something you want to do?" Sadie asks.

"I thought so. Life has taken a different path for a while now, though. That's part of what I'm trying to figure out. Currently I am a homeless, part time yoga instructor and lab rat."

"Never give up on your dream. Even if it is delayed for now, you'll never erase it from your heart, not if that is what you are truly wanting from life."

"I think it is going to be paused for a while longer. But, you're right. I won't give up on it."

"I wish we had somewhere to learn yoga around here. They used to have classes at the rec center, but I'm not sure what happened. Maybe the instructor moved. I took a few classes, really enjoyed it."

"You can teach it, Clover!" Poppy jumps in. "You should move here. You and mommy can be friends. She could go to your yogurt classes and then you can get coffee from our shop. That would be soooo fun!"

"Wow, Poppy. That's a big thought," Sadie is thinking, I can see the wheels spinning. "Honestly, it isn't a bad idea. If you are in the middle of figuring things out....there is a room to rent above the café. We could fix it up for you. You could checkout the rec center about teaching lessons."

"You two are wild thinkers this evening!" I add.

"Just trying to help out a friend. I am not kidding. You seem to like the area. You would be closer to your grandmother. There is a definite need locally for a service you are able to provide. Maybe it *is* something to think about. We'd be here to help you settle in."

"Huh, all of that is true. I'm not sure though. I have....well.... my one good friend, Reese, in Chicago. She was looking for me to help her with her business for a while. It is something I would really need to think about."

"Just think about it. Wait a while before you rule it out entirely.

You never know where life will lead you." She has such a way of saying things. It is inspiring.

"Sure, I'll think about it." Poppy's face lights up. "But no promises, okay?" I add, remembering her mom's way of protecting her from let-downs with her father.

We clean everything up. I wash a few of the dishes sitting in her sink and we have another drink, play music, and dance and sing around their kitchen. Poppy loves to twirl around and do fancy ballerina moves. I have a remarkable time.

"Time for bed, darling. It's getting late." Sadie gestures to Poppy to go upstairs and get ready for bed. "Say goodnight to Clover."

"G'night. I had fun. So did mom. She hasn't danced with me in the kitchen in a long time."

Sadie shrugs at that.

"Good night. I better walk back too, it is getting late. Thanks again for tonight. I had a blast. I will probably see you in the morning for my caffeine fix."

"Sounds good. Enjoy your evening. I hope to see you soon!"

She walks me to the backyard. I cut through the neighbors' yards and around the bushes to the garden. I missed the activities outside this evening around the fire. I guess it is later than I expected. I get back to my room and change for bed. I do a full body wiggle and shake, expending the last bit of energy in me. It was like a happy dance, and I let out a tiny squeal of excitement. I'm not sure what that is about, maybe an internal vibe from the Reese voice in my head.

I flip the switch to shut off the overhead lights above the bed. The staff have graciously turned down the bed again. I enjoy the chocolate gift they left. I reach over to plug in my phone to charge for the night and see another notification at top.

EVERETT: You overeat and already tire out?

Hmmm. Do I have the energy to stay awake for a chat with him? I did tell him I'd call. Maybe just a quick chat, then I am ready for a good night sleep.

Before dialing Everett's number, I wonder if I should fill in Reese on my dream of the day. She would be getting to bed soon, and I wouldn't want to wake her. I decide not to call, or maybe never tell her about that. It was overwhelming and confusing. I don't think I can handle getting Reese's matter of fact interpretation of it tonight. I'll hold off for now. I wouldn't mind getting her thoughts on Poppy's idea of me sticking around here for a while. Maybe I'll call her tomorrow. Wow, indecision may or may not be my problem.

I scroll through my contacts to call Everett. Each time I do that, my heart sinks a little bit as I pass Elliot's name in the list, see his contact picture of him playing at a gig, smiling enthusiastically. How long do I keep it in there? Everett decided to keep the service turned on for a while, maybe another month, in the chance of any business reaching out to him. I let him take the phone. I didn't want to mess with that. There were times I wanted to call it for old times sake, when I was feeling sad, maybe hear his voice on the message he had recorded for incoming calls. I knew if I started that, I would be down the rabbit hole calling it every hour to listen, breaking my heart each time.

Everett picked up the call right away. "Hello, Clover!" He sounded happy to hear from me. "How was your dinner?"

"It was very nice, thank you. I met this really cool woman, Sadie, who owns the café in town. I had burgers with her and her daughter tonight. It was nice to kickback and just hang out, like normal people do."

"Wow, Clover – that sounds like a blast! Quite the happening night life – burgers and beers!" he laughs mockingly.

"Do not judge, Mister Fancy Pants. That is what this trip is about for me. Relaxing, finding my way. Would it be better if I told you I went down to the local pub, got smashed, met a gorgeous stranger who is waiting outside my room as we speak. If so, I need to let you go!" Ha, take that!

"Wow, no. Please do not tell me that! I would be crushed."

"Crushed, really?"

"I am supposed to be looking out for you. That scenario would not reflect highly on my progress."

"Everett, you are crazy! I do not need a protector. I am a big girl, I'll be fine." I feel like that sounded convincing.

"Sure, sure. Trust me. I know damn well you are a grown woman."

"And what is that supposed to mean?" He is flirty this evening. I need to stop that behavior.

"Clover-, well....er, just that Elliot always told me how strong and independent you are. Nothing more, don't worry."

"Is that all he said?" Maybe I can get some answers to my confusing dream from earlier today.

"Innnteresting. I knew it!" he let out a few chuckles. "I knew there was something going on with you two."

"No, I just wondered if he ever mentioned anything else about me. About us? Brothers would have those conversations, right?"

"Not us, unfortunately. We kept in touch, but he never really opened up about stuff like that with me. It was a little too deep. I always questioned him and tried to get the details. He never really had more to say. I know he loved you deeply, thought you were an amazing person. You made him happy Clover. He was very happy, that I am certain. With someone like you around, how could he not be?"

"Are you getting all sentimental on me, Everett?"

"No. Just telling the truth. And I meant what I said about protecting you. You were Elliot's rock. You've helped me through all of this. The least I can do is be here for you, help you out when you need it. I will protect you, you know that right?"

"Wow." I choked up a bit. "That is very sweet, Everett. Thank you. I wish your brother knew this side of you a bit more. Or maybe he did, and didn't share with me. The brotherly love needed to keep up the caveman façade."

"I'm afraid he didn't. I never showed him my weaknesses."

"Being sentimental and sweet is not a weakness, Ev."

"I'm learning that now. You are helping me find myself. This entire experience is making me look at life from a different angle."

"I am glad you are learning a new perspective. I am too. I've only been here a couple days, but I am starting to see through the fog too. Actually, my new friend is trying to get me to move here. She has a place I could rent, and there is work potential. I do kind of like it here. This place makes me feel at home. I know I need to think about it. Like *really* think about it before I make any big decisions right now."

"That would be awesome, Clover. We would be less than an hour apart. I would love to have you closer than Chicago!" He seemed a little too excited about this opportunity.

"Well, I'm not sure what I'll do. Too much to think about. Maybe my time on the road to Savannah in a day or two will help me sort it out."

"Clover, you are driving to Savannah? Are you sure that is a good idea?"

"Yes, I need to get down there to visit. It has been too long since I saw them. While I'm on a break from work, and dealing with all of this, I imagine it is the best time for me to see family."

"That's true. But you are not going alone, I will go with you."

Well that is demanding, and surprising. My plan is to spend the travel time thinking through tough decisions that are ahead of me. I enjoy time alone. "I don't think-"

He interrupts me. "Clover, I'm not taking no for an answer. You let me know when you want to go, and I'll be there. I am in between big cases, and someone else can cover me if needed while I'm away. I could use some time away too. What do you say?"

Hmmm. I know he has been struggling too. I do not doubt that he could use a break. I am not completely convinced this is a good idea. If his intention is to find himself and help a friend out, that is fine. I am still not certain of his motives – guys are always confusing to me (with one obvious exception). However, if he really needs this time to heal, how can I say no?

"I guess so, if you insist. My plans are still up in the air. Not tomorrow, but maybe plan on leaving the following morning. Early – like four. Is that too early?"

"I will be there." His voice has calmed down now.

"Okay. I will check in with Ruby to see if that works out alright and confirm with you."

"That sounds great. I am excited to spend some time with you and meet your family."

"Yeah, me too. But, I really should let you go. It has been a long day and I'm exhausted. I'll get ahold of you tomorrow with details."

"Sure, Clover. It was nice to hear your voice tonight. You sound good. I hope you have a good night's rest. Until tomorrow.."

Holy cow. I am tired. I am more confused than earlier in the day. I am not certain what was going on with Everett on that call. He was actually being super sweet. My sexy Elliot dream earlier, and now this strange conversation with Everett. What is my brain trying to do to me? I feel better knowing Elliot never spoke to his brother about wanting more for us. That means everything between us was real, always out in the open. No secrets. As I think about it more, I am sure I had no desire for our relationship to change either. This is all a fluke. A brief, and grief, blip of confusion.

I need to get some absolute deep sleep tonight, so I can start tomorrow off refreshed and clear minded. I would like some chamomile, but that will take too long. Call me lazy. Maybe just a small melatonin dose will help out. When I did my unpacking, I thoughtfully placed them in the nightstand drawer. Convenient. I reach over and open the drawer to grab one. I hope this helps. I do a few deep breaths, pull the duvet up tighter, and slowly fall asleep.

CHAPTER 8

I WAKE TO THE sound of voices outside the window. It is after eight, but the sky is gray so it looks pre-dawn. It sounds like a party outside. There is music playing and laughter. I need to check this out before I miss something fun!

I rush through my shower, skipping the aromatic shower bomb. A quick shampoo and suds-up with the citrus cream shower gel is plenty to energize me today. As I get dressed, I am humming again, always our John Hiatt song. It was one of my favorites, and Elliot played it for me all the time. Since he passed, it seems to be the only song that gets stuck in my head. I slip on my shoes, and leave the room, a skip to my step. It is going to be a good day. I can feel it.

Outside, the owners have a mimosa party going. They are making omelets on the outdoor griddle. It smells delicious. My appetite is definitely recovered. I am easy to please. A simple ham and cheese omelet is my favorite. If you put too much into an omelet, the flavors just blend together to me.

Most everyone is seated, and I am the last one at the counter, waiting for the eggs to cook up. Hayley and her husband, Josh, run the bed and breakfast. He must be inside tending to the rooms. She has been the one typically cooking. Her technique at the griddle is impressive. I have only spoken with her a few times, but she has been so nice. I take the opportunity to bring up Sadie's coffee.

"Hi, Hayley. This is a fantastic gathering! You really know how to start off the day!"

"We're glad you decided to join. I am trying to come up with ideas to get our guests outside and maybe interact with each other more. This is a bit more time consuming to get set up, so mimosa mornings are only once a week. I have been trying to do the evening snacks to get everyone outside around the fire, too."

"Yes, the fire is really wonderful. I saw your s'mores out the other night. I was too full to sample, but they looked fun! Very creative."

"Tonight we're doing grilled pizzas by the fire, and Josh is going to play guitar. He is not extremely pleased I volunteered his musical talents." She laughs. "He'll get over it. I told him he doesn't have to play long. Last week a guest took over for him and did amazing!"

"That's very cool. Hey, do you know your neighbor, Sadie? She lives a couple homes down. She walked over yesterday – had to grab her dog who ran off. No worries, he's friendly. Sadie also thinks this place is great and was admiring the garden." I try to open the window to bring up the coffee idea.

"Yes, I think we have met. She runs the café downtown, right?"

"She does! As a matter of fact, we were talking and thought you may be interested in serving her coffee blend here?"

She smiled. I hope it is a "that's a great idea" smile. I don't know her well enough to decipher. Either way, I cannot imagine her getting upset by my asking. She may just change the subject; she stalls before replying. In a minute she is plating my breakfast, turning back to me.

"Here you go! I hope you like it. Maybe a better cup of coffee would complement it? I know that is something we could improve around here. I would definitely speak with her about buying beans from her. We try to carry local products here as much as possible. I didn't know she was doing sales outside the shop?"

"Honestly, the idea just popped up yesterday. Your coffee is fine here, but that may move the bar to exceptional. And, she could use the extra advertising. Not to sound desperate, but she is raising her daughter on her own and trying to grow her business. It is a lot.

I just thought, maybe neighbors could help each other, if it works out alright."

"That is a great idea, truly."

"I'm going to sit and eat this enormous omelet. It smells great. If you want to get in touch with her, let me know. I would be glad to bring her by."

"Yes, please. Tell her anytime. Josh and I have also been thinking about opening the place up to local traffic for certain events, not just guests. I wouldn't mind getting another business owner's perspective on that, perhaps she could help out with something like that. Like an open coffee hour with more full service. I can see it happening weekly. Throw in some local storytelling or open mic poetry…..hmmm….we're on to something here!"

"Ooooohhh, I feel the energy! You are on a roll!"

"The day is full of energy!" she says. She walks out between the patio tables and raises her champagne flute. "To a lovely day, with new friends and good vibes!"

"Here, here!" everyone responds. I wish I had been out here more to meet with some of the other guests. Everyone is interesting. It is refreshing to meet and talk with them, hear about what they do, where they're from, what brought them to town. I just tell them I am here for some R&R. No need for details, not wanting the pity party. The evening around the fire is something to look forward to. I would like to hang out with everyone again tonight.

I finish my breakfast and enjoy the company, grateful to not be dining alone. It feels good to spend time around new people. I am relearning to break out of my shell. The clouds start to dissolve, the sun is trying to peak out. There is a hint of pink and blue sky behind the dreary grey. It should be a nice day, a bit cooler than previous days. I help clear my things off the table and walk them to the counter. I say goodbye to the other guests and thank Hayley for a lovely morning. Now, up to my room to work out the gameplan.

I need to inform Ruby of my intent to visit. I wish I could be there when she tells my grandma that I'll be visiting. Hopefully that will lift her spirits knowing I'll be there soon. She'll be surprised to hear I will have company with me. I text her.

ME: Good morning, Ruby. How are things?

RUBY: Today is a good day. Any news for us???

ME: I think we'll be leaving 4ish tomorrow. B there early afternoon if we drive straight.

RUBY: Who's we?

ME: Sorry. Elliot's brother, Everett, is joining me. He didn't want me to travel alone.

RUBY: Well, well. That is lovely. Look forward to seeing you. Going to tell mom right now.

ME: See you then!

I sit down, grab the tour book to pick out something interesting for the day. I know there are more historical sites to check out. I'm not sure if anything can top the church visit from yesterday, in more ways than one! It looks like the Winstead Hill has a lot to see. As long as the weather holds out today, that looks the most interesting to me. If it rains, I'll use the museum as a back-up.

I glance out the window, still partly cloudy. I fill my backpack with the basics. I head to the front of the house. Hayley is there putting out some fresh flowers. They smell amazing. I think they're lilacs; they add just a subtle aroma to the corridor. "Can you help me with something real quick?" I ask her.

"I will certainly try. What can I do?"

"I am thinking about visiting the Winstead park. Is that far from here?"

"It's maybe three miles. You can call a car to get you there."

"Is it a rugged three miles? If not, I may just take some time and walk it. I could use the fresh air and exercise."

"I am sure you can manage it. But here's a card for a local driver if you need to be picked up." She walks to the nearby desk to grab the card. She ruffles through a few papers in a drawer in the old oak desk. It looks custom made, lots of built-in letter slots and cubbies. It is a gorgeous piece. Eventually, she locates the number and hands it to me.

"Thanks, I'll hang on to this. My plans never seem to go as expected!" I laugh.

"I understand. I'm the same way. I hope the weather stays nice. If you're into history, you'll love it there. Even if you're not, it is a beautiful area. I am certain you'll enjoy the visit."

"Thanks! My friend was the huge history buff. I find it interesting, but really like to see new things and people watch. I am sure I'll enjoy it." I wave and head out the bright blue door.

"Have a nice day!" she waves back and closes the door behind me. It reminds me of my grandmother walking me out for school in the morning. She always held the door open and then stood there and waited until I got on the bus, giving me a wave bye. Mornings were our time together. She usually worked in the evenings or overnight. Ruby or another neighbor would watch me until she came home. As I start walking down the sidewalk, I think about how difficult it must have been raising me alone. She had to be so tired after working late and then getting me up early. I imagine Sadie feels that way too, at least she has some control having her own business.

I decide to stop in and grab a coffee on my way through town and give her the update on my chat with Hayley. I walk into the shop and catch Poppy eating whipped cream off a spoon. I cannot blame her, that is something Reese and I have done a thousand times, only directly from a can!

"Well that looks delicious!" I tell her. She puts the spoon down quickly and folds her hands behind her back, playing innocent. "I do it too. I just love whipping cream!"

"I know, I have seen your coffee drinks!" Young and witty. The girl is just adorable.

"Ha, ha. You're funny. But that is very true!" I wink at her and we both giggle.

Sadie comes from the back office and shouts, "Hey, Clover! It is nice to see you. Did you have a good evening?"

"I sure did. I cannot wait to tell you the news!"

"Can I get you anything while you share? Something different today, or do you have your heart already set?" She points to the menu. It is handwritten on big paper scrolls draping down the wall. Very creative. A bagel shop near our loft did something similar.

"I would love another frappe like yesterday. It was to die for!"

"Coming right up!" she starts moving around behind the counter so swiftly. The coffee smell in here just settles my soul. The espresso beans grinding give off such a complex aroma, nutty and smoky with that hint of caramel sneaking through. I take a deep breath in, enjoying the scent. It reminds me of the apartment Reese and I had above the coffeehouse. We had good times there. It may be nice staying with her for a while when I return to the city.

"So? What happened that you cannot wait to share?" She is handing me the calorie rich, whipped beverage of the heavens. I take it from her hand, give her my cash and lean up against the counter. She wipes things off behind the big, shiny copper accented espresso machine.

"Oh yes! I talked to Hayley, the bed and breakfast owner this morning. Over mimosas, I managed to present the idea of selling your coffee roast at the house. She seemed excited about the opportunity, told me to bring you by anytime! Isn't that great? Hayley and Josh have been thinking about doing more gatherings there and thought a fancy coffee hour may go over well too."

"Really, she was truly excited? That is wonderful. I would love to team up with them on something like that. It sounds like they have great ideas – especially coffee related!"

I was happy to see her so elated. "After I do my touristy things today, I can get a hold of you. You could stop by and maybe catch them to talk more about it. Or you can contact her anytime, I'm sure. But it may be fun tonight. They are cooking outside and having some music. It could be a good time?" I am working hard to convince her. Sadie and I have similar personalities, and it would be great to get to know her better.

She glances over at Poppy and looks back at me, holding her finger over her lips. Apparently, we were heading into secret mode. Poppy wasn't even paying attention. She has been reorganizing supplies in a cabinet staying busy. I crack. "What's the secret?" I lean in closely and whisper to her.

"I've set up a sleepover for Poppy with one of her friends this evening. She doesn't know yet. I am going to surprise her. I thought she could use some time to hang out with someone else her age. It is hard for her when school is out. She spends most days here with me and around the public. *Adult* public. I try to get her involved in sports or something, but nothing has really grabbed her interest yet."

"Well, she is going to be excited! Did you already have plans for yourself then? I understand if you just want to hang out, you don't get much quiet, alone time I am sure."

She looked surprised by my answer, her eyes bugged out of her head. "Oh my goodness…no! When she is at her dad's I am always alone. And it is always quiet at night when she heads to bed. I could use a night out. I would love to join you!"

"It's settled then." I hand her my phone. "Put your number in here and I will call or text you when I am back this evening." She snatches the phone out of my hand briskly, with a mischievous grin. "Is there something I'm missing?" I have to ask, I am having trouble figuring out her implied gesture.

Sadie shakes her head back and forth, still grinning. "Any cute single guys there?" I see where she is going with this.

"Um – not that I have noticed. Mostly just endearing couples on a getaway. There is one older gentleman I saw reading outside the other night. He may be solo." I laugh and roll my eyes. "But I highly doubt he is your type. If you want to go out and find some nice, handsome, single young men…we can detour the plans and hit a bar later."

"Oh my, no. Not around here. I think I've met all of the eligible men around my age. Trust me when I say: nothing to write home about. I was hoping there would be an outsider staying at the bed and breakfast worthy of my time."

"Maybe you should expand your age limit?" Hmm, perhaps I'll get a better idea how old she is. Honestly, I still have no idea. She looks so young. "Twenty-two, -three? Might as well have some fun!"

Sadie throws her head back in laughter and reaches over to slap my arm. "You are hysterical, Clover! I am too close to thirty to date a toddler like that. But it would be fun!" She is still cracking up at my comment. "You have my number now, just text me whenever. A calm night around a fire sounds like fun too! Plus I can corner Hayley and her hubby about figuring out a deal. Thank you again for getting that started. You are a life-saver."

"No problem! I should get going if I am walking out to the park." I act like I'm stretching out my legs in preparation. "It is going to be an adventure!"

"Oh, please! You have no need to stretch out those yoga legs of yours! Enjoy your day. I'll see you later. I better get back to work!" A young, teenage couple just walked in holding hands. Sadie flashes a squeamish look over at me. I laugh back, and wave as I step out the door. I am looking forward to what the rest of my day brings. I cannot help but smile.

CHAPTER 9

I'M SO THRILLED, MY first steps are more like dance moves. I secure my small backpack, check that I haven't missed a zipper. It is the sort of day when I am unable to decide if I need sunglasses. I rest them on the top of my head so they are ready if the sun makes an official, and welcome, appearance. The air is calm, just a faint breeze hitting me straight on to keep me cool on this walk.

I chose not to read all of the information about the park I'll be visiting. I like to keep some of it a surprise. Plus, I never trust online reviews. I generally feel they are either overly positive by those who have something to gain out of it, or they are the few who write to complain about some random and rare event in an anonymous and unhelpful fashion. I'll keep my opinion unbiased until I experience it myself.

I walk along, passing through the rest of the downtown area, including all of the small businesses and several prominent historical locations. I enjoy seeing local owners doing well, having unique spaces. This area is untouched by chain stores and I find it refreshing. It is clear the owners work hard designing creative storefront window displays; some have elegant free-hand window art. Lovely bursts of color surround me, including large potted plants on street corners.

As I head further out of town, there are a few industrial sites, but they are masked with a large amount of greenery and trees. The road I am following has a lot of traffic, and areas without sidewalk, but drivers here are polite and leave me a gracious amount of space as they possibly can. There are spots where I can see tree line in the distance, but I feel anxious to get out to the park area, more into vast open space. Elliot would not have enjoyed this walk. He would rather drive and have more time to spend looking around.

I see the sign to the park entrance a few yards ahead. I pull out my phone to check my timing. It took me close to an hour. Considering I was checking out my surroundings closely at more of a leisurely pace, I feel I made good time. I also note a text from Everett came over. Shoot. I forgot to send him confirmation about tomorrow. I finish the walk, entering the drive area off the main road and look for a safe, quiet space to sit and send him a reply.

There is a bench nearby, and I take a seat. I grab the water bottle from my pack and take a refreshing sip, stretching out my legs in front of me, twirling my ankles in small circles. I love the sensation of post-workout stretching. However, glancing at the vast green space in front of me, it looks as though I have a lot more walking ahead of me. Hmmm, I may need to rethink the walk back. I finally decide it is going to stay cloudy and put my shades away too.

EVERETT: Are we still on for 4 tomorrow?

ME: Yes! If you arrive at 4 we can leave right away. Plan on me driving, since you have to drive here.

I see he is reading my message and dots appear while he is typing.

EVERETT: Clover, it is only 30m for me to pick you up. I can drive.

ME: I know. But it's an early start. I don't mind.

EVERETT: We can figure it out when I arrive. We will def take my car.

ME: Oh, fancy! Sounds good. Thanks! I'm at a park now, then hanging at the BNB for dinner with my new pal tonight.

EVERETT: Sounds fun. Talk soon. Enjoy ur day!

ME: :)

I'm glad I have an open afternoon to spend here. There is a walking trail to navigate the park on, and an observation area to enjoy the scenery. I have not spent much time in open, green space for quite awhile. I feel uplifted and refreshed as I start off on the path. It is spectacularly maintained. The air is crisp and clean, the scent of fresh-cut grass strikes my senses. I have missed that! I used to help out push-mowing lawns in the neighborhood as a teen. It provided me exercise and a little pocket money to spend on clothes or a movie with friends. But the time I spent mowing, listening to music, was more than a job to me, it was therapeutic. I did some of my best thinking on those afternoons. This day may prove the same.

The park is quiet today, very little foot traffic. From afar, I can see a couple of families enjoying themselves, someone walking a large great dane, and a few individuals using the trail for an afternoon jog. I suppose it would be busier on a sunny day. I can take my time, walking at my own pace. I listen to several songbirds for a while, until the breeze picks up and their calls come to a halt. I put on one earbud so I can play some music and continue on my journey. I stop at the information stations to read more about the history of the battlefield; Elliot would have done that. There is a lot of history here, stories to read. I think I would like to investigate the other sites around town too.

I try to picture myself coming here regularly, walking this track. The few joggers here seem to enjoy the space. It is so close to town, very convenient. The walk here from the café and a single lap around this track could easily get my ten thousand steps in for a day. I may agree with Elliot on this; I would rather drive here and spend more time walking in the serene location. Strangely, I can see getting around Franklin would be similar to my habits in Chicago, even though the size of each city is very different. I rarely need my car, my ancient 2004 Civic which Reese named Jezebel, when I am home. Walking and public transportation take me anywhere I need to go. My car has really only seen one path from home to Savannah. I can envision myself walking and biking a lot if I stayed here. Town is small, easy to navigate. I wonder if

Sadie drives much? I'll have to ask her this evening about that.

There are many other things I would need to figure out. From what I have learned already, townspeople here are very gracious and accepting. I feel like I could adapt quickly. I am not certain what the space above her café looks like, but it is worth taking a look at. I would have to find work, and quickly. Neither Elliot nor I have been good at saving over the years. Rent was obscene in the city, and we liked to enjoy ourselves seeing shows, concerts, and dining out a lot. I worked as much as possible but also have been paying off the few student loans I have. Luckily, I only have a few months left on cleaning those up. I have no idea what salaries are like around here, but I imagine living expenses to be much more reasonable.

Am I really contemplating a move? Besides one new acquaintance bringing up the idea, why would I want to leave the city I love? Reese reminded me to not make major decisions while my mind isn't the clearest. I cannot move in order to run away from my heartache, my loss. I understand that does not lessen based on where you are located. The longing to have known my mother, or to meet my father, or spend time with my grandfather always casts shadows on me wherever I am. Relocating would change nothing about this added heartbreak of losing my wingman.

It would be difficult to leave Reese, she and I have such a wonderful friendship. She is more like a sister to me than a best friend. However, things are progressing with her and Nick quite well, and I know she would be fine. Their business is growing too. Whether I live there or here does not change the fact that we would need to make time for each other. And, as Sadie already pointed out, I would be much closer to my grandmother and Ruby, my only family. I would be closer to Everett, who has been a great support through all of this change. He can be annoying, but I think all of this has been a wake-up call, and he is trying to grow-up.

I take a seat, as I feel I have walked this path two times now, but I truly have no idea. My legs are going to be sore tomorrow. I have not been as active these past weeks, finding it too difficult to teach any classes at the studio; my mind unwilling to focus. My practice in the garden here was refreshing. Perhaps Josh and Hayley could let me lead a yoga group for guests if I moved here? Hmm, my brain is seeing new potential.

I hear the start of Buddy Miller's "Wide River to Cross" pop up in my playlist. The song has always touched me, but sitting here this afternoon I cannot control the depth of emotion it generates. Tears form in my eyes. I lean my head back, close my eyes and just listen closely to the lyrics. At a crossroad in my life, I must stay focused on anything positive. Look for answers in things that will help me grow, help me find myself. Be happy.

Before I left on this trip, Reese had stopped by the loft to check on me. I was an absolute wreck. We sat on the floor of the living room talking, having a few beers. I explained how I just felt deflated, lost. Life was not taking me to where I felt I should be. I didn't know how to articulate it. I looked at the cold, dark red, exposed brick wall. It always looked raw and vulnerable; I told Reese that was how I felt. I remember her calm reply.

"That wall has withstood the test of time. Decades and decades of supporting the building, experiencing changes, suffering damage and cracks. Yet, look at it. Closely. It is still so elegant, strong, and *real*. You are no different."

I am not certain how she thinks of these things, but she could always drive home her points in such a graceful manner. Her ability to read my emotions and thoughts, her level of empathy, made me love and admire her so very much. She encouraged me to take a trip, talked me through different options, and then helped me settle on Franklin. Reese understood the link it would have for me to see things Elliot and I planned on seeing together. More importantly, she challenged me to come here and find myself again. To not worry about anything or anyone else. Focus on myself. My breath. My soul. This is that journey. This day has made me feel more myself than I have in such a very long time.

My reasons for staying in Chicago solely relate to Reese. I would miss her. I do not want to let her down. She has mentioned opening another studio several times and having me run it. If she needs me, I should be there for her. I could talk these things over with her. Following her advice, I try to eliminate how others impact my decision. What do *I* want?

Eventually, I would love to get back to school, actually study medicine. Dr. Clover Sheehy, M.D. That was my dream, if I am completely honest with myself. That life goal has been paused for a long time. I have allowed all of life's ups and downs become an excuse. I should take my MCAT soon if I want to see this come to fruition. I need to start somewhere. No more excuses. Clover, it is time to get your act together!

If I get through that step, I need to apply to several schools to increase my odds of getting in. It is possible I would not end up in Chicago for school at all. I will try to not put weight of furthering my education on my decision of where to live. Whichever place I choose may only be temporary.

There are too many thoughts flying through my grey matter. Restlessness takes over, I jump up with the urge to move. The energy boost is invigorating. As I get walking, the heavy clouds become overwhelmed and a light rainfall settles all around me. I laugh to myself. This place has helped me open my thoughts, see more clearly. The cool rain misting my face as I look up to the sky seems to wash my sadness and fears away. The child in me throws her arms out to the side and I begin twirling, my eyes closed. I feel light and alive!

I am standing on the trail twirling as my fingertips catch the hood of one of the joggers' jacket mid-spin. At the same time, lightning strikes and an immense crack of thunder startles me. I swear the electricity went directly through me. Dang! I'm such an idiot, I totally hit that guy. The man keeps going, and as I shout to apologize, he turns slightly back to face me while still jogging ahead. I see his hand wave in one quick motion, dismissing the incident. But as he turns ahead, his navy blue hood falls back, draping over his neck. He is moving at a fast pace, probably trying to get out of the rain. Before he is too far out of eyesight, I swear I see a mark behind his ear. A feather.

The rain is coming down in sheets now. I am just standing here alone. I push my soaked hair back out of my face and wipe both the raindrops and tears out of my eyes, trying to focus. I glance again. He's too far away now, almost at the edge of the park. I cannot believe what I just saw. It could have been a tattoo, lint, a bug, a similar looking birthmark. Think logically. Calm down.

But I am unable to control the need to follow him. I throw my backpack over my shoulder and take off in a sprint. I do not want to look foolish chasing him, but at this point in time, I don't fucking care. My legs are so tired from my ardent walking earlier, I am struggling to catch up. I lose sight of him as he rounds a corner by the parking lot overgrown with bushes and trees. It must be close to a quarter of a mile in a sprint as I approach the parking area. Damn, this guy is fast! I finally make the corner, and I see him getting into a car. "Elliot!" I attempt to yell. With my voice in shock, weakened and shaky, and the rain and wind, he apparently does not hear me.

As he lowers into the vehicle, he glances up over the roof. I barely catch a glimpse before he's in and driving off. But in that single second, I made eye contact with him. Sea blue topaz and green eyes sparkled back at me. My mind could not focus on anything else, but his eyes. *Those eyes.* The car is already down the street. I fall forward to the ground on my knees. The ground digs into my kneecaps, implanting gravel that may be there forever. My hands cover my face as I weep and hyperventilate. My lungs are on fire, but my heart burns even stronger.

I thought I was having an enlightening afternoon, finding myself, clearing my mind to work on crucial life decisions. I just took a big step backwards. Perhaps it is only appropriate I am chasing ghosts here at this battlefield. This is a place of loss for many. Nature cannot even control itself today. I have much to process but need to seek shelter. The weather is nasty.

I use all of my energy to pull myself off the ground. I pick out a large rock from my knee, seeing it has drawn blood. I spin my pack around to the front, and find the card Hayley gave me this morning, and call the driver for a ride. Luckily, he is free and only a couple of minutes away. He arrives in no time, helping me into the car. I ask him to take me back to the bed and breakfast as he handed me a few tissues to wipe my face, another holds pressure for a minute on my knee and helps clean it up.

He hurries me back into town and helps me up to the door under his umbrella. Is it possible that everyone in this town is so courteous? Josh opens the door to give me a hand. I'm trying to dig out my cash from my backpack, but Josh takes care of the payment before I can get to it. The driver thanks us and wishes me well before hustling back out to the car.

"Hayley, can you give us a hand?" Josh shouts out, looking at what a mess I can only appear to be. She hurries down the hallway from the kitchen.

"What do you nee-" Hayley stops abruptly as she finds me there in a puddle of water looking like a drowned rat. "You poor thing! Here let me grab you a towel." The corridor closet contains the linens for the house. She hands me one to clear my face, while placing another one around my back and shoulders. "Let's sit you down in here."

I am ushered to the dining room, which is all tile and will be easily mopped up. Josh pulls out a chair for me and sits me down. The two of them don't ask questions but act quickly. Soon my knee is cleaned up with an ice pack on it, and a cup of hot tea is sitting in front of me.

"Please don't worry about me. I'll be fine. I am so embarrassed! Look at this mess of water I've trailed in! I will help you get it cleaned up."

"No, no. You just take it easy. It is no big deal. We can take care of it. Are you okay?"

"Yes, just got caught in the rain. I was out at the park and was trying to get back to the main entrance in a hurry, and I fell. I'm a klutz, that's all." I am not sure how to explain the other events of the day. I keep it all to myself.

"Why don't you sit here a moment and catch your breath. I'll take your tea up to your room. Perhaps a warm shower will be soothing." Hayley is the perfect hostess. For once, I will go online to give a review, and it will be twenty stars out of five if I can do that. They treat everyone like family here.

"Thanks, I think a warm shower will do me good, and help my body recover from that run!" I follow her upstairs, my legs shaking with fatigue as I go. On the way, she grabs a couple of bandages from a cabinet for my knee.

"Your tea is on the nightstand. Let me take these dirty towels. The fresh ones are already in the bathroom. Try this eucalyptus spray on your sore muscles, it should help. But careful, not around your knee." She gets things organized for me and starts out the door.

"Hayley, thank you. You are an angel, heaven-sent!" I give her a big smile as she closes the door behind her. She doesn't say anything back, just smiles and nods her head. So incredibly humble.

CHAPTER 10

THE HOT WATER FROM the shower fills the entire room with a dense steam. The mirror on the vanity, the shower stall glass, and the overhead skylight are completely fogged up. It could be the setting from a horror film. With my recent ghostly experiences, maybe it will be. As the hot water flows over me, I have the first quiet moment alone to analyze what happened earlier. I angle my neck to allow the high pressure showerhead massage some of the tension out of my shoulders, and I eventually slide down the marble wall to the floor and take advantage of the sauna-like space. The water and warmth slowly help me relax.

I close my eyes and all I can see are his beautiful eyes staring back at me. I try to recount what happened, what I actually saw. The marking by his ear, the eyes, and the electric shock I felt as the thunderbolt came from the heavens at the exact moment we touched. I promise myself, and my inner Reese voice, to not overthink this. As my bestie explained on the phone, the mind imagines what it wants to see in times like this. In the several occurrences I have recently experienced, I have had glimpses of Elliot, or Elliot-like images. However, I have never seen his face, to recognize him. He has never responded to me. That would validate all of it. For now I remind myself I have only extrapolated the bizarre conclusion in my head, my heart. I mustn't make a fuss over it. Doing so will only hold me back, stretching the sorrow further.

I shake the uncanny thoughts out of my mind, physically rattle my head back and forth. The heat and steam have fully saturated my soul, my breathing steadies. I stand up and turn the water off and encourage myself to move on. The day began splendidly, I will get back to it. I have plans for the evening involving Sadie that I need to move on to. I do not want to let her down due to my inexplicable nonsense.

I walk back downstairs. This time my legs do not feel as wobbly, but my knee is fairly sore. I may need to let Everett start the drive tomorrow and let this rest a bit more. In the kitchen, I see Hayley and Josh preparing for the evening meal.

"Hi, Clover. You feeling refreshed now?" Josh inquires.

I walk over to the island and smell the fresh cut vegetables around me. There is a wide variety here, putting an exquisite array of colors on display. I pick up one of the yellow peppers, spinning it around in my hand. "I am, thank you. Could you use a hand with anything?" I offer. It is the least I could do considering how nice they have been to me.

"No, no. We've got this! After doing this for so long, we have a system worked out. It goes quite smoothly" Hayley informs me. I watch as the two of them work in unison. They look like dancers swaying back and forth. Hayley and Josh are an amazing team, and they always seem to be enjoying each other's company, smiling and laughing.

"Could I ask for another cup of that tea? It was wonderful. Just point me in the direction, and I can make it."

"Absolutely! The teapot is on the stove already. Feel free to heat up some water. The tea leaves are in that canister just next to the stove." She points me in the right direction. I open it up and enjoy the fragrant tea, it has a hint of peppermint to wake up my senses. "It looks like the rain is clearing. The front moved past us faster than anticipated. We should still be able to dine outside around the fire this evening. Of course, we will move into the sunroom if anything changes. We try to stay prepared!"

"That is great, I am looking forward to it. I may go drink this tea and do some reading upstairs for a bit, prop my feet up. I'll be back down in a short while. Everything smells wonderful; I cannot wait to try the woodfire pizzas."

"See you in a bit," Hayley smiles, still gracefully moving through the kitchen. Josh gives me a thumbs up and then goes back to placing the next prep bowl in front of her. Cooking is such a talent. I loved to watch Elliot at work in a kitchen, home or the shop. He knew the dance well.

In my room, I take a seat on the edge of the bed. I need to get a hold of Sadie. She should be back from taking Poppy to her friend's house by now. I reach for my phone and look up her name. She put her contact info as Sadie & Poppy. How cute! I love that she included her daughter. Even on a phone, they are inseparable. I need to get their picture to attach to the contact. I love seeing everyone's face as I scroll through and receive messages.

ME: Sadie, cookout is still on for this evening if ur up to it?

SADIE & POPPY: Of course! :) What time?

ME: I think cooking starts in 1 hr. But I'm here, if you want to walk over early.

SADIE & POPPY: Great. I'll be there soon!

ME: Sounds good!

I decide to text Everett to see if everything is good for tomorrow. I know how much he dislikes last minute changes in plans.

ME: Hey- still good for tomorrow?

I don't hear back from him right away. He is probably out on a date, knowing him. Or packing his things and detailing the car. He is always busy doing something.

Anticipating Sadie's arrival, I go back downstairs. There is a comfortable sitting room, with a rustic looking stone fireplace. On the mantle they have pictures of the house over the years. Like having school pictures of children, it shows how the home has evolved and matured over time. I love how they even printed the modern photos in black and white so they all match the originals. I spin around and sit at the game table. A large chess set sits out. I saw Hayley and Josh playing the other morning over coffee when I first arrived. I never learned how to play. It is on my bucket list. Both learning to play and finding that special someone to have morning coffee with over a game.

Along the wall are several bookshelves stocked with the house library. The top shelf must be favorites, as it is tagged "PLEASE KEEP HERE." The other shelves are marked as "TAKE ONE, LEAVE ONE!" My fingers run along the bindings of the books on their top shelf, keep-here editions. Whenever I am in a used bookstore, I have a habit of checking if my favorites are there. Unexpectedly, they keep a copy of Anderson's *Winesburg, Ohio* here. That is in my top five. If time permits, I will have to read it during my stay.

"Clover, your friend Sadie has arrived!" Josh acknowledges from the sunroom. Wow. She didn't waste any time walking over. I am glad she is going to hang out tonight.

"Wonderful, thank you!" I say as I get up and walk that direction. I love how this place is warm and inviting. Everyone treats it like the home it is, calling from the other room like you would for family. I have always been turned off by sterile, contemporary places like many of the new hotels are designed. As soon as this trip was discussed, Elliot had picked this place out in advance. If he only knew how perfect it was!

When I arrive to the patio space, there are several guests already sitting outside. The fire is lit, a cherry wood scent lingers in the air. I see Sadie in a chair already chatting up with one of the guests. I find the open chair next to her and take a seat.

"Hey, girl! Glad you made it," I tell her.

"Yes. Me too. This looks like fun!" She does not hold back her shining smile. I can tell she really needed an evening out.

She tells me how Poppy was overjoyed with her slumber party surprise. Of course, she checks her phone every five minutes in case there is an emergency. I hear about her busy day and let her vent out the remaining stress so she can hopefully enjoy the night without any lingering tensions. I am so impressed by her drive to succeed.

She worked very hard to make her dream come true, and had many obstacles to overcome along the way. She and Reese are very similar. They have that entrepreneurial instinct. Although Reese could have taken a handout from her family to get her business started, she turned it down. She wanted to be independent, to accomplish it for herself, on her own. Even now, her mother hopes if Reese and Nick tie the knot, that Reese will decide not to work and become more of a socialite. Reese has nothing in mind of that nature.

Hayley is rounding with the guests, grabbing drinks for everyone. When she brings us a couple of beers, she pulls up another chair alongside Sadie. "So, about this coffee deal? What do you think?"

"Wow. You've already moved to deal territory?" Sadie cannot control her excitement. Her smile stretches from ear to ear. "Yes, of course. I would love to work something out."

"What do you have in mind?" I know Hayley has already thought through a hundred ideas but kindly lets Sadie give her pitch.

Sadie goes on. "Well, my thoughts are quite simple. I am interested in taking a new angle on advertising to help keep business steady. Even more, I just want people to enjoy my coffee. I understand you do great business here; by serving my roast to your guests it would hopefully do both. I know I could beat your competitors' prices, sell to you wholesale." She has not had much time to work on this pitch, but she nailed it.

"Sadie, I love your coffee. I go to your café often. I think it would make a great addition here. This could become a growing trend!"

She paused a moment. "Actually, I am not looking for a trend beyond this. I know my limitations and would like to keep this as a solo deal, at least for now. I would love for you to be the only external location. It will give me the advertising advantage needed and give your place a uniqueness."

"Either way, we think it is a great plan! We have also thought of doing a special weekly coffee hour. Is that something you could help develop?"

"I would love to help! I can write up some ideas and maybe meet up in a week or so. Does that sound good?" Sadie asks.

"Absolutely! Great chat, I love progress! But I need to tend to the drink situation out here. It is way too quiet. Time to get this party started." She walks away collecting empty glasses and bottles from the crowd that has now grown out here. Josh is already walking out with replacements for everyone.

Within an hour everyone had some delicious pizza. They had such a variety of toppings to choose from and the flavors were top notch. I think it would be impossible to not enjoy the evening in a space like this, surrounded by these fine people. It has great energy, but at the same time is so relaxing. What a great way to set one's worries aside.

We all chat, play a couple of games around the fire. Sadie is so much fun to be around. I am not sure how many drinks we've had when Josh starts playing guitar. The two of us get up and dance around, eventually others join in. I haven't been around live music since Elliot's accident. I tried to make as many of his shows as possible, but mostly I heard him play while he was writing in his room. Some nights he played specifically for me, letting me pick the songs while we sat on the couch together. I could listen to his playing for eternity. Josh had more of a limited playlist, but he was doing well and everyone enjoyed it.

I run to my room to grab my sweatshirt and use the restroom. As I reach the bottom of the staircase, I see someone entering the front door. "Hey, beautiful!" I hear. At the door, Everett is standing with his arms outstretched to me, his bag sitting next to him.

"Uh, hello!" I walk to him and give him a hug. "What are you doing here so soon? I thought we planned on leaving tomorrow morning."

"Well, you said you would just be hanging out here tonight.

Instead of driving so early in the morning, I thought I would come down this evening and get a better night's sleep." He shrugs with a grin. "Not a good idea?"

"Of course, it is a fine idea. You just took me by surprise, is all. Do you have a place to crash? I don't think they have any availability here…it has been quite busy."

"I called earlier, spoke to a Hayley? I told her who I was. She said your bed is plenty big."

"Excuse me?" I am certain there is a major look of, not fear, but shock on my face. Hayley does not know that much about me, nor can I see her agreeing to such a thing.

Everett laughs. "I'm kidding, Clover. It's just a joke. I did call to see if there was room; they are full. I booked at the hotel just up the street. However, Hayley told me you had a not-so-great afternoon and invited me to join the festivities tonight to help cheer you up."

"Uh-huh. I see. Well, welcome to the party! My new friend Sadie, and other guests, are out back." I notice he has his bag with him, which is odd though. Why bring that in? Oh boy. Everett. What are you thinking? "Do you want to put that in your car?" I ask him.

"Oh, I brought a sweatshirt and a bottle of scotch. Wasn't sure what they'd have available. You know I am a picky drinker. I actually walked here from the hotel, I already valeted for the night. It was easier to carry in my pack. Can I set it in your room for now?"

"Sure, of course." I am getting a little annoyed now. He follows me back upstairs. Damn my knee is stiff. I open my room, and he sets his bag on the chair and takes a look around.

"Nice place. It doesn't look that big from the street though." He stands there, turns to me and takes my hand. He is standing a bit close. I know we have done a lot of hugging at the hospital, and the loft, but this feels weird. "I'm glad we're taking this trip together, Clover. Thank you for inviting me. I think it will be good for both of us." He has a gentle smile on his face, his dimple appears up on his chin.

"Well, hello!" Sadie is standing in the doorway and sees the two of us so close. "Clover, you've been gone a while, I just came up to check on you. I thought you were bailing on me. I see you are *busy*. I will go back downstairs." She starts to walk backwards in the hall.

I call her back promptly. "Sadie, wait!" She spins around in her cute flowery sundress; it is flaring out at the bottom. She places her hand on the doorframe, peeks her head in the threshold.

"Yessss?" I think the beer is making her a little dramatic, she wiggles her brows up and down. She is sort of silly!

"I want to introduce you to my friend Everett. Everett, this is Sadie. The woman I told you about."

"The hot one." He laughs in his charming way. She blushes, not knowing the entire story.

"That's meeee!" She giggles. Oh boy. The night is going to be interesting.

"Nice to meet you, Sadie. Shall we?" Everett gestures his hand toward the staircase. We all venture back downstairs; I hobble the way down.

"You okay there, Clover? What the hell happened to you?" Wouldn't he like to know.

"It's a long story. I can tell you on the road tomorrow. But I may let you drive when we leave." He nods in agreement, certainly happy to get his way.

We all make it back to the patio. The fire is blazing now. Someone has stacked a lot more wood on it. Josh has tired out playing, but a radio is on to provide a nice variety of music. Sadie, Everett, and I sit down at a little round table closer to the koi pond. Everett introduces himself to Josh, thanking them for the invite.

The three of us laugh and tell stories. Even though she is tipsy, I can tell Sadie is really enjoying Everett's company. He plays it cool and keeps conversation going evenly between all of us, avoiding awkwardness. Sadie does not let it spoil her fun, continuing to flirt and giggling like a schoolgirl. I am happy to see her having fun. Actually, I am pleased to find we all are letting our walls down and having a good time. If I made the move here, the three of us could hang out like this more often. I could get used to it, honestly.

After another round, the crowd begins to disperse. Sadie looks at the time, and decides she better leave. Her excuse is that she has to pick up Poppy in the morning. But, she also nudges me, and winks, looking back and forth between Everett and me. I give her a glare, and a quick nod of *absolutely not*.

Everett will not allow her to walk the short distance home alone. He is very much a gentleman. "I can walk you home, Sadie. You need to get there safely," he insists. Everett will take her home, and then he is only a block to his hotel. She accepts his offer.

"I'll see you in a couple days," I tell her. "And you, we still going to make it at four?" I'm looking to Everett for his reply.

"Of course. I haven't had that much to drink!" he replies.

"Okay, then. Goodnight you two. It has been fun! Be careful out there!" I say as they walk around the bushes at the back of the garden. I go back inside. After staring at the steps, again, I generate the energy to climb them. Man, oh, man. I am tired.

I cannot wait to get back to my room and crash. I have already paid for the week here, so thankfully I do not need to pack everything up before heading to Savannah. I just need to set a few basics aside in my small duffel. I finish up in minutes, prepared for the road trip. I brush my teeth and change into my pajama shirt and crawl into bed. I flip the switch to dim the lights.

I am tired, but lay in bed going over my day again. My thoughts drift to seeing my grandmother and Ruby. I try to stay calm so I am able to sleep. I want to avoid a melatonin, since it is only a few hours before I have to get up in the early morning. Also, I am fearful of dreaming tonight. With everything going on, who knows what my imagination could invoke.

I am almost asleep, and I hear a knock on my door. What in the world? It is insanely late.

"Hey, Clover, it's me. Everett." I hear him through the door.

Seriously? Why is he here? I crawl out of bed, my legs cramping up as I walk to the door. I open it and see Everett standing there with his cheek propped up against the doorway, his face smashed. He has his puppy dog eyes going. Damn, Elliot could give that face too.

"What is wrong, Everett?" I ask.

"Sorry to bug you. I left my bag in here."

"Like I couldn't have given it to you in the morning?" I say sarcastically in my drunken, tired voice.

"Not really...... my hotel card is in there. I threw it in there earlier when I grabbed the scotch. It was driving me crazy in my pocket."

"Oh. Right. Here, let me grab it."

"Clo – honestly I didn't plan this," he tells me as I am looking for the chair that his bag was sitting on.

"Of course. Who said you did?"

"I am sure you are thinking that. But, I really didn't. Maybe it is fate," he smiles again. I hand him his bag, he is stalling. It is blatantly obvious.

"What do you want Everett?" my patience is running thin.

"Can I just crash here? It started to sprinkle again on my walk back from Sadie's. I don't want to walk it in the rain." After my rainy travels today, I do not blame him. "I promise to be on my best behavior." He runs his finger in a cross pattern over his chest.

"Yessssssss, Everett. I guess you can. The chair is small. Can you be a gentleman and stay on your side of the bed?" I am being extremely serious now. There is no humor or flirting in my tone. He needs to know where I stand.

"Have you ever known me to be anything other than a gentleman?"

"Um, actually yes. Your brother told me plenty of stories," I spout back to him. "Need I say more?"

He clears his throat and glances down in shame. "Nope. Got it."

He set his bag back on the chair where it sat previously. "Nice shirt by the way!"

Crap. My oversized night shirt is baggy and comfortable, but not extremely long. Now I'm embarrassed. I need to recover from this one. "Your brother could handle me wearing it around the loft. I am sure you can deal with it too." I curtsy, hopefully distracting him from my blushing face.

He just laughs. I crawl back into the bed, staying on one side. "I'll even the score," he says as he sits on the edge of the bed and takes off his shirt and jeans. Good Lord! He is extremely built. I have to tell myself not to stare. Thankfully he has boxers on! He gets into the bed, making an obvious effort to stay on the other side, drawing a line with his hand to show me he understands.

"Goodnight weirdo," I tell him. "Cute shorts…did they have batman or something on them?"

"Do you want to see?" he stalls and then laughs. "Just kidding. Best behavior. I promise. And Clover – thanks. I really had fun. Your friend Sadie is nice. It was a great night. You seemed happy. That makes me happy."

"You're welcome. I had fun too. The days are getting better. The nights are always tough, it gets so quiet."

Everett rolls over toward me, lightly kisses me on the top of my head. "I know what you mean. I'm glad we have each other. Um, Clover……Is it okay if I hold you? Nothing weird. I know you and Elliot were close, and he once told me how he would hold you when you were sad. It made him feel like he was helping, and it helped him in return. I don't want you to be sad anymore, and maybe it will help me sleep too. I'm not usually a cuddler. I don't have many sleepovers."

"Wow. Really? That's a lot, Everett. I think the Scotch is making you sentimental again. And yes, you can hold me. I miss that."

Everett holds me all through the night, one arm wrapped gently over my waist, spooning. We both sleep soundly and don't move an inch. When we wake to the three-thirty alarm in the morning, it is not strange or awkward like I thought it would be. He casually sits up and gets dressed. "I'll go shower and grab my stuff at the hotel and will be back with the car," he whispers to me. I roll onto my back, rub the sleep out of my eyes. "Will that give you enough time to have some privacy and get ready?"

How thoughtful. "Yes, I'll meet you out front. Thanks, Ev."

"Okay, see you in a bit," he quietly says. I'm not sure why he is still whispering at me, I must wake up anyway. Maybe he is just being considerate of other guests, although I'm on the end of the hall.

I get showered and dressed quickly, tiptoeing around so I don't disturb anyone else. I grab my already packed bag and go downstairs. My legs feel better this morning after a good night sleep, though my knee is going to take time to heal. The kitchen has some dim lighting on through the night that I can see my way with. I do not know where the coffee is stored and decide not to bother. We can grab something on the road.

I walk out to the front porch, taking a seat on the swing. The sky cleared overnight, and the stars are now twinkling above. I notice how quiet it is outside this time of the morning here. In the city, there is always noise coming from somewhere, sirens, trains. Eventually you get acclimated to it, but when you sit down and actually listen, it is always there. A known constant. I delight in hearing the silence here.

Everett pulls up on the street in his car. The sleek charcoal Mercedes suits him well. He grabs my bag and opens the door for me. "My Lady," he says jokingly as I enter the car. When he gets in, he looks over at me and grins. "I have something for you!" He hands me a reusable to-go cup that has an image on the outside that makes it look like it is full of some nasty, green juice concoction.

I chuckle and ask, "What is this?"

"Do you like it? Elliot always told me about your love of sweet coffee drinks and your embarrassment of that. I remember that crap you were drinking at the hospital. Now you can get your fancy drinks in this, but it will look like you're drinking a healthy, grown-up beverage all the time!"

"You are kidding me? This is amazing! Thank you, this is very sweet. Now we need to get it filled, like pronto," I instruct him.

"Agree. Let's roll!"

CHAPTER 11

CONSIDERING WE SLEPT WELL, but not for long, I am surprised how invigorated we both are this morning. Everett is quite chatty, even before we stop to fuel up and grab our coffee. I hope he is not the type to talk the entire time on a road trip. Sometimes I simply enjoy watching the scenery go by around me, take in the landscape.

"If we do not hit any major construction or jams, we should make it there by, what, one- thirty?" he asks. I glance over at his speedometer. He has a lead foot. We may make it sooner than that.

"Yes, probably. I usually have one place I like to stop for brunch on the way, near Atlanta. They have the best grits. If you feel like it, we can stop there?" I say, hoping I get a yes reply. I drank more than I ate last night. The hunger will hit me in no time.

"Sure, that sounds good. I'll be ready for some food by then." Some time goes by in silence, as we both drink our beverages. My truck stop cappuccino is decent, and now disguised in my new mug Everett got me. I'm going to miss Sadie's coffees while I'm away. She could make great drinks, even better than the coffeehouse below my old apartment.

"So what did you think of Sadie? She's nice, isn't she?"

"Yeah, she is. So what is her deal? You said she has a daughter?" he asks. I wonder if he is genuinely curious about her, or if he is simply replying to pass the time.

"Yes. From what she's told me, it is the three of them: Sadie, Poppy, and Chance, their dog. She's divorced for a few years, unattached. Very successful. She runs her own business, a cute café downtown. And she's pretty too, right?" I know Sadie seemed attracted to Everett last night. Maybe it is time to see what he thought.

"Oh, she seems great, and very attractive I might add." Interesting. Maybe he did sense something there. "It was fun hanging out with her. She's a very happy person. Lots of energy. But-"

"Let me guess. You already have someone, or several someones that you can pick from at home when it is convenient? Or she's pretty – but not your type? Or, how about, you aren't comfortable with someone as successful as you are? Or maybe she's got too much baggage?"

"Is that what you think of me, honestly? I'm not a complete scumbag, Clover. Yes, I do like women. Have known many of them. I have never taken the time to really get attached to just one. Maybe I have never found the right one yet? I'm not sure what my excuse is. My job makes it difficult. I am always busy and meet a lot of different people. I have never had a desire to slow down, settle down. Am I that different from you, really? You don't have anyone." He throws back to me.

"I had your brother, asshole!" I am now mad and upset, and the tears start to well up in my eyes.

"You know what I mean. You've never let anyone in. I am not sure why, and I do not think Elliot knew why. He said he tried setting you up with some really brilliant and extremely nice guys."

"Yeah, well. I'm screwed up. That's my excuse. I probably always will be."

"Hey, that's not true. I am sure there are reasons. You're not messed up. Maybe you're just afraid. Maybe you've known too many guys, well, like me? I'm sorry I upset you. Clover, look at me." He grabs my chin and turns my head his direction. "I'm sorry. Really." He brushes the tear off my cheek.

"Don't be. I'm just an emotional wreck. I go from one extreme to the other. Happy, sad, angry. You haven't said anything that is not true. I am the one who is sorry. I didn't mean that crap. I barely know you. I know you have been nothing but nice to me through all of this, yet I go and say nasty things to you."

"No worries. It's okay. I know it has not been easy. Trust me." His nurturing tone is helping me calm down. "Let's change the subject, shall we?"

"One thing, Everett. So what were you going to say before I verbally attacked you? You like Sadie?" He did start to say something, now I'm curious to know.

"Well, I was just going to say she is all of those things. But, I should probably keep my distance. As you mentioned in my list of faults, I do not have a great track record. She has a lot on her hands, and a child. She deserves, well *they* deserve, better than me. I should not show interest when I'm trying to figure myself out. Learn what I want in life. She needs someone who has his shit figured out. I am not that guy, yet." He scratches the top of his head. I sense the disappointment in his voice.

"Everett. Geesh." I reach over and put my hand over his, squeezing it gently. "You *are* finding your way. Maybe you don't need time, rather someone to believe in you, that can help you on your journey," I encourage. He squeezes my hand back. "You're going to get there. Have faith. Trust in your angels to guide you."

Maybe I need to do more of that. I've always found my way, eventually. I'm finding my way now. "Dare to be strong and courageous. That is the road. Venture anything. Be brave enough to dare to be loved." The quote from *Winesburg, Ohio* jumps in my thoughts. This trip with Everett may help us both do that. I promise myself to try. To be open.

We both have said a lot, and we sink into a long wave of silence. I frequently glance over to make sure he is alert while driving. He plays with the radio dial often and taps his fingers on the steering wheel to the beat of the music. Other than that, neither of us makes a sound. The miles and hours pass quickly. I wanted this solitude, but it is allowing my brain matter to entertain new ideas. I continue the debate in my thoughts, between living in Illinois and Tennessee, and as we are traveling to Georgia, I have to recall Ruby's encouragement to move back there as well.

My childhood was difficult, but not horrible. We did not have a lot in Savannah. Our home was small, but well-kept. Our cars were not fancy, but they ran. I stayed busy with school and did well, but was not popular. Mostly, I remember the good times with my grandmother. We would play in the yard, have picnics. Our staycations included dressing up in costumes from far away lands and cooking their cuisine for our meals. We would read books about the culture and history. We always made the best of it. It is sad to think grandma cannot remember all of that now, or only in small passages of time. But whenever I see her, I tell her about those days and how happy she made me. Sometimes I break through to her, others I cannot. I will never give up trying. I owe that to her. I miss both Ruby and my grandmother dearly. However, I am not sure it is the right place for me to call home. Not at this point in my life.

I wonder how it was growing up for Everett? On rare occasions, Elliot would talk about his childhood, but when he did it was limited. "Everett, what is your favorite childhood memory?" I break the silence. Maybe I should have started with something more casual, lighter.

"Wow. Well, let me think." He sits for a few moments, clearly putting some effort into choosing the right memory. "There was one time, the only time, my father came to one of my baseball games. I scored the winning run. I didn't know he was going to be there, and when I slid into home I saw him in the stands. He was clapping and smiling and yelled, 'That's my boy.' I hardly saw him then, or now, and he's never seemed that interested or proud of anything I have done before or since." He continues staring straight ahead at the road, without blinking once.

"I am sure that made your day. I can only imagine how hard it was for you going through all of that as a kid."

"Sure, it was, I suppose. I learned to push through it. For many years I tried to do anything to gain his attention. For a while that mostly included getting into trouble. Then it was sports. Hell, I even became an attorney because he was one, and I thought it would make him proud."

"Do you like what you do?"

"It depends. I make good money, I get to meet interesting clients. But I am not sure if I ever feel really satisfied. You know? Do you think if I heard the words from his mouth, it would change that?"

"Is that the only thing stopping you from being happy? Waiting on that approval or admiration? I am sure he is proud. Elliot was proud of you. I am proud of you. I have often thought how hard your job is, and yet you make it look so easy. If that is all you need to make yourself happy, to feel accomplished, you have it."

"I guess so. Do you like what you do?"

"Ha! We don't have time to get into that. I'm hungry, and the next exit takes you to my favorite grits."

"Well, maybe later. I've just spilled my guts. You owe me an answer."

"I also owe you a meal!" We take the exit, driving up to the next stoplight and into the lot of the diner. I look at the clock. "We're making really great time, Everett. It's only eight fifteen. If we get out of here by nine, we'll be there by one-ish. Well, maybe one-thirty, with my driving."

"If I let you buy, can I finish the drive? Not that I am worried about time, but I like driving and your leg is pretty banged up. You ever going to tell me what happened there?" He points to my bandaged knee as we walk into the restaurant.

"Let me get some breakfast, and we'll see." I am not sure how much I should share about my knee. If I get too detailed, I will end up sharing all of the weird events I've encountered in Franklin.

"Deal!" He says, following me to the booth.

We both know what we want, and get our order in quickly. While waiting for the food I decide to skip over my knee story and go back to my career path. He listens carefully as I discuss all of the obstacles through the years. How I ended up with my part time jobs. My plans to get back on track, take the MCAT and eventually back in school if all goes well.

"Clover, that is amazing. I have always known you're smart. But med school, that would be awesome, right? And if you decide to move to Tennessee, you could go to school in Nashville or nearby?"

"Yes, I've thought about all of that. Vanderbilt has a great program, if I could get in."

"Can you picture it? You're going to be a doctor. Damn, we'd make one hell of a power couple."

"Whoa, whoa. What the heck is that all about?" I am not sure how to get out of this one. I know we are getting along, sharing more. But that is one ginormous leap ahead! "Don't you know, I am going to fall for one of my professors....or maybe the dean?" I finish with a smirk and laugh.

"Right, right. I'm going to seduce an up and coming songwriter who has an amazing …..er, voice. We can live in the same neighborhood."

"And start families, and our kids will go to school together?" I have said these words before, not so many years ago. Elliot. I miss him. I'll miss that. I miss dreaming together.

"Clover, you okay? Did I say something wrong?"

"No. Elliot and I had already made these plans together. It's going to be so different now."

"Hey, Clo. It's going to be okay. I can fill in for him." He reaches out to take my hand. "Not replace, just fill in. There's a difference. I get it." Then he winks at me. What? Not that kind of difference. I thought I had veered him away from those thoughts. I do honestly hope Everett and I will know each other for a long time, and hang out chatting like this. I decide not to overanalyze things. Stay chill.

"Thanks, Everett. You're a good friend." I smile.

My smile grows bigger as the food finally arrives. I ordered several of my favorites. Blueberry pancakes, with whipped cream.

Grits. Toast. Bacon. I am starving. Everett got the biscuits and gravy and some sausage. I look around and the entire tabletop is full of food. We are going to need a nap after this feast! The conversation pauses while we both shovel the food down our throats. I think he was more hungry than he thought. As if we have been dining together all of our lives, he reaches over and steals a piece of bacon. It gets me thinking.

"Hey, Everett. When we get to Savannah, will you go to dinner with me?"

He shakes his head, mouth full of food. "Were you going to make me dine alone?"

"Oh no, that is not what I was thinking. Sorry, let me explain. Will you take me somewhere that starts with a *P*?" I ask him. He looks surprised and confused by my request. I spend a few minutes telling him about the system Elliot and I were using to choose our dining options. He thinks it is a great idea, and promises to help me finish the alphabet, even when I travel back to Chicago. I get a bit upset that he grabs his phone, now, while we are eating. That is a pet peeve I have. No phones at the table. It makes me sad to see couples out together who never have a conversation, or share in a glance across the table, as they stare at their screens.

"Everett. What are you doing? That is not nice."

"Sorry, Clover. I was finding us a place to eat in Savannah. I found one. Patsy's Pub. That's two P's. Does that count double?"

How sweet, he was already searching. "Well, it isn't like we keep score. It's more for fun. But Patsy's is the place. Count me in!"

"Awesome! It looks….um, interesting. That's all I will say." I ask him not to show me. I want it to be a surprise. And I don't want to see the online reviews. My weird glitch again.

We finish up eating and get settled back in the car. He insists on driving. I won't argue. If he is okay with it, I may try to nap. I tell him to put on some tunes, or an audiobook if he wants. He would rather do radio station searching the entire time. Eventually, I dose off.

The huge breakfast settles in my stomach, and I soon am out cold. I was unaware of lane changes, songs turned up for jamming purposes. I was basically dead to the universe inside the benz. About an hour and a half into this portion of the drive, Everett taps me on the shoulder to wake me.

"Clover, hey – wake up. Sorry. Your phone just beeped with a text. I thought you may want to check it and reposition. You've had your head just hunched forward for like the past thirty minutes or so. I don't want you to get a neck ache." As I tilt my head back, and roll my head around to loosen it up, he reaches over with his hand and begins to rub the back of my neck. My word, he is strong. He kneads some of the tension out while I grab my phone from the floor where it slid down.

RUBY: Darling, haven't heard how the trip is going? Let me know.

I read the message and then clear my throat as Everett pulls his hand back to the wheel. I point at my neck again with a big grin. He takes the hint and works on my shoulder for a while. He also has a weird smirk on his face. I guess maybe he is surprised at my encouragement. "What are we looking at for time, you think by two we'll get into town?"

"Oh yes, definitely. Maybe a bit sooner. Is she waiting on us? I can step on it if we need to make up some time." He revs the engine a few times.

"Um, no. We're fine. She is just curious."

ME: Hi! It looks like we'll be in shy of 2. :)

RUBY: Excellent. You'll be glad to know she is having a good day so far. I think it is your arrival that cheered her up!

ME: That's wonderful news. See you soon!

"Everything okay?" Everett asks. "You okay? You tensed back up for a minute."

"Yes. I'm good. Going home just feels bittersweet. I am happy to see them, but I always fear my grandma won't recognize me. Each time, after she calms down, we have a good time. But it is just hard. I just wish they could all be good days. It almost feels like when I moved away it happened so suddenly. I can only wonder if that stress began the process."

"Clover, you cannot think that way. It has nothing to do with you, or your move. It is just a shitty part of life, of growing old for some of us. But you can't beat yourself up over it. You have been a wonderful granddaughter to her."

Even after hearing it, I still don't entirely believe it. I know Everett has experienced similar feelings. Elliot told me once how Everett always felt like his pending birth was the reason their father left. Claire and Elliot had to continuously tell him it had nothing to do with him. Elliot despised his father so much for leaving, for making his little brother feel that way. He said he felt like they never had anything in common, he and his father. Everett didn't spend much time with his dad, there were a few visitations he attended. Elliot felt Everett's traits and personality resembled his father's more. Everett often sought his father's approval and attention. Elliot could care less.

In attempt to cheer me up, he reminds me of our dinner date we planned. "Girl, you are going to have a nice time. You can have a wonderful visit with your family. We will go to Patsy's and have some fun later. I will guarantee this is a fantastic trip, I promise you that."

"Thanks, Everett. I know we'll have fun. Let's just get there." I feel the car speed up and move into the passing lane. I have created a monster. He lets out a subtle, evil laugh.

CHAPTER 12

WE ARE APPROACHING THE road I grew up on. I offer to switch and drive when we get to town, so I don't have to give the details while I enjoy my return. Everett said he is fine finishing the route. I won't argue. He doesn't enjoy my instructions, which relate to landmarks, rather than directions like left, right, north, south, and the like.

I almost miss telling him to make the final turn while I text Reese to update her on our whereabouts. He had to correct quickly, and stares over at me with frustration.

"Oops. Sorry about that! I was distracted." I explain.

"At least we are almost there. You could've waited until we arrived to send that text." He cannot still be upset about it. Geesh.

"Yes, but I didn't." I give him my smartass grin. He takes the bait and laughs. I am so grateful he has a sense of humor.

"Anything I need to know before we go in there? Secrets to share? Advice on how to fit in?" I cannot tell if he is being truthful about this. Is he honestly nervous to meet my family?

"No, nothing really. Just be yourself. They're going to love you."

"Really? Love me, huh? I'm that good, aren't I," he winks. We pull into the driveway out front. Before we can fully stand and stretch our legs, Ruby is running out to greet us.

"Get over yourself and prepare. Here she comes!"

She is wearing a cute pair of jeans, shaped just enough to show how fit she stays, and a baby blue, short sleeve sweater. Her hair is in a French braid down her back. She has always been talented at braiding, especially her own hair. I open my arms to encourage her upcoming bear hug.

"Cloooverrr! It is so great to see you!" She gives me a tight squeeze, pulls away a moment to take a closer look at me, then back into the hug. "And who do we have here?" She now turns to look at Everett. "Aren't you handsome!"

"Down girl," I laugh. "This is my friend, Everett. He's Elliot's brother."

"And this is your......sister?" he says, knowing exactly how to get in her good graces.

"I like him," she replies, winking. "No, I'm her favorite Aunt Ruby. Lily is in the house – it is naptime. Greg is out back, he'll join us in a second."

"Of course. It is wonderful to meet you," he says.

"And, she is my *only* aunt." I clarify. They both laugh. Everett grabs our bags from the car, and we all walk up to the house. I take in a deep breath and glance around. Ruby and her husband have kept the house up nicely. The flowers out front have grown. The grass is nicely groomed. I notice some new sidewalk stones in a path from the street up to the porch, which is now screened in. The shutters have a recent coat of paint on them.

"Everything looks great, Ruby. You and Greg have been busy. This porch looks great. I love how you enclosed it!"

"Well, darling. Lily spends a lot of time out here, and we thought it would be good to keep the bugs out since we are actually using the space more. It was an easy weekend project."

"This place is really lovely. I can picture you growing up, playing in the yard here, Clover." He glances back out to the yard as we walk across the porch and into the house. When we get inside Ruby reaches for our bags. There is a questioning look on her face. Everett notices as well. "Uh, is there something wrong?" he asks.

Ruby smiles, shrugging. "Well, I am not sure of the bag situation. I apologize. Do they both go in the bedroom? Or should I put his by the hide-a-bed? I am not old-fashioned, I'm only a few years older than she is. I will not be offended if you share the room."

"Ruby! Really? Soooo not like that!" I exclaim. "No sense crowding up the living room for now, if we'll be hanging out for a bit. We can put them both in the bedroom. We'll sort it out later."

"Now that's what I'm talking about." Everett laughs. I swat his arm for acting so ridiculous. "What, did you tell your aunt we slept together last night?"

Ruby stands in front of us, rolling her eyes and starts belly laughing. "You two are hilarious. It sounds like you have more than luggage to sort out! Ha!" She looks back at me with accusing eyes.

"Not what you think, Ruby. Not at all. However, we all are grown adults here. The poor guy stayed up late with my friends and I drinking. He slept for a few hours, and woke up in the middle of the night and drove all the way here. If anything, I owe him the bed and I can take the hide-away. I can be a good host."

"I'm the host, and I also think we *are* all adults. I say the bags go in the bedroom." She carries them both upstairs while Everett and I laugh away the awkwardness. As odd as it seems, it didn't matter where we ended up. I felt we both handled the previous evening just fine. And I know that couch has a terribly thin mattress on it, and I don't wish that on anyone.

I walk through the house to check things out, see what other cute changes they may have made in the past few months. It all looks familiar and nothing seems too different. It looks like home. Everett is watching me, and my reaction, more than checking out the place himself. It surprises me when I notice, because he quickly looks away. Ruby and Greg enter the room, followed by a half hour of introductions for Everett, over some sweet tea at the kitchen table. Everyone is relaxed and enjoying the moment. I am so glad to see my family. I am still urgently waiting for my grandmother to wake. Ruby reads me like a book and prompts me to go ahead and peek in on Grandma. I excuse myself from the table. Everett looks at me with a slightly anxious look on his face. I jokingly ask Ruby to be gentle to Everett before I part.

I walk down the hall, to the downstairs bedroom where my grandmother now stays. It used to be my mother's, and then Ruby's after my mom passed, until Ruby moved out. My grandmother used to be in the larger room upstairs, but it was getting too difficult for her to get up and down the stairs. Ruby used the master room occasionally when she stayed part time, but now she and Greg stay full time. My room became mine after I stopped sleeping in the bassinette near Grandma at night. I carefully crack the door open, opening it slightly and peek my head in.

Grandma is sitting up in bed, awake and looks over to me. My heart drops in anticipation if she'll recognize me. She smiles and pats the edge of the bed, inviting me over to sit. I walk in and sit next to her.

"Hi Grandma!" I hesitate giving her a hug, until I get an idea of how she is doing at the moment.

"Hello, Clover! Look at you so pretty!" She runs her fingers through my messy hair and then runs the back of her hand down my cheek. She takes a moment to look me over, and sits holding my hands. "I have missed you, child. When Ruby said you were coming I was ecstatic. How are you?"

"I'm doing okay, grandma. It is so wonderful to see you." I give her a gentle, but loving hug. "I am sorry it has been a while since I made the trip. You know, a lot has been going on."

"Yes, yes. I know. I'm so sorry. You look well considering all you've gone through. I have worried about you and prayed for you to stay strong. I am sorry you have suffered so much loss in your life, my dear."

I start tearing up. I know this is our first in-person chat since Elliot's accident, but I'm ready to move the conversation along. "Thanks, grandma. I'm doing okay. You know about my trip to Franklin. That has been going well! And my friend Everett is here, he wanted to meet you!"

She seems content and well. Ruby does a great job keeping a schedule for her each day. She looks so pretty, her hair is soft and wavy, she has a few dark strands still showing within her grey. She never used much make-up, I suppose that just took extra time she didn't have in her day. But nowadays, my aunt gives her a touch of blush to brighten her face, and sometimes a nude lip gloss. Her nails are painted today, I notice, in a pale mauve.

"Do you want to go in the other room and chat? I can introduce you to my friend!"

"Oh yes, that would be lovely. Thank you!" she is exuding excitement, already reaching out to me to give her some support while she stands up. I hear her sigh, I'm certain her body is stiff from resting for a while. I put my arm around her, hold her hand and walk her out to the living room. We take a seat on the old couch.

"Hello, Lily. I'm Everett," he reaches out his hand to take hers. Rather than shaking it, he slowly leans over and kisses the top of her hand. "It is a great pleasure to meet you. I have been hearing a lot about you!"

"Well, hello, young man. The pleasure is all mine." She pushes me down the couch a bit, and prompts him to sit next to her, between us. "Sit, sit. Let me look at you. Ah, yes! You are a handsome young man, aren't you."

"Grandma, please do not encourage him!" She laughs at my reaction.

"What? I can tell him that. You should too, isn't that right, Everett?" Oh boy, first it was Elliot that she fell for, now it is his brother. I hope she does not get any ideas.

"Huh….no. Clover has a mind of her own. Very stubborn, that woman," he points at me.

"Well, he has you pegged, doesn't he Clover dear!" I can tell the two of them are going to have a fun time visiting. I sit back and watch it happen. Ruby and Greg come in and sit down across from us. Everyone is drilling Everett, from his career, to gossip about music stars, and my grandmother keeps inquiring about a special someone. He quickly informs her he is single. She pats him on the arm when she hears.

Greg jumps in. "So I hear you two are going to Patsy's later? That should be a good time."

I look over to Everett who must have already informed them of our plans. He is grinning. I did not intend on telling them about our plan until I knew if they had other arrangements made. They may have already made something for us, since it is our first night in town. "That's perfect. I didn't have time to shop yet today, so nothing prepared except leftovers tonight. But I'll run later and get things for tomorrow. Mom, do you want anything in particular?" Ruby asks Grandma.

"Why don't we make pan fried chicken and some fritters, just like years ago!"

Wow, she is sharp today. And that sounds great. "I like that idea a lot, grandma. Ruby, do you need a hand getting things? I can run to the store for you?"

"Why don't you come with me. The guys can stay here for a bit with Lily while we run. Would you be okay with me having some alone time with my niece, Everett?" He is nodding in agreement. "Do you play any games? Lily is great at spades or checkers. Or she loves to read, if you would like to do that?"

"Ruby, please do not talk about me like I'm not even here. I am capable of passing time with your two lovely gentlemen. We will figure it out!" Wow, sassy grandma is out to play. Everett covers his mouth trying to hide his laughter. It does not work.

"We will be fine, you two go ahead. I think Lily and I may converse over some competitive checkers." Everett has made her day. And he is in for a challenging game. She loves checkers.

"Well, I guess it is settled then." Ruby casually peers around the room, clearing her throat. I believe she is also amused at grandmother's outburst. "Clover, shall we?" she looks at me and then signals toward the door. I nod in agreement, and we head out to the car.

Ruby drives to the store, allowing me a pleasant trip through town, recalling some of my favorite places. Everything seems so familiar, as if I hadn't moved away for several years. I can see the sun shining through the cables on the bridge over in the distance and can barely see the flag atop the dome of city hall through the trees. I would love to drive through the historic district, but that would be out of our way. That may be something Everett and I can do tomorrow while grandma naps.

Ruby starts to say something. I can imagine what she is about to say, and I'd rather not have those discussions. I interrupt her, and plan to block any of the awkward chit chat. "Stop. I will say three things to you. One. Everett and I are only friends. Two. I still have not decided on where I want to live right now, and I do not need any help making up my mind. Three. I am working through the losing Elliot bit. I am not great at it, but I am working on it. You don't have to worry about me."

"Hang on missy." She lifts her hand away from the wheel for a moment. Ruby has always talked with her hands. "I was going to say something about the house."

"Oh sorry. I've been in this attack mode for a while. I guess my emotions are just elevated. Please, go on." I have noticed my mood swings are terrible lately. I know I have a lot going on, but it is no reason for me to be down-right rude to people, especially to people like Ruby and Everett. I need to get myself under control.

"So, I was saying….Greg and I have been talking. I know you are up in the air about living situations, and this is in no way a persuasion tactic or to be taken into consideration in your decision. We just have been struggling keeping up both houses. We would like to eliminate some of the waste, both time and money, and maybe sell ours. We live with mom full time now anyway."

She continues on between the options they have thought through. They know if I stay in Chicago, or even Tennessee, they only need the one place. If I move back, I would need their help, especially if I get back into school. I could stay with them or maybe get my own place close by so I could have my own personal life. I laugh at that point. Me, a private life? I already know in my head what I think about it all. We have pulled into the market parking lot now. I can tell she is tense, unsure how I feel about all of this.

"Look Ruby. I appreciate all you have done and do for grandma while I've been away. I think you should sell your house. I'll sign my half of grandma's over to you and Greg. You deserve it. *If* I move back down here, I agree, I think it would be better if I had my own place. Either way, you should have the house. You do not need to wait more on your life because I cannot make a decision about mine."

"Clover, that is not what I meant by all of this!"

"Oh no, I didn't take it in a bad way. But it is the truth. I am figuring out my place in the world. You already know yours. I am not going to stand in the way of making your life simpler."

"Oh, honey. You'll find your way. Think about the house situation. No rush on a decision. And we would buy out your half, don't be ridiculous!" She is trying to put me at ease, but I'm not anxious or fearful about any of these choices. It makes sense to me.

"Ruby, I'm serious. The house is all yours. Sell your other one. It makes sense. And you can just have the house. I do not need anything. You grew up there, she's your mom. It should be yours and Greg's."

Tears well up in her eyes. I can tell she needed to get this out in the open. We both sigh, hug while we are still seated in the car. "Hey, we should get inside so you can get back. Don't you have a date?"

"That was my first point. Did you forget!"

We both laugh and go in the store. It doesn't take long to grab the few items on the list and drive back home. As we pull up, I look at the house and feel relief. I've made another decision; I've put a few more pieces of my life's puzzle together. We walk up the stone steps. Everett has fallen asleep on the couch. Grandma and Greg are playing cards at the table. I say hi in the kitchen; Grandma is back in quiet mode. I don't want to startle Everett, so I lightly rest my hand on his shoulder.

"Ev-, hey. You get a nice nap in?"

"Hi, uh, yeah I did. You just get back?" he says sleepily while stretching his arms to the side.

"Yes. I'm going to go upstairs and freshen up. I shouldn't be long. Then we can head out. You need anything?"

"Is there room in the shower?" he smiles, winking at me. Such a guy. "Just kidding. I'll be up in a minute. I just want to change my shirt. Cool?" he says, standing up. He walks to the kitchen, I turn to go upstairs. I quickly shower, it feels invigorating. A nap could have helped me out, but no time now. I'm dressed and putting on my necklace, Everett knocks on the door.

"You decent? I just want to change real quick."

I open the door to let him in. I sit on the bed to put on my shoes. He changes his shirt giving me a show of his six-pack abs galore. He tells me about his nice visit with my grandmother this afternoon, teasing me that he learned some good gossip. I highly doubt that. Honestly, there is nothing extremely wild or crazy from my past here. He is trying to get a reaction out of me. I don't bite. We both appear ready to go, and run downstairs to say goodbye to the others before we go out to Patsy's.

Everett agrees to allow me to drive there, as I know the way and he is not confident in my direction skills after our trip in today. He thanks me again for asking him to complete the alphabet restaurant challenge. I am glad he is looking forward to it. I am too. I now have a few things established for my future. Many more to go, but I'm trying to celebrate each achievement. As we reach the pub, I am ready for another fun evening.

CHAPTER 13

PATSY'S IS VERY BUSY this evening. It is an older pub with a huge antique wooden bar, complete with the large mirror and built-in shelves on the side. The glasses and stemware hang above the bar top in racks. All the glassware is sparkling in the dim lighting. There are close to ten or twelve stools surrounding the bar; they are all full. We look around for a place to sit and pick out a table in the far corner. It is nice enough, somewhat secluded. The lights from the nearby jukebox gleam on the tabletop. Everett orders us a few beers and asks for the menu. Unfortunately, the kitchen is closed and all they have is tavern pizza.

Just a minor setback. I don't mind what we eat. I just know it has been a while since our feast of a breakfast, and my stomach has begun to grumble. I pick out the pizza and ask for a bowl of bar pretzels. Everett is not a fan, but I don't care. I watched them be poured fresh, and I need a snack.

I focus on the patrons all around us. This old neighborhood pub has really pulled in the younger generation, it seems like quite a hot spot. Everett finds a dartboard hanging and asks if I would like to play. I am awful, but it will be fun, so I agree. He apparently plays often, but does not lead me to believe that at first. He eventually admits to having one hanging in his office. He plays to help him think.

The rounds keep coming, and eventually the pizza. They must have one oven to cook in. But it smells wonderful, and tastes even better. As we eat, we talk more and hear of each other's trials and tribulations. Elliot and I always found fancier, eclectic places to dine in Chicago. But the vibe here, with Everett is great. We relax and are having a blast. Maybe we can finish the ritual at more casual locations. This will be fun.

I order a couple of shots. I am not sure why, but I feel like letting loose like the first night I met Reese. We had so much fun, and it felt good to let all of my worries go for the night. I challenge myself to do the same this evening. The shots definitely speed that along. I walk over to the jukebox and request a couple of songs. There must be a long playlist before mine, they are not playing right away. Everett continues on about his wild bar experiences, especially in college. I inform him I typically only went to bars to see bands. I have never really just hung out like this, being able to carry on a conversation, at a bar.

"What else have you done in your life, Clover? Elliot told me a lot about you, but I don't know your whole story. Tell me more." He seems genuinely interested.

"Wellllll, let's make this more fun. Want to play two truths and one lie?" I ask. This has always been a fun game. Reese and Nick would always come over to the loft and play with Elliot and me.

"I am not sure how to play. Explain please." Everett is intrigued. I tell him the rules. One person lists three things, two are true and one is not. They can be anything you wish to share. The other guesses which is the lie. If they guess wrong, they drink.

"I'll start. I am afraid of big boats. I once had a pet iguana. I took piano lessons until I was eight." I see he is in deep thought. "Come on, you only get ten seconds!"

"Are you making up rules as you go? Give me a moment." He rubs his chin in the thinking mode. "Okay. I'm going with the boats."

"Ha! Drink up big guy. You are wrong." I hand him his beer and make him drink.

"Your turn."

"Wait, do I get to hear the story first? That is lame!" He laughs, setting his beer down.

"Oh yes. I forgot! The tequila is getting to me. So, I do not like boats and I took piano lessons. I never had an iguana, but I always wanted one. I imagined naming him Theodore." He bellows out a laugh. "It's not that funny. Now your turn!"

"Okay. But that is kind of cute." In just a few moments he gives his statements. "Okay, okay. I think I have this right. I have never smoked in my life. I secretly listen to Taylor Swift. I went skinny-dipping once with my brother's girlfriend." He stares me down, singing the Jeopardy countdown music.

I think it through a while. I already know the answer. That means...wait. "You pig!" I throw a couple of pretzels at him, he blocks them with a hand. Quick reflexes considering how much we have had to drink. Then, I hear my song start. I jump out of my chair and grab his hand.

"Wait, don't you want to hear my story?"

"Not now! I want to dance!" It doesn't matter no one else in the place is dancing, like at all tonight. "Brown-Eyed Girl" came on, and I have to move. Everett does not hesitate and proudly takes my hand. We find some space in between tables and dance foolishly. He is spinning me around and we're both laughing, enjoying the moment. Eventually, the trend catches on and a few other couples join the fun. Towards the end of the song, my sore knee buckles a bit, I am a bit uneasy, and drunk, and Everett catches me. He holds me close and helps me back to the table.

He scoots his chair closer and grabs his cold beer and holds it over my knee. I take a quick breath in; the cold sensation shocks me a bit. He smiles, running his thumb down my chin almost apologetic. But then, he leans in close and kisses me. Gentle, but full of desire. I stop him, lean back in my chair, and put my hand over my mouth. I am stunned for a moment. He follows my lead and sits back.

"What the hell was that?" I ask. Drinking means no filter for me.

"I'm sorry, Clover. We are just having an amazing time, laughing. You look so gorgeous dancing and happy. I couldn't help myself."

"Everett, you know how-"

"Yes, I know what you've said, you *have* made the friend comment enough times now. I can tell by your reaction I was in the wrong. But I just rolled with the moment. Besides, Elliot said he saw us together. Didn't you hear him that day, just before...well, before." He sinks down at the memory.

I am stunned. Truly. "Do you think he was actually in his right mind at that moment?"

"How am I to know, Clo? I don't know what to think about it. What else could he have meant? He always said he was your wingman, would connect you to someone. Someone more." We both take a long drink. "What do you think?"

"I sort of blocked it all out of my head. I am not sure what he was saying. I thought he was dreaming. Or maybe had an out of body experience in surgery and saw us waiting together. He may have confused your consoling embraces as more. There *are* other options. I highly doubt he had predicted the actual future." He's running his hand through his hair now. I feel bad, sort of. I don't want to hurt him.

"I'm so sorry. I just have really enjoyed spending time with you and getting to know you better. I thought if he prophesized us together, maybe it was his hope for me to be here, to protect you."

"Everett, that is very sweet. And I do want you to be here. I like hanging with you too. But now is not the time. I'm just not in the right headspace for this. I hoped I was being clear about that all along. You know?" I try to say it gently.

"Yeah, I get it. Can you forgive me? Friends?" He holds out his arms to bring me into a hug. I comply. We hug for a moment, he kisses the top of my head again and rubs my shoulder.

"Friends, of course." I smile at him. "But, one thing. Enough of the weird sexual innuendos too, got it?" He smiles, and nods back. I think we're okay. I don't want to lose him; we both need each other right now. The waitress interrupts and asks if we want another round. We decide against it, and settle up the tab. The two of us finish our beers.

"So, why did you call me a pig….er, before all of this happened?"

"Oh yes, I forgot. Well, Elliot told me once about you stealing cigars from your stepdad, Number Two. That had to be your lie, as I assume you smoked them? Which leads to the fact you swam naked with his girlfriend?"

"Well, it is true, but she was my friend first, then he started dating her. I really hated him for it. She and I still hung out, there really wasn't much to it. Actually, it was her idea. I just played along. He found out and was so pissed." He points to a small scar just under his chin. "Brotherly love."

"I think the Taylor Swift may be worse, though." I joke and pat him on the arm. I think we'll be fine. The casualness is already sneaking back. We are both ready to leave. I know I should not drive. I ask how he is doing. He seems fine now. The rejection must have sobered him up. But the house isn't really that far, so we decide on leaving the car and walking back. It's a nice evening for a walk.

At the house, everything is quiet. Ruby left a light on for us on the porch. He follows me up the stairs, steadying me so I don't fall. We giggle a few times as we get to the room. He looked at me with a raised eyebrow, questioning the next move.

"Ev- you can stay in here. I trust you. That couch is horrid to sleep on. We're good." He asks two more times if I really don't mind. I don't mind. I go to the bathroom to change, he is already in bed when I return. He is laying on his stomach, arms folded up underneath him, his head turned my way. I crawl in and do the same. For a few minutes we just stare at each other.

"Was this how it was for you and my brother?" he asks.

"Um, you mean like this right here?" I pause thinking about

Elliot. "Yes, sometimes. It is not like we slept in the same bed all the time. We were able to be close like this, platonically, and really be there for each other. It was never complicated by anything more. We were just comfortable together. He truly was my best friend."

"I know. I'm sorry, I hope this doesn't make you sad. I didn't mean to bring it up. I just hope to be a good friend to you. I know it will never be the same, but I will be here for you."

"Thanks, Everett. You're very sweet. Now, to change the subject...in the car today you had the funniest smirk on your face when I woke up to Ruby's text. What was that about?"

"Oh, right! So, I woke you up actually. You were sound asleep for a while and dreaming."

"How do you know I was dreaming?" Now I'm worried.

"Well, you said something in your sleep and I am fairly certain it was not meant for me!" Oh gosh, I am blushing now. The alcohol is also not working in my favor. Everett is still calm, head on his hands, smiling.

"Dare I ask?"

"You were telling someone 'I love you too' and you had the most adorable look on your face."

Holy crap. I was dreaming. It must have been a repeat of the version with Elliot and I in bed together. How mortifying! I rub my face a few times, trying to clear my head. What do I say to that?

"Do you care to share? Was it some crazy fantasy?" he says teasingly. "I am correct, it was not intended for me, right?"

"Of course not. Honestly, I was dreaming about your brother. I had the same dream once before." I am not sure why I feel the need to tell him about it, but if I do not he will only continue to bother me about it. "It was quite vivid, futuristic, and sensual." Why, why, why am I telling him this?

"So, you did feel more for him?"

"No, I think my mind has just been playing tricks on me lately. A lot of tricks. The dream was like we were together, years from now. *Together*. It is not real. Was never something I thought of until now, when it cannot possibly happen anyway. And I've been imagining he is near. I actually chased some guy down in Franklin because he looks like him. That's how I banged up my knee, in the rain. Everett, I'm just a wreck." I don't know whether to laugh or cry. I think I'm doing both right now. Freaking tequila.

Everett reaches over and holds my hand. "You're not a wreck. It's just a lot. You're going to be okay. You will have that with someone, someday. You're too great a woman. Your Mr. Right will appear when you least expect it. Who is it, the handsome dean at school? He'll find you."

"I suppose so. You'll find someone too. Maybe we both already have."

"You think?" he points back and forth between the two of us. "I'm only kidding again, Clover. Let's get some sleep." We fall asleep holding hands.

The morning starts off loud. Greg has breakfast started. There are pots and pans rattling around the kitchen. My hangover head is not agreeing with the noise. Oh my! I walk down to see if I can help. Even though he is not a quiet cook, he is proficient. Everything looks good. Ruby is already up getting grandma ready for the day. I go to her room to see her. "Good morning ladies! Don't you two look stunning today. It looks like breakfast is almost ready, shall we go eat?"

Ruby looks distressed. My grandma doesn't answer me, she just stares out the window. "I think I'll bring her breakfast in here today," Ruby says, eyeing the door to ask me to leave. Oh no, she is not well today. I have learned on my previous visits if it is a bad day to give her space. Sometimes I confuse her, with looking similar to my mother. I walk back to the kitchen and sit with the guys. Ruby comes in and makes a plate for Grandma, apologizing. It isn't her fault. Why does she do that? I assure her it is okay. Everett and I can find things to do. We will leave them alone for a bit.

I show Everett around town for the afternoon. He has never been here and enjoys my mini-tour. We walk the brick streets in the historic district. The day is really perfect. Weather is great for being outside. I explain my love of window shopping. He is not the greatest at strolling along. His pace is a bit quicker than mine, and I am slower with my lame leg today. I continuously ask him to slow down. We spend several hours walking, stop for a sandwich at a cute little deli. While eating, he asks what I like about Savannah.

"It calms me. Chicago is exciting, fast-paced and full of adventure. Savannah feels more natural, friendly and comfortable. It is easy to feel at home, take your time, enjoy the people and beautiful places around you. Here, you celebrate each day."

"So they are opposite in the way they make you feel?"

"Yes, I love them both dearly, but miss the other when I'm away. Do you know what I mean?"

"Sort of. I've really lived in only one place. It will always be home to me. I visited Elliot in the city a few times. It is fun, but not for me. He loved it there, embraced it from day one. I never felt the desire to leave. What do you think about Tennessee?"

"Well it is a balance of both places in a way. I haven't spent a lot of time there. That time or two with Elliot to see you and your mom. These past days in Franklin have opened my heart to it a little more. There is a lot to do, the people are kind. I feel inspired there, but not rushed like in Chicago. I do like it."

"Enough to move there? Could you find happiness there?"

"Maybe. When I think about it, I do get butterflies. When I get into Savannah, my desire is to see my family. But I have a difficult time seeing my future here. It just doesn't feel the same. I had sort of a plan in Chicago, but that seems out of reach now. Things are definitely different. In Franklin, I have already envisioned my future. Not that it wouldn't be a transition, but somehow it makes sense."

"I think you may be closer to your answer to finding what you want and need out of life. I know you will be successful wherever you choose. But I have seen you light up when talking about moving. I saw you happy with new friends around a firepit the other night. I like how you have let yourself relax there. Do you think you can find that again in Chicago?"

"I am afraid I won't. That makes me sad, because I have had good times there, met great people. I need to make changes, get on the right path. I think I may be ready for something different." We finish up and walk back to the car. On the drive through town back to the house, both of us keep to ourselves. I am not sure what Everett is thinking but I am going through a checklist in my head of what I need to make happen in Franklin. I think my mind may be made up. I still need to talk to Reese about all of it. She can help me sort it out. She knows me well.

At the house, it seems a meal and more rest has brought my grandmother out of her spell from the morning. We all chat in the living room for a while. Everett has everyone laughing, and things seem good. Ruby, my grandmother, and I eventually go to the kitchen to start making the corn fritter batter. It always tastes better if you let it sit a while before you fry them up. We have a grand time cooking together. I remember doing this as a child. We loved to make dinner and sing and laugh. This feels like the old days.

Everett comes into the kitchen, curious to see us acting so childlike and free. He sits and watches as our meal comes together, enjoying the show of the crazy ladies making a mess and throwing flour around. I know he had few times in his house growing up that looked this wild. Girls are different than boys. I decide to bring him into the fun and toss some flour on his head too. He should not be the only one here looking so clean. It doesn't faze him, and he joins in the fun. The kitchen is a disaster by the time we finish cooking dinner and have a legit food fight.

The chicken tastes exactly as I remembered, and the fritters even better. I am in heaven. None of us hold back, the food is devoured. Everett helps me clean up while Ruby takes grandma to wash up for bed. Greg finds a game on TV he is more interested in. I don't want Everett to miss the chance to see more of town, but he agrees to staying in. We all hang out, watch a movie and enjoy each other's company. I feel good spending some much needed time with my family. I am pleased that Everett is here too.

Night comes quickly and we plan on leaving early in the morning, around six. I go to sit on the porch, enjoying the cooler evening and reminiscing about my younger days spent here. Everett goes upstairs grabbing a shower. Eventually he finds me outside and sits next to me. As if he can read my mood, we just sit in silence. We can hear the locusts. A young mockingbird is singing a tune for us. It is peaceful. Eventually we go upstairs to get some rest. Everett opens the window so we can keep listening to nature's creatures outside.

The early morning arrives soon. I go in to say goodbye to my grandmother. She is already awake, reading. It takes everything inside of me to not feel sad or tear up in front of her. I tell her I'll visit again soon and call often. She brushes my freckles, like I am still a small child. After a few moments, I give her another squeeze, a kiss on the cheek, and I close the door behind me as I leave. Everett is standing outside the bedroom in the hall. He hugs me, knowing this is so difficult for me.

A quick cup of coffee with Ruby and Greg in the kitchen, and Everett and I walk out to the car. He insists again on driving. I do not argue, he knows the way now. The drive back to Franklin seems faster than the route down. Perhaps I am more at ease this way. As the buildings and trees fly by me through the window, I know I have made progress. I feel good about handing the house over to Ruby. Everett and I have strengthened our friendship. I think I made a decision about where I want to live.

"Take me home," I tell him.

"Home?" he raises his brow and asks to get more clarity. I think he is shocked.

"Yes, home." I smile. He smiles back, and reaches to hold my hand.

We drive straight through, only stopping for a quick bathroom break and refill on beverages. I promise to take him to late lunch when we get back. Home.

CHAPTER 14

As we pull up to the bed and breakfast it is two-thirty. As usual, Everett makes great time. We make plans to catch up later. Right now I want to put my things away, take a hot and relaxing shower. I still need to check in with Reese. There is a lot to discuss. Everett wants to get some rest too and agrees to text me in a couple of hours after he chills at the hotel for a while. Sounds good. He walks me to the door, carrying my bag for me. As I open the door, Hayley is waiting on the other side. She is happy to see us.

"Good afternoon! I hope you had a lovely trip. Come in, both of you. A few of us just grabbed a seat out back. It is lovely today. Annnndd, there is sangria!" I am not sure if I can say no to her kind invite. I look over at Everett with weary eyes. He smiles, shrugging, and walks inside. I guess that is decided. "Oh goodie!" she exclaims, in her cute way.

I ask if he will be okay for a few minutes while I run my things upstairs. He is fine. As we part, I hear Sadie from the sunroom. Oh! I did not know she was here. I tell her I'll be right out. Everett follows Hayley, and the three of them join the others outside. I climb the stairs, my knee is feeling even better today. I place my duffel down. Continuing my new promise to myself, I quickly unpack all of my things into their appropriate place.

I grab my phone and text Reese.

ME: Hey, girl. Just got back to Franklin. Much to tell you. Can we chat later?

REESE: Oh, yes. Cannot wait. I have gossip too.

ME: Everything okay?

REESE: Yes. It can wait. Love you girl!

I peer out the window. Everyone is chatting outside. Everett looks content. I decide to take a quick shower and change out of my travel clothes. Within minutes, I am ready and go outside. Josh pours me a glass of a tasty berry sangria. Wow, that is good. I take a few more sips. I walk around a bit, stretching my legs out. The car time over the last days was grueling. I glance over and notice Everett and Sadie are sitting together and appear to be enjoying the company. I stall to give them some uninterrupted time. They both seem so at ease I would hate to spoil it.

Hayley walks up to me by one of the flower beds. "So, Everett said the two of you had a good time?" I sense she is trying to get some information out of me.

"Yes, we did. It was really great of him to come along, and drive. He is becoming a great friend. My family loved him too."

"A friend, huh? It is really none of my business, but the two of you seem to have a connection. No?"

"Yes, we do. We share the bond we each had with his brother. We are trying to get through all of this together. But, Hayley...please no matchmaker games here. He and I have already worked through that. We are good as we are. Okay?"

She smiles, nodding in agreement. Then she looks over at him seated with Sadie. "What about that? I can tell she is interested. I haven't seen her smile like that in a long time." Hayley may be onto something here. The two of them look good together. "Maybe you should go investigate," she's giggling.

"On it," I tell her. I walk over and pull up a chair. They are talking about scuba diving, which I know nothing about. Everett is bragging about places he has been diving, of course. Sadie is listening intently, adding she has only been once, on her honeymoon. A solemn look appears on her face. I decide to interrupt and change the subject.

"Sadie, have you thought more about the plans to host coffee time here?" I interject.

"Yes, before the two of you got back, I was going over things with Josh. I think we can get it worked out and maybe begin in a month or so. Still have fine-tuning to complete. But it will be great." Her pride and commitment to her work brings her smile back.

"Well, I hope I am invited to the inaugural event?" Everett chimes in, winking at her. She blushes and confirms he is on the list. He admires her determination. We had talked about that in the car. They continue in conversation, as he asks her what inspired her to open the café. She gladly tells the story of the plan, design and opening of her place. She really worked hard to manage all of that and take care of Poppy.

I clear my throat. "About that space?" I ask her.

"What about it?"

"Do you think we could check it out? I believe I am needing a place to rent." I explain.

Both Sadie and Everett sit up straighter, showing their excitement. "Really?" she seems childlike in her tone, like a young girl being handed an ice cream cone before dinner. I smile. "Yes, of course, Clover! I can show you any time. Like I mentioned briefly before, it is not a huge space and it'll take some work. Just promise to keep an open mind when you look at it. I have often thought about getting it ready for a tenant, but other projects have taken precedent. Timing is good, especially so *you* can move in!" She is now doing little mini-claps.

Everett adds, "I think you are making the right decision, Clover. I am happy for you. You are going to like it down here. I can help get you settled too. Until you find a place, you can crash at mine if you need to. Whatever you need, I can help."

"Thank you guys. I really appreciate the encouragement. I'll figure it all out." I grab both of their hands. It really means the world to me that the two of them have come into my life right now.

"I've picked up a few handy-man skills through the years. I can help with the apartment, if you need it. I could use something other than work to stay focused on right now," Everett offers. "Do you ladies want to go check it out now? My car is still here. Maybe stop for some of your wonderful coffee, Sadie? Or have dinner afterward? I am at your service."

Sadie's expression changes from her excited, animated self. "I need to go pick up Poppy in a half hour. She went to the park with her friend. Maybe tomorrow? But you are leaving later, aren't you Everett. Dang."

"We could pick her up on the way," he looks at her, "if you like?" Her grin returns, even larger this time. Hmmm, what is Everett up to.

"You don't mind? I totally understand if you want to postpone," she hesitantly adds.

"I think that is a wonderful idea, Ev! We have a half hour to finish this glass of sangria. Then we can pick up Poppy, check out the apartment, and grab dinner. I'm excited!" I grab my glass and lift it up. "To new friends and new adventures!" I toast. They clink with me. Immediately, everyone on the patio lifts their glass and chant, "Here, here!"

The sangria is refreshing and doesn't last long. We walk out to the car. Everett explains that my legs are shorter than Sadie's, persuading me to sit in the back. He gives me a little wink as he says it. He first opens the front passenger door, allowing Sadie to get in. She hilariously yells, "Shot Gun!" as she climbs into the car. I don't mind getting my own door and do so before Everett has a chance. We arrive at the park and find Poppy playing with friends. Sadie meets her and thanks the mother who was watching them. Sadie gives Poppy a big hug and walks her back to the car.

"Hi everyone!" Poppy announces once she is buckled in next to me in the back. Everett and I simultaneously return her greeting. She leans forward up to Everett's seat and rests her chin on the headrest. "Hey, it's your cute boyfriend!" she grins mischievously, then looks back at me. Everett immediately laughs out loud. I correct her for the millionth time. "Yeah, yeah. I know." Everett confirms what I have been telling this girl all along. Sadie is thrilled to hear it from his mouth, unable to control the joy on her face. I have never been so happy that another individual is glad I am not in a relationship.

It is only a few minutes' drive to the shop downtown. Sadie informs Everett there is private parking in back he can use. We enter the door in the back of the building. On the left is the narrow, wooden staircase to the apartment above. The four of us walk up in a grade school single-file fashion. At the top, Sadie unlocks the deadbolt and welcomes us inside. It is a small, studio type apartment. A small kitchen area is to the left. It is clean and bright, and it has retro metal cabinets that are fun and funky! There is a stove, but needs a refrigerator. Across to the right is a small bathroom. Sadie says the shower does not work great and will need fixed. There is a nice vanity with mirror, and white subway tiles all around. The rest of the space is open. The tall windows on the front allow a lot of sunlight through the space. I can picture some breezy long sheers hanging over them. The room has hardwood floors. They are a bit rough, but bring a nice warmth to the area.

Sadie flips a light switch on and off, noting the canned lighting needs bulbs, but one works so it appears the wiring is fine. Sadie adds, "If you want more of a private area, we can put up a wall to divide the space more?"

Everett looks around. "It doesn't look that bad, Clover. We can find a fridge, refinish the floors. Bathroom updates would be simple. I could do the work; it may take me a couple of weeks, but is doable. Totally."

"If you are not impressed or if it isn't your style, it is okay too. I can help you look for something else if you want. Please don't feel obligated. You need to be comfortable and find the perfect space for you. But if you like it, it is all yours." She is so thoughtful.

I look around a little more. I walk to the front windows and

I can see all of the same colorful storefronts and awnings that I noticed while walking the other day. I spin around, throw my hands into the air. "I love it! I really do!" I twirl around a few times. Poppy joins me, giggling. "Do you think it suits me?"

All three exclaim, "Yes!"

"Okay. It's a deal. Wait….can I afford it?" I look to Sadie. We haven't discussed financials yet. "I can pay for the repairs. I know this wasn't on your agenda right now."

"Don't be silly," she says. "I can take care of getting it ready. Maybe with Everett's help we can keep those costs down." She looks to him to confirm he meant what he said. He does. "I will be happy just to have it occupied. Until you find some work, you can help me out downstairs if you want. I can always use a hand. But you cannot drink the profits." She laughs, but most likely means it. "I do not need a deposit, advance or anything. Maybe eight hundred a month? Is that reasonable to you?"

"That would be amazing, Sadie. Thank you! I'll take it." We shake on it. Poppy is running around the space in excitement. I feel like running around too. So much to do. "Should we start planning?" My mind has a mass of ideas circling through it. I think we could do the work fairly quickly. Not a lot of major repairs are necessary. I could be in my new space in a matter of weeks.

"Let's start with dinner, what do you all say?" Everett asks.

The four of us enjoy a dinner at a local eatery. The restaurant serves amazing farm-to-table delights, family style. It is a tranquil and unique experience. Poppy chooses to sit next to me. I think I am her new favorite person; I clearly bought her affection with that first lollipop. Because of her seating preference, Sadie and Everett sit across from us. They appear quite cozy. Everyone is passing the dishes around as I notice Everett is using this to his advantage. I catch him gracefully brushing up against Sadie's arm on several occasions. Perhaps he is changing his outlook. I hope he is realizing he deserves to find happiness too. Sadie is so sweet and gracious. She could help convince him of that. It may not take long before the walls he has built up over time tumble down at her doing. From the sparks I see at our dinner table this evening, it may already be well underway.

"Sadie, do you have a number for the recreation center in town you mentioned? Now that I found a place to stay, I need to get some work lined up. I still don't mind helping you out at the shop, but I need to find some other work too. If I plan on going back to school, it is imperative I start saving up as much as possible."

"Yes, we can go over there tomorrow together if you would like, so I can show you the way."

I feel like I have already taken too much of her time. I hope I am not too intrusive, but I am so grateful for her help. "If you are available, that is fine. But if not, I'll be okay going alone. You can let me know in the morning." She nods and mumbles agreement, still chewing her last bite. She has a bit of food on the corner of her mouth when she smiles. Everett notices and sweetly takes the corner of his napkin and wipes it away.

"Ladies, when we're done here I will need to get you all home so I can get on the road. I hate to be a party-pooper but I really need to get into the office tomorrow. Clover, you have a couple more days at the bed and breakfast?" I shake my head up and down. "Let me know when you need to head my direction. I can clear my weight bench out of my spare bedroom and get things ready for you. It will be fun having a roommate for a few weeks."

Sadie has a bizarre look on her face. "Will that work out for you?" she asks me. "If you get work lined up, I mean." I see what she is saying. If I find work soon, or even start helping her, that extra commute time from Nashville could limit the time I have to work on the apartment and study for my MCAT exam.

"Yeah, it may be a little difficult. I guess I could ask Josh and Hayley if they have room for me for a while, maybe ask for a discount for more of an extended stay. Would that upset you Everett, if I stuck closer around here? We will still hang out, especially if you give us a hand with the apartment." I do not want to appear ungrateful or make him think I am not interested in hanging out. We've had some good times together lately, and I really love being around him.

"You do whatever you need to, hun. I'm fine either way. If it easier for you to stay in town, then you should do that. But, paying for a room for several weeks is kind of expensive?" I think he is still hoping to convince me to stay at his place.

"Stay with me and mommy!" Poppy recommends, looking at her mom, then quickly covering her mouth as if she should not have dared to say that.

I laugh, she is such a cutie. "That is nice, Poppy, but I will find a place to stay. It is only for a short amount of time."

"No, she's right," Sadie adds. "No point in you paying for a place. We have an extra room. It could work out great, save you some money. I don't mind. We would love to have you." She looks across to me, reading my expression.

I crack. "Really? That will be lovely. Thank you." Poppy squeals and I lean toward her and bump shoulders.

"Well, that is settled," Everett adds. "Sounds like we have a plan. This is good. I will be able to visit with you all together that way!" He is looking more at Sadie than me now. I see a little spicy grin appear on his face. Hmm, very interesting. It isn't his silly, goofy, flirty look that I have seen before. This is more serious in nature.

He drops off Sadie and Poppy first. He drives around the block to take me to my room. I wish him a safe drive home. Everett gets out of the car, walks around to me and gives me a crushing hug and kisses my cheek. "I'm really happy you're sticking around here."

"I bet you are, big guy!" I nudge his shoulder and then point behind me in the direction of Sadie's house. He blushes. Yep, he's well on his way.

"Stop it," he says while he raises up onto his tiptoes and back down a couple of times. He is unable to control his excitement. How adorable. "I will be in touch. We can work on your place next weekend. K'?" He leans in for another hug.

"I can't wait!" I begin to tear up. It must be a combination of my excitement to get into a new place, happiness that my new friends are here to support me, and bittersweetness that my trip with Everett is ending. "Thanks, Everett. You've been so good to me."

"I'll always protect you, Clover. Never forget that." He takes my hand, squeezes it gently and then steps away. I don't move. As he walks to the car he turns back to wave at me, and blows me a sweet kiss. I catch it in the air and giggle. Bye, friend. The cool Everett returns and revs the engine a couple of times, and does a burnout as he takes off.

CHAPTER 15

As I walk into the main hall, the bed and breakfast is quiet this evening. I see one new couple playing chess in the sitting room. I can hear Hayley and Josh in the kitchen laughing as they clean up from the dinner rush. I peek my head in and wave hello. It looks like the older gentleman who I always see reading is taking a nap while seated in the sunroom. The others could be out enjoying the evening air. I am beyond exhausted. It has been an extremely productive day, but I feel the need to hop on my bed and relax.

When I reach my room, the bed is already turned down for me. They did that early tonight; I bet Hayley readied my room knowing I had a long day. She may be a mind reader, if not the best hostess in the universe. I'm going to miss this hospitality when I get into my new apartment. Heck, I have never consistently made my bed daily. I challenge myself to start. It will need to be done if my bed is visible from the main areas in the studio apartment. I am still not convinced I want to add a privacy wall.

I drop my bag on the chair, throw on my pjs, and prop my pillows up so I can lounge in bed and read. I grab my phone to send out a couple of updates. I send a quick message to Ruby to inform her we made it back safe and sound. The next is to Everett asking him to text me that he made it home, and thanking him for everything in the past few days. Now, I promised Reese we would chat. I wonder if she is home? For a moment I feel anxiety set in. I have a lot to tell her.

ME: Reese, you up for that chat?

As soon as I hit send, she is already calling me. I see her goofy picture on my screen.

"Hey Reese! How are y-"

"I'm getting marrrrieeeeeeeed!" She shouts.

"What? Oh my goodness, Reese! I am so happy for the two of you!" I am ecstatic that she and Nick are finally doing this. They are adorable together and make each other so happy.

"I know, right!?! He asked me last night at dinner. I am totally in shock. It is going to be soon. My mother would drive me insane if we planned for a year or more. So, we are thinking in a month, two tops? Nothing too fancy. Will you stand up for me, be my maid of honor?" She is speaking a million words a minute.

"That is amazing. Of course, I will!" Holy crap. There are so many things I need to be tackling in the next few weeks. It is going to get crazy if I have to go back and forth and help with the wedding. Breathe. This is for Reese! She has always been there for me. I will be there for her, no matter what.

"Thank you, thank you, thank you! When are you coming back so we can start?"

Oh, my. How do I tell her this? I do not want to spoil her excitement. I have already made this decision. I have thought it all the way through. She did tell me to take care of myself, think about what I need, not what others think or want.

"Well, that is what I needed to talk to you about. A lot has happened in the past few days."

"You're getting married too?" She is not laughing. She cannot be serious.

"Ha! Um, no. That is not it. Not even close!"

"Dang it. When you first went on this trip I called Everett to check on you. He seemed more interested than just checking on you, if you catch my drift?"

"I cannot believe you did that, but you are wrong. He and I are friends. On our road trip we have become closer, but not like that. So thank you, I guess. What I need to tell you is ... I have decided to move here."

"To Franklin? Really?" She pauses for just a moment. "If you will be happy there, I think you should. Not that I want us to be in different cities, but you do need a fresh start, Clover. I am not sure if you have ever been in love with Chicago. As long as you have thought it through, I'm entirely behind you, love."

"Thank you, Reese. It is not that far away; it may be temporary anyway. I'm going to go back to school. I need to move on with my life. For the first time in ages, I feel I'm back on track, not just stuck in the mud. I can feel the momentum. It feels right."

I hear her tearing up. This is not something Reese does often. She is a rock. She loves hard but typically doesn't wear her emotions on her sleeve. "Reese, are you okay?"

"Yes. Better than okay. I am just so happy. It seems both of us are growing up; our dreams are coming true. I am proud of you, Clover. You are going to do amazing things. You are destined to. And I have Nick and a business that I love. I am feeling a bit emotional."

"Tell me about your dream dress. What kind of wedding do you want? I cannot believe you are getting married, you wild child!"

We talk for hours. I hear the entire proposal story. She tells me about what she envisions the wedding to be like. I tell her about the apartment, the work to be done on it. I ask her thoughts on how I can nail a job at the rec center, and she practices a speech if they call for a referral. She asks me to entertain the idea of opening the second *Arise* studio in Franklin. I am not sure I want to get into that with school on the horizon, but I promise to think it over. I realize I still have not told her about my afternoon in the park and my outrageous Elliot dream.

"Reese, I know it is already pretty late, but there is something else I need to tell you. Can I keep you for a bit longer?"

"Sure. I mean, we need to practice these long calls since you are leaving me!"

"Wait, please do not lay the guilt on me like that."

"I'm just messing with you, Clover. This will be fun. We'll be like teenage girls on the phone for hours! Please, go on." She is quite curious what this is all about.

"So, you know how I saw a guy in town the other day, and I sort of freaked out?"

"Yes, and I told you that the mind can play tricks while you grieve."

"I know, I listened to you. But something else happened. I saw a guy...er, the same guy, maybe?" I give her all of the details, explaining what I saw and how I chased him down again. The mark by his ear, the eyes. I tell her of my dream about Elliot and me. I feel inundated with emotion as I relive these moments. She calms me and reiterates that all of this is normal, that I should not freak out about it. The dream could just be echoes of my tie to Elliot, the trust I had in him, that type of intimacy. My brain just warped it into a sex dream. But she believes I need to move beyond chasing down strangers. How could anyone understand those moments? I know how deceiving the mind can be, especially under emotional spells, but I was lucid and clearheaded when they happened. I may not have responded logically, but it does not change what I saw, how I felt. To prevent additional psychoanalysis I refrain from sharing those details. Right now I just need to vent to my friend. I don't expect to obtain advice that would make any sense of it.

I promise Reese I will call if I have any other extreme visions. We both are getting sleepy and decide to call it a night. After hanging up, I lay in bed with my mind going bananas. This will be a long night staring at the ceiling. From the window I can see the sky is clear, stars are twinkling. I walk downstairs and quietly prepare a glass of chamomile tea. I walk out to the patio and curl up on a chair. The night is calm, a slight chill to the air. I tilt my head back, looking to the stars. Maybe there are answers in the heavens for me tonight. I see a quick flash of light in the corner of my eye and discover Hayley walking over to me.

"You okay, Clover?" she asks with a worried look on her face.

"Oh, yes. I am good. Just clearing my head. It is beautiful out here this evening."

She sets down a small candle on the table between us. "Do you mind if I sit?" she asks pointing to the chair beside me. "If you need alone time, I won't barge in."

"Please, join me." I see she chose a glass of wine to cap off her night. "What brings you out here?"

"I walked down to close things up for the night out front and heard the garden door when you came out. I thought I would check if you needed anything. This candle can help keep any bugs away too."

"Thanks, that is very kind. I felt a little restless in my room, I just wanted to check out the night sky here. You can see a lot more stars than in Chicago. I like it here. Did you hear I've decided to move? Here, to Franklin." She turns more my way and taps my arm with her hand gently, smiling. I see the flash again. I notice it is her necklace. It is a gorgeously detailed Celtic tree of life with a small diamond in the branches. I can't help but stare at it, mesmerized. It reminds me of home.

"That is delightful! I am so glad you'll be around longer. We have enjoyed having you here and getting to know you. I believe Franklin suits you. Please let us know if you need anything while you make the move. We are more than happy to help!"

"I will, thank you. Sadie and Poppy have asked me to stay with them until we get the apartment above her store remodeled, then I'm going to rent it from her. I am excited." Her necklace sparkles again. "On another topic, your pendant is stunning. Are you also Irish?"

"No, no, I am not. Josh gave me this for our anniversary this year." She gently takes hold of the pendant, pulling it away from her neck so we can both closely admire it. It is clear she is very fond of it; both the pendant and her face sparkle as she holds it.

"It is a lovely piece. You wear it well. My grandmother always hung a Tree of Life in our rooms. She said they guide us to grow stronger. One of her old-school Irish customs."

"That is very sweet, what a lovely tradition."

"Yeah, I guess so. I will have to put one up in my new place. It can represent my leap into the next phase of my life." Saying that makes me feel happy, calmer. I cannot help but smile.

"What a great idea! I cannot wait to see the place when you have it all finished! That is a great location too, right in the middle of town." I nod and think about how fun it will be to be in the new space, make plans with my new friends, get to know the area and more of the wonderful people who call it home.

We both sit in silence for a while, just relaxing and staring up at the night sky.

"Clover, if you are fine here, I'm going to go upstairs. It has been a long day. I'll see you in the morning, okay?" She sips the last bit of wine from her glass.

I stand up with her. "Sure, of course. I am good. I should do the same, actually. I'm pretty exhausted now that I think of it. I'll follow you in momentarily." She goes inside, while I stand and stretch a minute. I look at the glimmering stars one last time and exhale deeply. I made it. Another day. I'm going to be okay.

My sleep is uninterrupted, unimaginative, and very restful. I am full of energy and want to solidify plans today. First, I take time to go online and schedule my MCAT exam. I plan to give myself about ten weeks of solid, devoted studying. I find a date to register that fits my timeline. I submit the registration. If all goes well, I'll take it in three months, and know a month later how well I performed. Next year at this time I hope to be interviewing and praying some school will take my old ass.

More thoughts fly through my head as I shower and get ready. I text Sadie to see if she still wants to accompany me to the rec center. She is flexible and asks me to meet her at the café whenever I am ready. My energy is skyrocketing this morning. I decide on a professional, yet fun sundress for the day, and tie a lightweight sweater around my shoulders as a fashion statement and for unexpected inclement weather. I pull my unruly red hair into a twisted low bun. I cannot seem to get it just right, but it looks better than the frizzy mess I had before. I grab my stuff and head out for the day.

As I walk downtown, I envision the apartment in my head making mental notes of what should be priority, things I need to pick up. I feel mildly overwhelmed at how many tasks have accumulated. I refocus on the surroundings as I walk. I see an open storefront for rent just a block from the café. The dark stained wood front is rich and makes the large diamond beveled, leaded glass windows jump out. It is charming. I could see Elliot picking out this place for his patisserie. I pause on the sidewalk and close my eyes to picture it finished to his perfection. Little spotlights would shine on the details of the windows, making them sparkle. A black and white striped awning would hang above the door. It is classic Elliot, spectacular really. It only takes a moment to realize daydreaming about his goals and dreams is pointless. I try not to let the sadness pull me in and force myself to keep moving forward, physically and emotionally.

I arrive at Sadie's within minutes. She is sitting, scratching her temple and doing paperwork at a window table. As soon as I walk in the door, she jumps up and begins preparing one of my favorite beverages. The aroma blankets me. "Thanks again for taking time out of your day to go with me. Maybe later I can start some training in here. I have no problem drinking these beverages, but making them might be a different story," I chuckle.

She grins, handing me the mug. "Clover, you do not have to rush into this. My goodness, you still have days left of a planned vacation. You came here to take time for yourself. You should do just that. We can get started whenever you feel ready."

"No time like the present. I am ready. I need this, to keep going. It makes me feel good to be motivated again, alive. Can you please do this for me?" I sound needy. I am afraid to go back to the dark place I had been trapped in, with too many emotions pulling me further down. I need to prevent my mind from tricking me, giving me false hopes for things that will not be. I must stay focused on the future.

"Sure, of course. If you feel that strongly about it, we can start today. However, if you find it is too much too soon, just say so. I can have Jared show you the ropes this afternoon. He's worked here since I opened, the best barista we have. He comes in at three, if you want to plan to meet him then?"

"Yes, yes, yes! I will be here. Thank you again for everything, Sadie. You're the best!" I give her a big hug. I sip my drink, discretely poured into the faux green-drink mug that Everett gifted me. "Are you sure you have time to go with me this morning? I totally understand if you are busy." Although it would be nice to have her accompany me, I can see she has a lot on her mind.

"Clover, would you mind if I did stay here? I am really behind on paperwork and have a shipment arriving later this morning that I need to tackle. I do not want to disappoint you, I know I said we'd go together."

"Truly, Sadie. I'm fine. I can do this solo, no worries! You take care of things here, that is priority." I look at the coffee mug shaped clock on the wall and see I should get walking if I want to arrive a few minutes early and check out the area. "I'm going to leave you to your paperwork. I'll text you how it goes!"

"Sounds good. I'll update Jared so he knows he'll be doing some training later. Good luck!"

"Thanks again!" I smile and step back outside. The weather is cooperating today. The sun is shining, there is a light cool breeze. I think about how pleasant even the winter months would be here. I know it gets colder, but nothing like in Chicago. I certainly will not miss all of the snow.

The recreation center is only a few blocks away. I pass several people on the sidewalk. Some are business people, dressed in suits and carrying briefcases; others are tourists closely looking at street signs trying to find their next destination. One woman is staring at her phone and turns in front of me to enter a store. We almost collide but she swiftly moves out of the way and apologizes for her distraction. I smile back and notice she is headed into the jewelry store with the sparkly window displays. Everything looks gorgeous. I wonder if this is where Josh bought Hayley her pendant. My grandmother would love something like that, but I'm sure anything similar would be well out of my current budget. Someday, when I have a physician salary, I'll be able to do things like that. Cross my fingers. Right now I need to find work.

The recreational center is a newer structure, but it was designed to blend in with the traditional buildings surrounding it. My confidence is waning as I walk up the steps into the building, and my palms begin to sweat. I locate the main office and ask for Ian, the gentlemen I spoke with earlier this morning when I phoned. Within minutes he is available and steps out to greet me. I try to subtly dry my hands on my sweater hanging off my shoulders before he looks my way. We make our introductions, and he directs me to have a seat in his office.

Taking Reese's advice, I start with my experience teaching yoga, the styles I have practiced, and my more recent trials of organizing the studio schedule, and coordinating staff training. I hope my limited local contacts can help me get something going here. Although he is listening intently, I can sense Ian is going to burst my bubble. His very calm demeanor shows no sign of excitement or intrigue. Maybe this is how he always acts? There is an arrogance in his motions that puts me on edge.

"Wow, Miss Sheehy. You have a lot of experience and I absolutely love the energy." Perhaps I read him wrong; this might turn around. "As your friend mentioned, we did offer a yoga program here for a short timeframe. However, the instructor moved away and we never had a strong enough interest in the classes to pursue a replacement. None of our current employees were interested or certified to teach. We try to keep a variety in the programs we offer, but we felt that one just did not fit our community's needs."

Crap. What do I say to that, or how do I make a dignified exit now? "I understand. Do you think it is something worth a trial to see if new interest is out there? From speaking to some folks in the community, I really think it would be beneficial. Perhaps some short, beginner classes and advertising could get it started? I would be willing to help with that. I really would love an opportunity." I am begging and feel like a complete ass now.

"Miss Sh-" he begins.

"Clover, please." I encourage him with a smirk. Maybe trying a more personal level will better my odds. Almost immediately, I feel regret for that addition.

He smiles, but I still sense disappointment coming my way. "Clover....I do find you to be very driven, smart. I think you could help us out here. However, our high energy classes and competitive team programs tend to do better with our demographics. Would you be interested in helping with any aerobic or spinning classes?"

I really need a job. However, I am not totally excited about the offer. "I am sorry you do not feel a yoga program is worth taking a chance on again. I am sure I would have no problem catching on and teaching the other classes-"

"Of that I am certain," he interrupts. My creep alert just went off as he gives me a strange stare up and down. Nothing coy about it. I tug my sweater tighter around my shoulders. Ian adds, "So would you be interested?" He leans over and brushes my hand. This now feels nothing like a job offer.

I stand up and curtly reply, "I will have to decline. I am sorry I have wasted your time today. My interests are very specific, and my passion is for yoga." His expression has now changed to a sullen pout. He got the hint. "Please excuse me," I say as I pass by him and exit the office.

That was all unexpected and disturbing. Did I overreact? Dammit. I really needed that job. What the hell am I going to do now? Should I really be taking chances like this? Moving here? It is not too late to change my mind. I haven't wasted anything on the apartment yet. I could go back to Chicago, figure it all out- help Reese and Nick with the studio, help her plan the wedding, face my fears and get on with my life.

I walk back to the bed and breakfast to change into more casual clothes with comfy shoes to wear while Jared helps me train this afternoon. Hayley has sandwiches and salads out for lunch. I grab a caesar salad and sit down outside under the pergola. Josh walks over to me and asks how my day is going. I tell him about my meeting with Ian.

"That guy is a jackass, Clover." He tries to console me. "Don't let his actions steer you away from your goals."

"Really? You don't think I overreacted? I know my emotions are hypersensitive at the moment. Did I lose a chance at a job because I am unable to handle a guy hitting on me?" If he was hitting on me, that is. I cannot even tell any more. I have closed my eyes to all men for so long, to minimize my risk of getting hurt.

"Don't sweat it. You'll figure it out. Plus, you read that guy like a book. He is weird and creepy, and hits on any available women every chance he has."

"Gee, thanks!"

"Sorry, I didn't mean it like that." He nods back and forth. "You are a lovely woman! But he thinks he can charm anyone. I am glad you saw through him. It sounds like your emotions are spot on. You deserve to find a nice guy. He is not a nice guy. You also deserve to find work that you enjoy."

"Thanks, Josh." Maybe it is from being so close to Elliot for years, but it feels good to get a man's opinion, it is comforting. "You're right. I will figure something out."

Hayley walks out, "What are we figuring out?"

"Oh, just that my life is a disaster, that I have awkward social skills, and I still have no job. No worries!"

"Girl, you are not a disaster! Sorry it didn't go well today. We'd still like to have you do some yoga sessions here each week. I think it will be fantastic! That's a start, right?"

Why are they so darn nice? What have I ever done to deserve their kindness? "Absolutely, that is a definite start. Let me know when and where. Thanks for everything!" The two of them pick up a few dishes from nearby tables and go inside. Hayley turns back and gives me a quick reassuring wink. The afternoon sun is soothing. I grab my phone from my pocket and see I have several messages.

REESE: So?????

EVERETT: How's ur day? Job yet?

SADIE & POPPY: Any news?

Wonderful, now I get to explain this to everyone. I reply to Reese first and then copy the message and send it to the other two. Basic, to the point, with a partial lie at the end.

ME: No job. I'll be fine. Working on plan B.

I lean back in the chair, stretch my legs out and allow the warmth of the sunlight to cloak me in positive energy. There is no need to completely change my plans, but I do need to find some employment soon. I know I can be at the café a couple of shifts per week to help, thanks to Sadie. It seems I can teach a yoga session or two privately here at the BNB as Hayley mentioned. I can look at a few other places, maybe a smaller gym or dance studio would be interested in hosting. I'll start asking around. For now, I need to head to the café and start some training. At least I have something lined up, as insignificant as it seems right now. Baby steps.

CHAPTER 16

JARED RUNS THE CAFÉ for Sadie in the evenings most days. Sadie has informed him of my training session beginning today. As I walk through the door, I see him working quickly behind the counter. He is a sharp dresser, has on nice jeans with a white dress shirt and grey checkered button up business-type vest. He glances ahead and waves at me, flashing his open hand up to me, wiggling all his fingers, and mouths "*five minutes.*" There is a line of several people waiting at the counter. I can give him a few moments to catch up.

I take a seat at one of the tables and wait. I scroll across my phone, but no messages await me. I drop the yellow phone into my bag, no need for distraction while I train. I catch myself drifting off as I stare out the window. I imagine how different this trip would be if Elliot were here with me - things we would do, what he would find most interesting. I may never have met my new acquaintances or taken time to learn more about them. I miss him dearly, but in a way am glad I am here alone. It is forcing me to be more outgoing, try new things, meet new people. He and I could get trapped in our own world so easily.

I can see a moving shadow on the floor; it is the visible dance from the heat outside. The heat waves, thermal radiation, amaze me. How strange to have something you can feel, only indirectly see, and cannot touch. I stretch my arm out and interfere with their movement. I think about the moments of my recent, how should I say it.....Elliot visions. I suppose they are no different than these lurking shadows of heat. They happened. I know they were real. I can feel the impact of them, but I cannot seem to connect to him completely. He is out of reach but still shows his presence. I feel comforted, but also melancholy. I close my eyes to help pull myself together.

I hear footsteps shuffling and open my eyes to see Poppy skipping toward me. She stops and hops onto the chair next to me.

"Why are you sad again?" she asks.

"You think I am sad again?" This girl never ceases to amaze me.

"Yep. I can just tell," she shrugs her shoulders, tilting her head to the side so nonchalantly. "Won't you tell me why?"

I clear my throat trying to fight the tightness it has forming within. "Same reason as the last time we chatted about it. I am missing people. This time it's my best friend. His name was Elliot."

"I am sorry you miss your friend. I can be your friend. Will that make you happier?" she questions so sweetly.

"Of course, that will make me happier!" I smile.

"You have other friends too. My mom and Everett. I am glad you and my mom are friends. She gets sad too. She doesn't know I can tell, but I can. She stares off just like you just were. I think she gets lonely. I wish I could make you both happy."

"Oh, Poppy, you do! You are such a lovely young lady! You make everyone around you smile!"

"I try. You know my mom worries about me. I've heard her talking. I shouldn't be nosy, but sometimes I can't help it. She thinks the divorce is too hard for me. But I worry about her more. I still get to see my dad and talk to him. She doesn't have that anymore." Poppy's eyes lower a bit as she thinks to herself a moment.

"Poppy, you shouldn't worry about your mom. She is a strong lady. *You* give her happiness. She loves you very much."

"Yeah, I know that. I just wish I could help her not be so lonely. But I am glad I found you and now we all can be friends. And I'm glad you are going to stay with us. That will be fun!"

"Yes, me too, Poppy. I'm glad too," my smile widens as I see her excitement gleaming. "Is your mom in back?"

"Yes, she's around here somewhere. I'm supposed to be doing my chores before we leave for the day. I'm almost done."

"Good job, Poppy. I need to walk over to Jared and start my training. You better get your tasks done. I'll see you later!" She hops back down and runs to the back room.

Jared is ready and now waves me over. The crowd has lessened to just one woman who is still staring at the menu deciding what flavor she wants in her latte. He finishes her order and then focuses on my accelerated training.

We start with the simple things. He explains the equipment, how to operate and clean it. He wants me to just watch him this evening when he makes any drinks. I think I'll have homework studying the main recipes. I get the tour of where all the supplies are stored. He creates me a login for the register and shows me the basics; it is fairly easy to use. Jared recommends a few coffee tutorial videos that go into how beans are prepared. I am good at the reading, watching. I am truly fearful of the steam wand. I know there is an art to making the perfect beverage.

He is extremely patient with me, reviews things slowly and explains in great detail. I can see why Sadie involves him in training new team members. It is also very evident he is good at his job and takes pride in it. In between customers and training, he asks questions about me and I bounce several back to him. I find out he is only a few years younger than me, working on his masters in mechanical engineering at State. If I am being honest, it makes me feel a little under accomplished.

I remind myself I am making progress. I am moving here, studying for my now scheduled MCAT, and finding work. My plan is underway. I let the smell of the coffee awaken me. I get back to focusing on Jared. He is very agile as he prepares drinks. We spend some time on their coffee and tea varieties, how often and when the daily flavor is brewed. I feel like I'm walking in circles trying to keep up with him. After several hours, he tells me I can be finished for the evening. I ask if I can return tomorrow, if I passed the first level of training?

Jared informs me to meet him at the same time tomorrow, which sounds great to me. I promise to complete my homework and be prepared for the next round. I walk to grab my bag, but it isn't at the table any longer.

Oh, no! Did I leave it there unwatched; was it stolen? I cannot see any of the patrons taking it, but maybe I'm being too trusting. I look around a bit and do not see it. I walk in the back and see it on the desk in the office. I know I did not move it. Perhaps Poppy kindly placed it in the safer location before they left. I suppose it doesn't matter how it got there, but more importantly that it is still in my possession. Big sigh of relief.

I thank Jared for his help tonight, grab my bag, and walk out the door. I realize how tired my feet are from standing all night. The evening air is settling in, it has cooled off some. I stop and turn back for a brief moment, glancing up at the apartment windows above the café. I try to picture what it will look like when I'm settled in, the windows open, warm light glowing from the living space. I am quite excited about it.

I turn back around and start walking, passing a couple of the familiar spots on my way back to the BNB. As I approach the front of the cute rental where I envision Elliot working I stop again. This time, I move in closer and peer into the glass on the door, hands cupped around my face. The interior is one large open floorplan. It looks like a long, but somewhat narrow space. There are tall ceilings, maybe twelve feet, which seems atypical for the buildings around here, and definitely for this space. Although it is disproportionate, it does make the room look larger, it would surely allow more light to travel through. I am not certain why I care so much, perhaps just the thought of Elliot having a location like this? Either way, I must look odd peering into the old building.

I really should get back to my room, have some dinner and start studying. The clock is ticking now to prepare for my upcoming exam. One thing I am good at, unlike frothing milk, is getting organized to study. I speed up the remaining portion of the walk back.

As I enter the blue front door, I hear several guests in the sitting room chatting and playing games. I peek and say hello. Since my initial walk through, I have not returned to the library to retrieve the book I originally noticed. I quickly find it on the shelf and take it with me. I am excited for the re-read of one of my favorites. I pass Josh in the kitchen. My late arrival has me missing the formal dinner time, but he helps me find a sandwich and some fruit to get me started studying. He asks if I will join the crew outside for dessert around the fire, but I need to limit my distractions. I explain my plans and take a raincheck.

I hike up the stairs, truly sore from my day. I am happy to switch into my night shirt and get comfy. The desk isn't extremely large in here, so I spread out a few notebooks onto the bed and glance over what notes I have already prepared. The sandwich is tasty, a nice lean roast beef and provolone on a crusty French bread. I should have grabbed two of them, as this goes down quickly.

I flip through my study guidebook pages in earnest, jotting down notes on index cards. I spend a couple of hours refreshing. I know there are many online programs and resources to use, but they cost a lot of money, which I do not have as a luxury. I will invest in a practice exam program, but the bulk of my studying I will need to do old-school. It is nothing I cannot handle if I stay focused and stick to my schedule. When I get through it all, hopefully I can enjoy the spoils of my hard work.

I stand for a few moments to stretch, attempting to stay alert while I study. I take a second to check my phone and see a missed call from Reese. I never did message her the details of my disappointing morning. I don't want to bother her after our extended conversation last night, but a quick text won't hurt.

ME: Reese, it was a no go at the rec center. Started training at the café tonight tho. I'll figure it all out. Started studying tonight. Miss you!

I put the phone down quickly, knowing how it can be an evil distraction. I sit back on the bed, grab some of my popcorn I bought at the store several days ago. It seems like an eternity ago now, but it really hasn't been long. Not for all the things that have happened. I continue for another hour or so, but as the words begin blurring together I decide to call it a night, at least for the studying. I grab my book from downstairs and begin reading, easily jumping back into the stories.

As I read about the struggles of each character, I try to analyze my own life. I am the only true enemy I have; I have been the one standing in my way to growing and moving on. I have never been good at letting go of the past. It is something I will keep high on my self-improvement priorities. Living in the present. I understand the importance of zen living, concentrating on the present, but never put effort into practicing it for myself. Until now. Maybe it can really help me if I give it a shot.

My phone vibrates, I can see it light up. It must be Reese getting back to me. I reach over, nearly falling off the bed trying to grab it from the bedside table. I see Everett's face on the screen. Hmmm, he is up late this evening. I swipe to answer.

"Hey, Everett – what's going on? I didn't think I would hear from you so soon."

"What – you don't miss me yet?"

"Of course I do. I thought maybe you would have gotten tired of me!"

"No, not yet at least," he lets out a mischievous chuckle. "I am sorry to call so late, but I thought you might be up. I need to ask you something."

"Okay…what is it?"

"So, strange thing happened tonight. I received this really weird text from an unknown number. After I read it, I *think* I know who sent it, but it is really bizarre."

"Hmmm, I'm intrigued! What did it say?" he has really piqued my interest.

"So basically it read: 'You are super nice, and cute, and funny. My mom sort of likes you. Do you like her?'"

Immediately I am laughing. I know exactly who sent it. "Everett, that is the cutest thing ever! You *do* know who texted you, right?" How Poppy managed this one, I am not sure. But I will get to the bottom of it.

"Well, I didn't know the number. I have gone out on a date or two with a single mom before. But with it being so recent.....you think it is about Sadie, right?" he sounds nervous.

"That has to be it, Everett. I mean, it is blatantly obvious, isn't it?"

"What's obvious? That it is about Sadie, or that she.....eh, likes me?" now he sounds like a young boy, his voice jittery.

"Both, actually. I'm certain Poppy sent you that text. And I'm also certain that Sadie is interested. What is not so certain is how Poppy managed to get your info." It dawns on me. Wait a minute. She moved my bag today at the café and had easy access to my phone in there. She most likely looked him up. What a little shit! I laugh out loud.

"What is so funny....this has me freaked out a bit! Clover, I need your help!"

"Calm down. I am laughing because I think I know how she got your info." I explain to him the events earlier this evening. It all makes perfect sense. Plus, Poppy and I were just talking about her mom being lonely. She is playing matchmaker, the little genius. "So what has you freaked out, exactly?"

"Well, first I am just really shocked – shocked at how this girl sent me this message. Shocked at how the message made me feel, um, nervous. This could go bad. If I reply that I do, indeed, like Sadie – and her daughter misconstrued her attraction to me, I look like a fool. If I reply that I do, but then I screw it all up because I am an emotional imbecile, I not only look foolish, but possibly hurt *both* of them. See where I'm going with this?"

"Wait a minute. In none of these scenarios do you say you do not like her, correct?"

"Honestly, no. But that doesn't mean I should act on it. You know I'm not ready. I explained that to you already."

"Trust me, she likes you Everett. And so does Poppy. Imagine how Sadie is going to feel when she sees that text on her phone. Right now, she is either unaware that this has happened, or is currently scolding Poppy for sending it and trying to figure out her next step. No matter how you reply, you'll save her the embarrassment of having to send you another text without her knowing how you feel. Your court, mister. Play ball!"

"Fuck. What do I say? Can you talk to her for me?" he pleads, clearly on edge.

"Ha! You are kidding, what is this middle school? Heck no, I am not talking to her for you. Cowboy up, you can do this!" I hope this motivates him. I am not as good at pep talks as Reese.

"I don't know about this. I feel stupid. How do I even start it? Do I address Poppy or Sadie? For heaven's sake…this is sooooo flipping confusing!" his frustration makes his tone sound sharp, jagged.

"Eliminate that issue. Just call her. Be honest with her. What do you have to lose?"

"I'm not just worried about the two of them, or myself here. If things get weird, I do not want to screw up the plans with helping get the apartment ready for you. You are involved in this too, in a weird way…ya know? I promised to protect you too. There is a lot to lose here. Don't make it sound so simple." He tries to explain all the layers of his fear. The depth of his concern for me still shocks me at times.

"Thank you for worrying about me, but that should not be part of this decision. I trust you. You can handle this. *Call her!*" I instruct him while trying to still sound gentle.

"Yeah, yeah. Got it. I'll call her. When…when should I call her? It is late. I don't want to bother her now, do I?" the uncertainty still remains in his reply.

"You can do this, Everett. Figure it out. You have got this!"

"Now or never, I guess. Wish me luck." I know he doesn't need luck. Sadie really likes him. I'm excited to hear how this goes. I tell him good night and hang up.

All I can do is sit here thinking what that conversation will be like. Oh my Lord, if Sadie hasn't seen the text Poppy sent yet, it will be quite a surprise to her. I wish I could be a fly on the wall in her room! I know Everett is scared and anxious, but I think he is ready. From the stories Elliot used to tell me, Everett has never been attracted like this to anyone. Nothing that made him nervous like a teenage boy. If he has allowed himself to feel that connection, there has to be something to it. He is ready to find the real thing. I think the two of them would be cute together.

I shut off the light and lay down. My thoughts are about Sadie and Everett, then about Reese's upcoming nuptials. I allow myself thirty seconds of pity, wishing fate would step in and help me find someone. I shut those negative thoughts down quickly. I am happy for all of my friends. Anything good I eventually (hopefully) find will be worth the wait. I've been waiting sooooo long. It better be damn good when it strikes me. To that I start to drift asleep.

CHAPTER 17

APPARENTLY, I WAS NOT too tired to eliminate dream activity last night. I wake before six from my new repetitive Elliot sex dream. I need to get this under control. I am not sure why my brain activity keeps going back to that. I thought all of this weirdness was to help me heal, move through this grief. Leave it to me to be stuck like a scratched record, with that image replaying over and over. I should be doing better than this. I have already thought through my concerns about our relationship, my longing to see him again. Could this be about something entirely different? Was this more of a need to have that kind of attachment or experience? And if so, why does it have to be Elliot portraying the role. Can't this be sorted out in a different manner? Ahhhh! I just want to scream out loud. I can be so damn frustrating. Again, I become my own obstacle.

Maybe this would be a good time to do some Zen meditation. I grab a pillow and seat myself on the floor, lotus style. My poor attempts to psychoanalyze, overthink, and tear every thought apart have not been working. I'm going to try to do this another way. Breathe, I repeat to myself. Think about not thinking. My solution may never be found through logical reasoning. I am going to work on being in the present, going off intuition. I spend nearly an hour clearing my thoughts, allowing my soul to speak. I slowly walk my thoughts back to my body and blink several times to allow my eyes to adjust to the morning light now peeking through my window.

I stand slowly, stretch for a minute and readjust to the room, my surroundings. I feel better. Calm. I will let the answers come to me in their own way, their own time. I vow to not waste energy on seeking them out. I can use that on things that are in my control, the tasks I have set for myself, not the emotions.

I would like to get some exercise today. I really need to get back into a routine. When I walk downstairs to grab coffee, I see Hayley finishing some things in the kitchen.

"Good morning, Clover! You're up and about early this morning!" she greets me.

"Hi. Yes, I am well. Ready to see what the day brings! I might go for a walk or jog." I pour a cup of coffee, adding a ton of cream and sugar to it. "What are you up to this morning?"

"Actually, I am heading out myself. Josh has things under control here. I was going to ride my bike to the store and pick up a few things. Would you like to join me?"

"Good to know; I wondered if many people biked around here! It seems like a nice area to do that. If you need a hand, I can go with you, but I don't have a bike." Maybe that could be her out if she was inviting me just to be nice.

"Well, we could either walk together, or you can use my bike and I'll take Josh's?" Hmm. Guess she really wouldn't mind hanging out for a bit.

I choose the bike option, so I don't slow her down and I can learn how some of the locals get around town. She grabs her things, a small list of items to pick up, and I quickly go to my room to change. Within a few minutes we are set and on our way. She takes me on a detour first, around a couple of blocks here in the residential area. We pass Sadie's house, a park on the corner down the lane I hadn't noticed before. There are a few kids playing on the swings, their mothers close-by, chatting with each other over coffee.

On the ride, Hayley tells me more about how she and Josh acquired the bed and breakfast, how they didn't really plan on it – but when they saw the property it just sort of happened. They put a lot of work into getting it remodeled, keeping its historical charm. I tell her more about my plans to go back to school, living here until I hopefully get accepted somewhere next year.

As we continue on the journey, Hayley is waving at many people we pass. She is so friendly and has many friends and acquaintances here. We make one quick stop on the edge of the business district, where she picks up some fresh blooms from the florist. She adds them to her bike basket. The arrangements are colorful – starting to see tones of autumn coming through, not just in the décor selection but all around us.

There is a lot of foot traffic already in the shopping area. We hop off the bikes and walk them for a few blocks until there is more room for us. She knows a great deal about the area, the history and shares her knowledge with me, like my own personal tour guide. She must get a lot of practice answering questions and telling stories to their guests all the time. I show her the church I visited, and I learn more about it as we pass.

She runs into the tourist center briefly to collect a few brochures to have for handing out at the BNB. Glad to see they are opened today. While she's inside, I wait patiently directly in front of where I saw the black sedan drive off the other day. I still cannot explain logically what has been happening here. But, maybe I am not supposed to yet. Maybe I should just enjoy the day, my next steps, and more importantly getting to know these new wonderful people in my life, and this beautiful place.

The pamphlets are now added to her basket, and we walk onward through town, turning a corner, passing the monument in the center of town. Our pace slows as we enjoy some window shopping. Next, she stops in an apothecary store, walking me through. I am introduced to the shop owner, Charlotte, who is the brilliant creator of the shower bombs Hayley keeps at the BNB. Good to know! When I am in my own place I definitely want to keep those on hand. They smell wonderful!

We end up passing the theater and I pick up their schedule of upcoming movies. That could be a fun thing to do one evening, when I am not studying. It may be difficult to remain focused on important tasks when there are so many things to do here. Reese loves the movies – well, more like she loves movie theater popcorn and tolerates the movies. I cannot wait for her to visit and check this all out with me too.

Hayley asks if we can make one more stop, as she needs to drop off Josh's watch to have the battery changed. I am in no hurry. I explain my only plans today were to see more of town, study, and be at the café for training by three. We have ample time to tackle whatever she needs to do.

Another block and we're at the shop. Again, in front of me is where I first saw the Elliot look-alike in the street. So weird. No ghosts around today – perhaps the fresh air is finally clearing my head. We walk into the store and the woman who I almost literally ran into yesterday is standing behind the counter. She knows Hayley, and they chat for a minute, Hayley handing her the watch needing repair. While they catch up, I look around. Everything sparkles and glimmers in here. Their collections are just gorgeous. I stare through the glass at some stunning rings as Hayley finishes up and walks back to me.

"See anything that you like?" she inquires.

"Yeah, of course. Everything in here is absolutely gorgeous. Doesn't all of it speak to you in some way?" The spotlights hit her pendant she's wearing again. It really is beautiful. "Is that from here? Someday I would love to find something similar for my grandmother, Lily. She would adore it."

"Well, there may be something similar, but I think he had this piece made for me. We can ask, hang on." She calls over the lovely lady behind the counter. "Sydney, do you know if you carry anything like my pendant here, in stock?"

This is really out of my league. I can tell by the extravagant display cases that I couldn't afford a thing in here. I am more of a fifty percent off sale at the mall jewelry store kind of gal. Make it sixty percent off sale.

The young woman, Sydney I guess is her name, walks over. "Let me see. Well, that is definitely a Louis piece, but not from the collection. It is a special-order item, yes?"

Hayley replies, "Yes, I think it is. Do you have anything similar though? My friend may be interested…someday." She looks over to me and winks. At least she understands I cannot afford anything like that currently.

After opening up a case on the other end of the store, hopefully the cheaper end, Sydney pulls out a small rack and sets it up on top so we can view it. There is a variety of trinity knots, and claddaghs in pendants, earrings, rings. They all are beautiful, detailed items, nothing like the pendant Josh bought Hayley, but still very elegant. I hover my finger over an item or two. Maybe it is static electricity from the velvet stand or lighting, but you could hear the shock it sent me.

I jump back a second. Hayley giggles at my reaction. "That pricey, huh?" she adds.

"Huh…well, I haven't even looked at that yet. I guess I do not even need to," I laugh in response. "Thanks for showing me these. When it is closer to the occasion, I'll check back in and see if you have something then. These are all very stunning though."

I thank them both for helping me look, then nod toward the door and wait outside for Hayley to join me. Within minutes her business is complete, and we are back on our way. One last stop at a small produce stand where she gathers several items finishes up our tour. She needs to get back to the house to help Josh prepare for some incoming guests and set up for lunch.

As we pass by the quaint storefront for rent where I picture Elliot working, I cannot help but stare at it again. Hayley notices and asks me what caught my attention.

"It is silly, really. When I first walked past this place, I could picture my friend running his business there. He was almost done with his culinary degree, and wants – er, wanted to open his own pastry shop. That place would have suited him. I am not sure why I keep obsessing over it."

"Maybe it is meant to be *your* place." She directs back to me.

"My place? I do not follow," the confusion is evident in my reply.

"Yes, your place. Don't you want to do yoga somewhere here? Maybe that is your place." Hayley smiles at me and then drops the subject, continuing on our ride back the last few blocks.

Huh......my sign? I only have peered into the windows admiring the space, imagining it as a small French pastry shop. Never did I imagine it could be anything else, anything involving me. Hayley is imaginative. As we pull up to the front of the BNB, we again hop off our bikes. I help her with the items from the baskets that we've collected on our journey this morning. She pauses for a moment, standing under the ivy arbor out front.

"This is where it happened for me. I stood right here, closed my eyes and knew it would be our place. Our adventure. You never know, Clover, the same may happen to you!" she snickers.

Wow, now I really need to sit down and think through some things. I make my exit up to my room. I kick off my shoes and jump out onto the bed, stretching to fill the entire space. Laying on my side and staring out the window, I watch the trees dance in the light breeze. I close my eyes and reflect on these newly inspired thoughts. I do not have to expand on what Hayley said too much. I think her point was quite clear. I reach for my phone.

I find the silly picture of Reese in the list and hit call.

"Hi, beautiful! Guess what I'm doing.....picking out a venue!" Reese announces. "What are you doing?"

"Hey! That sounds like fun. What are you thinking? A fancy church? Downtown? Industrial? Suburbia garden?"

"Well, actually....close to home. There is an amazing venue in Lincoln Park. It has the date we want, luckily someone's wedding was canceled – the poor saps. If we keep guests to under fifty, we can totally afford it. They do everything...the ceremony, hors d'oeuvres, meal, full-service bar, cake. I mean, everything! I ran over there this morning to look at it. The patio is gorgeous. I'm taking Nick back tomorrow."

"Wow, that sounds amazing. I wish I was there to look with you! I cannot believe you're tackling all of this already?"

"I am trying to get stuff finalized before we even tell my parents about the engagement. Sneaky, I know."

"I get it, though. If you know what you want, don't let them change your plans. It's your big day!" She sounds busy doing planning, and I am sure she has another class to get back to in a bit too. Maybe I'll wait to bounce my ideas off her.

"Did you need something, Clover? Everything okay? Anymo re.." she clears her throat, "um, anymore… sightings?"

"I'm good. No worries. I did want to chat about something if you have a minute."

"Yes. What's going on?" Reese never hesitates to help out. Even if she is juggling umpteen things, she makes time.

"Well, so I have an idea. Maybe. You know I didn't get the hours at the rec center, right? I have started training at Sadie's café, but still need another source of income. If you still think you want to open a studio, I think I found a place. It is not huge, but it is nice. It is right downtown here. Lots of foot traffic, close to residential area, and a lot of close local businesses. I know it is a lot…but I wanted you to check it out, think about it."

"Seriously? I was hoping you would want to get involved up here. But it can totally work there too. Especially if nothing is offered in the area. Are you sure you are ready? I understand you will have school starting soon…but you can help get it going, and then we can find some other help. There will be time to get established first."

"I know it is a gamble for you, with it being here. But I can do this. And I really love this space. It speaks to me in a way. I have no idea what the commercial space runs here, but will check it out if you want me to?" I cannot believe all of this is spewing from my mouth. What in the Sam Hill am I getting myself into?

"Sure, send me pictures, the address, any info you can find. I will check things out as soon as possible. Maybe a road trip soon. Your birthday is coming up anyway….I'll need to see you." Reese talks faster and faster as she gets excited.

"Oh boy…don't remind me about the birthday!" I had completely forgotten about that. Super, another year older, another year without major achievements.

"Oh, I plan on reminding you! Can we chat later, my *fiancé* is beeping in. Ha!" She is so adorable in her excitement.

"Yes, no worries. Thanks Reese, for everything! Talk soon." I hang up as she sends her predictable smooch sound through the phone.

This day just took an interesting turn, didn't it? I wonder what other surprises are lingering on the horizon?

While my mind is still occupied on the studio space downtown, I look online to see if I can find the rental listed. After a few sites I finally locate it. There are not many details, but I can see the basics and the contact for the property manager. I send the information on to Reese for her to check out. I already have a list of ideas about the space. We could structure it similar to the Arise studio in Chicago with a small lobby area, studio space, locker room, and refreshment area.

Wow, that makes me think…maybe Sadie would want to become involved and help in the refreshment arena. That would be another small location to display her product and get some more advertising. I could speak with Charlotte about helping us; we could use her items to find the right aroma for the space and enlighten our senses further during our practices. This list keeps building. I record as much in messy scribbles on the back of one of my notebooks before I lose my train of thought.

For due diligence, I look up comparable spaces in the area. I learned plenty watching Reese and Nick look for the perfect locations for both their yoga studio and his new office. Two or three are very similar in square footage, traffic patterns, parking. I'll send those to Reese as well. I need to keep emotion out of business decisions as much as possible. However, I cannot help the new obsession I already have for the space. How wonderful it would be if it worked out and we opened in *that* space.

With Reese and Nick on board, and help from my new friends like Everett, Sadie, and Hayley and Josh, I know this could be successful.

Man, thinking of Everett and Sadie! Why have I not heard from either of them. I wonder if he chickened out and never called her. But, I still think I would have heard something, right?

Curiosity gets the best of me. But, I promise myself to do this one thing, and then I must study. I have a few solid hours to work my way through more of the study guide before I need to meet Jared this afternoon.

ME: Sadie, how are you today? Anything new with you?

There. I will leave it at that.

As promised, I concentrate on my notes. I set a timer for one hour to remind me to stretch. I have a habit of immersing myself too deeply when studying that hours can go by where I do not stand, move, eat or drink, even use the bathroom. This timer became a study tradition during finals week my junior year and it seemed to help me both physically and mentally. It is vitally important when I am not at a desk; times when I'm scattered all over a floor or bed like today.

When the alarm goes off, I jump up, not feeling like an hour has passed already. I decide to walk around, head downstairs and grab a peppermint tea. I round the corner into the kitchen and see Hayley and Josh cutting the stems from the blooms purchased earlier this morning. They are laughing and act so childlike as they work together, placing them into several vases.

"Hi guys!" I try not to interrupt their fun and sneak by to quickly prepare the tea.

"Oh, hello!" Josh replies. "How is the studying going?"

"It's good. I'm staying on task at least. There is a lot to review. It has been a few years for me."

"Kudos to you, Clover. My brain never worked like that. I'm such a hands-on learner; I don't think I could handle studying for hours on end like that. You amaze me," Hayley says so genuinely. At the same time Josh tickles her on her side. She pushes him away, slightly blushing with embarrassment.

"She's a hands-on learner, alright!" Josh laughs. Hayley elbows him in the ribs.

"You guys are a trip!" I join the laughter and admire how strong their bond is. They are an inspiration. Give people like me hope, honestly. "Well, you may not be the studious type, but your outside-the-box thinking today may have helped me on my journey," I inform Hayley.

"How so?"

"Well, I think we may move forward with a yoga studio here. Screw that prick, Ian. We don't need him. I sent my friend, Reese, the info on that commercial space downtown. I have no idea if that will be the spot, but now that the wheels are turning I know we will have a place here. So, thank you for the inspiration. Truly."

"That is wonderful! I am excited for you. Let us know if we can help. Hopefully this does not mean you will be too busy to hold a class here every now and again?" Wow, she really wants to see that happen.

"You say when, and I'll do it. It is the least I can do."

"How about next week?" Josh lifts his brows.

"Seriously? Next week! I will totally do that. What are you thinking?"

"We've talked about it a bit. Would you be willing to do a couple morning sessions, and maybe one afternoon? You can pick the times and days…but we will post the times for guests. We would like to pay you a flat fee for each session. You let us know your standard rates. We'll cover it for guests, but if you want to advertise locally, maybe a separate drop-in rate for them? What do you think?"

"I think you should help me manage the studio. You really have a knack for this stuff. And yes, I think that all sounds wonderful. I could do a Tuesday/Thursday morning hour class and maybe a Wednesday afternoon thirty minute? Let's just say fifty bucks for the hour class and I'll do the Wednesday pro bono just for helping me out. Seriously, this will be great advertisement."

"Sounds good. We have some time with decent weather. As it cools, we'll have to find a space to accommodate. If we clear the sunroom, we may be able to continue, if participation is not too high. But once I post the class info on the message board at the rec center, we may have issues finding room," an evil grin appears across Josh's face.

"We'll cross that bridge when it comes. Who knows, maybe I'll be in a formal space by then. We could just have a discount for your guests to drop-in? There's time to figure all of that out."

"I think it is amazing. All of this is amazing. We are so glad you're sticking around!" Hayley pulls me into a hug.

"Thanks. I am not sure what else to say but, thank you!" I see the clock on the wall. "Shoot, I have gone beyond my break time. I really need to get back to the books before my night at the café. I'll leave you two to your projects."

"Don't work too hard!" Hayley replies, handing me my cup of tea.

"I will try not to."

I return to my room and prepare for another study session. I figure I should get ready for my evening of training at the café first. I know I'll get studying and run short on time. I quickly freshen up, change.

While I am sitting back down, picking up my notebook, my phone rings. I see SADIE & POPPY appear across the screen. Well, well. Look who is calling.

Then again, who *is* calling? Sadie or little Miss Poppy who is so proficient at using her mother's phone now. I giggle. This day is getting better and better.

CHAPTER 18

I QUICKLY SWIPE TO answer, before it goes to voicemail. "Hello?" I address the caller generically, still unsure who it may be.

"From your text, I assume you have some idea what is going on. Something new with me? Really? You are ridiculous."

"I seriously cannot believe you have waited to get a hold of me. You're killing me! Spill it!"

I hear a large sigh. Uh-oh. I hope things are okay. I thought I sensed an excited, spirited Sadie at first. Everett better not have jacked this all up.

"So, I'm sound asleep last night and my phone rings. Strangely, it was not plugged into the charger where I placed it, but sitting on the far edge of my nightstand. It was a random number, so I just silenced it and rolled back over. About fifteen minutes later, the damn thing was ringing again...same number. I was prepared to chew somebody's ass out when I answered it."

Oh my. Poor Sadie had no idea about the text yet. I just know it.

"I start with, 'Who calls people this late at night? Don't you have any consideration to those of us who actually need to wake up in the morning?'"

My laughter builds, and I try to cover the phone so she cannot hear the humor I am finding in the story that is unraveling.

"All I heard back was a man's deep voice saying, 'Sorry.' And then, click. He hung up. For whatever reason, I decided to give him a taste of his own medicine. I called the number back immediately, but he answered saying my name. All I could think was who is this guy? Why is he calling me so late?"

"I would have done the same thing! So what did he say?"

"I am assuming you already predicted this is Everett? Yes?" I mumble my agreement. "Okay, he told me who it was, and that he just called to talk about the text message he received. He read off the message while I immediately confirmed on my screen what he was saying was true. What was Poppy thinking? Humiliation to the n-th level. All I could do was apologize over and over that she sent it.

"But after my apologies he bluntly asked me if it was true. If I like him? Talk about putting me on the spot. And why was he being a coward and not starting with how *he* felt. I was dumbfounded. But, it is not in me to lie so I just blurted it out to him, 'Yes. It's true, I like you.' There was a lengthy pause, neither of us knew what to say next. Eventually he got the balls to say something."

I am now squealing! "What did he say?"

"He said that he was glad because he is growing fond of me too. What the hell does that mean, fond of me? I didn't know what to think. Does that mean he likes me in a friendly way, or something more? I mean he is calling me in the middle of the night, you would think he would have more to say than that, right? I am too old to have this kind of confusion in my life. I knew if I didn't clear it up, I wouldn't be able to sleep. I didn't want to wait until I see him again. 'What exactly do you mean by fond?'

"He chuckled and said, 'Wow, um, ….okay. I mean I like you too. You are gorgeous, sweet, caring. I mean I like spending time with you and want to get to know you better. You make me smile and laugh. I'm amazed at your accomplishments, the way you raise your daughter. I *like* you.'

"I was speechless. He just threw it all out there like that, Clover. Can you believe it? Here I thought he was into you at first. I mean, I knew he and I were flirty, but I didn't think it would be anything more than silliness. This totally shocked me. I took a few minutes to replay it in my head, and he just sat there waiting for me to say something. He finally interrupted my silence and asked what I was thinking. All I could do was say thank you, and that was the sweetest thing anyone ever told me. Clover, we talked for hours. I am running on like two hours of sleep right now. This is nuts."

"That is so great! I think it's awesome. So did you make future plans?"

"Well, he will be here tomorrow to start on the apartment. He asked us to dinner when he gets in town."

"Oh, hell no!" I cannot believe that was their next move.

"What? What is wrong with that?"

"You will absolutely not be going on a kid-friendly first date. You are going just the two of you. I'll watch Poppy. She can help me get my things situated at your place while you two go out. I am still planning on staying with you right?"

"Crap, yes. I forgot tonight is your last night at the BNB. I haven't even done anything in that room. I can this evening."

"You do not have to prepare anything. Please don't treat me special. I can do laundry and linens. It will be fine. Poppy can help me. We'll have fun. I'll order take-out. It'll be a blast. And....you can have a nice time out with Everett."

"Really? You sure?"

"I won't take no for an answer."

She giggles. I know she is thrilled. It was clear that the two of them have great chemistry. I am glad Everett got over his nerves and actually reached out to her. I am surprised I haven't heard from him yet today. Maybe he wanted me to talk to Sadie first, so I can give him her perspective of things. I will do my best not to be an in-between person.

"Sadie, what happened with Poppy?"

"Well, that girl should not have done what she did. But I cannot really punish her for something I am now happy about, can I?"

"I agree, give her some slack on this one. She meant well. She just wants you to be happy."

Poppy is a go-getter. It did not take much for her to get a gameplan together. I know exactly when the thought first crossed her mind, in the afternoon at the café. She saw the chance and went for it. With that drive, she will do great things in her life!

"Hey – I need to go, it's getting busy in here. I'll see you in a little bit? You're still meeting with Jared?"

"Yeah, go ahead…get back to work. I need to finish up a few more pages studying, and then I'm on my way. See you soon!"

"Later!" she exclaims, the joy still evident in her tone.

I have a few loose ends to tackle quickly. Maybe I can borrow Hayley's bike again to get to the café to save me a little time. First thing…I need to touch base with Everett.

ME: Ev – I heard you made the call. Good job, buddy!

EVERETT: You talked to her?

ME: Yes, and I refuse to share each other's secrets. I will only get involved under dire circumstance.

EVERETT: Got it. Thanks for the talk last night. Ur a lifesaver.

ME: Anytime! I'll see you tomorrow at the apt? Oh, and I'm watching Poppy so you two have some quality time together.

EVERETT: Thought you weren't getting involved?

ME: I'm not! Just helping indirectly.

EVERETT: Got it. See you tomorrow.

Now, what next? I don't think my mind is clear enough to continue studying. I will just walk to the café and arrive a few minutes early. I contemplate taking some index cards in my bag in case it gets slow, but I should probably use any downtime to start practicing on my own.

Lately I have been reaching my exercise goals with this added walking around town. I will have an extra block onto the walk starting tomorrow. But, once I'm into the apartment, it will just be steps downstairs to my new part time gig. The yoga sessions beginning next week will help. By the year's end I could be holding a few sessions daily, if things move ahead with the studio possibility.

So much for concentrating on the present. Dang it. Note to self:

One day at a time.

The stroll to the café draws me toward the apartment, both mentally and physically. Everett will be here tomorrow afternoon. The plan is to walk through it again, going over the renovation schedule. He is bringing tools and some supplies he has at his place which we could potentially use. The next day he is willing to entirely devote to working with us. I mean, honestly, that could change if he decides to squeeze in additional time hanging with Sadie. Maybe I can get his thoughts on the commercial studio space too? I have no idea how handy he is, but if things go smoothly at the apartment, maybe he and Nick can talk about design plans for the studio.

There I go again, jumping the gun. It does feel good to have some of the fog lifting. The last month has left me blank, unable to think clearly. I never realized how I just checked out. Losing Elliot had left me drifting in nothingness, like a spell was cast on me where I just disappeared. I vanished from my life, just as he did. He would not want that for me. I look up at the sky and whisper to him, "I won't be afraid anymore. I won't let life pass me by." If he is here listening, I hope he hears my vow. I hope he believes I can do this and helps me along any way he can. He always promised to be my wingman. I believe with all my heart he will not steer me wrong.

I pass the studio space. I now try to picture *me* working in there. I picture smiling faces walking out the door, yoga mats slung over their shoulders. The people walking near me on the sidewalk could be the first folks to sign up. Reese better hustle. I have plans for this town!

I arrive to the café and find Jared waiting. He held off doing his normal routine at the start of his shift in order for me to see the process one more time. I think I'll be able to handle most of that checklist. He explains the business card drawing held weekly, which is for a free drink of their choice.

My bigger concern is learning all of the different names of

things, recipes, and ultimately the technique to prepare them properly. There is a lot to know, and it seems every person walking through the door has specific preferences. I pray I learn quickly because these never seem to be made the same way twice, at least not this evening.

Jared is willing to let me tackle a little more on my own, but with him close-by supervising. If I am struggling with the ratios in a drink, he helps out. When he asks about my previous coffee knowledge, I share I know how to order the ones I like, sort-of, and I know what an Americano is. That was Elliot's favorite. He said I'll be able to take care of two returning customers with that knowledge, that he knows of, and laughs at me. Great. Must everyone be so fancy?

Just as the previous night, time flies by. By closing, I can tell my brain is on overload for the day. I try to finish up with more mundane tasks, so I don't screw anything up. I follow Jared out the door as we lock up. He has a couple of days off, and I will start working on the apartment tomorrow, so that works out well. I wish him a good evening and walk back to my room to get some rest.

My things, what few I have here, will be easy to gather in the morning so I can check out. Josh already told me I can keep my stuff stored as long as I need until I am ready to head to Sadie's house. In the short time I've stayed with them here, I have been able to get to know them and appreciate how hard they work. I am grateful I will only be a few houses down and get to see them next week at my first yoga session in the garden. They have made a difference in how welcome I have felt in this new town, fortifying my decision to stay. I will be forever grateful.

I spend the evening inside, trying to keep myself busy to avoid the anxiety over hearing from Reese. I review the material Jared suggested I take a look at, next an hour is spent back on my study guide, after which I pass time with some leisure reading.

Eventually the phone rings. Thank God, Reese is finally getting back to me.

"Hi lady! Long time no talk. What are you doing?" I decide to not lead with a bunch of questions about the studio.

"Hey, all is well. Nick and I are just getting ready to have sushi and watch one of our shows. What a day, am I right?"

"Yes, it's been a long one, but decent. Yours?"

"I think so. Things are moving quick. We told my parents today. I couldn't risk them finding out elsewhere. They're happy for us. I have a last-minute trip planned now to NYC for the weekend, dress shopping. My mother convinced me that is her designated assignment of the wedding. She wants it to be perfect. I'll let her treat me, I suppose."

"That sounds like fun. You two haven't done anything like that in a while, you'll have a good time. I feel terrible I'm not there to be helping you. Is there anything I can do from here for now?"

"Yes, but not related to the wedding planning. I need you to meet the property manager tomorrow on that studio. We already looked over the details you sent. Of the spaces you listed, the one you like seems to be the perfect choice. Would you have time to do that tomorrow?"

My stomach flips. I am excited. "Really? Yes! Yes! I can. Send me the appointment time. I'll be there. Anything in particular you need me to check out?"

"You can handle it. Besides looking at the structure, let me know if the layout is workable for what we'll need. Plus, we have already decided that Nick and I will both head down to see you next weekend. If it looks decent, we'll do another walkthrough and see if we can make some progress. Plus, then we can help you celebrate your birthday!"

"Seriously? That will be so great. I am looking forward to seeing you both. I miss you guys!"

"I bet…. Miss I'm moving away."

"That's just mean, but I forgive you."

"I forgive you too. Everything is going to be okay. This is a good thing. How have you been doing otherwise?"

"Can't complain. Tomorrow I'll flip over and start staying at my friend Sadie's house. We are going to start the work ASAP on the apartment. Everett will be in town, I can see if he can arrive a little early and walk through the studio space with me. He probably knows what he's looking at."

"Is he still looking…. at you?"

Shoot I haven't updated her on that. "Um, no. Definitely not. I think there is a spark between Everett and Sadie. They have an official date tomorrow."

"Go, Ev! That is cool. Seems he finally caught on, ha!"

"Yes, I think they could be good together. Everyone seems to be finding someone. All I find are imaginary boyfriends."

"Girl….just you wait. Yours will be epic. I know it. Have faith!" she has a seriousness in her voice now.

"We'll see. I'm concentrating on myself now. Income. Studying. Studio. Apartment. I'm fine."

"And Lily? She good?"

"Same mostly. I need to call and check in, but no better, no worse. But, hey – you have an evening to get back to. Watch your show. I'll let you know how tomorrow goes. Thanks, Reese! And I cannot believe you'll be here in a week. Totally stoked."

"Me too, girl. Me too. Have a good night." Smoochy noises follow and then the click.

I fall asleep while preparing checklists for tomorrow, things I need to look at in both the studio and the apartment.

CHAPTER 19

AFTER ANOTHER NIGHT WITH ample and, thankfully, uncomplicated, dream-free sleep, I awake early and decide to join the other guests downstairs for breakfast. I'm feeling a little emotional about this being my last day staying at the BNB. Josh and Hayley have made me blueberry pancakes as a special treat. I am not certain how they found out about my addiction to them, but I have a feeling Everett may be connected. I'll have to thank him when he arrives in town later today.

Rather than rushing through my meal, I take time to chat with other guests. There's a few new couples who arrived in the last day or two, and others who have left which I regretfully missed saying goodbye to during my recent hectic days. Hayley and I go over my plan for the day, and I tell her I have a meeting this morning, and then will return to pick up my belongings. We both act like it is no big deal. The good news is that I will only be a block away! My, how things have quickly changed in the last week.

After breakfast, I return to pack up the remainder of my things and get prepared for my "move" later in the day. Perhaps I should consider it more of a shuffle. I glance through my notes of things I need to discuss with the property manager. I devote a few minutes for a quick meditation to help clear my mind. As I am sitting on the floor, cross legged, my phone rings.

"Sorry to bother you, I know you're probably studying, but I'm in a bit of a bind," Sadie explains with a slight sense of worry, and definite tiredness in her voice.

"No bother at all. Is something wrong?"

"Well, here's the deal. Poppy was up most of the night, sick with stomach flu. She still is not feeling great. I've tried getting a hold of her father. Of course, he is not available to help out. I know Jared is busy, and he specifically asked for these days off. He never asks for time off. Is there any chance you could help me out? I'm going into crisis mode here."

"Well, I am not going to be of any help at the café, with only two days of training under my belt. It will be better if you cover there and I watch Poppy. Let me see if I can reach the property manager to cancel my appointment this morning. Can you give me two minutes to call them and I'll call you back?"

"Yes, sure. Thanks, Clover. I really appreciate it. I hate to throw this on you, I know you are swamped," her desperation is not as evident now, but she sounds so tired.

"It is not a problem. That's what friends are for." I am so glad I may be able to give her a hand. She has already done so much for me. "Let me confirm I am able to cancel, and I'll call right back. Talk soon."

After hanging up, I grab my notepad to look up the property manager number. As I'm scanning my notes, Everett texts.

EVERETT: Ready for the day? I can't wait to meet you guys at the apt.

As I read his message, I wonder if he would be able to help me out.

ME: Hey, I am excited – but one hiccup. Have to cancel meet with property manager. Poppy is not feeling well, and I offered to watch her while Sadie works.

EVERETT: Do not cancel. I will go for you. I can check it out, get the basics. If that will help?

ME: Well, I guess you can. I can send you the details I'm needing, and you can look at the guts of the space.

EVERETT: Consider it done. Send info.

ME: XOXO

I immediately call Sadie back, explaining our plan. She is grateful we could work it all out. She will man the café until her other back-up worker is available in a few hours. I will watch Poppy, and Everett can go to my meeting. What a great team. I text Everett a picture of my notes; that's easier than typing it all out. He responds with a thumbs up and is already on his way to town.

I grab one of my bags before heading downstairs. Josh looks surprised that I already have some of my things with me. I explain my change of plans for the day. After hearing Poppy is not feeling well, he quickly gathers some things in a bag for me. There's yogurt and bananas from this morning's breakfast, some leftover chicken noodle soup that they served at lunch yesterday. It is the sweetest thing. As my arms are already overflowing, I decline the sandwiches he was meaning to pack up. I guess I will be arriving well prepared.

It is probably a good thing my departure is rushed this morning; it eliminates the chance to get emotional as I leave. I will have to stop by at some point later to retrieve my other bags, so no need to think about it too much. I grab all the goodies and walk down the block to Sadie's house. She is happy to see me and takes the food into the kitchen while I set my bag down in the living room.

"Poppy is still in bed, watching some dog movie for the hundredth time. She is feeling a bit better but is still a bit queasy and just really weak. I told her you were coming over and her energy improved drastically!" Sadie said, sounding more at ease now than on our call earlier.

"We will have a good day! You need to get going. We're fine here. Truly." As I say this, I begin to feel my confidence differ from what I'm actually saying. When have I ever taken care of a sick child? I have no siblings. I never did any serious babysitting as a teen. What if something goes wrong? What if she gets worse? Oh my Lord! I agreed to watching Poppy this evening, but that was meant to occur when she is in perfect health. *Get it together, Clover.* You want to be a doctor. You can handle this.

"Thanks, Clover. You're a lifesaver!" she smiles, grabs her purse and keys and flies out the door. I glance around the house. It is quiet. I walk down the hall to check in on Poppy. As I peek into her room, I see she is back asleep. The movie she had been watching is over, the credits playing. I grab the remote and shut it off. I walk over to her and check her forehead to see if she feels warm.

As I reach out to her, she opens her eyes. It takes her a moment to realize it is me standing at her bedside. I hope I didn't startle her. Sadie told her I was coming over, but after napping she may be a bit foggy.

"Hey, Miss Poppy. How are you feeling?" I sit down next to her on the edge of the bed.

She returns a sweet smile and says, "I think I'm better. I don't like getting sick, though."

"No, I bet not. I don't either. It is not fun. But we'll try and make the best of it. We can veg out and watch movies, play a board game, whatever you want to do." I am totally winging it here. Besides watching television, what else can we do that would be calming for her, so she doesn't get wound up and relapse?

"Thanks, Clover.... for helping my mom." Of all things, while this young lady is feeling absolutely lousy, she is concerned about her mom. She has such a big heart.

"I'm here to hang out with you! And I'm happy that helps your mom. We all just want you to feel better. Everett too, he told me so." I thought I would put in a good word for the guy.

"I know, he already called me this morning." She smiles.

The surprise on my face is evident. "Oh he did? That was very nice of him!"

In my rush to head over here so quickly this morning, I didn't have time to think about anything besides gathering my things, updating the property manager on the change of who would be meeting him, and walking over. I know Everett dropped everything to help me, but he really was concerned for Poppy and Sadie too. How sweet of him to call and talk to Poppy to check on her.

It has made her day.

"I like him, he is very funny. And my mom likes talking to him too."

"He is very funny." I leave my comment to that. Again, I try to be an adult and protect her from the what-ifs of the situation. I am sure Sadie has not said or done much in front of Poppy that could get her hopes up, out of concern to shelter her from any more disappointment in life. If there is a way to prevent her heart from being hurt, that is the only way. Poppy sees and hears plenty, and she is extremely smart and can imagine enough on her own, without extra encouragement. Watching Sadie's responses to Poppy, and recalling how my grandmother acted in similar ways throughout my life to protect me, I am hyper aware of this instinct. I am certain when I have kids it'll be the same.

Poppy takes the bait and left that conversation alone. "Do you think I could just rest for a little while before we do anything else? I hacked all night long and just want to sleep."

"Sure, of course. You rest. If you need me, I'll be in the other room reading, okay?"

"Mmhmm." She rolls over and snuggles into her pillow, and wraps an arm around Chance, who is keeping close watch on his best friend.

I walk as softly out of her room as I can, trying not to disturb her. I leave the door open so I can hear her if she needs me. Unlike my room at the bed and breakfast, the house has a little more space to move about. I open the door to the guest room which I'll be spending the coming weeks in. I am not sure how she accomplished it, but Sadie has the room tidied, the bed is made up. I notice she cleared off the desk in the corner and set up a cute lamp, knowing I'll be studying a lot. The space will be perfect while I'm here. I walk out and grab my bag. Without knowing how long Poppy may be asleep, I may as well put some of my things away. I find some empty hangers in the closet so I can unpack. Awesome!

Time goes quickly as I set up in my next temporary home. I

unpack the items I managed to carry over this morning from the BNB, organize my paperwork and take advantage of this quiet time to study while Poppy is resting. I pop my head into her room a couple of times to check on her, the poor kiddo must have been completely exhausted from being up all night. She hasn't moved an inch from this morning.

Everett should be finishing up with the meeting at the studio space with the property manager. Although I am anxious to hear how that went, I'm content hanging out here and feel lucky that I am able to lend a hand. Everyone around me has been going out of their way to offer me help lately: an open ear, places to stay, employment opportunities, and the list goes on. It is quite overwhelming. I must have "Please Help Me" stamped on my forehead. I will do whatever I can to pay back all this kindness.

I scan through the items Sadie has in the refrigerator, checking if there is any combination of ingredients that may come together for dinner, even with my lack of culinary skills. I am not certain how Poppy would feel about our previously planned take-out tonight, now that her stomach has been acting up. But it's slim pickings in the icebox. Just as I think she may sleep through lunch so I can offer her the soup Josh sent with me for dinner, Poppy calls my name softly from the other room.

"Poppy, I'm coming," I announce as I hurry down the hall to see what she needs. As I enter her room, she's sitting up in bed, rubbing the sleep from her eyes. Chance is smooshed up against the wall and peeks one eye open like we are really annoying him as he tries to nap. "How you feeling pretty girl?"

"I'm better. How long was I asleep?"

"For a couple hours. I bet it felt good after being up all night with an upset tummy. Can I get you anything?" She is so cute when she wakes up, just taking her time talking, big sighs – like it all takes great thought and effort.

"I'm sort of hungry, I think," she rubs her belly in circles. "At least for a little snack, maybe?"

"Of course! Do you just want some crackers or would you like to try some delicious soup that our friends sent over for you?"

Poppy scoots over to the edge of the bed, looking a little more alert, and gradually stands up slowly as I help steady her until I am certain she has enough strength to move around. She has a determined look on her face and nods to me like she is alright to move on her own. I step back a bit and release her arm; she returns a big grin and starts walking toward the door. Okay, maybe I'm overreacting a bit. "I feel like going out to the couch – that way you can sit with me and we can watch TV. Come on puppy!" She motions to Chance to follow us out of the room.

She makes a quick stop to use the bathroom and then meets me in the living room. I get her situated, let her scroll through channels as I warm up some lunch. The two of us sit at tv trays with our soup and watch a documentary on penguins. It has us both interested, and we spend a large portion of the show belly laughing at how ridiculously silly they are. I'm glad she's starting to feel a little bit better.

I pause the program to take the dishes to the sink and Poppy insists helping dry if I wash. She then calls Chance to the back door and lets him out to run and do his business for a bit. Sadie has worked miracles teaching this girl the importance of responsibility. As I am draining the sink and wiping off the counters, my phone lights up, ringing. Poppy grabs it to give to me, but I ask her to swipe it to answer since my hands are wet.

"Hi! This is Poppy answering Clover's phone. Who's calling, please?" she professionally asks – back in her British accent. Where does she come up with this stuff? I wonder who it is. "Oh, hi. Yes, it is me…..again." she giggles. "I'm feeling much better, thank you. Do you want to talk to Clo?" This is the first time I've heard her refer to me by my nickname. I cannot help but smile, and place my hand over my chest as she tugs at my heart strings.

I quickly dry off my hands with the tea towel and she hands me the phone. "Hello?" I ask, still unsure who is calling.

"Well, I see Poppy is making a habit of using your phone," Everett explains, chuckling. I still cannot believe she played matchmaker. "Glad she is doing better. How are you holding up? Getting settled?"

"Hey, Everett. Yes, things are good here. She seems to be gaining some energy. How was the meeting? Where are you?"

"The meeting was good. I think he answered most of your questions. The building itself is old, but in decent shape. I'm not sure exactly what y'all have in mind, but I think the space could be easily adapted. Doug, the manager, said the owner specifically would need to approve any major changes. I have his contact info if you need any other information. He said just get in touch with him after you and Reese make any decisions."

"Perfect, thank you!" I'm glad that went smoothly, but I knew Everett would handle it.

"I just heard from Sadie. She's handing off duties at the café and will go unlock upstairs. I'm going to meet her there. She said we could do a quick walk through again, and then she'll head back to take over with Poppy so you and I can get to work in the apartment."

Now I am torn. Although I *really* want to get started at the apartment, I also have been enjoying my afternoon hanging out with Poppy.

"Everett, when you meet Sadie, please tell her the two of you should just stay and work together at the apartment. We're good here. And I'm sure the two of you won't mind getting a jump start on some alone time." Knowing Everett, he will not object to that idea one bit. Crap, I forgot Poppy is standing next to me listening to my every word.

"Are you sure, Clover?"

"Yep. My mind is already made up. It's a girl's day here." He doesn't argue and hangs up.

CHAPTER 20

ONCE THE PLAN FOR the afternoon is settled with Everett, I need to decide how to spend the coming hours with Poppy. I finish the last bit of cleanup in the kitchen and return to check on her in the family room. She is nestled by the arm of the couch; Chance is on the floor beneath her, his head flexing up so he always has eyes on her. Her color is back in her cheeks, and she appears more attentive to the cartoon on the television than before lunch. Josh's soup must have been what she needed.

I plop down next to her, and she scoots over to me, resting her cheek on my shoulder with a grin. "Thanks again for staying with me today. I already feel much better."

"That's good to hear, Poppy. And I am happy to be here. What do you feel up to for the afternoon? Would you like to pick out a board game or something?"

She contemplates for a minute, brushing the sole of her bare foot against Chances back below her. Eventually, she sits up, more alert, and turns to me. "Can we just talk for a while?" she asks softly. I know Poppy is brilliant, mature for her age, with a mischievous streak. I have no idea where this conversation may be headed. Still, as long as she is comfortable hanging out with me, I'm okay with whatever she needs.

"We sure can! Do you want to hang out here and chat, or we could go to your room? If you want some fresh air, we can sit outside and let Chance run. The weather seems perfect out there. What do you say?" Honestly, I hope she chooses outside because

I think it will help her feel better, and the vitamin D won't hurt either.

She scoots off the couch and walks over to grab Chance's collar, slipping it over his head. I guess she is picking outside. She leads the way, and I follow closely behind, asking if she wants a glass of water or apple juice. We both settle on water and find a comfy spot on the swing in the backyard. The dog has plenty of energy and occupies himself with a stick he discovered near the bushes.

"So, what do you want to chat about, my friend?" I'm unsure if she just wanted to make it a proper girl's day and chill and share stories or if she had something on her mind. She hesitates at first and then decides to open up.

With a bit of shyness, she bravely asks, "Clover, I need to know everything about Everett. I know he is your friend, and my mom likes him, and I think he likes her. But I have to know if he is good. I think he seems nice. But how do you really know?"

Well, shit. This is more than I expected. Huh. I thought caring for a sick Poppy would be the most frazzling thing on my nerves today. Totally got that one wrong. My hesitation to reply keeps her gazing my way, waiting for an answer. But I still don't know exactly what to say.

"Hey, I know this is probably very new for you to see your mom excited about talking to a man. Someone who hasn't been in your lives very long. Poppy, I'm going to be honest with you..." I pause to collect my thoughts. I owe her honesty, but am I the person she should be speaking to about this? What if I steer her wrong? I don't want to cause this sweet girl any reason to hurt or doubt. I try to focus and just tell her what is in my heart. "I have known Everett for several years. We had never talked a lot through that time until recently. His brother, Elliot, was my best friend. I knew the kind of person Elliot was and how much he cared for his brother. And since Elliot went to Heaven, Everett has become a closer friend to me. I really think he is a nice, caring man. I can tell by the way he asks about you and your mom, how he checks in and wants to help, that he wants to get to know you both better, that he cares."

"I know all of that. I do. But how do you know for sure, like *for sure* for sure? I want my mom to be happy. I'm tired of her being alone. But what if he stays for a while and then leaves?"

Geesh. This kid is not going to cut me any slack here. I want to offer her more than words and flimsy reassurances in the face of her fears. I know what she has been through with her father not being around much. I want to tell her adults are not always perfect. That they can make mistakes. That even the best relationships can change. But I know she is only eight years old, and her understanding of the world is different. How can I ease her fears but not get her hopes up?

"Poppy, I don't know exactly what the future holds. I wish I did. What I do know is that your mom loves you and will always be here for you. And I know that Everett is a kind person. I don't know if they will be friends, or more, or for how long. But maybe we need to let him make her happy right now. She wants to be happy, and sometimes that means she has to make choices that might be scary at first."

When I picture their mother-daughter bond, knowing it will get them through any situation they face, the phantom pain I'm familiar with flares up. I relive that sensation as the fragile part of me breaks, shattering again into a million pieces, leaving behind the hole in my heart. I have to give it my all to fight back the tears. Poppy must sense it.

"Are you okay, Clo?" she looks at me with concern, ignoring her own fears for a minute and now worrying about me. "What's wrong?"

"Don't worry about me. I'm okay. I just was thinking about my mom. Did you know I never knew her?" For a second, I'm not sure why I just told her that. This could be a little heavy for her. Hell, most days, it is too difficult for me to comprehend.

"I know. My mom told me. She said you never met her. You

know what I think? That doesn't mean you don't know her. She's here. Just like my mom says she'll always be with me. And that my dad is always here too." She places her hand over her heart. I swallow the tears back more. "How did you handle the scary times?"

"Well, sweetie. It wasn't easy. I cried a lot. I was scared. I felt alone." Poppy just takes my hand in hers and nods. It's like she knows I need to say this. I'm unsure if I've ever told anyone about my mom like this. I think I told Reese and El bits and pieces, but not like this.

"So, now, you're just okay with it?"

"No, not okay. I still miss her. I still wonder what it would have been like having her there for every birthday, every important moment of my life."

I felt all those empty spaces were bearing down on me. Then, I recalled a story my grandmother had told me. *"Heartbreak, my dear Clover, is like a storm trying to tear you apart. If you can endure it, you will become stronger, more resilient, and more beautiful."* And that is what I had done. I had learned to be strong and to rely on myself. I had learned that life could still be beautiful even without a mother by my side. Just like I'll learn to continue without Elliot by my side.

"But you're happy now, right?" Poppy asks, her eyes searching mine.

I take a deep breath, smile, and say, "Yes, I am. I am happy. And I know, even though it feels scary now, you and your mom will be happy, too. And maybe, just maybe, this is a chance for you to learn to be strong too. You can do it. Trust me, you are stronger than you think."

As I look at her, a flicker of understanding seems to light up in her eyes. At this moment, I know she isn't just hearing my words; she is learning that even though life presents challenges, we can grow stronger to push through them.

We are not defined by our heartache but by our strength in overcoming it. We are not defined by the absence of those dear to us but by the resilience that blooms in their wake. We are, in our own way, survivors. And survivors, I realize, are not broken but beautiful.

"Yeah, okay. I'm glad you are happy. And I'm scared about my mom moving on. But I'm happy she's trying. And I'll try to be strong. But if he makes her cry, I'm going to punch his lights out."

And just like that, our conversation ends, and she hops down to play with Chance. Her energy isn't quite up to her usual level, but it is better. The heaviness of our discussion does not seem to weigh her down. I know she is a strong girl. I admire her tenacity. She looks back at me and smiles. "Thank you, Clover," she adds. My worry that maybe our talk was over the top dissipated. I think she needed to hear something real without the sugar coating. She needed to hear someone trust her with their own fears about life. To know she's not alone. To understand she has people to help her through this, even if it is just having a chat on the patio on a sunny afternoon.

Yep, she's going to be okay. And so am I.

CHAPTER 21

AFTER AN EMOTIONAL AFTERNOON at the house, a light dinner for Poppy, and an early bedtime, I sat alone at the desk in my bedroom at Sadie's house.

The white noise machine I had turned on at Poppy's bedside purred loud enough to hear it from the next room. It helped me clear my mind so I could use quiet time to review some study cards. Even in the peaceful silence of the evening, I was struggling. Trying to keep the laws and equations of Coulomb, Faraday, Lenz, and Maxwell straight has my eyes zigzagging across the cards and further confusing what I had learned about electromagnetism years ago.

At one time, this was all easy for me. Now, it seems my only understanding of the concept is that of the magnetic force and electric currents surrounding me during the strange encounters here in Franklin. Maybe applying these abstract concepts to the real-world situations I've been challenged with recently will help me retain some of the material.

As I press the pads of my fingers against my closed eyes, creating swirls of starry patterns in various colors, I am startled by the sound at the mudroom door. I hear keys drop down on the counter, light steps into the living room, and the couch creak. Sadie let out a wearied groan as she sat, a sound expressing the sheer weight of her exhaustion. She had to be so run down after helping Poppy through the night, running the café for hours, and then meeting Everett to begin work on the apartment. Rather than rushing out to meet her and see how the day went, I gave her a few minutes to unwind and settle.

I turn off my study lamp, knowing it is probably all I will tackle for the day, and tiptoe to join Sadie on the chair beside her.

"Hey, how are you?" I quietly ask. Her eyes flutter open slowly, and she just waves to show she's alive. I let out a little chuckle. "Gonna make it? Can I get you anything?"

"I swear, I must be turning into one of the creaky old floorboards we've been working on," she groans, collapsing further into the couch with a sigh that would have made a dying whale jealous. "My joints are screaming; every muscle is protesting. I think I pulled a hamstring wrestling with that last stubborn drawer in the kitchen. Seriously, I'm practically a ninety-year-old granny in a twentysomething's body!"

My lips are twitching with amusement. "What are you talking about? I'm sure you were a whirlwind of energy all day. I swear, you are practically vibrating with excitement." I wink, trying to send some cheer her way. It is a start, even if I only get a subtle giggle from her.

"Yeah, well, that was before I realized my body had decided to stage a full-blown rebellion," she explains, rubbing her aching back. "And then there was Everett... you know, Mr. Stamina himself, just going non-stop like this damn project has to be finished this weekend. Like seriously, what the hell is the matter with him. Does he not understand how fu-, I mean how flipping exhausted I am?"

"I don't think he realized how hard you worked today before meeting him there. Plus, the guy is used to not sleeping; he's a workaholic. Did you tell him you needed to stop, relax, and recover for the night?"

"Yes, several times. But he just told me to take a seat, and he could finish up what we had been tackling. But I couldn't just sit there and watch him work. Eventually, when I started whining about being sore and tired, he caved."

"So, what happened?"

"Well, he offered me a nightcap, 'To celebrate the progress we made on the first day,' he said," and I noticed a little blush creep up her cheeks. "But my brain, apparently as exhausted as my body, had interpreted this as 'Let's go party all night long and stay up into the wee hours of the morning.' So, I politely declined, mumbled something about an early start, and stumbled off towards the stairs feeling like a total loser."

"Come on, you're not a loser," I said, patting her hand. "You worked your butt off all day. You deserve a rest. Besides, I have a feeling Everett will still be there tomorrow."

"But what if he thinks I'm some old, cranky, exhausted mess?"

Oh, my goodness. She is dramatic this evening, I chuckle. "Honey, you're not old; you're just tired. And besides, that man probably thinks you're amazing for handling all this renovation work, keeping your business going, and caring for Poppy. I know I am amazed at how well you can juggle a thousand things at once. You just need to recharge your batteries, and you'll return to your vibrant self in no time."

"You think so?" she asked, a flicker of hope lighting up her eyes. "Maybe, just maybe, if I could find a way to teleport myself onto a secluded island for the next few days and get some serious sleep, I could forget all about this whole exhausting moment."

"Exactly," I give her a warm smile, trying to be encouraging. "Now, how about I go make us some tea, and we talk about how much fun we'll have going back there tomorrow?" I glanced her way, and she glared at me. "Too soon?" I laugh and walk toward the kitchen for the tea I promised her. In all honesty, it is the very least I can do. Ultimately, her busy day was all because of me. She is exhausted because she is trying to help me.

As I return with some chamomile, I sit next to her on the couch. "How was Poppy doing tonight? I need to peek in on her and give her a goodnight kiss. But I don't know if I can walk that far. Plus, I don't want to wake her."

I feel incredibly guilty that she is so physically exhausted at my expense. I am so grateful that she has this space and is willing to renovate it so I can move in. But I don't want to be a burden on her life. I've leaned on many people lately, trying to overcome difficult times. I won't forget that Sadie has her own struggles and is trying to raise a sweet girl, run her café, and combat life's other challenges. I hope she feels supported more with me and Everett around now. I can help with Poppy whenever she needs it and pick up hours at the shop. Everett is offering to help with the renovation and hopefully bring some much-needed joy and laughter to her days as well. We both can be here to lift her up when she needs it. But I need to hear more about how she feels working with Ev.

"You know Poppy asked me today about Everett? She worries about you and wants to be sure he is a good guy. Whenever I think I have her figured out, she surprises me."

"Welcome to my world. Ha! That girl. What did she say? I don't need her worrying about this. It is hard enough being a kid these days. Maybe I need to think about what I'm doing and talk to her about it more first." Although I understand what she is saying, I don't necessarily agree with her. I know she is enjoying time spent in Everett's company.

"Sadie, she just wants you to be happy. She asked me what I knew about him. I told her. I explained how life can be scary, but you must be brave sometimes. She is a good kid. Strong. She's okay. If you want to know the truth, I think she helped me more than I did her. And then she threatened to punch him if he hurts you." I laugh out loud. Then we both tear up and laugh some more.

"After today, how are you feeling about it? Is he good for you?" She looks back at me, putting effort into how she will reply.

"What do you think, Clover? I get so confused. It has been so long since I even thought about moving on. I am not comfortable letting my guard down. I can't do that to Poppy. It's like I only worry about protecting her from life's what-ifs."

"Well, I'm truly no life expert," I say. "But you know what I do know? Life is full of scary shit. We just have to learn to be strong and find the courage to keep going, even when it feels like the world is falling apart. And that's what you're doing, Sadie. You're being brave, putting one foot in front of the other, and showing your daughter how to be strong. That's all that matters."

"It's not easy," she whispers, tears filling her eyes.

"I know," I said, squeezing her hand. "And that's expected. But you have to give yourself some grace. You're still capable of loving and being loved. You're allowed to want to build a new life and be happy. Just because you're scared doesn't mean you're weak. It means you're human. That's what makes us strong, Sadie. It's not about being fearless; it's about being brave."

I know these words I'm saying aloud are for both of us to be reminded. I'm not sure where all of this sentimental psychobabble came from within me today. I must have been listening to all the advice and support I've heard over the years from my grandmother, my aunt, and Reese.

"I know I have let this fear paralyze me to stop me from moving forward. Fear of another failed relationship, fear of seeing my daughter get her hopes crushed. All of it. But I think you are right. It's time I stepped into the light to see if more is out there for me. I need to let the chance of happiness be worth the risk of pain." She takes several deep breaths, wipes the tears from her eyes, and gives me a big grin. "I think he is good for me, Clover. I really do. I think it is worth seeing where it goes. Thank you for everything. Thanks for jumping into the rescue this morning without hesitating. Thank you for listening. For being a good friend. For supporting Poppy through all of this. I know you have a lot on your mind now, too. But somehow, you are still this beacon of light for us. I hope you see that. Truly. Now, if you don't mind, I'm going to say goodnight to Penelope, shower, and hit the hay."

I'm unsure how to respond to her, but I must say something. I treasure the friendship we are building and am grateful to have Sadie around during this part of my life. "Hey – Sadie. It was my pleasure to help. All you ever have to do is ask. Remember, you deserve all the good things in the world. Now, go hug your girl. Text your man. Take your shower and get some well-deserved rest. I'll be here in the morning. I'll take care of Poppy and Chance and get breakfast ready. You relax, please. Okay? Good night, friend."

"Goodnight, Clover. Glad you're here. Please make yourself at home."

With that, Sadie headed down the hall, spending several minutes in Poppy's room. Eventually, I heard her continue to her bedroom for the evening. I grab our teacups and place them in the sink for me to clear up in the morning. I let Chance out again, glancing up towards the dark sky. Clouds hide the stars above, but the moon is trying to peak out. I can smell smoke from the garden firepit that Hayley and Josh had going this evening.

It is so peaceful—just the footsteps of the dog and the gentle rustle of leaves in the yard. It's a welcome change from the constant noise that echoed through the city I'm choosing to leave behind. There, every day was a rat race. In this small town, the pace is slower, the air calmer, and the people kinder. I find myself without the usual knot of anxiety in my stomach, replaced instead by a sense of calm and contentment.

Here, I am not just another face in the crowd. I am becoming a part of something, a community. I am getting to know my neighbors, and I feel a sense of belonging that I need. It is a comfort I didn't realize I craved. I am finally breathing, truly breathing, for the first time in years.

A part of me still feels guilty, a tightness in my chest, at the thought of moving forward without Elliot. But another stronger part knows that staying trapped in grief won't honor his memory. He'd want me to live, to love, to find joy again. So, I allow myself to feel the evening breeze on my skin, savor new friends' laughter, and embrace the challenges and uncertainties ahead. It isn't a betrayal but evidence to the enduring power of his love. It is a leap of faith, a risk I am willing to take, a chance at happiness that I owe to myself and to the memory of the friend who had taught me to embrace life, even in its most painful moments. I need to do this. I hoped Sadie was inside now, having a similar revelation. And I smile to myself for the first time in a long while. Really smile.

After getting the dog inside, I walk into the guest room—my room here for the coming weeks—and settle in. I glance at my phone and see a text awaiting me.

EVERETT: It was a busy day. I think I wore her out, and she left suddenly. Is she okay?

I wonder how much information I should share. I promised myself not to interfere, but I think some things are safe to say.

ME: She's okay. Tired. We had a good talk. Check in with her tho. She needs it.

EVERETT: I didn't want to disturb her if she was resting. But U R right. I should. Thx

ME: You are a good guy, Ev. Take care of them. They r special.

EVERETT: I know. So are you. Night.

ME: Night. See you in the AM.

For the first time in over a month, I do something brave. I scroll to the number on my contact list above Everett's and hit call. It goes straight to voicemail, as expected. As my eyes sting with unshed tears, I hear his voice.

Beeeeeep. "Hey, this is Elliot. If you're calling to ask me to join your band, I'm already taken. If you're calling to get my opinion on the latest TikTok pastry recipe, hang up now- we are no longer friends. Otherwise, just leave a message. Or, you know, maybe try sending a carrier pigeon. Those are pretty cool. 'Kay. Bye."

I don't know why tonight is the night I must do this, but I have this strong sense that I need to. Electromagnetism draws our souls back together, even for a brief moment.

"Wingman. It is good to hear your voice. It feels strange to talk to you like this, knowing you can't hear these words, but maybe you can because my heart still yearns to tell you everything. The world feels a little dimmer without your laughter, your warmth, and your presence. Every corner seems to hold a memory of you, and it makes it so damn hard to keep going. But I'm starting to find my way again, bit by bit. There are days when Grief feels like a lead weight in my chest, and I just want to curl up and disappear. But I know you want me to move on. So, I'm trying. I'm trying to be brave enough to laugh again and embrace the new adventures that life throws me. It's not easy, but it feels right. It's a promise I'm making to myself and to you. I know you'd be proud of me. You'd tell me to keep my chin up, to never forget how much I'm loved, and to keep reaching for the stars. And that's what I'll do. I'll live with a piece of you always in my heart, a reminder of the amazing times we shared, and our unique friendship. Rest easy, my friend. I'll never forget you. I miss you so much, and I love you even more. Bye, Elliot."

A strange lightness fills my chest as I hit END on the call. It isn't a sudden burst of joy, but more subtle. Like the darkness is not entirely gone but less scary. It is a feeling of acceptance, a quiet acknowledgment that moving on doesn't mean forgetting. It means carrying his memory with me, a warm presence that doesn't dim but instead guides my path. Grief is still here. But a sliver of sunshine is beginning to seep through the cracks, a hopeful promise of a brighter tomorrow, a tomorrow where I could honor his memory by living fully, embracing the world with open arms, and always carrying his spirit with me. I close my eyes with a sense of calm and a feeling of excitement about what tomorrow will bring.

CHAPTER 22

I WAKE UP ENERGIZED, and it is early—still dark kind of early. I do my best to tiptoe, use the restroom, and grab coffee. An hour or so of studying helps me feel accomplished. Then, I grab my notebook and review my To-Do list for the upcoming week. I'm sure the next two days with Everett here will be chaotic. After that, I'll have work to do on my study guide and a few shifts at the café. I need to plan my yoga sequence for the BNB session I'm starting Wednesday. I need to review ideas for the new studio space and have an updated list prepared for when Reese and Nick come to town next weekend, plus call the property manager and schedule another walk-through with them. Maybe work on a plan for fun things we can do when they arrive. It will get busy, but it will be rewarding and fun. I like a full agenda. I have missed feeling productive.

As I get the batch of cinnamon muffins out of the oven, Poppy joins me in the kitchen. She looks like she is feeling better today. She is standing taller, no longer has a green hue to her skin tone, and has a big grin as she smells the sweet baked goods with a big inhale.

"Good morning. That smells delicious!" she greets me as she dramatically licks her lips, sitting at the small table. "Did you make those all by yourself?"

I pour her a glass of apple juice and set it beside her. "I did. My friend Elliot's secret recipe. You'll love them. How are you feeling this morning? You look more like yourself."

Her feet swing under the chair as she pulls the paper off the bottom of one of the still-warm muffins. "I feel good. Mom not up yet?"

"No, I figured we should let her catch up on sleep. If you want, we can take a walk, maybe down to the park in the neighborhood, and give Chance some time to run around a bit."

The idea makes her face light up. "Yeah, that's a good idea. Sounds like fun!"

I give her a chance to enjoy breakfast and help her pick out her clothes. As we tie our shoes by the door, my phone chimes with a message. Everett already has a start on the day and said he is at the apartment, that we can join him whenever we're ready. I noticed the message was only to me, so I asked if he had messaged Sadie. He tells me he is on the phone talking to her, so she knows. Although I hoped she'd get more sleep, I'm glad they're talking. I have Poppy run her a muffin and coffee into her bedroom while she is still relaxing on the phone.

Poppy and I walk in silence to the park, not much said, as Chance runs alongside us. As the sounds of kids playing get louder, I see Poppy's pace picking up as she recognizes her friend Maya's mom's car parked in front. "Hey, you want to run over and play with Maya? I can hang on to Chance while you visit. I don't mind." It doesn't take her long to skip over to the group of girls playing by the merry-go-round.

I take the opportunity to introduce myself to some of the parents sitting at the picnic table. Everyone is super kind, and I even manage to do some networking. Several moms and even a dad seem interested in the yoga session. I told them to keep an eye out for fliers on when and where I'll be having classes. I'm still not sure how Ian didn't think there was a community interest for the rec center to host. Oh well, his loss, the arrogant ass.

Maya's mom asked me if Poppy could go with her and a small group of girls to play goofy golf in the afternoon. Before texting Sadie, I pulled Poppy aside and asked if she wanted to spend time with friends. But she is very excited about helping at the apartment today and tells her friends she'll take a raincheck. I'm glad she is making more friends and getting involved. I know Sadie was concerned about that. I think Poppy just needs some time to break out of her shell.

After the short stroll home, well, back to their house, the sun shines bright, a nice breeze sways the tree branches, and the day looks inspiring. I leave Poppy with Sadie and decide to walk down to the café, grab a coffee, and then go upstairs and start working on renovations with Everett. The girls can spend some mommy-daughter time alone and meet us later.

As I arrive at the apartment, Reese is blowing up my phone with pictures of dresses her mom is having her try on in New York. She may not be thrilled with most of the fancy, princess-puffy styles her mother has her in, but she is beautiful, and I'm glad they are spending time together. Sometimes, I think she takes it for granted that they can have those moments. I just texted her back that she is gorgeous and to enjoy their day together.

"Hey, Clover. You're here early. Are you excited to get working?" Everett pulls my attention from my phone. I set it down.

"I am. I saw how you tired Sadie out last night, so I figured I should put in some effort today to compensate for her extra energy spent putting up with you."

"I didn't mind. At all." He snickers. "It was fun. Although I couldn't get her to take a break, Clo. She just kept going. She put all the new hardware on the kitchen cabinets and washed the windows. I kept asking if she wanted to stop for the day and grab a bite, but she insisted we keep going."

I was curious what his perspective was on the night. I'm not going to cave and tell him what she said. I hope they talked it out this morning. I think they were both nervous about spending time together alone. Even though it wasn't dinner and a movie, they still were working on a project alone for the first time. If they can figure out how to do home renovations early on in a relationship, they can make it through anything!

As I put my work gloves on, I glance around the space. I can see changes in it already. Sadie's work on the windows has the daylight shining in, cheering up the abandoned space. I can see dust swirling around me like a dust devil. I cough, swatting at the motes of grime, my nose wrinkling at the musty scent. It is very different from the loft Elliot and I had in the city, which used to be my haven. With its uneven floors, faded paint, and musty smell, this run-down flat feels right somehow. It feels like a blank canvas, an opportunity to create a different life that isn't shaped by the shadow of loss as I look around and see the progress already coming together.

The new friends I've made and my old support system give me the tremendous courage to escape that despair. They encourage and challenge me like a lifeline back to brighter days. They help me heal, breathe, and rediscover myself.

Everett plays music on a small speaker and gets lost in his work. The bathroom fix he's in the middle of has tools and a bunch of small plumbing parts scattered all over the floor. I am fortunate he is handy and is helping out. Sadie kept this hidden gem tucked away, the old space screaming with potential to be brought back to life. It's a good project, a challenge, and is the perfect antidote to the stagnation that had settled over me.

Now, standing amidst the dust and the faded wallpaper, the familiar sting of grief is softened by the shared laughter echoing from the stairway. Sadie and Poppy arrive and wear old clothes, already splattered in paint, with bandanas tied atop their heads. It appears they have discussed their game plan. As soon as she says a quick hello, Poppy goes directly to the kitchenette and starts washing down the insides of all the cabinets, actually crawling into the lower ones to scrub out the far reaches. Sadie grabs a long roller and gets busy painting the ceilings a bright white. Everett wanted those done before we worked on redoing the floor. I worked on replacing lightbulbs, painting trim, and shampooing an old couch that sat covered in the corner.

We sing, laugh, joke, and work nonstop for hours. The space is slowly transforming into a cute little haven. As we wind down, Poppy is sitting on the counter, Sadie is leaning on the windowsill, staring out to the street, admiring the foot traffic heading into the café below, and Everett... well, he doesn't wind down. He's finishing up the new toilet seal. We all have hair plastered with sweat, dirt or paint under our nails, but smiles go from ear to ear.

"Well, everyone. I think it is time to call it a day. Seriously, look how great this place is. I want us all to stop before we are too exhausted to go out and enjoy a well-earned dinner, my treat. Y'all are awesome. I am so glad to have you as friends," I say as emotions build up.

"Good idea. It's time for some fun. We totally killed it today," Everett chimes in. As he throws his tools into a big orange bucket, the girls pick up rags and do a quick sweep. We take a few minutes to see what materials we'll need tomorrow so I can stop at the hardware store. Everett called Josh and asked if he'd be willing to give us a hand tomorrow with a few tasks requiring more muscle power, and he agreed. With a glance around and a flip of the light switches, Sadie locks up, and we all go downstairs to the parking lot.

"Can we all take an hour, get cleaned up, then meet for dinner? Poppy, why don't you pick where we eat? You are just getting your appetite back, and I want you to enjoy it."

Poppy looks at all of us, then announces, "I know you all think since I'm a kid, I'll want to get pizza. But can we go to Sprout? That food was sooo good last week."

She's right; the food there was great. It is the farm-to-table place we all went to last week when Everett and I returned from Savannah. We all had a great time there. The environment was family-friendly and relaxed, and the food was terrific. Maybe that could be our new hangout. "I think that is a great idea, Poppy. What do you all say? Everett, you want us to pick you up at the hotel when we're ready?"

Nods of agreement from all and the plan is set. I chuckle as I look around at our current state. We look like a Jackson Pollock painting come to life with an extra dose of dust thrown in for good measure. And I just lose it at the sight; an uncontrollable fit of laughter roars out of me. Within seconds, the others join until happy tears trickle down our cheeks. It feels good, real good. We all needed this moment. With laughter came a balm on our raw souls, a gentle cue that joy and friendship can still find a way to bloom even in the face of hardship.

Everett drove back to his hotel, and we made it to Sadie's place and cleaned up in record time. I haven't spent much time recently working on my appearance. I took care of myself, but it wasn't like I made an extra effort to get dolled up. But tonight, I felt more like me. I wore a lovely summer dress and applied some make-up: natural shadow, mascara, and a pretty peach gloss. I noticed Sadie looked extremely pretty, too. So Poppy didn't feel left out, I gave her a little blush and some clear gloss. The three of us stand together in front of the large vanity mirror, proud of the strong ladies we see in the reflection.

"Alright, ladies! We are looking good tonight!" I shout. Sadie is standing in the middle and reaches out to grab a hand from Poppy and me with a big grin. The three of us giggle and dramatically bat our eyelashes at each other.

Poppy squeals, "Okay, let's go conquer the world!" and pulls our arms above our heads. "Or at least a big plate of chicken nugs."

Sadie and I laugh and follow Poppy to the door. Like I've been doing it for years, I check Chance's water dish to ensure it is full and scoop his dinner kibble. He wags his tail goodbye as his favorite girls take off on their adventure.

I text Everett, so he knows we'll pick him up shortly. Then, an incoming call blares through the car speakers. After a loud, animated group conversation, it is arranged that Poppy will go to a sleepover at Maya's house after dinner is over tonight. She looks pretty excited, but I hope she has enough energy to enjoy a slumber party after working so hard with us all day at the apartment.

I know kids have insane amounts of energy, but I understand it can turn sour when it runs out suddenly. Sadie must think the same and asks Poppy not to overdo it tonight since she is also getting over the flu. We know she is feeling fine today, but I'm glad she mentioned it.

Within minutes, we had Everett with us and were on the way to the restaurant. When we pulled up to the hotel, he looked worried we wouldn't all squeeze into Sadie's little Yaris coupe. I decided not to budge and made him join Poppy in the back. I thought they could bond for a few minutes during the short drive.

The backseat was tiny, but Everett somehow managed to bend himself. His knees were practically in his ears. His arms were squeezed against the windows, and his head was precariously perched against the roof, a human pretzel in a car-sized bread-basket. Every time Sadie hit a bump, Ev let out a muffled groan, his face contorting in a mixture of pain and amusement. Sadie, struggling to keep her laughter in check, assures him that he is fine, but the way his shoulders bob with every pothole and his elbows poke out like awkward wings make it impossible to take her statement seriously. With an animated grin, Poppy decides to further his pain and begins to tickle him while he has nowhere to run. A fit of giggles explodes from them both. Sadie is watching via the rearview mirror as Everett, in his contortionist state, plays along with Poppy's silliness, and he hoots and hollers. This is the best car ride ever.

A car stopped in the lane next to us at a red light, and a group of teenagers stared at us, laughing and pointing. I assume we look nothing less ridiculous than one of those tiny cars filled with clowns. To add to the mischief, the teens rev the engine jokingly, but as the light turns green, Sadie is going to rev back, but she removes her foot from the break and takes off with a big jolt, sending Everett's smooshed body forward suddenly, smacking his nose into my headrest.

"Ffuuuuuudge!" he shouts, covering his nose with his hand. Poppy looks like a deer in headlights, and Sadie asks if he is okay. His eyes are watering from the sting of the impact, but he is fine. No bloody nose, no whiplash. Honestly, the car didn't even go that far; it was just a rapid, jerky launch when his body was too big for the tiny seat and belt to hold him in. I laugh uncontrollably for the second time today, and eventually, the others join in.

"Thanks for catching the language, Everett. That was a close one," Sadie chuckles and looks back at him through the mirror again.

"Yeah, sure. What, are you trying to kill me off or something?" he jokes.

For a moment, his face goes blank, and she sees it. Then she frowned as she looked at me, but I just nodded with a slight grin back. I know what they are worried about, but I'm tired of people tiptoeing around what they say. Worrying that it will upset me reminds me of the loss we just went through. I need to let them know it is okay. I'm glad Everett can act his usual kidding way again, not even giving what he said a second thought before it came out. To break the awkwardness, Poppy chimes in, "No, silly, she likes you too much to do that!" Then she pauses and adds, "So do I, even though you're like a baboon tucked in back here."

And then the giggles ensue.

CHAPTER 23

THE AROMA OF ROASTED garlic and rosemary lingers in the air, a souvenir of the delicious meal we just shared. We've decided to go for a drink at a new pub downtown here. Poppy is excited to go to her friend's house and watch movies. Rather than all of us squishing back into the car, Everett and I walk the block to the new hotspot. Sadie drives Poppy to Maya's and plans to meet us there. We say bye to Poppy before they leave and head down the sidewalk to the next destination of this fantastic day.

The walk is refreshing; the air is cooling off, and stretching after that filling meal feels good. Everett starts the conversation, "Things seem good, don't they? I mean, you have a lot of puzzle pieces falling into place. Good, right?"

"Hmmm. Yes, I guess they are. It is sort of crazy to think in such a short timeframe, I'm making these decisions to move, help renovate an apartment, learn a new skill at the café, prep for my MCAT, and check out a studio. I mean, what the hell, Everett? I thought the world was ending a month ago, you know?" Saying it out loud makes me feel even more insane but in a good way.

"The whole thing seems to have transpired in the blink of an eye. Something magical happened to set things in motion. Clover, you are getting stronger. I kid you not. Witnessing your bound-less energy and infectious smile today was truly awe-inspiring. It warms my soul to see you finding joy in life again."

"Are you getting all mushy on me, buddy? I'm doing okay. I know I'll be fine, and I'm glad to see you having a good time with

Sadie....and Poppy, too. You're good for them." I mean that. I see him growing up, showing his true colors. There is more to him than his past.

"I'm trying to be a man deserving of them. I'm just glad to have a chance to get to know them better. I haven't had anything like this in a long time, Clover. You know that I've always been a lone wolf, but I'm okay with it like that. I didn't need anything too serious; definitely no one too close, but there's something about this that feels different. I don't mind leaning in a bit to trust. It is kind of exhilarating."

"Be careful, Everett; all that gooeyness could attract bears," I chuckle and give him a little push on his arm. "I'm happy for you too, Ev. It's nice to see this side of you. I know Elliot is looking down at us right now, thinking about how awesome we are." With our final steps as we approach the awning at the pub, he just nods in agreement. Then he pushes me back.

"Can we get a drink now? Enough of the heavy. Deal?"

"Yep, you got it!" I agree.

Sadie is parking her car right across the street and walks up. "Oh, Queen's Alehouse, here we come!!!!"

As the three of us head inside to find a table, I notice Everett hovering his hand near hers, a silent invitation as they walk in. It's like he leaves it hanging there as an unspoken question, waiting for her answer with the gentle touch of her fingers. Without effort, she clasps her hand into his. From steps away, I watch him turn back slightly and give her a gratified smile.

He steps into the crowded tavern and stretches his other arm out to clear a path so we can get through the cluster of people blocking the way. We found a high top with a few stools and took it. It is bustling here; the newness of the place attracts a lot of traffic. The atmosphere is comfortable and modern but warm. It has a more traditional pub feel, with some modern conveniences. You can check out the draft list and order beer flights electronically from the tables via small tablets, and servers bring them to you. They have a separate specialty cocktail area, with a sign above that says Queens Elixir. There seems to be a large bridal party taking over that area.

As we settle in, we all preview the menu and get an order placed; Everett leans to me and says, "Do you think we can count this for the next alphabet outing? We had Patsy's last time. Q is next, right?"

"Oh my goodness, yes. This counts. Great idea, Ev. I just hope you behave yourself tonight." I give him a wink. There is no need to delve into the awkward events of that night out, especially with Sadie here. He just returns a knowing smile and chuckles.

"No worries, I already have my sights on someone," he reaches over and takes Sadie's hand again. It is so loud in here, and I am sure she didn't exactly hear what we said, but she is happy to have his attention.

I decided to give them some space. It almost feels like the night Reese and Nick met. I was never really made to feel like the third wheel, but I know when a new couple needs some time to talk and get to know each other, "Hey, I'm going to find the restroom and maybe check out the elixirs offered. I'll be back in a few!" With that, I hop off the stool and start wiggling my way to the back of the place.

I find the corridor to the restrooms, but with the crowd, there is a short line to the ladies' room. I see a place in line and take out my phone to catch up on things while I wait. Reese said yes to a dress, and Ruby and my grandmother had a fun afternoon planting a windowsill herb garden. I am glad to see everyone enjoyed their days. I miss all of them but feel encouraged to know Reese will be here in less than a week to visit, and I will now be much closer to Savannah so that I can get there more often, too. I send quick replies to both and promise to send apartment update pictures soon. As the line shrinks, I put my phone away.

I leave the bathroom a few minutes later and return to the elixir bar. I usually stick to the basics: a shot or a beer or two. For once,

I decided to give it a go on something new tonight. Why not? I look at the drink choices and pick one or two decent options, both of which have berries in them. As I wait for this queue to thin, I glance around the bar.

The sight of Everett and Sadie up front, so cozy in their chat, makes me grin and melts my own heart. It's adorable to watch their bond grow, an indication that even after loss, new love is possible. But it seems a familiar sense of loneliness, a flicker of grief, creeps in my chest. I continue to feel hesitant, but they are discovering their path, destiny, and reason for being.

The bar is buzzing with energy, the air thick with the scent of beer and sanitizer. I see couples on dates, friends catching up, and bridal parties making memories. My gaze drifts through the crowd, a mix of some familiar faces I've seen around town and many strangers. I can't help but wonder if I would ever find someone to share a story with, a drink with, a life with.

"So, tell me. You here alone tonight, with friends?" Ian steps closer, moving away from a few guys he was chatting with. This is not the mystery man I would dream of bumping into this evening.

No, Ian is that kind of guy who seems handsome at first, charming, maybe. His face, though not unpleasant, has a permanent smirk, as if he's just won a game of life he hadn't even played yet. The way he surveys the room, eyes scanning for someone to impress, radiates a kind of arrogance that chills me. Ian is the epitome of that particular brand of "gym bro" confidence like he's better than everyone else. There is an undercurrent to his charm, a sense of entitlement that makes me want to run in the opposite direction. He is the kind of guy who wouldn't be satisfied until he has everyone in the room bowing at his feet. I, for one, am not interested in being part of his audience.

I've seen him at work, with his creepy gawking eyes during my interview debacle, unable to see a bigger picture beyond his own needs, which sours my stomach. Josh even told me to stay away from him and to trust my instincts on this guy.

"With friends." I give a curt reply and turn around to face the bar and try and get the bartender's attention.

"Oh, that's cool," he adds, running his slimy hand down my arm. "Can I get you a drink while we catch up? I was surprised you never called back to take that job offer. I thought you could use a chance like that. You know, try to get ahead while you set down roots here. You are moving here, right?"

Ugh, he is grating my nerves. Before I can hold it back, I blurt, "Look, Liam, I am sure you are pretty popular, but I'm not really into that whole 'looking-down-at-everyone' thing, okay? Now, please....run along," and I wave my hand to shoo him away.

The look on his stunned face before I take another step away has me internally high-fiving. My bite is back, and it feels good. So good. Astonishingly good. Until it turns not so good.

"Feisty, huh? I like it. And, my name is Ian, which I think you remember, you crazy bitch." Now he grabs my arm tightly, "What's your problem, any way? I thought you meditative, yoga, zen types were mellow and agreeable. Maybe you need to be taught a lesson," he whispers to avoid further attention.

His hand, rough and clammy, tightens on my arm. It is a grip that seems to be more about control than affection, a power play. He hadn't even asked; he just assumed I'd be okay with his touch. My anger flares, and a sudden surge of adrenaline courses through my veins. If I don't act, he'll harass me further, so I will do the only thing I can. With a surprising amount of force, I rip my arm free, his hand slipping away like a limp fish, and give him a sturdy push away. Surprised by my unexpected defiance, he stumbles back in his tipsy state, flabbergasted. I take the opportunity to step back, my gaze unwavering. "Don't you dare touch me again," I spit, my voice calm but firm, a steel edge to my tone. He opens his mouth to say something, but I don't give him a chance. I swiftly sneak around two other large men standing in the back and zig-zag away in the crowd to find the back exit.

The fresh air hits me as the door flies open. I'm sure several patrons watched my ungraceful exit strategy, but I just had to get out quickly. It would be too far to crawl through the crowd to get back up front, near Sadie and Everett. But back here, it's quiet. No one seems to be around, and I can catch my breath and calm my nerves before I head back inside. I cannot believe that prick. What an asshole! I guess my gut instinct was pretty accurate, even if my reflexes were slower to catch up.

I give myself several minutes to breathe and relax. I text Everett that I'm out back and okay, in case he begins to worry. I've been gone a while. Of course, I'm sure he and Sadie are having a good time and don't notice the passing of time. As I walk back in, I look around to confirm Ian isn't close and pray he found his way back to his group of friends, way the hell away from me. I spin around a few times and see a scuffle going on in the corner. I can only see the tops of some heads, but I know Ian is pushed up against a wall, and someone appears to be in his face. Then, suddenly, he pushes free, and I watch as he progresses through the onlookers toward the exit. I quickly lean up against the bar and act like I'm giving my order, my back to him as he passes by me. Just when I think the coast is clear, I sense him.

"Couldn't just fight your own battle, huh? Had to have your boyfriend threaten to kick the shit out of me? You'll regret this, princess!" He seethes in my ear and then turns back as he goes outside. I look around at the people near me and act like I don't know what he is talking about, shrugging my shoulders.

The bartender looks my way, sets a shot glass before me, and says, "On the house. It looks like you could use it. I already texted the door guys to ban that creep from coming back. You alright?"

Embarrassed but not exactly upset, I down the shot and hold it up for a refill, "I'm okay. Thanks. He's just an idiot that couldn't handle rejection." The next shot burns going down a bit, but it is a nice tequila and I enjoy it. As I turn around to return to our table, I catch just a brief smell of that familiar cologne, the one linked to the mysterious man I've seen around town. It's almost too subtle to separate the fragrance from all the other typical bar smells, but this stands out to me. It makes me feel that zip of energy, that electromagnetic pull. My gaze scans the space, wondering if my Elliot doppelganger is here somewhere. The man with those cerulean green eyes. Almost dizzy from my twirl to look desperately in all directions, I don't recognize one person back here. I figure it is time to reunite with my friends and ask Everett what the heck he said to Ian. He obviously put some well-deserved fear into him.

Approaching the table, it appears only Sadie is sitting there. She is nibbling on her nails, nervous about something. "Hey, Sadie!" I say as I walk up and give her a brief hug. "Where's Everett?"

"He went looking for you. You sent that text a while ago, and he wanted to check on you. I told him I'd stay here in case you made your way back first. We saw some argument in the back and were worried. Are you okay?"

I smile at her, trying to assure her I'm alright. "Yeah, I'm okay. I ran into that Ian prick from the rec center. He gave me a bit of a hard time, but he left. I'm okay." I grab the glass of water on the table and drink the entire glass down. Maybe I'm more shaken up than I thought. More concerned about allowing myself to wish I would see my Elliot look-alike here again and not so much about the run-in with Ian.

Sadie stands from her barstool and waves high to catch Everett's attention. He smiles and waves back, seeing we are both back at the table, and weaves his way through the growing crowd to join us.

"You okay, Clo? I'm not sure what was happening back there, but it looked a little rowdy."

"Yep, all good. But how much of that shitshow did you see? And what the heck did you say to Ian? He was even more pissed when he left." Even as fit as Ian is, Everett towers over him. I'm sure he didn't have to say much to scare him off.

"You saw that idiot here? What did he say to you, Clover? Do I need to go shake him up a bit?" He looks equally concerned and pissed. I know he is protective of me; Elliot was the same way, but now I'm confused. I thought he already had a chat with Ian.

"Wait, what? I thought you already made that idiot piss himself. After he harassed me, I went outside to get air, and that is when I texted you. When I returned, someone had him cornered and was giving him a taste of his own medicine. I couldn't see much, but I assumed it was you. When he left, he insinuated I was weak because I had to have my 'boyfriend' fight my battles. So, that wasn't you?" None of this night is making sense.

"Clover, no. It wasn't me. After you texted to say you were getting some air, I wasn't too worried, but then I heard those guys arguing, and I thought I should see you were out of the way in case anything escalated." He is scratching his head now, just as confused. Sadie is just looking back and forth between the two of us.

"That's weird," she adds. "I wonder who the other guy was?"

"That's the thing, Sadie. I don't know anyone else here. Not just here, in the whole damn town! So, who the heck would have stood up for me like that?"

It was the most unexpected thing to know a stranger was standing in the bar, minding his own business, but when he saw what was happening, he stepped in. From behind, I could see his bold stance; from afar, I could hear the warning in his voice. Suddenly, I felt protected. I felt I wasn't alone. This stranger's act of kindness left me both shocked and grateful. Even in the world's chaos, some people still cared and would stand up for what was right, even when it meant risking something for a stranger. His actions gave a glimmer of hope. I was initially grateful and comforted, thinking it was Everett stepping in to protect me, but knowing it was some stranger elevates my gratitude to the next level.

"So, you didn't see who it was? I'm kind of pissed he took my chance at showing that jerk who was boss, but I'm glad he was back there when he was. I wish I could shake his hand," Everett confesses, still scanning the room.

"I wish I could shake his hand too. Believe me," I add.

Sadie is still standing there, taking it all in. Once her head is wrapped around what happened, she playfully says, "Clover has a secret admirer, a knight in shining armor!"

I'm not sure what I have exactly besides a vivid imagination. An imagination that is currently thinking about a variety of impossible things. The day began with fun walks in the park, hard work at the apartment, a laughter-filled dinner with friends, and joy watching two of my friends fall for each other. But I'm not sure what to believe about how it is ending. Wait until Reese gets a load of this!

I laugh, trying to brush off the comment about having a secret admirer, but the thought of finding "the one" seems too far-fetched and slightly unrealistic. But as I looked at Everett and Sadie, their faces lit with happiness, their hands intertwined across the table, I couldn't help but wonder if maybe, just maybe, there was still room for a bit of magic in my own life, a little hope for a happy ending.

Our night out is salvaged. We order another round and get back to having fun. It whirls by, filled with laughter, conversation, and the warmth of shared joy. I meet a few interesting people, share a few jokes, and even dance a little. As the night winds down, I realize that maybe, just maybe, this new chapter, this new town, this new life, is not about finding "the one" but about embracing the journey, the possibility, the joy of being present in every moment. It is about finding happiness in the bonds we make, the friendships we nurture, the stories we share, and the laughter we create. And maybe, just maybe, that will be enough.

CHAPTER 24

MY DAYS ARE A combination of caffeine and chaos, sawdust and study guides. The café turns into my sanctuary, my refuge. The aroma of the freshly brewed daily coffee and the gentle hum of conversation fills the air, a constant soundtrack to the days. I know Sadie thought I was doing her a favor by picking up hours here, but it was more of a Blessing to me. Between the latte art I was working on and customer talk, I am always mindful of my next chore, my next project. I use the downtime to study, sort through index cards, and attempt to get as much information back into my head as I can manage. Though I fight fatigue continuously, I push on because I am fiercely determined to accomplish my goals.

Then there is the apartment. With the walls painted in cheerful tones and the chipped furniture we were able to rescue, polish, and restore, the renovation is moving along gradually. The bathroom renovations are finished, and a new refrigerator has been moved upstairs and put in place because of Everett and Josh. It is a continual source of fulfillment and a reflection of the effort and commitment we all put into it. However, it also entails spending hours transporting supplies, wielding paintbrushes, and removing intractable screws. My hands are always smeared with paint, my muscles hurt, and I'm frequently covered in a thin layer of dust. However, there is also a certain happiness in the mess—working closely to bring it all together.

Between the physicality of the apartment work and prepping for the yoga sessions I have to plan, my body is screaming for a vacation. But there is no time for rest. I asked Reese for advice on some sequences for newbies of all ages and backgrounds. The planning and input from her turned the first two sessions into a great success. So far, both days have had a good turnout of guests who participated, including drop-ins from Sadie and Poppy. Hayley and Josh even attended the first one. I think it will be a good addition to the activities offered at the BNB. Their outdoor space worked well, with all the fragrance from the flower gardens and the serene sounds of the koi pond. Though some of my energy was used up in class, it also recycled a lot of it into a new source of excitement and has me looking forward to checking out the studio space this weekend.

And then, of course, there is the anticipation of Reese and Nick's visit. Their arrival is just days away, and my mind is already racing with plans. I had to make sure that Hayley has a room reserved for them at the BNB since the apartment won't be ready, and the guest room at Sadie's is already occupied by yours truly. I stocked up on their favorite treats to put in their room for arrival and a fresh bouquet of flowers. Josh and Hayley would have helped with that, but I want to create a welcoming atmosphere where they can recharge, relax, and feel comfortable. They've both been busy wedding planning, working, and hauling my storage boxes here, so I want to do anything I can to make them feel at home. It has been a bit daunting, but I embrace it with enthusiasm.

I am exhausted; there's no denying that. My muscles ache, and my mind is in constant overdrive. On the other hand, I am pumped up, enthusiastic, and full of purpose. I am making the most of every moment, seizing any chance that comes my way. And amidst the chaos, I find a strange kind of peace and satisfaction in knowing that I am making progress, that I am building a life that is uniquely mine, a life that is full of friendship and a touch of organized chaos.

***

After finishing at the café one afternoon, I walk upstairs to try and tackle the closet rack system. I have brackets, rods, and baskets scattered all over the floor in a big mess. Sadie stops upstairs to assist with the instruction sheet in some language neither of us has seen before, as well as pictures that require a magnifying glass to which we currently do not have access. While working on the project, she asks about the weekend plans.

"So, I hear your birthday is this weekend, Clover. Do you want to do anything special? Nice dinner out, quiet evening in, dancing at a club, favorite cake? I can help with plans if you want."

"Oh, I wasn't really thinking about that. We have enough going on. Plus, with Reese and Nick in town, things will be busy, showing them around town and touring the studio. And honestly, I want them to have a little downtime to just chill, you know?"

She sighs a bit, giving me a stare down. "But, it's your biiir-rthdayyyy!! We *have* to do so something to celebrate. And I must tell you, I've been put on the spot to ask. And if you don't have a preference, Everett told me that he and Reese will plan something for you. So, speak now or whatever...." she chuckles, waving her hand back and forth.

Great, now Everett and Reese are in cahoots planning. I know what Sadie is saying will be confirmed. Those guys are not going to let me get away without some celebration. So, to make them happy, I'll just agree. "You know what? Let them surprise me. I've never been big on surprises, but I'm turning over that new leaf. Letting in joy. I suppose what better way than to celebrate my birthday with friends."

Hesitantly, she says, "Really? You don't want to make a suggestion or anything? Just surprise you. Honestly, I'm a little scared of what the two of them will come up with. Oh my gosh, you are one brave woman."

"Oh, come on, it won't be that bad. No scarier than these closet instructions." I start to giggle, looking around at the pile. I'm not sure I'll ever get it sorted out.

"Okay, I'll let them know." At that, she grabs her phone and sends text messages, several in a row. Her phone starts buzzing to life.

I glance over at her with a questioning look. Her phone is literally going off one notification after another. "How bad is it?"

"Girl, you have no idea what you have just unleashed! All I'm saying is the two of them are on a roll. I see words like epic, A-game, mariachi. They are literally going insane right now," she giggles, bringing her fist to her mouth. "Everett is kind of cute when he talks party planning."

"Uh huh, cute. Right. When else is Everett *cute?*" I get no reply out of her, just a shy shrug and more giggles. It seems they are texting and calling each other a lot. He hasn't been here since early in the week, but I know they are making weekend plans. "Are you going to Reese's wedding with him, or do you want to be my plus one?"

"Well, he's mentioned going but hasn't officially asked me. So, I'll let you know. I had better find a dress just in case, I suppose. If he doesn't want me to go with him, I'll just show up with you. That'll teach him!"

"Oh, I feel the love. Second choice Susie here. But I'm good with that plan." I haven't been in the mindset to think about finding a date. In the past, I always had Elliot to go to events with me. This will be new.

The week went by in a flash, and now here it is Saturday morning, and I am upstairs at the apartment doing minor cleanup from projects Sadie and I were able to handle solo the past few nights. Reese just texted and said they are only minutes from town and would swing by here first to see me before checking in. I'm so glad to see them again!

I hear footsteps on the stairs and then a knock announcing their arrival. As I am perched on a stool, moving things around on the top closet shelf, I hop down and rush to the door, my heart doing a happy jig. Reese, ever the fashionista, is a vision in a floral maxi dress, her hair now a subtle pink shade growing longer and flowing in perfect waves. Nick, looking dapper in a linen shirt and khaki pants, is holding a massive duffel bag emblazoned with the words "Reese's Stuff: Don't Touch."

"Oh my gosh, you guys!" I squeal, pulling Reese into a hug. "It's so good to see you!"

"It's been too long!" Reese exclaims, her voice bubbling with excitement. "And look at this place! It's amazing! How are the renovations going?"

"They're coming along, but I need a miracle to gather the energy to finish it all up," I admit, gesturing at the floors we still need to refinish and the non-existent decorating. Then I pull Nick into a hug,

Suddenly, a booming voice echoes from the doorway. "You mean a miracle named Everett?" Ev starts to enter with a box of more materials and a big grin.

"Welcome, welcome!" I invite him in.

Nick laughs, "I'm not sure I'm up for a full-scale renovation, but I'm happy to help unpack. Reese has the car packed up with all of your stuff."

Without hesitation, Everett and Nick turn to begin the process of bringing my boxes in and stacking them up on counters and in the shower, out of the way from where we will have the floors being worked on next week. With the added activity, Sadie must have heard us while working downstairs on paperwork. Moments later, she and Poppy walk into the apartment, holding a large catering coffee jug.

As the girls meet in the main space, Nick and Everett return with another stack of boxes. I introduce Reese and Nick to Sadie. Reese is immediately struck by Sadie's vibrant energy and infectious laugh, which turns into a vortex of warmth and kindness. Watching them interact, I feel encouraged. This is it: the mix of old and new, the steady support of friendships, and the fascinating thrill of making new ones.

"It's so nice to meet you, Reese!" Sadie says, her smile bright. "I've heard so much about you!"

"Well, there's a lot to tell, I'm sure. We've been friends since before time began," Reese jokes, throwing an arm around me. "We've shared so much together. But I'm stoked to hear all about your adventures here!"

Sadie, eyes twinkling, takes a step back. "Well, I'm definitely up to taking it easy this weekend and getting to know you all better!" she says, her hand on her hip. "Poppy will want to hang out, too!"

With that, Poppy darts out from behind Sadie. "Hi, I'm Poppy! I'm Clover's new best friend!" she declares, clutching a stack of to-go cups in her arms. "Want some coffee? I just helped brew it myself."

Reese kneels down, her eyes meeting Poppy's. "Hi, Poppy! It's nice to meet you. I think we're going to have a lot of fun together. If you give me one of those cups, you'll also be my new best friend!" She steals a cup off the stack in Poppy's arms and fills it under the jug spigot.

As everyone shakes and hugs, I can't help but feel a deep sense of gratitude. I am surrounded by love and support, with old and new friends all joining me on this exciting new journey. And now, I cannot wait to see what the future holds, especially the weekend ahead.

After the entire group helps with carrying all my boxes upstairs, I take Reese and Nick on a swift tour of town. We make the stopover to get them checked into the BNB late in the morning. With a bit of time to spare before we go see the studio space, I try to make them welcome. I watch Reese and Nick unpack their bags in the cozy guest room, a twinkle in their eyes as they tease each other about who packed the most and the apparent winner. Reese admires the flowers I had prepared for the room, leaning over to smell the fresh arrangement, and then finds the basket of snacks I set on the nightstand, already opening the licorice bites.

"This place is so great! I love the vibes here! So colorful and cheery!" she adds while pulling the curtain sheer back to take in the view of the back garden from upstairs. "Nick, look at this awesome outdoor space. It reminds me of the patio at the wedding venue!"

I've only heard about their booked event space, but it sounds lovely. I am so looking forward to their big day! Both are special to me; Reese is a treasured friend, and Nick is the closest I've ever had to a brother. I hope their wedding is absolutely magical since they are the most adorable couple.

But then, a surge of uncertainty falls on me. Without Elliot, I have this big question mark in my life. And with sparks flying between Everett and Sadie, I am sure I'll be attending the wedding alone. I know I should be happy for them, but sometimes I just feel… lonely.

Even though I'm slightly envious of Reese and Nick's happily ever after, I wouldn't trade our friendship or their happiness for anything in the world. I'm determined to celebrate them and let them know how much I love them. I'll be there, front and center, my smile as bright as the wedding lights.

I introduce them to Josh and Hayley as I guide them downstairs; they meet with friendly smiles and knowing looks. The four exhibit a camaraderie that begs me to question what they're up to. I swear I see Hayley wink at Reese, and Josh and Nick share a mischievous smile. I'm pretty sure they're all in on some grand scheme, and I have a strong feeling it's related to the birthday celebration they're planning for me tonight. I can't wait to see what they've got in store, but for now, I will simply enjoy the comfort of good friends and the promise of a fun-filled evening.

We are joined by Everett and make our way to the appointment to see the studio space. The property manager waits outside while we do a walk-through. Reese and Nick have put a lot of thought into their vision of how the space could be converted, having done this with the original studio. They address some of Everett's worries during their conversation with the pragmatic man. "The electrical needs to be updated, and, well, the back wall needs tuckpointed."

As I make my way through, an overwhelming sense of enthusiasm washes over me, unrelated to Elliot or anybody else. It's about me. At last, the room, the idea, the ambition, is starting to take form, with it a new sense of independence. I've always been linked to other people's plans; this is unique to me. It's my own dream that I can work into reality.

The light streams through the windows, illuminating the dusty floorboards and the peeling paint. I see the potential, the possibilities. This isn't a space to impress, fit in, or please someone else. This is a space to inspire, uplift, and share what I have to offer with the world. This is a space to be me, to be free. "If we do this, you guys, I'm all in. I'm ready. But I have one condition..." The three of them look my way, awaiting my point. "I want to name it Uplift. Not Arise, or Arise II. It has to be Uplift."

"I love it!" Reese, ever the cheerleader, declares. "Nick and I will support you however you need it, but it'll be your baby!" She runs over to me and squeezes me into a bear hug. The kind I've missed for too long.

With Nick's blessing and an agreement from Everett to help get it going, a new level of excitement fills the air. The property manager reviews the paperwork, and things become official quickly. With the help of my awesome friends, I feel like that's another major step to moving forward. Allowing more light to filter through the cracks in my soul. It is definitely uplifting.

Later that afternoon, after a delicious meal cooked by new friends at the diner in town, I watch Reese and Nick unpack box after box of my belongings from storage. We only tackle the items that can go into the kitchen cabinets and clothes that make their way into the recently assembled closet. While going through the boxes, Reese finds a gorgeous coral yoga mat and a couple of yoga blocks.

"Hey, do you remember this?" Reese smiles, "Your first yoga mat ever!" It's just been sitting around since college.

"OMG, Reese!" I said, running my fingers over my old mat, feeling nostalgia and excitement. Awesome! "It's kind of a sign of how much I've grown."

And as I gaze at the mat, I can't help but anticipate what my future is starting to look like. With my friends by my side, I am ready to create something truly special. I know it will be a success and take me to even greater things.

CHAPTER 25

THE PATIO DOOR SLIDES open, and I'm greeted by a burst of lively music, a joyful mix of laughter and cheers. A mariachi band is playing an upbeat tune, and the garden at the BNB is glowing cheerfully with paper lantern lights. My friends, all gathered in this cozy space, are smiling at me, their faces gleaming with playful happiness. A big smile spreads across my face. They've done it! They've organized the most enthusiastic birthday party, which is exactly what I needed.

Hayley and Josh have turned the area into a fiesta-themed fantasy. The flattop griddle is sizzling with fajitas, the drinks are flowing, and the air is filled with the aroma of spice and laughter. I lose myself in the music, bobbing together with my friends and dancing enthusiastically.

Everett clears his throat and greets everyone, and then looks toward me. "So, Clover," he begins, a smile softening his features, "I've known you for a little while now, and let me tell you, you're one of the most incredible people I've ever met. We've had visits prone to disaster and arguments about life and family. We've spent time on the road to visit your grandma and got to know each other better. I've allowed your family to school me in cards, and throw flour in my face. This new renovation at the apartment has shown messiness to another level, but also laughter so hard we have tears rolling down our faces. You know, these are some of the best times I've ever had in my life. You have a way of finding joy in the most unexpected places, in times I never thought I could smile."

He paused, glancing around the room, his eyes lingering on each of our friends. "I'm also so excited about the alphabet restaurant challenge now that you are moving closer, and future games of two truths and a lie with you and friends. It's going to be epic! But seriously, Clover, I'm truly grateful for your friendship. After Elliot... well, things were hard. You welcomed me into your group with open arms and never made me feel like I was intruding. You're the kind of friend who makes you want to be a better person, a more worthy friend, just like my brother was."

His voice softened, and a hint of sadness flickered across his eyes. "I know Elliot would be so proud of you, Clover. He always talked about how amazing you were and how you always saw the good in everyone. You truly are an inspiration."

He takes a deep breath and looks around the beautiful space to the amazing people surrounding us. "Thank you, everyone, for being here tonight, for celebrating with Clover. It means so much to all of us. Elliot would have loved this, and I know he's here with us in spirit. Happy birthday, Clover! We all love you so much!"

His words resonated around me, and we all raised our glasses in a silent toast to Elliot, the friend and brother who had touched so many lives.

A lump forms in my throat.

Everett's remarks warmly remind me of the love that still unites us and the legacy Elliot left behind, even though I miss my wing-man dearly.

Reese intervenes before the atmosphere grows gloomy. Ever the charismatic one, she begins, "Clover, happy birthday! You know, there's a reason they call you Clover. You bring luck and joy to others, and even if it means searching through a dumpster, you always locate the most incredible things."

Her mischievous eyes sparkle as she pauses. "Do you recall when you discovered that beautiful chipped porcelain teacup while we were thrifting in that dusty old store? I thought it looked like something a cat had puked on, but you maintained it was a 'treasure.' And you know what? It was. You transformed it into a gorgeous coffee table centerpiece. And as of this afternoon, I'm happy to have moved it back into your area," she laughs. "Clover, you have a touch of magic. You have a way of turning the ordinary into extraordinary."

She winks at me while our friends are all laughing. "And, if I'm being honest," she whispers, leaning in close, "that's exactly what you do with your life, too. You turn chaos into beauty and make everyone around you feel like they're a part of something special. Happy birthday, my dearest friend."

Everyone crowds around me to offer hugs and birthday wishes. I'm overjoyed with this fantastic group of people in my life now. They have lifted me up in ways I cannot describe and have become my light on the darkest days.

Soon, Poppy presents me with a hand-drawn picture of a little figure practicing yoga on a mat, with a dog ten times larger than the person licking their face. It's the sweetest gesture, and I'm overwhelmed by her thoughtfulness. Then, my friends surprised me with a lovely gift—a plush, new couch for my apartment. Everyone has pitched in to make this happen, and I'm just blown away. Looks like I won't be going dumpster diving with Reese for more furniture.

I'm hanging out with my friends, and I can't help but feel super grateful. This is the life I've always dreamed of – a life full of fun and adventure.

As the night goes on, the music gets softer, and the vibe of the party starts to chill. Maya's mom grabbed Poppy, and the adults huddled around a cozy fire, swapping stories and laughing together. The soft light from the lanterns, the cozy warmth of the flames, and the chitchat all came together to create the perfect, happy cocoon.

I snuggle into the couch, my heart full of warmth and contentment. Reese, Nick, Sadie, Everett, Josh, Hayley– this is my tribe. This is where I belong. I wouldn't trade this for anything in the world. We make plans for Sunday. It is a blend of things that need to be done, but it is also a chance for all of us to take a break and relax, and I hope all of my friends can get to know each other better. Hayley and Josh are already planning a delicious breakfast spread, and then Reese, Sadie, and I will catch a matinee downtown while Everett and Nick do some of the dirty work at the apartment. We're planning a picnic in the park in the late afternoon for all of us to meet up, and Josh is bringing a variety of sandwiches and snacks. I'm not sure I'm ready to revisit the park where I got caught in the sudden downpour and bloodied my knee chasing after a ghost. It's become a running joke, a glimpse of the absurd, beautiful moments that make life extraordinary. It is supposed to be great weather, and there will be more space for all of us to have fun, play some games, and unwind.

I'm already looking forward to the day. I know it will be filled with laughter, friendship, and a touch of magic.

Sunday does not disappoint. The morning goes by quickly, filled with good times and many new memories I'll remember forever. For a birthday I hoped to ignore this year, everyone has made it special for me. We have breakfast at the BNB, as Josh and Hayley still have actual guests that deserve attention. Reese and I splurge on theater popcorn, loaded with delicious oily butter and a dash of salt, while a vintage Marilyn Monroe film is playing at the downtown theater. It was one of our favorites in college, but Sadie had never seen it, so it was fun to introduce her to something from our long-term friendship and strengthen the bond between us all.

From there, we meet Everett and Nick at the apartment and review plans to finish it. They were able to prep the floors so the crew that refinishes them can get started first thing Monday. Hopefully, they will be done, and it will have a chance to seal before I return from my trip to Chicago next weekend. On the way, we pick up Poppy and take two vehicles to the park to find Josh and Hayley occupying a shelter with picnic tables. Sadie also brought some yard games like bocce ball and badminton.

Josh outdoes himself on the meal; although simple, the flavors are amazing, plus he brought cupcakes for dessert. As my friends all engage in conversation, Poppy turns cartwheels in the field, and Chance stays close by, watching for table scraps. I walk down the path and sit on the bench in the clearing where I sat just weeks before. A lot has changed since then, but it feels good to sit here and feel more focused and put together than the last time I found myself seated in this place, overcome with unrest.

The wind is calm today; the sky is clear. The grass is still green, but the air has a cooler feel. I see Everett stroll in my direction, giving me a wave and feeling out the situation to see if I want company or need a few minutes. Before our recent time spent together and all of the help he's given me, I'd probably prefer to take some time alone. But Everett has shown me he is a good friend, a willing listener, and a sturdy support system. I have also learned that even tough guy Everett needs to vent sometimes. So, I'll be here for him if he needs me too. I give him a sure smile and wave him over.

When he approaches, he has both hands in his pockets, looking almost childlike with nervousness in his expression. He leans in, his eyes searching mine. "It's really a great place, isn't it?" He scans the park and lets out a heavy sigh.

"It is. It's a good place to sit and think. And seeing our crew out here having fun today has been nice. But I have a feeling from the look on your face that you have something else on your mind. Everything okay?"

"Yeah, I guess I do. Clover, you're not going to believe this." He takes a deep breath, his voice low. "I got a voicemail on Elliot's phone."

My heart skips a beat. I'm struck with panic. What if Everett heard it? The message I left, the only one I recorded to that number, was full of raw emotion. I recall everything I said, meant only for my wingman, tears welling in my eyes as I reflect on it. Those words were meant for Elliot, no one physically able to hear them, or truthfully, just meant for me to say one last time. Just so they were spoken aloud.

Everett sees the fear on my face and gently squeezes my hand. "Don't worry," he says, a reassuring smile softening his features. "I wouldn't invade your privacy like that. I wouldn't listen to any personal messages. I saw that call on the log from your number - but just left it alone."

I let out a sigh of relief, my tense muscles relaxing. "What was it then?"

"It's from a business in Chicago. Some kind of custom order," he explains. "The message said Elliot placed an order but never picked it up. It's a pick-up notice."

My mind races, trying to recall what Elliot could have ordered. It doesn't make sense. He wouldn't have just left an order unclaimed. Unless he was scheduled to pick it up......after. He never mentioned anything to me, but it could be anything. "Did it say where?"

"They didn't give information on the order. Just the name Axel & Stone, an address, and the order number. Nothing more specific."

"Never heard of it, but I guess it could be anything. Maybe something for the shop or Elliot's boss. I'm going back to Chicago next weekend for Reese's bridal shower," I say, my voice tinged with a hint of curiosity. "Maybe I can check it out. It might be something important."

"Good idea," Everett nods. "I dug through boxes in the storage unit this week, looking for a receipt or anything to show what it was, but I came up empty-handed, with no clue in his records. It's definitely worth checking out if you have time while you're back in town."

A sense of mystery hangs in the air. After Elliot's passing, there are still pieces of him to be found, remnants of his life waiting to be discovered. And I'm determined to find them.

Everyone packs up the picnic and heads back to town.

As the day wraps up, Sadie and Poppy head out first to take

Chance home. The evening is winding down at the BNB as Reese and Nick get ready to head out. I feel a bit sad as I hug Reese goodbye, wishing they didn't have to head back to Chicago just yet.

"No worries, Clover," Reese says, squeezing my hand. "We'll see you next weekend for the bridal shower! My mom is really going all out; it's going to be wild!"

I can't help but chuckle, imagining Reese's mom going way over the top.

I'm super excited for next weekend's shower, and I can't help but feel a little thrill inside. I've got this nagging feeling about checking out Axel & Stone, the shop Everett talked about. I'm not usually into surprises, but that voicemail has me intrigued. The chance to uncover a hidden part of Elliot's life is exciting.

"Hey, Clover, we should grab lunch next week," Everett says, his voice warm and comforting. "I'd love to hear about your trip to Chicago and all the craziness of the bridal shower. Also, I can help you wrap up any little things that need to be done at the apartment. But I think most of the work should be done by then. It'll be chill. You'll have a nice place to stay when you get back."

I smile, suddenly feeling super grateful. This weekend has been a crazy ride, but it really showed me how awesome friendship is, how great it feels to share moments together, and the strong support we can offer each other, even when things get tough. I can't wait to see what next week unfolds.

CHAPTER 26

MONDAY MORNING, THE SUN spills through the window and lands right on my face. I stretch, and the familiar ache in my hips is welcome proof of the flow state I reached at the end of yesterday's yoga preparation. I'm teaching three classes this week at Josh and Hayley's place. Hayley's been texting me enthusiastically about it. I think she will embrace the tranquility that yoga can bring to her life.

I roll out of bed and grab my phone. I quickly scroll through social media and text Sadie to ask about her availability at the cafe this week. She's got a lot going on with trying to develop the pop-up coffee hour at the BNB and is working with a new tea distributor to add some new variety, so I'm happy to pick up some shifts.

SADIE & POPPY: Two days, Wednesday and Thursday. And maybe a couple more if you're up for it???

ME: No problem

I'm happy to help out, and the extra income will help me put the finishing touches on the apartment and possibly start getting some things going at Uplift.

Wednesday afternoon, I'm behind the counter at the cafe, the familiar hum of the espresso machine a comforting backdrop to the bustle around me. The cafe is surprisingly busy, even for a Wednesday. I've been trained well, though, so I'm feeling confident. I'm even managing to hold my own with the orders, and I've only made three mistakes so far. Sometimes I get a little confused, but eventually figure it out. For example, when a lady asks for her chai to be extra spicy, I just wing it and add an extra dash of cinnamon and ginger. Her first sip as she walked towards the door she threw me a big thumbs up; I must have guessed right.

Later that afternoon, the cafe's chatter is interrupted. "Hi, Pardon my manners. I haven't had my noon caffeine yet. You're…
…um….Clover, right?"

I turn to see a familiar face. "Yes, that's me." I recognize her now from my shopping day with Sadie. "You're Sydney, Sadie's friend from the shop downtown?" I ask, my smile wide. She orders a pistachio latte. I've grown to like these, too, and make extra while I prepare hers.

I hand her the latte and ask, "I haven't seen you around town much. But I guess I've been crazy busy, so we probably wouldn't have bumped into one another."

"I have been out of town. Sometimes, I have to go back and forth to our other store. I'm back for a day, but something urgent came up, and tomorrow, I must return there for a week," she replies as she grabs a seat at the table closest to the counter. "I'm hoping the traveling stuff is finished soon. I'm sort of over it."

"That sounds hectic. I get it. I travel back to my hometown quite a bit. The drive can be brutal at times." I add while working on the next man's order.

"How is your grandma? That's who you go there to see, right?"

"She's doing well," I say, my heart warming at the genuine concern in Sydney's voice. She seems like a lovely woman. "Thanks for asking." We find ourselves in conversation for a while amidst the afternoon rush. But I enjoy her stories about growing up here. After she departs, the day goes by in a blur of activity. But all with a very positive, optimistic buzz to keep me going.

The cafe is quiet after closing. I sit at one of the tables, my textbook open before me. I'm trying to cram in some studying before I check upstairs to see what progress was made. The sounds penetrating through the ceiling here today made it seem like the floor guys got a lot accomplished. I hope to move my stuff over there when I return from Chicago this weekend.

I scroll through my phone, checking my emails. The lease for the studio is almost finalized. The property manager said the owner seems excited about the idea and has been very accommodating. I'm really looking forward to getting the keys in about two weeks! Everything is happening quickly; it's a bit much to take in!

The cafe door swings open, and Sadie steps inside. Her face shows some weariness, yet she beams with a bright smile. "Hey there!" she says, her voice soft with tiredness. "How is your day going?"

"Busy," I reply, a smile creeping onto my face. "But good!"

Poppy walks in behind her. I bend down and share a high-five with her. "Hiya, Miss Poppy," I say, feeling her arms wrap around my neck.

We sit at one of the tables, exchanging stories about our day. Sadie looks relieved to have a moment to relax, while Poppy is fascinated by the sugar packets scattered across the table. I am finding solace in her innocent presence.

Later that evening, Everett comes by with a pizza. "I know you're all probably swamped," he says, handing Sadie a slice. "But I wanted to see you gals."

"We appreciate it," I say, stealing the pizza box from his hands and diving into the melty, cheesy goodness. "It's good to see you. It's even better you brought dinner." Poppy leans over me and grabs a slice for herself.

We hang out for a while, giggle, and tell stories. Everett and Sadie sit on the couch seeming very comfortable. Poppy and I hang out on the floor with a Connect Four™ game. It's a simple moment but feels exquisitely bigger to me. In this quiet moment, surrounded by the people I love, I feel a sense of calm fall over me. It's a sign to look for the quiet in all of the craziness.

Thursday morning, the smell of coffee and pancakes fills the air as Hayley and Josh usher me into their cozy kitchen. We're talking about Uplift, and the nervous energy buzzing inside me for weeks starts to settle. Hayley enthusiastically rattles off a list of local PR opportunities – a pop-up yoga class at the farmer's market, another at the local health food store, and even a free class for first responders. Her generosity and the support she and Josh offer overwhelm me. They are truly wonderful friends.

Later that afternoon, I lead the class at the BNB, a familiar routine now. The energy is high, the sun streams down on us, and for an hour, we are all lost in the flow. Afterward, I race over to the cafe, swapping places with Sadie so she can take Poppy for her physical. School's starting soon, and she needs to get the paperwork sorted out.

The evening is peaceful, which is a pleasant change after the chaos of the previous days. I spend a few hours catching up on my studies, with Chance's snoring as background noise. When Sadie returns, we sit on the patio, discussing life, love, and the uncertainties ahead. She tells me how she fell in love so young, believing it was an everlasting love, a happily ever after. But she came to see over time that it was only a stop on the road to becoming the person she is now.

Her comments ring true to something deep inside me when I consider them. Later, I fade off to sleep and find myself pulled back into the same dream, tormenting me with relentless frequency. The golden brilliance of the morning sun bathed Elliot's face. We're young and carefree, and our love is a burning fire in our hearts. We're meant to be, the dream whispers, and the feeling of his hand in mine, his eyes filled with love, is almost accurate enough to reach out and touch.

Friday morning arrives, the first rays of sunlight jarring me awake, the dream still clinging to the edges of my consciousness. I get a chill from the jolt of that familiar sensation, the tug of the past. A recollection of how specific memories continue to have an odd hold on me even as I move on. Today, I need to try to live in the present. Today, I need to focus on the future, on Uplift, on my path, a path that may still be tangled with threads of the past, but a path that I'm determined to walk with my head held high.

The sun is warm on my face as I walk down Main Street. My mission: find the perfect dress for Reese's bridal shower. I browse the boutiques, my heart beating with a mix of excitement and anticipation. The air is alive with the sounds of laughter, the clinking of glasses at the diner, and the happy chatter of townsfolk. A familiar warmth spreads through my chest, a sense of belonging growing stronger with each passing day.

Then, I see it. Hanging in a charming little shop window, a dress pops in the afternoon light. It's a flowy floral print with a tight waist and a skirt that falls softly around my knees. The color is a vivid coral that will stand out against my skin. I knew immediately that it was the one.

As I pass the diner, I gesture to the owner, Chuck, who smiles and nods. Across the street, the Reflecting Stone Jewelry display window sparkles with diamonds and jewels. Sydney is inside, working with a customer. Once I grab her attention, she throws me a big smile, her face lighting up with recognition. I wave, experiencing a burst of warmth from the relationships I am building.

My walk concludes with a bittersweet feel. Elliot and I had planned to visit this town, but we never got the chance. The plans altered in the blink of an eye, and now I'm strolling these streets alone. But as I reflect on the route that led me here, I recognize Elliot steered me in an unusual way. When I left Chicago, I expected a visit to this little town to haunt me with the dreams torn from our grasp, a magnifying glass held to what could have been. It's strange how life works. Instead, it has delivered an unusual sense of calm. Maybe it's the serene beauty here, the welcoming people, or the leisurely pace. Perhaps it's an opportunity to escape the hectic pace of city life and rediscover who I am. Whatever it is, I haven't felt this peaceful since..... well, before everything changed.

I calmly realize that the road we were on and our imagined future was different. And will never mean I'm ignoring the hurt or betraying our relationship. More like it's a release. The realization that certain roads take unexpected turns and that it challenges us to welcome the changes and find comfort in the unknown. Realizing this means letting go of the familiar, which can be both terrifying and liberating. Reese pushed me to be brave on this trip and her constant support helped me regain my footing and rediscover who I was.

Returning to my apartment, I pack a weekend bag; my emotions vary bittersweetly. I am thankful when I contact Aunt Ruby and then speak with my grandmother, whose dementia is relatively subdued today. She is having a clear day; her voice is strong and full of laughter as we remember past summers and life's little pleasures. "Ah, Clover," my grandmother's voice is soft, a whisper of the wind. " You've got your mother's spirit, you know, that same fire that burned bright even in the face of hardship. She wouldn't be surprised, my brave girl, to see you standing tall, your heart filled with strength as enduring as the ancient stone walls of our Irish heritage. You're a warrior, Clover, just like the women who came before you, facing down every storm, every challenge, with a spirit as strong as the emerald hills of Erin." She shares more stories of our family and then tires out, so we have to end the call.

I'm grateful for this time with her, this unexpected gift of clarity, knowing it's a precious moment, a fleeting glimpse into a past she may soon forget. I will return to Chicago tomorrow with the comforting memories of this community, my grandmother's wisdom, a feeling of belonging, and the optimism of a fresh start.

CHAPTER 27

THE DRIVE BACK TO Chicago is full of unnecessary honking, never-ending orange barrels of construction, and a whole lot of road rage. It's crazy. The drivers here think they're in a demolition derby. There's this one guy in a beat-up truck with a bumper sticker that says, "I brake for squirrels," who practically sideswipes me on the interstate. I swear, the poor squirrel would've had a better chance if I'd hit him. But that's Chicago for you.

At least Reese's bridal shower is a welcome change of pace. Her mom has gone all out, transforming the venue into a paradise of nude pink, pampas grass, and cream roses. The tables are draped with shimmering pearl chiffon runners, and the air is filled with the scent of fresh flowers. Reese looks absolutely radiant, though I suspect her mom has had a hand in her outfit choice. It's a beautiful dress with too many ruffles and lace for Reese's usual vibe. But she has her own little rebellion: a new delicate tattoo of a horseshoe peeking out from under the shoulder strap of her dress.

The shower is an elegant affair, a champagne-soaked celebration of Reese's love story. It's lovely to see her mom looking genuinely happy and relaxed. She keeps sharing these little, knowing smiles with Reese, and it seems like they're really enjoying themselves, which is quite a sight to see.

The best part is when Nick arrives and crashes the party. He shows up late, and Reese nearly leaps into his arms. It's one of those moments, you know? You just feel so happy for them. They deserve all the good things life has to offer.

I offer to help with the cleanup, but Reese's mom waves me off with a dismissive smile: "No need to worry, everything 's all good." She's got this calm confidence, and her efficiency is almost ethereal. I don't want to step on her toes, so I let her take care of things while I enjoy watching the last details of the party being cleared away.

Nick and Reese grab my attention, "Hey, Clover, why don't you come have dinner with us?" Nick says. "We're off to our favorite Thai spot!" Reese adds, "We want to celebrate with you while you're back in town." I can't resist their enthusiasm, and soon, we're piled into Nick's car, heading off to a night of delicious food and even better company.

We discuss their wedding plans over steaming bowls of pad thai and spicy green curry. It's a whirlwind of excitement and logistical nightmares. Nick confides in me about the surprise honeymoon he's planning for Reese: a week in the Greek Isles. He's got this mischievous glint in his eyes, and I can tell it will be something special.

Back in Chicago, the familiar cityscape feels strangely foreign. It's sensory overload, the air thick with the smell of exhaust fumes and the city lights washing out the stars. I'm trying to adjust but feel a new energy pulling me. It's about that custom order I have to inquire about, the one Elliot placed months ago at Axel & Stone. I googled it. Luxury jewelry store. That's a lot of money. What did he buy? Why didn't I know about it?

The thought of it is more exciting than daunting. Who knew he'd have more surprises in store for me. It feels like a little piece of him, patiently waiting to be discovered. But what could it possibly be?

An idea flashes in my mind, and I impulsively ask Nick and Reese, "Did Elliot order something for your wedding from Axel & Stone?" Their faces are blank, their expressions puzzled.

"No, why would you think that?" Nick asks, his brow furrowed. I try to explain, but my words are jumbled. I update them on the voicemail Everett found on Elliot's phone. I thought maybe he was doing Nick a favor.

"It's just… the timing is off. He couldn't have ordered anything before you got engaged. Unless it was your engagement ring. But I know Nick did all that on his own. He… He ordered it before you got engaged. That didn't happen until after the accident." The room falls silent, the silence punctuated by the clatter of dishes. The truth hangs heavy in the air, a weight I hadn't anticipated.

But then, I smile. It's a mystery, a puzzle waiting to be solved. It feels like a small anchor to Elliot, some tangible evidence of my wingman that still links us. This town is now leading me down a path that's both exciting and intriguing, a path that might just lead me to a treasure I didn't even know existed.

Nick and Reese's condo is a haven of warm memories and familiarity for me. We sprawl out on the plush sofas, sipping cocktails and reminiscing about the good old days. It's so nice to share laughs and jokes with people who enjoy those shared memories and the warmth of real connections.

So, we start chatting about ideas for the yoga studio, and I'm honestly surprised at how fast everything seems to fall into place. Reese and Nick are helping to brainstorm ideas, devise marketing strategies, and envision a space that feels inviting and inspiring. It's super exciting and a bit scary, but I can feel that spark returning; my passion for this dream is alive again.

We chat about the wedding and my possible return to school. She can see that I'm on the cusp of something big; I give off a vibe of endless possibilities. Her enthusiasm just makes me smile. Her optimism about the future is so infectious that it just spreads to everyone around her.

Eventually, though, exhaustion settles in. We bid each other goodnight, and I crawl into the guest room, the silence of the condo a stark contrast to the lively chatter of just moments ago. I lie awake, the echoes of laughter and shared dreams still ringing in my ears. But then, a different melody begins to play in my mind, a soft, familiar tune. I can make out the gentle strumming of a guitar. It's

Elliot, his soft voice carrying the melody of our song, resonating through the corridors of our memories, proving that love remains nestled in the depths of my heart.

I close my eyes, feeling our bond slowly retreating into the stillness of the night. The future unfolds before me, a blank canvas filled with endless possibilities, evoking a mix of excitement and apprehension as I prepare to embark on this journey. Yet, I feel in my heart that the journey I'm on, the life I'm creating, truly belongs to me. It's like a galaxy emerging with explosions of affection, heartache, and resilience, a universe that continues to unfold yet is beginning to radiate beauty and hope.

As we rise on Sunday morning, I watch Reese preparing for her yoga class. Over the years, her classes have brought me confidence and energy, a gentle cue that even when life presents its challenges, there is always a path to discover balance and inner strength. Today, I found myself in need of that gentle nudge, so I chose to accompany her.

The studio is alive with the familiar scent of sandalwood and the gentle hum of soft music. As Reese leads us through the poses, I feel my mind clearing, the stress of the past week dissolving like mist in the morning sun. I hope our new studio will create that space for others, offer a haven of peace and renewal, and help them find the strength they need to face whatever life throws their way.

After class, we walk through our old neighborhood, the streets filled with memories. We reminisce about late-night talks, secret crushes on professors, and the dreams we held close to our hearts. It's a bittersweet stroll, mementos of lives we've lived and the paths we've taken.

Reese leads the way to an area of the city I haven't been to in a long time. I never had reason to venture into the Gold Coast very often. As we walk past the jewelry store, Reese points it out. "I thought you'd want to check it out, Clover. So when you go inside tomorrow, you'll be less nervous. I know how you get your knickers in a twist. And I'll be here for you if you need me. Stay as long as you want. I'm sure whatever this is will stir up quite a bit of emotion." She giggles to lighten the mood, but I know there is so much truth to what she's said.

"I'm staying the extra day," I say, "Just for the jewelry store. But then I need to get back home."

Reese's face breaks into a warm smile. "It sounds funny hearing you call another place home. But I'm super stoked for you. This new start is going to be amazing. Speaking of home, you planning any trips to Savannah soon?"

The thought of a trip to Savannah, of seeing Grandma and Ruby, fills me with a sense of ease. "You know, I should return to Savannah soon to see my grandmother and Ruby. I shouldn't wait too long. Why don't you tag along? Maybe after you shed the cocoon of newlywed bliss and join real life with the rest of us."

"I'll go with you, but I'm keeping the cocoon. I like it in here. It's warm and cozy. Filled with love and kisses and soooo many illicit pleasures," Reese adds with a garish laugh.

"Sounds like a plan. I'll let you know when I can find a break for a few days and go." With that, we continue our walk back to the condo. But as I look back, the flashy sparkle from the sign hanging outside the jewelry store sends a bolt of emotion to the center of my soul. I am not sure what tomorrow may bring, but I have a feeling there is no amount of yoga or pep talks from Reese that will help me. I will put on my big girl pants and confront it alone. Well, maybe not entirely alone. I know in some dimension, Elliot will be by my side to give me strength.

The afternoon fades, and we find ourselves back at Reese and Nick's place. The kitchen smells of the roasting prime rib. The day was a perfect blend of solo girl time with Reese and the warmth of another evening with the couple. I find a quiet reassurance that even amid uncertainty, life offers unexpected gifts, moments of promise, and a chance to find solace in the company of those we love.

CHAPTER 28

THE GLOW OF MORNING filters through the blinds, painting stripes across the guest bedroom floor. My stomach is already in knots. Today is the day. The day I confront the mystery of Elliot's custom order at Axel & Stone. What could it be? A watch? A cufflink set? A diamond ring? In a way, I don't think what it is really matters; it's only the fact Elliot picked it out. I only hope I can get that information.

It's not like I have any legal rights to his belongings. We weren't married or engaged, so they have no legal obligation to tell me anything. But still, I pray they'll take pity on me when I explain what happened. I am not sure I could walk away if I don't find out what this is all about.

I pull on my most comfortable outfit, the softest cashmere sweater Reese gifted me years ago in a camel color, my well-worn jeans that feel like home, and a pair of sneakers for all the walking ahead. It's a simple outfit, but it's imbued with the warmth of shared memories and the confidence I need to face whatever awaits me.

Today, though, it's about Elliot. It's about taking a glimpse into the past, discovering a piece of him I never knew existed, and maybe, just maybe, understanding him a little better and capturing a piece I can take with me through my life.

The polished glass of the Axel & Stone storefront gleams in the morning sun, reflecting the bustling city life outside. I stand here, staring at the heavy oak door, my heart beating rapidly in my chest. My palms are growing sweaty, and cold chills erupt on my skin.

For minutes, I seem caught between the anxiety of the unknown and a strange, magnetic pull that draws me towards that door.

It's a feeling I can't quite explain. Some part of his essence is here, whispering to me, drawing me inside. Maybe it's a foolish hope to reconnect to him somehow, but I can't shake the feeling that this jewelry store holds a piece of him, a piece of our shared past.

With a deep breath, I try to calm my frantic breathing. I inhale slowly, filling my lungs with the crisp air, and then exhale, letting go of the tension gripping my shoulders. One foot goes in front of the other, and then another, and suddenly, I'm moving, my feet carrying me toward the door.

With a heavy push, the door pries open, and cool air glides over me. I step inside with anticipation. I'm surrounded by a world of sparkling gems and shiny metals, a grand display of elegance. The store is massive, much bigger than it appeared from the outside. The whispers of the staff and the soft piano playing through the speakers create an inviting atmosphere. I'm ready to face the mystery that awaits me and maybe, just maybe, find a piece of Elliot that I never knew existed. To many, I'm sure it would appear I'm getting too emotional, overreacting to simply picking up a purchase he made. But to me, it is everything. This is big.

Losing someone is like having a book slammed shut before you reach the end. It's a conclusion that makes you desperate to turn the page and reveal what lies ahead. It's not merely their absence but the fading of the chance for new memories to be created. Every day that goes by without them feels like a cherished moment lost, a chance to discover something beautiful about them slipping through your fingers, a page torn out and destroyed.

Yet, in the grief, there's a faint glimmer of hope. Something emerges, an overlooked memory that reveals a deeper side of the one you held dear. A fresh perspective. And in that moment, the book gently unfolds, showcasing a new page.

It cannot fill the void left behind or heal the remaining pain.

But it presents an opportunity to lighten the burden of sorrow. That testimony that love doesn't disappear with death but remains in our memories.

And at those times, a new strength shows up—a strength born of resiliency, a strength that says, "I will remember you, I will cherish you, I will carry your spirit with me, always." In time, it will become stronger than the loss.

Inside Axel & Stone, the air is infused with an energy of luxury. Driven by that spirit, I drift and stare at the gorgeous details of every piece. The store encompasses workmanship and functions as a gallery of outstanding artistry. Emeralds glitter like the green flecks in Elliot's eyes; diamonds flash like galaxies, rubies like coals of fire. Every item promises to share a story.

For a while, I lose myself in the beauty. But the nagging question, the mystery of Elliot's order, draws me back to reality. I approach the counter, a cool, polished dark marble. I wait, my heart thumping out of control, hoping for a sign, a nudge, a confirmation that I'm on the right path.

A familiar face emerges from around the corner. It's Sydney, the woman I chatted with just days ago at the cafe. The Sydney who works at a jewelry store in Franklin, who had to travel for work this week, who somehow found her way to Axel & Stone.

Surprise washes over me, but it's quickly replaced by a surge of relief. Maybe this is a sign; perhaps this is the boost I need. Maybe Sydney, with her working relationship with the team here and having already met me, can help me navigate this unexpected path. I hope so. I pray so. As she approaches, a bright smile lighting up her face, I find myself filled with a sense of hope that, in the process, I might just find something unexpected, something beautiful.

"Sydney? Oh my goodness, it is great to see a familiar face," I say with surprise.

"Clover! What are you doing here?" she replies, her eyes widening at the realization that I'm standing here. "Chicago is the last place I expected to see you."

We both laugh, the absurdity of the situation sinking in. My mind plays a quick recap of our recent encounters, the intro from Sadie, the cafe, the walk down Main Street, and the serendipitous twist of fate that has me here in this unexpected setting. I pull out the scrap of paper with the order number Everett gave me, the one he said was the key to finally unraveling this mystery.

"I never realized you were talking about Chicago for your work travels. Small world, I guess. This is where I lived before abruptly picking up my life and relocating to Franklin. I just needed a fresh start. Which, oddly enough, has brought me here."

She looks at me and smiles. "Definitely a small world. But it is good to see you. What can I help you with today? I assume you came here with something in mind, not just to visit with me," she kindly redirects the conversation back to the task at hand.

I can only imagine what is running through her mind. When I met her at the Franklin store, she knew I couldn't afford even the smallest item. And here I am in the flagship store surrounded by luxury, clearly out of my league. As I peer around, I recognize that everyone here is dressed to the nines. And I stand in my jeans and sneakers, hair pulled up messily on my head into a bun, with ringlets already making their escape. My confidence begins to waver, but I tell myself to keep going. Sydney is a lovely woman; I'm sure she's understanding.

So I continue, "Well, it's a bit of a story. You see, my friend passed away a couple months ago, Elliot. He was my best friend, my roommate. My everything, really. And then suddenly, he was gone, complications after an accident." I pause to pull back the tears forming in my eyes. I don't know why, but I am okay with discussing him with friends and family. However, I get rattled when I tell the story to strangers who don't know him.

"I'm sorry, Clover. That must be so difficult," she says, looking like she may also shed a tear.

"Well, his brother Everett received a voicemail from your store on Elliot's phone. Thankfully, he kept it active all this time," I explain, my voice dropping to a whisper. "The message was about a custom jewelry order he placed here but never picked it up. I'm trying to find out what it is, what I need to do to settle a bill, or if we can even take whatever it is."

Sydney nods, her eyes filled with concern. "I understand," she says softly. "I cannot imagine how hard it must be to come here. You are very brave, Clover." She disappears behind the counter, returning a moment later with an old notebook. She flips through the pages, her brow furrowed in concentration. "So, let's see what I can find out for you. Give me a moment," she says, "I'll check the custom order log."

I wait with a nervous burning in my stomach. I can't believe this is happening. In the next moment, I may reconnect with Elliot in some way.

Sydney steps around the corner and returns moments later, her expression thoughtful. She holds papers and a sleek, dark green velvet box. It's a beautiful box, the deep green almost black. It's larger than a ring box, too large for earrings. Maybe it's a pendant, a necklace. The possibilities dance in my mind.

My heart races with anticipation, a mix of excitement and apprehension swirling within me. I try to calm my nerves, taking a deep breath, but the feeling is almost unbearable. The box, nestled in Sydney's hand, looks heavy with unspoken promises and untold stories.

As Sydney sets the box on the counter, my eyes meet hers. In that shared look, I see a flicker of understanding, and charged emotions. It's a silent acknowledgment of the power of the enduring nature of memories, of the healing that can emerge from the depths of loss. And in that moment, I know that the box before me, with its mystery, holds more than just a piece of jewelry. It's a window into Elliot's heart, a piece of his soul, an indication that joy can find its way back to you in ways you may never imagine.

Sydney runs her finger over the date on the order. "This was placed almost six months ago," she says in a hushed voice. "It seems he was pretty determined to have it ready by a specific date." She points down to the requested completion date. Even upside down, I can read that line.

"My birthday, the first of September." I barely get the words out. She nods in understanding.

She glances at the note again, her lips curving into a gentle smile. "I can see why he wanted it done by then," she says, her voice laced with a hint of tenderness.

"This note...it's beautiful." It's the custom order form Elliot filled out. I can see the scratchiness of the lettering and the angle of the pen strokes. Even the heavy dotted I's, the ink blotted in those specks. It is Elliot's handwriting, without a doubt. I want to reach out and just touch the paper, but I wait patiently as Sydney continues. Her voice fills with warmth and emotion as she reads the note aloud. "Please create a custom piece inspired by the Louis collection but with a personal touch. I would like a white gold cuff bracelet crafted with two feathers wrapping around the wrist. They should be delicate and feminine, overlapping gracefully at the top. Engraving on the back should read: 'Happy bday Angel. Always, your Wingman.' This piece is for the most special someone you'll ever know. A loyal friend, a true gem. Please make it beautiful, deserving to be worn upon her wrist."

I'm fighting back tears, a chuckle escaping my lips, as I hear his words, tenderness, throughout the room. "The store was in touch with him a few times," Sydney continues. "The notes on the order form show we spoke to him once to confirm the size, then again with the designer to discuss the finer details." She pauses, her gaze drifting to the box, a gentle smile gracing her lips. "Each call has a note to ensure it was done by the requested date, to make sure you got it on time."

The weight of his gesture and the thoughtfulness he poured into this piece surround me. It's a testament to the kind of man he was, to the depth of his love, to the connection he shared with me, a magnetism that still resonates. I can almost see him, his beaming smile, his voice filled with a warmth that made my heart soar.

The box holds so much more than just a piece of jewelry. It's a treasure, a legacy of beauty and grace that transcends time and loss.

Sydney slides the box closer to me. She gestures for me to open it, her smile encouraging me. I hesitate, my fingers trembling as I grasp the lid. The hinge is stiff from disuse, and it takes a delicate pull to get it to budge. A sliver of light spills through the opening, catching a glint of sparkle, almost blinding my eyes.

Then, the box is fully open.

My breath catches in my throat. The sight before me is breathtaking. A white gold bracelet, crafted with two delicate feathers, wraps around the velvet cushion. The feathers are exquisitely crafted, with intricate details that capture the grace of an angel in flight. The metal gleams with a cool, ethereal light, reflecting the soft glow of the store's chandeliers.

It's absolutely gorgeous, a masterpiece of craftsmanship. I'm speechless, overwhelmed by the beauty and the sentiment. My heart aches, a heavy weight settling in my chest. Elliot would have loved to see this, the sparkle in my eyes, and the surprise on my face as I unwrapped it on my birthday, as he intended. He would have loved to see it on my wrist, to know that he had created something so beautiful, personal, deeply meaningful, and special to me.

"Go ahead, Clover," Sydney urges gently, her voice pacifies the storm of emotions swirling within me. "Take it out."

I hesitantly reach out, my fingers brushing against the velvet. I gingerly take it out, and it's even more breathtaking up close. I flip it over, my fingers tracing the delicate engraving, "Happy bday Angel, Always, your wingman" is etched with exquisite precision.

I'm crushed by an assembly of grief, love, and longing—all intertwined. I slide the bracelet onto my wrist, and it feels perfect as if it was always meant to be there. It's a hug of love, connecting me to him.

The bracelet is breathtaking. I'm almost speechless, lost in the intricate beauty of the design. It's a magnificent piece of art, a masterpiece sculpted in metal, exhibiting the power of creativity. I twist it gently on my wrist, feeling the coolness of the white gold against my skin, the weight of its delicate beauty, the perfect balance of the feathers. It's flawless, truly flawless.

"It's stunning," I manage to whisper, my voice barely a breath. It's the only word that comes close to expressing the awe that fills me.

Sydney, sensing my speechless wonder, smiles understandingly. "It's marked order complete, paid in full," she says, her voice soft, her gaze lingering on the piece. "It's yours, Clover."

My eyes widen in surprise. She doesn't ask for proof, no photo ID, no questions about my relationship to Elliot. She simply trusts. I feel a deep sense of appreciation for her compassion and kindness.

"Thank you," I whisper, my heart overflowing with a mix of emotions. "Thank you so much." Now I'm almost shaking. My hands show subtle signs of tremor, evidence that I'm barely hanging on here.

"Hang on a minute," Sydney says, her eyes sparkling. "I'll get the paperwork sorted; let them know it's been picked up. And you're in luck," she adds with a knowing smile. "The designer, the master goldsmith who crafted this piece, is here today. Let me go get him. He gets very attached to his work, especially pieces like this. I'm sure he'd love to see it on your wrist, where it's so perfectly meant to be."

The possibility of meeting the artist behind this masterpiece sends a jolt of excitement through me. It's like another layer is peeled back, another puzzle piece falling into place. Even though Elliot is gone, his legacy lives on in the bonds he forged. And I, standing here, in the heart of this jewelry store, am about to be a part of that legacy. The possibilities, the emotions, and the whispers of the past all come together and hit me with immense force.

Time seems to slow down as I stand there, holding the bracelet, drowned with its significance. It was more than just a birthday present; it was a lifeline, a symbol of his devotion, a way to let

262

me know that even when he was gone, he'd still be my wingman, always by my side. I realize now that he knew I would need this security, this link to his presence.

Emotions well up within me, a mixture of joy, grief, and a longing that feels almost unbearable. I hear voices approaching. Sydney's voice is clear and warm, followed by another, deeper, more resonant voice. As Sydney rounds the corner first, I try to collect myself. I don't want to appear like a crazy, emotional, babbling idiot.

"Clover, this is Axel," Sydney says, her voice filled with a warmth that helps calm my anxiety. "He's my boss, our designer, and head goldsmith. I'm so glad to be able to introduce you." Before she makes her final steps toward me and clears the visible path to the man turning the corner behind her, I smell a woodsy, citrusy scent, like a blend of pine and bergamot, in the air. Memories flash in my mind at the familiar scent. The sidewalk outside the Franklin store. The church. The park. The bar.

And then, standing before me, separated only by the counter, is Elliot—or at least, a man who looks exactly like him, with the same captivating blue-green eyes, the same sun-kissed skin, and the same disarming smile that could melt a glacier. He smiles at me, his dazzling expression sending me a jolt of shock.

In that moment, my world shifts on its axis. I'm frozen, my mind struggling to make sense of this unexpected turn of events. The bracelet heavy on my wrist sends a visceral reaction to the impossible situation unfolding before me. I can't breathe, can't speak, and can't even process the sight before me.

And then, as if propelled by instinct, I grab the papers and the box and cling tightly to the bracelet on my wrist. With a sudden burst of energy, I spin, and without a word, I run. I run through the store, my feet heavy under me. I push open the door and run into the city air, my heart pounding, my mind reeling, the image of that smile etched into my memory. It's the beginning of a new chapter filled with questions and mysteries, a possibility that whispers of a truth I never dared to imagine.

CHAPTER 29

As I STUMBLE OUT of the jewelry store, my brain feels like it is in a fog, confusion swirled with grief. I caught a glimpse of the man—the spitting image of Elliot—who had stepped around the corner to the counter. My heart raced so fast that I could barely hear my own thoughts over the echo of his name in my mind.

I turn, desperate to escape what feels like a cruel twist of fate. The sidewalk seems to vibrate beneath my feet as I try to gather my thoughts. But before I can vanish into the crowded street, I feel him close behind me.

"Hey, are you okay?"

Taking a deep breath, I turn to him, the swirling emotions crashing over me like waves. I squeeze my eyes shut as hard as I can, thinking it will change what I see when I open them again. It doesn't. Tears well in my eyes, and I lose the battle as one slips down my cheek. Today was not supposed to be like this. *Oh my God. Oh my God.* "You look just like him," I whisper.

Axel furrows his brow, confusion flashing across his face. "Just like who?"

I'm standing stiff as a board, unable to move, think, or comprehend anything. Have I died, am I standing in front of Elliot himself? Is he reincarnated? I cannot fathom what on earth is happening. I realize I'm staring at him, or through him, or something. But I'm still just frozen here, and he, whoever he is, is staring back.

"Really, are you alright? You look like you've seen a ghost," he asks in a soft voice.

His voice is warm and unfamiliar, laced with concern. As I take a step back towards him, his eyes reflect a mix of empathy and curiosity. Those eyes—so familiar yet distinctly different—pull me in like a gravitational force I cannot resist, and I freeze for just another moment.

"I... I think I *am* seeing a ghost." I force a laugh, but the sound is brittle, much like this facade I am attempting to maintain. He tilts his head, a bewildered expression dancing on his lips.

"You look like my best friend Elliot. I mean exactly like him. Fuck. -er sorry. This is just so unbelievably overwhelming right now." I lean over, putting my hands on my knees, trying desperately to get some air and not pass out with this new revelation. As I stand back up, he moves a few steps closer to me, worry in his expression. A sense of protectiveness in his motions, something reassuring about it.

"It's okay, really. Calm down. You seem so spooked. You need to breathe. Slowly. In and out." His arm reaches out, his hand closes the final distance between us. As it envelopes softly around my wrist, around the bracelet he so beautifully created, I feel a complete sense of calm. His thumb slowly brushes back and forth against my open palm. "There you go, just breathe. That's it."

A small smile breaks through my haze as I feel this new draw to him. There is something inherently familiar about his voice, a comfort against the fresh wound of loss that has my gut in knots.

"More like haunted. You just... you look so much like my friend."

His brows furrow slightly, and I can see the wheels turning in his head—trying to absorb what I had said. I peer into his eyes as he searches my face for understanding.

"He... he passed away a couple months ago. Elliot......he's the one who ordered this bracelet you made me, before he died. It was to be a gift for me. I keep seeing someone who looks just like you—Jesus, this is just so crazy." I still cannot get my mind wrapped around all of it. My breathing has slowed, but I'm still teetering on the edge of a manic setback here.

"I'm sorry for your loss. If it helps, I'm not a ghost, I promise." He runs a hand through his hair, as he tries to lighten the mood. Yet, that simple admission felt like a gift—an invitation to share my burden rather than carry it alone, to try and unearth what all of this means.

Axel's expression shifts as he looks at the bracelet again, understanding dawning. "That's beautiful and tragic, all at once. I really am sorry for your loss."

In that moment, I feel the weight of my grief shift, a tiny release of hope breaking through. "You have no idea how much he meant to me. I thought I could sense him everywhere, in all kinds of places, old and new." I'm not sure why I start blurting all of this out to him, this stranger. Somehow my mouth decided on its own to spew out whatever my heart was feeling.

"Maybe that's his way of letting you know that you're not alone," Axel says so calmly. I mean why shouldn't he be calm. He has no idea what is going on here. I'm just some batshit crazy woman who picked up a piece of jewelry in his store.

"I'm not him. And I'm not a ghost. But I'm here though, if you need to talk."

With his words, and the touch of his hand still resting on my mine, I feel the fissures in my heart mend just a little. I recall every laugh, every tear, every moment spent with Elliot, and suddenly it doesn't seem so painful.

"Maybe we can talk," I whisper, letting the bracelet glint in the sunlight—a little relic of hope.

"Yeah, sure. Let me just run in and tell Syndey I'm going to be out for the day, alright? Are you okay here, or do you want to walk inside with me?" A brow lifts upward in question, a gesture so amazingly like Elliot's I still can't fathom the similarity.

"I'm okay. I'll wait here." I'm anything but okay. But I want to avoid the embarrassment I would find back in the store. A few minutes go by, and to pass the time I place the papers and velvet

267

box into my purse. I see a text waiting to be read on my phone.

EVERETT: Let me know how the day goes. Curious to hear what he bought me. LOL

Oh, Everett, if you only knew how the day is going. How will I ever explain this? My Lord, I cannot untangle it in my own mind. What should I say, "Hey Ev, things are good. He bought me a beautiful bracelet. BTW – the jeweler is your brother's mirror image. No biggie." I almost laugh at the thought of it, the absurdity. I put my phone back as Axel walks back out. "All good in there?"

He smiles at me, dimples light up his kind face. "Yeah, everything is fine. Sorry it took me a minute. Sydney is concerned about you and told me to be very nice to you or she'll kick my ass. So that's that. Anyway, where we headed?" I'm thankful he is so sweet, he is very patient, even though I'm certain he has his own curiosity running wild now too.

I can feel Axel's gaze on me, a curiosity that lingers even as I navigate through the people on the sidewalk. I'm sure he's wondering about my abrupt exit, my explosion of emotions. I can almost feel the questions hanging in the air, a silent query about the reason for my sudden flight.

But Axel is unwearied, a quiet strength emanating from him. He doesn't press, doesn't push, simply waits for me to find my footing, to regain my composure.

"I'm a little overwhelmed," I confess, my voice barely a whisper. "This is a lot to take in."

Axel nods understandingly. "I can see that," he says, his words a comforting contrast to the frantic beat of my heart.

"Would you….would you want to grab a coffee somewhere? I could use the distraction." I ask, needing a moment to gather my thoughts, to regain some semblance of control.

He nods. "I'd love that."

Axel points towards a quaint corner cafe, its windows filled with warm light, the aroma of coffee and pastries wafting out to greet us. "That's a good one," he says, his eyes meeting mine, his expression a blend of concern and something else, a glimmer of something deeper, something that sparks in my chest.

We walk, shoulder to shoulder, almost touching, the space between us charged with an unspoken energy. He wants to reach out, I know he does. I can sense it in the way he positions himself, the way his shoulder brushed against mine, the way his gaze stalls on my face, searching for a sign, a response. I almost wish he would be daring enough to hold my hand, to offer that comfort again, that show of concern that I crave so desperately right now.

But he doesn't. He simply stays close, his presence a sort of serenity in the midst of the city's bustle. I inhale, catching a whiff of his cologne, that unique blend of woodsy citrus, laced with his own personal scent. I have to admit, ever since I smelled it back in Franklin, I've been sampling scents in every department store I could find. Nothing compares. It's so unique, so distinctly him.

We enter the cafe, the air filled with the calming aroma of coffee. The chatter of patrons mingles with the clink of cups, creating a familiar background noise. We find a quiet table by the window, and settle in, waiting for a server to take our order. The moment stretches out before us, simmering with a trace of hope for this conversation, of understanding, of optimism I never thought possible.

I stare at him for moments, unable to collect my thoughts enough to speak. I look over his features, mesmerized by the resemblance to Elliot. By the look on his face he is curious what is going on in my mind now, but he lets me take this time for myself. Eventually I get the nerve to begin. "So, yeah, this is weird, isn't it? You must think I'm a lunatic." I say not in question, but as a matter of fact.

He slides his hand over the table, and brushes it over mine. "No, not a lunatic. I don't think that at all. But I would like to officially introduce myself. I'm Axel." He raises his hand to formally shake mine, and then holds them there, keeping them linked until they rest still connected between our coffee mugs.

"Hiya. I'm Clover. I guess Syndey explained that before I rudely darted away from you." I have to chuckle. I'm not sure what else to do in a moment like this. As I place my elbows on the table, I run my hands up and down my face with embarrassment and sigh. "Oh my God, get it together Clover," I say to myself, hopefully he didn't hear.

"Yeah, I got that much. And then after you ran, you said I look like your friend, Elliot. Wanna talk about that?" He presents an offer for me to truly open up. I'm not sure how much to share, but I feel drawn to him. To be as honest as possible. In return for his kindness, I owe him that.

His response was a fusion of confusion and intrigue; I could see it flicker across his face, and I couldn't help but feel a strange fire ignite within me. Yet, it seems undeniable, he is my flickering candle in the dark, sparking both despair and joy.

As we shift from small talk to the heavy truths of our lives, my words spill over like the coffee, steaming with remembrance and loss. I am tense with nerves. I feel exposed, but Axel makes me feel ready to share my truth.

"Elliot was everything to me," I begin, the weight of my words heavy with sorrow. "He was my anchor. My compass. We spent many great years together, through college and after, we crafted dreams, spun stories of our future – traveling, med school, pastry shops, families. He had a light that could pierce through the darkest days."

My voice trembles as I continue, memories surfacing like delicate bubbles. "He was my best friend, my partner in crime. But losing him felt like losing a part of my very essence. I've spent so much time treading water, wading through the grief, struggling to breathe."

Axel's gaze remained locked on mine, absorbing my sorrow as if trying to carry even a fraction of it for me. "I can't imagine how hard that must have been," he says softly.

"It was suffocating," I confess, tears pricking at my eyes again.

"The laughter faded—everything felt muted and gray. Every corner of my life felt empty without him. And the dreams we spun together… they felt like ghosts haunting me. I often questioned if I'd ever find joy again, if I could even chase those dreams solo."

As the words spilled from my heart, I could feel Elliot's presence playing in my mind—a guardian angel whispering encouragement. I took a shaky breath, willing myself to share the next part. "But my friend Reese convinced me to take this trip that Elliot and I had planned. She thought it would be good for me. What I've found, is sort of a new start. A chance to begin again. Not running away, but being strong enough to move forward, if that makes any sense. I think it helped me begin to understand that grief isn't about forgetting, but about remembering and honoring those we've lost."

Axel sits across from me, just absorbing every word I bleed out. "And this trip, it surprised you? How it morphed into this new beginning?"

"Yeah, I found a serenity there, in Franklin. The people are so sweet and caring. The place is enchanting. I've decided to move there. It helps to be closer to my family too. It just feels right. I felt drawn to Franklin, like it was his way of guiding me back to living again, like some magical bridge."

"I believe that," Axel replies, his voice thick with emotion. "You could almost say it's like he brought us together now."

Faith stirs within me, and I sense the warmth of Elliot's spirit surrounding us, helping me navigate through this raw and tender moment. My eyes meet Axel's, a curious dance of confusion and recognition, like two pieces of a puzzle that had never quite fit until now.

After doling out my struggles—losing Elliot and the rain cloud of grief that had shadowed every step of my journey, I feel the need to lighten the mood. There is much more I need to figure out, but right now I should offer him a break from the heavy. "You know," I say, "my friend Reese insists I'm a walking sob story, wearing 'Please Help Me' shoes. I guess picking up the pieces isn't as trendy as it sounds."

"All I see are your cute sneakers. I think you're doing fine, Clover" He laughs, taking hold of the switch in energy.

"So you met this handsome man, Elliot, here in Chicago?" A big grin stretches across his beautiful face.

"You think you're cute, huh?" I joke back. "Yes, I met the devilishly handsome man here." I was amazed at how quickly we hit it off.

"I see. And you say I look just like him?" his head tilts at an angle, and his grin deepens showing an emerging dimple. How cute.

"I think so, let me look." I take my hand, placing my index finger on his chin and turn his head from side to side, jokingly at first, until I notice something. Under his right ear, I recognize his birthmark. Identical to Elliot's. Astonished, I quietly gasp and withdraw my hand.

"Scary huh?" He thinks I'm just kidding with him. Like I found him uneasy on the eyes. But when I don't reply with any witty comment, and put my head back in my hands, he looks deeper at me. "Did I say something to upset you. Gosh, I'm sorry Clover. What is it?"

I glance up slightly to take another peek and he sees me looking and quickly rubs his marking of an angel. "It is a bit crazy. I mean, I doubt you'll even believe me."

"Try me," he encourages looking deep into my eyes.

"Well, you have the same birthmark of a feather, in the same location that Elliot did. Only his was behind his left ear…" I pause. I replay the moment I saw this mark during my breakdown at the park in Franklin. The rain pouring around me as I sprinted behind a stranger, because I thought I was losing my mind. But I wasn't, I realize. It was Axel.

He rubs the spot once again. "And, mine is on the right." Not a question. No hesitation. Just the simple statement. Maybe he doesn't think I'm nuts.

"Yep. Exactly. Yours is on the right. I don't understand. Are you sure you are not reincarnated or something? Did you just wake up one morning and not know who you were or why your life changed so dramatically?"

"Well, no. But after today, I'm going to wonder." I'm glad we can have a little bit of humor mixed into this very strange, and heavy conversation.

"So tell me about you. I need to confirm you truly are this Axel person. At this point in time, I'm not sure what to believe. How is it you became this talented jeweler? How did you meet Sydney? She seems to be the one affiliation I have found to you, besides the fact that Elliot ordered this jewelry from your store. But you didn't know who I was. Well, still don't, but you get the picture."

"Well, I grew up a military kid and moved a lot. I didn't make friends, so I worked on little projects. I liked making things for my mom. It started with a simple soldering iron and little silly jewelry pieces. But it grew over time. Eventually, I became an apprentice to my old boss here in Chicago. When he passed, I opened my own place. With its success, it grew hectic. As I looked for somewhere to put down new roots on a more serious level, I found Franklin. I hired Sydney there; she's been great. She really helped me get things prepared for the Franklin grand opening a year ago. So great, she heads to the Chicago store occasionally to help with bigger projects."

I am amazed at his ambition, and success. It really is remarkable how much he's accomplished. "That is really an achievement!" And I mean that, deeply. I know how stressed out I am about helping start up a yoga studio. As I explain the story of my move to Franklin, and about my plans for opening the studio, he interrupts.

"Wait – you're the one opening the yoga studio? Holy cow. This is just crazy."

"Out of this entire day, you find that to be crazy? Oh my gosh, that is funny." I literally start laughing, hysterically. I can't help it. It just strikes me like that. He joins in, and together, we giggle. I break through the chuckling to add, "Why would that be so crazy? I have done yoga for years, and helped my friend Reese at her studio since its beginning. I think I'm actually pretty good at it, and am really excited about this new experience," I defend.

"Oh. No, no, no. That's not what I mean. Clover, I own that building. I've worked with a property manager to handle things, but I bought that building thinking I'd put my store in it. But I just couldn't do it. It didn't feel right. There was something about it that made me feel like an intruder. So I found another building but kept that one as an investment." I start to realize what he is saying.

"Wait, so you own the building that we're putting the studio in? You. Like you, you, the guy in front of me, you."

He grins and grabs my hand again. "Yes, me. Me, me. I know it is strange. All of this is a bit beyond my understanding right now. But I think you and I were meant to connect at some point."

I think back on all the things I saw in Franklin. I know it was Axel I was missing in passing. It must have been. One more limb to go out on here. For some sense of closure. So I can tell myself I wasn't losing my mind in all those wild situations. I have to ask. "So, do you live in Franklin now or Chicago?"

"Well, I have a place here in Chicago, but rent one in Franklin. Eventually things will settle here, with Sydney's help, and then I plan on moving there for good. That's been my plan, it is just taking some time. But I spend a lot of time there, especially when I need a break from the city. I enjoy the calmness of it. I have a manager that is going to operate the Chicago store, and I'll only be there for big events, release of new collections, things like that." He explains, animatedly. He is so much like Elliot when he talks, yet he has a very different aura.

I sit for a moment taking it all in, listening to his continued story about his move. He talks about his parents and their close watch over what he does. How they worry he is alone. Even in his similarity to Elliot, my perception of him as I sit here is so very different. Sitting across from Axel, the air between us thrumming with silent electricity, I contemplate the nature of this new bond. This is in contrast to the bond I had with Elliot, a genuine and profound friendship that we developed through the trials and tribulations of coming of age and sharing life's events. We were each other's rock amid life's stormy waters—friends, confidantes, and cheerleaders.

But with Axel, there's something else, something I can't quite define. A spark, an ember of possibility. A hope, a longing, a chance for something more. It's unsettling, unexpected, but undeniably present. It's a feeling that makes my heart flutter, a feeling I haven't felt since…well, ever if I'm being honest.

Then, I'm struck, blindingly belted, with a memory. The words Elliot whispered just before he passed, the words that had haunted me ever since. The words that confused everything with Everett for so long. He looked at me, his eyes filled with a clarity that belied his pain, and said, "I see you with my brother." *Jesus, Mary, and Joseph.*

I'm frozen, the weight of revelation crashing over me. It was a cryptic message, a whisper of the future, something he couldn't explain but somehow knew was true. And now, here I am, face to face with a man who looks so much like him, feels so familiar, yet so different, so new.

The pieces of the puzzle begin to click into place. The flashes of him in Franklin, the custom bracelet, the timing, the inscription – all point to a link that transcends mere coincidence. It's a connection orchestrated by a love that knew no limits, a love that could see beyond the boundaries of life and death, a love that whispered hope for a future I couldn't have imagined, a future that, at this moment, feels both startling and exhilarating.

"Clover, what's going on in that beautiful head of yours?"

CHAPTER 30

HONESTLY, WHAT CAN I say? Is there even a possibility that Elliot had some strange vision of the future? And if so, what does that mean about who Axel is? What does all this mean?

The realization hits me like a tidal wave, washing over me with a force that leaves me breathless. I stare at Axel, my eyes wide, my mind struggling to process this revelation. The words tumble out of my mouth before I can stop them, a question that clings to the space between us, charged with a mix of disbelief and faint understanding.

"Do you have a brother?"

Axel nods, a thoughtful crease forming between his brows. He takes a sip of his coffee, his gaze lingering on me. The question persists, a silent acknowledgment of the mystery that has unfolded before us.

He sets down his cup, a slow, deliberate movement, as if gathering his thoughts, choosing his words carefully. "I don't know for certain if I have a brother," he admits, his voice a low rumble that sends a shiver down my spine. "It's definitely possible."

The air thins, the silence stretching out between us, a shared sense of intrigue and a flourishing sense of possibility. We've spent a couple hours together, sipping coffee, sharing tales, delving into the depths of our pasts. Some of our conversations were light and playful, others deeply personal, and some even flirted with the edges of something more. But now, with that question hanging between us, a new energy crackles in the air, a shift in the dynamics, a whisper of a truth.

He leans closer, his eyes locked on me, a flash of something unsaid in his stare. "I want to tell you something," he adds in a low whisper. "Something that's been weighing on me for a long time."

My heart races, my breath catching in my throat. The mystery, the intrigue, the unexpected turn of events, all converge in this moment. I lean in, drawn by his voice, his gaze, his enigmatic aura. I'm ready to hear his story, perhaps uncover the truth that lies at the heart of this remarkable encounter.

I know, with an almost chilling certainty, that the next words Axel speaks will be some of the most important I've ever heard. More than that, they'll be vital to him, a weight he's been carrying for far too long. That's what he said. My body trembles with nervous energy, a sense of unease that borders on terror. I know he's experiencing something far more profound, of a past that has shaped him in ways I can only begin to imagine.

I need to ease his worry, to offer comfort, to let him know he's not alone in this. With a sudden impulse, I stand, moving to the edge of the table, and slide onto the bench seat beside him. My fingers trace his arm, a gentle gesture of support, and then I turn to face him, meeting his gaze directly, a silent promise of understanding.

I reach out, taking his hands in mine, overlapping our fingers, the warmth of his skin a grounding force amid the rippling emotions that engulf me. I hold his hands, a pledge of trust, a signal that it's safe to venture down this path, that I'm here with him.

The moment our hands touch, a jolt of electricity courses through me, a spark igniting in the depths of my being. It's a feeling I haven't experienced since our brief touch in that park, a feeling that makes me feel alive, whole, a part of something greater, something more important. It's like a missing piece of my soul has been found, an essence that transcends words.

And somehow, I know my wingman, Elliot, has brought me here. To this moment. This exact place in time.

"Go on," I whisper, my voice barely audible, but filled with a strength I didn't know I possessed. "Tell me."

Axel takes a deep breath, a sigh escaping his lips, a sigh heavy of unspoken emotions. His grip on my hands tightens, his fingers digging into my skin, a silent plea for grace.

"I was adopted," he says, his voice raspy, a hint of vulnerability breaking through the normally composed exterior. "My parents told me when I was pretty young. I was okay with it. They're wonderful people, loving, supportive. I care about them deeply." He pauses, a tinge of sadness crossing his eyes. "But even as a child, there was a sense of longing. A missing link. Like something wasn't quite right."

He continues, his voice softer now, desperate almost. "I would get headaches, not because of stress, but for no reason at all. Stomach aches, inexplicable aches, that felt more like a deep, visceral feeling that someone I knew was hurting."

His gaze drops, his eyes searching for answers in the depths of his coffee mug. "I used to ask my mom about it," he says, still staring down. "But she'd always say I was just a loving boy, full of empathy. But I knew it was more."

He looks up, his eyes holding a trace of pain, a reflection of the years he's spent wrestling with this mystery. "As I got older, I asked more questions," he continues, his voice gaining strength. "But I hit roadblocks, walls of silence. Eventually, I decided to let it go. Focus on myself, be a good person, grow up, be successful. But lately, in the past few weeks, I've been in a dark place, a kind of depression, I don't even know why."

His voice breaks, a tremor running through his words. "It's like I'm being pulled back to a truth I've tried to bury, a truth that keeps whispering, 'You're not complete, you're missing something.' And I don't know what to do about it."

His confession is raw with a heaviness that seems to press down on us both. But it's also a release, a moment of honesty, a step towards understanding. I hold his hands tighter, ready to help him navigate this uncharted territory, this journey into the unknown.

I give him a moment to gather himself, to breathe, to let the uneasiness settle. My emotions are swirling within me, a flurry of shock, empathy, and a growing sense of certainty that something extraordinary is unfolding. I struggle to keep my own emotions in check, to be strong for him, to offer the comfort he so desperately needs.

"Axel, I think you need to see this," I say, my voice laced with a mix of apprehension and anticipation. "I need to show you why I reacted the way I did. Why seeing you, looking at you, was the biggest shock anyone could endure, to see an exact twin of someone you just lost, to imagine them standing right in front of you... It's life-altering."

I pull out my phone, scrolling through my photo library. My finger hovers over a picture, a memory of a happier time, a time before loss, a time before the world shifted on its axis. It's a picture of Elliot and me, sitting on our couch, wearing goofy, ugly Christmas sweaters, mugs with antlers full of cocoa, the biggest, cheeriest smiles plastered on our faces.

"This is Elliot," I say softly, my heart aching with a bittersweet longing.

I hand him the phone, my fingers brushing against his as I pass it to him. I watch as his eyes scan the picture, as his expression shifts from curiosity to surprise, to a dawning realization. I see it all reflected in his eyes, the shock, the qualm, the astonishment that's echoing my own.

He doesn't speak, but his silence speaks volumes.

The evidence is undeniable. The same eyes, the same features, the same smile. Elliot, the man who had a significant impact on my life, the man whose loss still leaves a devastating trail, and the man who looks exactly like Axel.

And as Axel looks at the picture, I can see the puzzle pieces falling into place, the recognition, the threads of a story that's been waiting to be told. This is not just a coincidence, it's a revelation, a truth that's about to change everything for Axel.

"I don't even know what to say. He looks just like me." He finally breaks the silence, with a soft reply. His hand hovers lightly over Elliot's face in the photo.

"He does, he most definitely does." I think about things for a moment. Trying to bring some sense to what is happening, to focus. "Axel, when is your birthday?"

As he looks away from the phone, he returns my stare, knowing answers to one of the biggest questions of his life are most likely within seconds of revealing themselves. "April eighth," he answers.

I give a knowing nod. A split-second when I'm both astonished and unsurprised. "And how old are you?"

"Do you really need to ask? I think you already know the answer to that." All I can do is nod my head in agreement. Of course, I know.

My gaze drops, drawn to his hands, still grasped to my phone. A shiver runs through me as I notice the scar on his pinky finger, a long pink mark that covers a good portion of the digit. I've seen this scar before. Not in this reality, but in the dreams that have haunted me for weeks.

The dreams of Elliot. Or so I thought.

The striking resemblance to him is undeniable. The eyes, the birthmark beyond his ear, the way his smile lights up his face. The similarities are endless, a physical echo of a man I cared for so deeply, a man who is no longer with us.

But this scar…this is different. It's a mark of a past I know nothing about, a past that seems to hold a key to the mystery that's swirling around us. And yet, I recognize it clearly, as if I've touched it before, with my own hand.

I'm jolted with a sense of disorientation that leaves me breathless. It's almost impossible to comprehend, this uncanny resemblance, this conduit that stretches beyond the boundaries of logic, this ounce of truth I never dared to imagine.

My heart pounds in my chest, a surplus of fear and excitement, of dread and anticipation, bubbling within me. The world, just months ago, seemed solid and familiar. Now, it feels like a shifting landscape, a canvas of uncertainty, where nothing is as it seems, and everything is possible.

I look up at Axel, my eyes searching his, seeking answers, seeking confirmation, seeking to make sense of the impossible truth that's revealed itself in this quiet cafe. He looks at me with his expression a mix of confusion and a glimmer of something else, something that seems to echo the storm raging within me.

"Axel," I whisper, my voice trembling, "Tell me, about this scar."

Axel chuckles, a low, rumbling sound. "I told you I was adopted, and that it is not impossible for me to have a brother, one who may very well be your friend." he says, his eyes twinkling with a mixture of mischief and a touch of self-deprecation. "And you're asking me about my scar."

I am sure it seems absurd to him. He thinks he uncovered an enigma to a long lost brother, and I am focusing on his scar. What he doesn't know is how that scar has affected me and my dreams over the previous weeks. It has provided me a glimpse of happiness, something to cling to while my world has gone dark. "Sorry, I don't want to downplay the seriousness of what you just confided in me. But I really need to know about your scar. If you don't mind sharing." I rest my head on his shoulder, still staring down at his hand. I didn't lean into him to persuade him to tell me, but it is a comfort I just needed to feel. Something to tether me into reality, while it feels like there is some mystical realm saturating every breath of oxygen surrounding us.

He shakes my hand gently, his touch pauses my anxiety. "Yeah, sure. I can tell you," he says softly, his voice filled vulnerability, "It's...well, it's a part of me. It's been there forever."

He takes a deep breath, his eyes gazing into the distance, as if reliving the memory. "I got it when I was a kid, six or seven maybe?" he begins, his voice laced with a hint of melancholy.

"Burned pretty bad when I was playing with a soldering iron. Ironic actually, to get a painful scar I'd have forever while I was trying to create beauty, to craft stories in metal. " He chuckles again, that modest sound hinted through it.

He pauses, letting the words hang in the air, "But it wasn't just about the craft. It was about an escape," he says, his eyes meeting mine, a raw honesty in his gaze. "An escape from the loneliness of being a military kid, moving every year or two. From the constant longing for that missing link that I never quite understood." He looked at the scar, a familiar marking etched onto his flesh. It was an expression of the pain, but proof of his resilience, his ability to find solace in the unexpected. It was a reflection of who he was, a boy who had found his own way through the haze of a nomadic life, and in the process, had stumbled upon a skill, a passion, and a scar that defined him in a way nothing else could.

His words reverberate through me, a shared journey of seeking a sense of belonging. I feel a sudden surge of empathy, a grip that goes beyond mere circumstance. His scar, a mark of a future I've dreamt of, whispers of a destiny that's unfolding.

I nod my head against him, a silent gesture of appreciation, of gratitude for his vulnerability, for the trust he has placed in me. The story, though simple, has resonated deeply, a reminder that we all carry our own scars, our own burdens, our own stories of searching.

"It's time for me to share something too," I say, my voice soft, but filled with a newfound strength. I explain about Elliot's words, the words he whispered just before he left us, a whisper that has haunted me ever since. "He said, 'I saw you with my brother.' He was so in wonder at his own words, in a moment of shock, he even repeated it. Like it hadn't even made sense to him.'"

The moment I speak those words, a shift happens. Axel sits up straighter, a subtle tension in his shoulders, almost possessive, as if he's instinctively defending something, something I'm only beginning to understand.

"Everett thought he meant he and I were destined to be together," I continue, the words tasting strange on my tongue, an echo of how that felt so wrong, so misplaced. "But I thought of it differently," I say, meeting Axel's eyes, "I imagined he was seeing Everett and me during his surgery, being supportive, standing by him while we were unsure what would happen. It was a vision of friendship, developed out of the trauma we lived through in that moment."

And then, I tell him about the dream, the dream that plagued me for weeks, the dream of a love so intense, so joyful, so real. The dream of Elliot and me, but not as friends. Not as the soulmates we'd always been. It was a romantic love, a haze of passion, a love that made me feel whole, alive, complete. I explain the strength of the emotions it evoked, the aching sense of longing, the wish for that level of joy, that desire, in my life. Especially as I saw new romance happening around me in Sadie and Everett. How I was witnessing Reese and Nick moving on, being happy.

The silence that follows is heavy, a palpable tension filling the space between us. The story I've just shared feels both intimate and dangerous, a world where dreams and reality blur, where love can take unexpected turns, and where the past and the present collide. "I never imagined he would mean *this*. How would he even know about you?"

It's a story that's been hidden deep within me, a story that's been waiting for this moment, waiting for the right person to hear it, the right person to understand. And in the depths of Axel's gaze, I recognize it may have been meant for him all along.

He squeezes me into a hug, a gentle embrace that envelops me in warmth and comfort. His arms wrap around me, his touch delicate. He kisses the top of my head, a sweet, tender gesture that makes me melt on the spot. It's so caring, so genuine, I don't want it to end.

But then, he breaks away, a playfulness in his eyes, his voice a soft murmur. "So, the scar, that's a clue? That was in your dream, wasn't it?"

My heart races. I hadn't meant to bring the subject up, not yet, not so soon. It's so personal, something I've kept hidden, a dream I've almost dismissed as only a figment of my imagination, even when it seemed so real.

"How did you know?" I whisper as I shudder with surprise.

He shrugs, his smile a touch mischievous. "Some dreams are hard to forget."

Wait, what? Can he mean he has had the same dream? I suppose anything is possible in my life right now. I'm not going to dive into that with him. I think I need to let it go for a minute. We can always go back to that topic later.

He leans in, his eyes meeting mine, a jolt of hope passes through me. "But I'd love to hear all about it. Tell me about your dreams."

I'm caught in the pull of his gaze, his warmth, his enigmatic smile. The truth, the mystery, the possibility, all swirl around me, an intoxicating cocktail of emotions. My mind races, trying to process the eruption of events, the twists and turns of a destiny that's been laid out before me. And as I prepare to discuss more of my life and hear about his, I can't help but feel a sense of excitement, a sense of anticipation, a sense of being on the cusp of something extraordinary.

I hold up a hand, my voice a gentle plea. "Hold on, Axel," I say, my heart still thrumming from the force of our shared revelation. "Maybe we can talk about my dreams later. Right now, I need to understand this. I need to know about your adoption."

He nods, his gaze searching mine. "I'm ready to talk," he says, his voice soft, a reassuring touch. "But I honestly don't know much more than that. I don't want to disappoint you."

"I'm so afraid," I say, my voice trembling, "that the missing link, the piece of the puzzle you've been searching for, that it bridges you to Elliot. That it's something deeper, something that will change everything."

"To find any clarity, any answers, any closure," I continue, "I need to talk to Elliot's parents."

I pause, my gaze shifting to the window, watching the city bustle by. "Elliot wasn't close to his father," I explain. "And his dad was even more distant to Everett. So that's probably not an option. I haven't heard from Claire since she went back overseas after the funeral, not for weeks. But she might be the only one who can help. Would it be okay if I reached out to her? To ask if she has any knowledge about you?"

Axel's eyes meet mine, a spark of hope lighting up his face. "I'm okay with that," he says, his voice filled with an emotion I can't quite decipher. "It's been so long. I've stopped searching, stopped hoping. But maybe, just maybe, this is the chance I've been waiting for. Maybe, after all this time, this riddle, the mysterious void I've dealt with, might finally be solved."

The silence that follows is charged with anticipation, and a bit of fear. This life, in all its complexity, holds a beautiful chaos within it, a symphony of twists and turns, of unexpected encounters, of love and loss, and a destiny that awaits us all, sometimes in the most improbable of ways.

We sit there, in the quiet embrace of the cafe, two souls intertwined in a web of shared longing, a web that's about to be unraveled, a web that promises a journey into the unknown. A journey that may offer me some closure about Elliot's final words, my dream. But the same journey may lead Axel to have a fresh wound on his heart. An understanding of his history, but new grief in his future. I'm not sure how to feel about this. But somehow, we'll conquer the mystery together.

The day has been exhausting, a rollercoaster of shock and revelation. My body is barely holding up, my mind buzzing with the weight of the new information. The fatigue must be apparent on my face, a weariness that reflects the emotional turmoil I've been navigating.

"I should probably head back to Reese's," I say, trying to find a way to leave gracefully, but I don't want him to feel isolated. "I need to explain some things."

I'm not sure what kind of support system Axel has, what his comfort level is with sharing this new revelation with his family. I'm hesitant to leave him alone, to leave him wrestling with the uncertainty, the questions that have been unearthed.

"Will you be okay?" I ask, my voice laced with concern. "Is there anyone you want to talk to? Someone who can offer support?"

He laughs, a low, reassuring sound, a ripple of warmth washing over me. "I thought I'd be the one asking you that," he says, a playful glint in his eyes. "But I'll be fine, Clover. Don't worry about me."

He reaches for his phone, a silent request. I understand. "Let's exchange numbers," I say, my voice catching in my throat. "You can text me anytime, anytime you need to talk."

"I will," he says, a serious note entering his voice. "And I'll be in touch soon."

Our paths are now destined to remain joined. Not only because of the questions surrounding Elliot and his possible tie to Axel, but also because we'll both be in Franklin soon.

"I'd planned on heading back tonight," I say, "but I think I'll get a good night's sleep and head back in the morning."

Axel's eyes widen in surprise, then a smile crosses his face. He hesitates, then asks, "Could I... join you? I'm flying back in two days, and honestly, I'm not sure I'll be able to focus on work with this... this... well, everything." He trails off, his gaze searching mine. "We'd benefit from the company, Clover. What do you say? Would it be weird, too soon?"

His request is bold, a suggestion that feels both daring and exciting. I look at him, and I can't help but smile. This journey, this unexpected adventure, this meeting that feels both destined and impossible, is only just beginning.

"Okay," I say, a smile brighter, my heart pounding with trepidation. "I'll be at Reese's. I have my car and can pick you up whenever you want."

We make plans to leave late morning, a tentative agreement that feels comfortable and strangely uncertain. He gives me his address, a simple string of numbers that reveal a truth I wasn't surprised to discover – he lives in a really nice building downtown.

As we stand at the doorway, ready to part ways, an awkward silence settles in the air. This goodbye feels unsettled, incomplete. I know I'll see him in the morning, but it feels strange ending the day with just a handshake and a "see ya later."

Axel leans in, his eyes foxy. He holds his arms open in a welcoming gesture. "Come here, Clover," he says, his voice a low rumble. "Come on."

He smiles, and I can't resist. I step into his embrace, surrendering to the warmth of his arms, the comforting scent of his cologne. I hold him tight, wrapping my arms around him, feeling the strength of his frame, the solidness of his presence. Deep in my soul, I feel this draw, a magnetic pull that transcends words, an attraction that feels extraordinary.

He rubs my back, a gentle gesture that sends a shiver through me. He hums a low, almost wordless sound, a sound that speaks of a shared understanding, a shared longing. After a moment, he leans back, his gaze searching mine. He kisses the top of my head, a soft, lingering kiss that leaves me breathless.

"You good?" he asks, his voice a gentle whisper.

I nod, unable to speak, overcome by the rush of emotions that surge through me.

"Okay, then," he says, his smile tinged with a hint of sadness. "We'll talk soon, okay?"

His gaze drops to my wrist, lingering on the bracelet that brought us together, that has coerced us into this new destiny. And I feel the same, a silent acknowledgment of a greater power that binds us.

CHAPTER 31

THE EVENING AIR FEELS cool and refreshing as I make my way back to Reese and Nick's place. I glance down at my phone, the screen a dazzling display of missed calls and texts. Reese, Everett, and Ruby. It's been a day. Shock and awe.

I'm not sure where to begin.

I quickly reply to Ruby with a "Hello, miss you guys."

I know I'll need to speak with Everett soon, but I think I better wait to get into the details until I hopefully have already spoken to Claire. Instead, I send him a quick message. I tell him it was a crazy day. That El had a bracelet made for my birthday, and I'll call him when I get back.

And finally, I call Reese. "Hey, I'm on my way. I hope you don't mind me staying one more night."

"I'd love that, you know you are always welcome. Except my wedding night. Boom chicka bow woooowwww. That's out. But seriously, you know I was worrying about you, having not heard from you all day. You okay? Things go well?" She asks, true concern in her voice. In the background I can also hear Nick asking if it is me and if I'm alright.

"There is a lot to unpack. I mean, *a shit-ton.* I don't even know how to begin. We'll talk when I get there. I'll see you soon, 'kay?"

She agrees and we hang up. The city lights begin to twinkle as the sun dips below the horizon. It's a beautiful evening, but my mind is racing, trying to make sense of everything. I can't believe what happened. The meeting with Axel, the revelation about his

288

adoption, the uncanny resemblance to Elliot, the gift, the story that's slowly unfolding before me. It's overwhelming, and yet, it's also exhilarating.

I spin the bracelet on my wrist, its cool metal a reflection of its beauty, of its significance, of the love that created it. As I replay the day's events in my mind, the details start to click into place, it all points to a larger plan, a plan that goes beyond coincidence.

I really believe, deep in my heart, that Elliot knew I'd be on this journey somehow. He knew I would need his support, his guidance. He knew that somehow, some way, I would find myself here, meeting Axel. And now, with this bracelet, this symbol of his love, I know, with an almost certainty, that he's here, guiding me, leading me on this beautiful and mysterious path. He always said he'd be the best wingman. That he would help me find true love and happiness. What if he was right all along?

The evening finds me sprawling out on the floor, a nest of pillows and blankets surrounding me, an ice cream bowl perched precariously on my lap. The words tumble out of me, a torrent of emotions that spills out the story of the day, a day that has upended my world and possibly started rewriting the narrative of my life.

Reese and Nick sit there, mesmerized, taking it all in, full of awe. Reese finally makes sense of all my unexplained doppelganger sightings in Franklin, the inexplicable pull I felt toward Axel, the uncanny resemblance, this powerful sensation.

But the story of Elliot's last words, the possibility that he knew about his brother, and the fact that I had a dream starring Axel, a dream I now know wasn't a bizarre depiction of a future version of Elliot, but a glimpse into a truth I had yet to grasp, that's what truly stuns Reese. It takes her time to process it all, to accept the possibility, the improbability, the sheer unbelievable nature of it all.

Nick sits on the side, his presence a steady anchor, offering silent support and hugs when we need them. He's always been our chill factor, the voice of reason in the face of chaos.

"It's crazy," Reese finally says, shaking her head, "But somehow, it all makes sense." She smiles, understanding washing over her face. "It's like everything happened to bring you here to this moment."

I nod, feeling a sense of peace settling over me. It's a strange peace knowing that I am accepting the unknown, embracing the unexpected, from knowing that even in the face of chaos, there's a beauty, a logic, a higher plan that we can't quite comprehend.

But even as I feel a sense of calm, a worry creeps in. What will this do to Axel? What if we really confirm he is Elliot's brother, and he'll never have a chance to know him? To have that relationship? And what about Everett? Where does he fit into this unfolding story? My heart aches for Axel, for that lifelong notion of being incomplete, for the answers he seeks, but also for Everett, because I know this will impact him in some extreme way. How can it not?

This journey, this discovery, this unexpected twist of fate, is only just beginning. And I know, without any doubt, that it will be a journey filled with challenges and revelations.

The exhaustion finally catches up to me. It's been a long day. I know I need to get some rest, to prepare for the drive home tomorrow, and whatever awaits me there.

I tell Reese and Nick goodnight, grateful for their support, their love, and their willingness to embrace the unexpected. As I sink into the fluffy pillows and stretch out, I reach for my phone. I text Sadie, letting her know I'll be back tomorrow. I need to check on the progress at the apartment, see if it's close to move-in ready, or at least ready-enough status.

Everett deserves to hear more, to know what's been going on, but I decide to wait, to share when there's hopefully more to explain. I quickly message him that it was an interesting day, and I miss him.

And finally, my thoughts drift to Axel. I can't reopen the door to any deeper discussions tonight, not with my heart still thrumming with the intensity of our day. But I feel the need to say goodnight, to reach out even if just for a quick text.

ME: Goodnight, Axel. I hope you're okay. I'm thinking about

you.

But when I don't receive a reply, I become concerned. He's been through so much, facing a truth that's been hidden for years, a truth that's been waiting to be revealed. I can't imagine the emotions he's grappling with, the questions that must be swirling in his mind. And the fact that he's not responding, not reaching out, only deepens my concern.

Hours pass, a restless night filled with anxiety and worry. Just as I'm about to give up hope, my phone lights up.

AXEL: Thank you. For everything.

Relief washes over me. His words, simple but heartfelt, are enough to ease my anxiety, to reassure me that he's okay, that he's processing, but he's not alone.

I drift to sleep, a peace settling over me. The journey I've begun, the new path I'm walking, it's a path filled with unknowns. But I'll manage. I know it will be okay. I have support from so many, and a newfound strength, renewed by the idea that this is all part of a plan, and Elliot will also be nearby as I find a way through it all.

The morning goodbyes with Reese and Nick are filled with emotional hugs and even a few tears. It's hard to say goodbye, to step away from the comfort of their love and support, to leave the warmth of their home. But I know I'll be back in a couple of weeks to celebrate their wedding, to share in their joy, to witness the start of their new chapter.

I navigate the city streets and pull up in front of Axel's skyscraper. I certainly do not miss driving in this traffic. He's waiting under the awning, a small leather bag slung over his shoulder. He looks magnificent, rested, but the stress in his eyes is telling.

The drive begins without any awkwardness. We fall into easy conversation, the tension of the previous day dissolving with each passing moment. He tells me he ended up calling his mom last night, and they talked for hours. He didn't get any new answers, but she offered him support as he digs further into his history.

"We should make the call to Claire," he says, his voice laced with a hint of hope.

We decide to give it a shot, but I warn him first. "We'll see if we can catch her. She's not the best at keeping in touch." I glance at the time and do the math. It's 10:30 here, so 6:30 in the evening her time. I ask my handsfree app to dial her number.

And then, the phone rings. Surprisingly, she answers on the fourth ring, concern in her voice. "Clover? Is that you, dear? Are you okay?"

"I'm okay," I say, my voice trembling with emotion. Before I lose my gusto, I just get right to the point. "Hi Claire, I have you on speaker, and I'm not alone. We have some questions."

And as I speak, I make a quick turnoff onto the next exit, a sudden urge to be able to park, aware of the possibility that this call, this conversation, could change so much.

"Who's with you?" Claire asks, her voice filled with confusion. Axel looks over at me, shrugging, unsure of what to say. Should he speak? How do we even begin?

The air crackles with tension. Claire is silent for a moment, her breath catching in her throat. "Everett? Are you there…?" She trails off, her voice filled with a mix of surprise and a hint of fear. She seems to be trying to understand the situation. This is not typical for me to call her out the blue. "Wait, oh my God. You know, don't you?"

But then, Axel interrupts. "I'm sorry, it isn't Everett. My name is Axel," he says, his voice firm, a hint of steel in his tone. "Although it sounds like there are things Everett needs to know, this is about Elliot. We have questions that may concern me. Related to the eighth of April? We could really use your help sorting through this, if you're willing?"

There's silent confirmation, a recognition that this call, this conversation, is about something more than just a casual catch-up. It's about a truth that's been hidden for years, a truth that's about to be revealed. And as I listen, my heart pounding in my chest, I feel a surge of anticipation, a sense of wonder and a touch of dread.

"You say your name is Axel?" Claire asks, her voice sounds dainty. "And you knew Elliot... how?"

Axel takes a breath, his voice steady despite the tension in the air. "Well, I never knew Elliot, unfortunately. But he sounds like a great man. I'm sorry for your loss, Claire. Really. But I need your help to understand some things. You see, I met Clover yesterday, in a strange set of circumstances, and she told me I look identical to Elliot. To add to the confusion, my birthday is also April eighth. You can imagine my shock. And hers."

The silence that follows is heavy, thick with the weight of unspoken truths. I can almost feel Claire's mind racing, trying to piece together the puzzle, to understand how these seemingly unrelated threads have come together. It magnifies the power of fate, the pull of destiny, the way it brings us together, even when it feels like we're worlds apart.

"Oh my God, Axel," Claire whispers, her voice shaky with shock. "I don't even know where to begin."

Axel's voice is patient, understanding. "How about the beginning?" he suggests. "Tell me about Elliot."

Claire takes a deep breath, her voice trembling slightly as she begins. "Well, when Joel and I first got married, we were trying to start a family. But it was a struggle, years of trying... And then we found out that Joel couldn't have children." She pauses, her voice catching. "It was devastating, heartbreaking. But we knew we wanted a family, so we went through the adoption process. And we had our precious boy. Elliot came to us through an agency. We didn't know anything about him, besides he was ours and his birthday. We brought him home at four days old."

"And then?" I interrupt, "you adopted Everett a couple of years later?" My stomach rolls. Because I realize now that can't be true. Because I've seen the pictures with Claire pregnant, and little Elliot standing beside her. The same picture Everett came to the loft to find in Elliot's belongings. It was the last photo of them before Joel left. So something is definitely amiss.

There's a beat of silence. Then Claire's voice comes back, "No, my dear. We didn't....we didn't adopt. He's mine. Everett is my biological son."

An explosion of shock hits me. Axel and I exchange a stunned glance. The pieces of the puzzle are starting to fall into place, but in a way neither of us could have imagined. This truth is a twist we never saw coming.

"Things were difficult at home," Claire says, a hint of sadness lacing her voice. "It was only a couple of months, but it's how I got Everett, but also how I lost Joel. When I found out I was pregnant, we were going to work through it. But then Joel decided it was too difficult, and he left. We wanted some stability for the boys, so Joel and I decided to raise them both as our own, but we separated."

She pauses, her voice filled with despair. "I never thought anything like this would happen. It just doesn't make any sense."

His voice a steady calm in the midst of the storm of emotions, Axel adds, "I think you'll understand more once you see my picture. I have a feeling it's going to be a lot clearer."

"Claire," I ask, "Did Elliot and Everett know? Did they know about any of this?"

There's a long pause, a silence that stretches on, filled with the weight of unspoken truths. Then, Claire's voice, soft, almost hesitant, breaks the silence. "They didn't know, Clover. Not a thing. Joel asked me to keep it a secret, for both their sakes. He never wanted to cause any confusion, any hurt."

Her words, though filled with a sense of regret, offer a strange kind of comfort. It's a relief to know that Elliot wasn't living with a secret, a secret that might have weighed on him, a secret that could have caused him pain. Pain that Axel knew all too well.

But still, a question echoes in my mind, a question I may never have the answer to. Did Elliot know, on some level? Did he have a sense of a missing piece, a missing vitality, like what Axel described living with all these years? Did he, in his final moments, experience a vision, a glimpse into a truth he never knew existed? Was it a gift he gave me, a message whispered through the veil of death?

I'll never truly know. And it's a thought that haunts me. If he did know, if he felt that void, that longing, did he keep that part of his soul hidden, from everyone? Did he have that heaviness follow him around?

Claire and I exchange a few more words, promising to talk soon, to keep each other updated. We both need time to process this, to understand the implications of what we've uncovered.

The call ends, and Axel and I remain silent; Claire's words now ricochet around the space.

"You okay?" I ask, reaching out to take his hand in mine.

He nods, his gaze fixed on the dashboard, unshed tears making his beautiful blue-green eyes shimmer. "Yeah, I think so."

The world feels different. The answers Axel's been seeking, the secrets that have been hidden for so long, they're slowly coming to light, unveiling a truth that's both beautiful and unsettling. And as we continue on our journey, I can't help but feel a sense of anticipation, a sense of purpose that I'm here to help Axel through it.

CHAPTER 32

THE MILES BLUR PAST, the landscape a kaleidoscope of colors and textures as we drive. The silence in the car isn't awkward, it's filled with a shared sense of curiosity, of a camaraderie that's only just begun. Axel asks me questions about Elliot, and the touch of sadness on his face makes my heart ache for him.

"Tell me about him," he says, his eyes searching mine, seeking to understand the man who was both his brother and a significant part of my life.

I tell him everything, about our years together, our shared dreams, our unique friendship, about his kindness, his compassion, his creativity, his talents, his unwavering spirit. I share stories that paint a picture of Elliot, the man I knew and loved.

I can see in Axel's expression, as I talk, that he has mixed emotions. There's a notion of relief, a sense of understanding, as if he's finally grasping the reason behind the void he's always felt, the feeling that something was missing. But there's also a darkness there, a level of grief that begins to emanate from him.

The realization that he had a brother, a twin brother he'd never knew existed, has arrived months after Elliot's death. The joy he could have experienced meeting him, getting to know him, getting to share a piece of his life, has slipped out of his grasp. In a way, it doesn't seem fair.

I understand how dark grief can be, how it can pull you under, how it can feel like you're drowning in a sea of sorrow. There's nothing I can say that will erase his pain, nothing I can do to bring back his brother, my friend.

But I can be here. I can offer my support, my friendship, my understanding, my memories.

"I'm here," I say, reaching for his hand again, squeezing it gently. "It'll be okay."

The remainder of the drive back to Franklin feels surreal. It's as if we're traveling through a dream, a landscape that's both familiar and foreign, a world that's been forever altered by the past few days.

We develop a plan for our arrival. My friends are waiting to hear from me, to know what happened, Everett especially. But the question lingers, how to share the shocking new information with him, the truth that he isn't Joel's son, that he and Elliot weren't biologically related.

An incoming text from Sadie throws my anxiety into overdrive. Axel reads it aloud to me while I drive. "We're all gonna hang at the BNB tonight, hoping you can join."

I'm still not sure how to approach all of this. We still don't have complete confirmation about Axel and Elliot, but the signs are pretty evident. Axel is going to do some more genetic inquiry to see what he can discover. Until then I don't feel comfortable holding anything back from Everett. The question is how to break the ice into this conversation.

I ask Axel to type a text to him to start the process.

ME: Hey, I'm going to be back within an hour or so. Can you meet me at the apartment? I need to check on the floors and see if it's ready to move in. And I need to talk to you about something.

It isn't long before the reply arrives:

EVERETT: Yes, sure, I'll be there. Can't wait to see your bracelet.

We go back and forth, debating whether Axel should be there at the apartment, or maybe go over to the BNB first. After all, that group didn't know Elliot, so they wouldn't be floored by the idea of seeing his ghost. Axel said he would do whatever I was most comfortable with.

A quick call to Reese for advice confirms our plan. We'll tell Everett together, and then go meet up with my friends. Reese thinks it's a good idea for Axel to meet everyone.

As we drive through the familiar streets of Franklin, the anticipation builds. We're about to face the consequences of our meeting. We're about to share a truth that will change everything for yet another person I care about. And while I can't help but feel a sense of apprehension, I also feel a tiny surge of hope. But, I'm having a hard time reading Axel. I have no idea what he is feeling, and he doesn't seem ready to share.

The stairs leading to my apartment feel strangely unfamiliar, even if they recently became the corridor to a new haven of peace and solitude filled with joy and laughter. But with Axel by my side, it's transformed into something different, something more. I can't help but feel a twinge of awkwardness that creeps in at the edges.

A flashback flickers through my mind, the day I met Elliot, the day he walked me back to that Chicago apartment. We stood at the door, our eyes and hands locked, a silent understanding passing between us. Then, he leaned in, and our lips met. It was a simple kiss, a sense of comfort, but lacked that sense of something more.

I wonder, what would it be like with Axel? Would it feel the same, that spark of recognition, that undeniable allure? Or would it be something entirely different, something more intense, something that ignites a deeper flame, a real passion?

Now is not the time to test it out. Not with the heavy conversation that awaits us on the other side of the door. Not with the revelations that hang in the air, the truths that we have to share with Everett.

But the thought endures, a sense of possibility, a spark of something that feels both exciting and terrifying. I take a deep breath, trying to push those thoughts aside, focusing on the present.

Axel is watching me, his eyes searching mine, his presence a comfort. He understands, I know he does. And in his eyes, I see a glimmer of hope, that feels both fragile and powerful.

We reach the door, the anticipation of the conversation waiting for us on the other side. I hesitate for a moment, my heart pounding in my chest, then I reach for the doorknob. It's time to send another person's world into a tailspin. I hate that I am the one to deliver such news. It should have come from Claire or Joel, even. But here we are.

I turn to Axel, my voice a hushed whisper. "Can you wait here on the platform, please? Just give me five minutes to explain things to Everett. I can't put another soul through the shock of thinking they're seeing Elliot's ghost standing feet from them."

He nods in understanding. I know he must feel nervous and uncomfortable, but he agrees. He leans against the railing, watching me with a quiet intensity.

I turn the doorknob, the sound of it clicking seems to snap my focus forward. I step inside, the familiar scent of my apartment enveloping me, with a subtle lingering odor of the new floor finish.

"Hey, Everett. It's good to see you." I give him the tightest hug ever, wishing I could protect him from the things I need to say. I start with the basics. I show Everett the bracelet, its exquisite craftsmanship, its delicate feathers, its gleaming white gold. He stares at it in awe, his expression mirroring my own when I first saw it. "Wow, it's gorgeous," is all he can say.

"Elliot ordered it for my birthday," I say softly, my voice trembling with emotion.

But then, I show him the engraving on the back. I hover my finger over the word, "wingman."

"He always said he would introduce me to that one person in the world, the one who could be my everything," I explain, my voice filled with a bittersweet longing. "He said he'd be my wingman."

"Yeah, I know he did. But I have a feeling, you are going to remind me that it wasn't me, like I first believed."

And then, I begin to share the details of how the week has upended my world.

"No, I don't think that was his plan for you and me. I'm not quite sure how he knew I'd find him. I'm not even sure if he understood it completely. But I know those last words he whispered as we were ushered out of that hospital room was part of a vision only angels could have shown him. I know it's astonishing," I say, my voice barely a whisper, "but you have to believe me." I take a deep breath, then glance down at the bracelet again. "The designer's name is Axel. And he traveled with me, because he wants to meet you."

I pause, my heart pounding in my chest, waiting for Everett to process, to understand, to grasp the impossible truth that's unfolding before us.

"Axel," I say, my voice cracking with nerves. "Come in."

I take a step back, offering Axel a path into the apartment. My heart beats faster, as I wait for his reaction, for the moment when two worlds collide.

As Axel steps inside, my eyes dart back and forth, torn between the two men. This new protectiveness for Everett grips me, a deep understanding that he's going to need me, that this moment, this discovery, is going to be incredibly hard for him.

Axel's face comes into view, and I become inundated with emotion. It is still hard for me at times to look at Axel, the resemblance to Elliot really is amazing. But I've also learned how different he is from his brother, and it allows me to create a separation, and the shock is tapering. I reach out, taking Everett's arm, offering a silent reassurance. He immediately tenses, his shoulders stiffening, and for a moment, I think he might drop to the floor. I use all my strength to offer him support, to hopefully keep him from shattering. I don't want him to go back to that dark place again.

"It's okay, Everett," I whisper, my voice barely audible, my hand squeezing his arm. "I know. Shocking isn't even the word. But we can explain, well, some of it."

I look at Axel, a sense of urgency filling me. "Axel, this is Everett, Elliot's brother."

I turn back to Everett, my heart aching with a mix of sadness and a strange kind of hope. "And Everett, this is Axel. Well, he's also Elliot's brother, his twin."

The words hang in the air, a deafening silence filling the room, a silent acknowledgment of the impossibility of the situation. I can see the shock, the confusion written on Everett's face. His eyes dart back and forth between Axel and me, trying to make sense of the truth that's been revealed, the truth that's reshaped their lives.

And as I watch, I can't help but feel a sense of empathy, a sense of understanding. I know what it's like to lose someone you love, to have your world shattered. I know what it's like to feel the pain, the grief, the loneliness. But I also know, with an almost certainty, that this bond, it's going to be a gift, a gift that will help them heal, a gift that will bring them closer.

Everett stands still for another minute, his expression still stoked with disbelief, and something else, something that feels like a glimmer of understanding. Then, he takes a step forward, closing the distance between him and Axel.

"I'm not entirely sure what the hell is going on here," he says shocked. "But holy shit, it's good to see you, man."

And with that, he pulls Axel into a hug, a hug that's filled with a warmth and a sense of fraternity that's palpable, a link that speaks volumes about the bond that's been spontaneously formed between them.

I try to fight the tears. I do. I try with all my might. But when I look at them, embracing each other, patting each other on the back, and watch as a tear forms in the corner of Everett's eye, the dam breaks. The wetness falls down my cheeks, a torrent of emotion I can't control.

After a solid minute, they step back, their eyes locked in a silent conversation that's filled with a lifetime of unspoken truths. Everett takes another look at Axel, his gaze intense.

"I knew my brother all my life," he says, his voice weak. "Damn, you look so much like him. *Jesus*, you look like him. But you're so different. Your eyes are darker, your build bigger, your hair parts different. You're him, but you are definitely not." He continues staring down Axel, trying to take it all in. "Now, I need to understand... how is this possible?"

His question hangs in the air, a question that echoes the sentiment in all of our hearts. Axel turns to me, his eyes searching mine, a silent acknowledgement of the bigger truths that still need to be shared, the secrets we have to crack open.

I nod, my heart aching for both of them, for the journey they're about to embark on. "Come on," I say, gesturing towards the couch in the living room. "Let's sit."

We explain the adoption, the unexpected twist of fate. Axel, with a newfound clarity in his eyes, shares how he knew all his life he was adopted, but never knew he had a sibling, especially a twin. He seems to feel a sense of relief, a piece of his puzzle falling into place.

I tell him how I met Axel, the shock, our conversations, the shared sense of intrigue, the bracelet, the impossible nexus, the strange Franklin sightings. I explain how I reached out to Claire, how she and Joel adopted Elliot, and then how, in a twist of fate, she wound up conceiving Everett in an affair, how they chose to withhold the truth from both boys, to protect them from the complexities of their origins.

Everett sits there, absorbing it all, his face bouncing from one extreme emotion to the next.

"So, Elliot wasn't my brother?" he asks, his voice tinged with shock, a sense of loss coloring his words. "And Joel... he's not my father?" I wonder how his body can physically handle the depth of this heavier level of grief. Not just losing Elliot, but the truth of losing him in an entirely different way. My heart is breaking watching him. But we will all get through this together.

We both reassure him. "Yes, you *are* Elliot's brother," I say, reaching for his hand. "That's all you ever believed, that's all you ever felt, and that will never change."

Axel joins in, his voice filled with empathy. "And Joel," he adds, "will always be your father. Just as the man who adopted me will always be mine."

"But my dad left because he couldn't handle the truth of what my mother had done." Everett realizes more of his past. I know he will have deeper conversations with Claire and Joel, on his own time, when he's ready. I just hope maybe this will help bring them closer together, offer some sort of healing. Especially to Joel and Everett. We still don't know about the details of who Everett's biological father is. I'm not sure Claire will ever share that. But I think she owes it to Everett to face the truth if he chooses that path.

Everett breaks down, tears streaming down his face. The weight of the revelation is heavy, the reality of a truth that has been hidden for so long is finally hitting him. But there's a sense of relief in his tears, acceptance in his gestures.

Axel speaks softly, his voice filled with a genuine sorrow. "I'm so sorry for your loss," he says, his eyes strained with sadness. "I know I wasn't lucky enough to ever know Elliot, but I think I knew things about him before I ever knew of him. And I'm really struggling with this loss too. But I'm hoping we can get to know each other. I didn't know our brother, but I'm not going to lose the chance to know you. I already consider you my brother."

His words are heartfelt, genuine, illuminating this kindship that's been kindled. It's a moment of shared grief, a moment of solace that whispers of a new beginning, a journey of healing, a journey of discovery, and the intricate syncing of family that fate has created.

Everett nods, his eyes shining with tears. "I'm grateful to meet you, Axel," he says, his voice thick with emotion. "To know I have another way to connect to Elliot, to discover a new bond with you. It's...it's like a piece of him I never knew existed."

I'm filled with a sense of pride, looking at the two men in front of me. They are strong, resilient, filled with a love that transcends loss, a connection that runs deeper than blood. They are the strongest people I've ever known.

As I circle the bracelet on my wrist, its feathers portray the love that brought us all together, I know in my heart that Elliot is behind this, that he orchestrated this meeting, that he's guiding us on this journey. I look up, sending a silent thank you to him, knowing he's watching, proud of the brothers he's brought together. He is proving to be the perfect wingman.

Outside, the sun dips below the horizon, bathing the room in twilight. It is the perfect balance of endings and beginnings.

We sit for another hour, sharing stories, tears, even laughter, unraveling the tangled threads of the past, piecing together the puzzle of our lives. As I recognize the healing that is happening here, I sense we are no longer just individuals navigating our grief; we are a family united by love and loss.

There are moments, of course, when Everett is taken aback by the similarities between Axel and Elliot. The same eyes, the same laugh lines, the same way they hold themselves. But just as I've learned to distinguish Axel's unique spirit, his strength, his warmth, Everett will too.

And then, we decide to head to the BNB, to meet up with our friends. I know Everett will benefit from having Sadie by his side. She'll be a source of strength and support. And I know our friends will welcome Axel with open arms, just like they did to me, with a warmth and acceptance that encapsulates the beauty of this small town.

As we walk out of the apartment, I pull out my phone and call Reese. I only catch her voicemail. I knew she and Nick were busy with his family.

"Reese," I say, my voice trembling with the events of the day. "It's going to be okay. Everything's going to be okay. We're just starting a new chapter, a new adventure. And I know, in my heart, that it's going to be beautiful."

CHAPTER 33

HOURS LATER, WE'RE ALL huddled around the fire, a group of friends, bonds created through different avenues, yet somehow intertwined by a mystical glue, a link with Elliot that resonates in our hearts. It's not shocking how everyone is getting along, really, because everyone here has been so overwhelmingly kind and gracious to me, welcoming me into their circle with a warmth that's both unexpected and deeply appreciated.

The fire crackles, casting dancing shadows on the faces around me. Conversations flow, laughter fills the air, and Axel and Everett are joking and carrying on as if they've known each other forever. And maybe, in a way, they have. They've been brought together by fate, by a twist of destiny.

There will be many new stories shared, many secrets revealed, many truths to uncover. I've already begun to share my dreams, my visions, with Axel, but for now, we need to simply feel relaxed, settled, at peace.

I walk over to the hydrangeas, their vibrant blooms a burst of color in the evening light. I stare down at the koi, listening to the water trickling around them, a gentle murmur of serenity.

Poppy approaches me, her eyes filled with intrigue. "You have that look again," she says, her voice soft, almost conspiratorial. "You're thinking hard."

"I am," I admit, a gentle smile gracing my lips. "I'm thinking about lots of things, people, life."

Poppy nods, her gaze steady. "But this time, you don't look so sad," she observes. "But are you happy?"

Her words strike a chord within me. There's a glimmer of joy, a spark of hope, a thrumming of promise, even through all of this uncertainty and sorrow. We've had this conversation not so long ago.

"I am, Poppy. Things have changed so much. I'm trying to learn to adjust to all of it. Do you know what I mean?"

"Yep. I do." She pauses, and holds my hand. Then she turns me slightly, so we are both facing the group all gathered under the patio lights. Our little family. And with the amazing wisdom this young girl always seems to hold, she adds, "Maybe this is your chance to learn to be strong. And maybe you need to just let him make you happy for the right now."

She turns the words I told her weeks ago back to me. I take it all in. I squeeze her hand. "Thank you, Poppy. I needed to hear that."

"I know you did. Now let's go back and hang out. No hiding. Okay?"

The evening settles over us like a warm blanket. Poppy and I return to the patio, the fireflies blinking their silent greetings in the dimming light. Axel, with a casual grace that belies the chaos of the past few days, picks up Josh's guitar that was on its stand under the pergola. The worn wood, the familiar feel of strings, seem to calm him, to ground him, to bring him a sense of peace. He holds it right-handed, the opposite of how Elliot would have grasped it.

He strums a chord, a gentle melody that resonates through the air. Then, he begins to play "Feels Like Rain," the John Hiatt song Elliot always played for me, with a grace that sounds like he's played it a thousand times before. He beautifully played the song that held a special place in our hearts.

An emotional tsunami came over me, but it's not sadness, not grief. It's awe, a sense of wonder as I watch Axel play, his fingers dancing across the strings, his expression filled with a quiet passion. He just looked down as he strummed, tapping his foot in rhythm, completely unaware of the many eyes watching him.

Everett looks over at me, his gaze filled with understanding, his eyes reflecting the same thoughts swirling in my mind.

I could analyze it, overthink it, try to decipher the meaning behind this unexpected choice of song. But then I decide, no. I don't want to overanalyze. I don't want to dissect the emotions, the layers of meaning.

I simply want to admire Axel, to watch him play, to listen to the music, to enjoy the sights and sounds of the evening. I want to feel the warmth of the fire, the coolness of the night air, the sense of peace that settles over me.

I want to be present, in this moment, with these people, with the memories, with the love.

And as I close my eyes, allowing the music to wash over me, I realize that Elliot's presence is merged through every atom of this moment, every shared laugh, every conversation, every comforting silence. And it is good.

This is a new chapter filled with uncertainty, with grief, with healing, with a love that transcends boundaries, a love that connects us all, a love that whispers of a destiny we're only just beginning to understand.

★★★

The coming weeks are a blur of activity, a whirlwind of emotions. I'm juggling my responsibilities at the cafe, helping Sadie navigate her busy schedule while trying to cram in last-minute studying for my MCATs. Reese and Nick are knee-deep in wedding planning, their excitement infectious, but also a little overwhelming. The grand opening for my yoga studio is looming, a challenge I'm facing with both stress and delight. I'm leading classes at the BNB, at two new pop-up locations in town, and trying to find time to be present for Everett, to offer him the support he needs.

We spend evenings chatting on the phone, swapping stories,

and offering each other a lifeline of comfort. On weekends, we're together, a blended family of sorts, with Sadie and Poppy adding their own brand of chaos and love.

Axel has been stopping by the cafe when I'm working, a quick hello, a smile that lights up the room. Sometimes we meet at the diner for lunch, gabbing about our experiences, catching up, enjoying a quiet moment together. I'm mesmerized by the way he seems so genuinely interested in learning about me, my dreams, my goals, not just stories about my past, about Elliot. He's been in contact with Everett too, offering support, building a bond that feels both fragile and powerful.

I want Axel to know more about my Chicago life, to meet Reese and Nick, to experience the warmth of their friendship. And as the wedding date draws closer, a decision takes shape in my mind. I'm going to invite Axel to the wedding. As my plus one.

It's a bold move, a step into the unknown, a gesture of faith. But I feel a deep certainty, a knowing that this is the right thing to do. It's a way of embracing the possibility of something more, something extraordinary. It's a way I can choose to be brave. I'm not sure what the future holds, what surprises await us. But I know, he belongs there with me. So I ask, and he accepts my invite with a sweet boyish grin. He flew us back, as he also had some business to tend to. We arrived in Chicago the day before the wedding.

★★★

The small rehearsal dinner is a beautiful gathering. It's intimate, filled with warmth and laughter, a celebration of love and friendship. I'd thought there might be a moment of uneasiness when Reese and Nick see Axel for the first time, when they first see the man who looks so much like Elliot. But in typical Reese fashion, she bypasses any awkwardness and pulls Axel into a hug, her warmth and acceptance a reprieve to any tension.

"It's so good to have you here, Axel," she says, her smile infectious. "It only feels right that you're here with Clover."

Nick shakes Axel's hand and gives him a big pat on the back. "Welcome aboard," he says, his voice filled with genuine warmth. "We're so glad you could make it."

Axel takes it all in stride, his strength and positive energy awe-inspiring. He never leaves my side all night, his presence the comfort I needed.

The night unfolds with a mix of laughter, hilarious stories, of tears and tender moments, of a love that's enduring. As I watch Axel navigate this new world, I can't help but feel a sense of pride. He's embracing it all with grace and resilience.

I'm grateful for him, for his support, for his love, for the way he's helping us all find our way back to each other. And I know, deep in my heart, that Elliot is watching over us, smiling, knowing that his legacy lives on, that his love has brought us together, that we're all connected by a thread of destiny that can't be broken.

The rehearsal dinner wraps up with a flurry of goodbyes and promises to see each other in the morning. Axel heads back to his condo, while Sadie, Poppy, and I make our way to the hotel. Everett has an adjoining room, a temporary arrangement that feels strangely comforting. We finish the night with popcorn and movies, staying up late, trying to find a semblance of normalcy amid our ever-shifting world.

Axel calls me later that night, his voice soft and genuine. "Goodnight, Clover," he says, his voice filled with a quiet gratitude. "I'm so grateful that you asked me to be here for the weekend, with you. And I'm looking forward to the wedding tomorrow." The warmth of his words settles over me, creating a stillness to the lingering anxieties of the day.

The next morning is filled with commotion. Axel and Everett entertain each other, their laughter echoing through the wedding venue's hallway, a reflection of the bond that's coalesced between them. Meanwhile, I do my best to make the morning perfect for

Reese, trying to keep her mother calm and composed. It's a delicate balancing act.

As the day unfolds, the excitement builds. The wedding is moments away, a celebration of love, a new beginning, a vibrant reminder of the power of human connection.

As the strings of love play tenderly, I feel a warmth enveloping me, a keepsake of all the memories I had amassed along this journey. Laughter and joy dance around us, my friends mingling with new faces, creating new memories together. As I stand here, watching Reese and Nick exchange vows, I feel a lightness in my heart—a resigned understanding that love never truly dies.

In this moment, I understand that my grief had not diminished my capacity for love. It had transformed it. I rub the feather bracelet on my wrist, a token of Elliot's love—and a reminder that he would always guide me.

Despite the ache of loss, I can almost see Elliot standing watch over me like a guardian angel. It is as though he is shining a light into my life, whispering words of encouragement to embrace both the new and the old—friends, family, and chances for love that awaited me just around the corner. To follow the path he is guiding me to, like only the best wingman can do.

The wedding ceremony is a blur of emotions, of vows and tears, of laughter and love. I exchange glances with Axel throughout the ceremony, each one a silent conversation, a mutual understanding transcending words. His smile penetrates my soul, a warm ray of sunshine that feels both familiar and exhilarating, healing me in ways I can't describe.

After the photos are all snapped, the announced walk into the reception area is a moment of pure joy. I catch Axel's gaze, and I notice his eyes following my every step, his expression stirs a need deep within me.

We find our way to each other on the dance floor, the music pumping through our veins, the lights swirling around us. He leans in, his breath a whisper against my ear. "I'm so grateful to be here with you today," he says, his voice soft, his touch sending shivers down my spine. It's a touch that awakens me in ways I can't quite explain, a touch that is so exhilarating, a touch that stirs a longing I haven't felt in years.

I lean into his touch, closing my eyes, sinking into the warmth of his presence. He brushes the bracelet on my wrist, a gentle gesture that makes my heart skip a beat.

"I didn't know Elliot like you did," he says, that sadness trickling through. "But I read his note he wrote when he ordered this bracelet. To be honest, I probably read it a hundred times. And I hadn't even met you yet. I felt the words he wrote on that paper. I felt it in my soul. And he was right. You are the most special person I've ever met."

He pauses, his gaze searching mine, his expression muddled with vulnerability and hope. "I know I missed my chance to know him, but I am so grateful for this chance to know you," he says, his voice filled with a conviction that resonates deeply within me. "I think you're amazing, Clover. Absolutely perfect."

His words are a solace, a magical notion that love can bloom, new connections can form, and happiness can be found in the most unexpected ways.

In this moment, with Axel by my side, with the music pulsing through our bodies, with the love surrounding us, I feel a sense of peace, a sense of belonging. It's a feeling that reminds me that life, in all its complexities, in all its twists and turns, can be beautiful. And as I lean into his body, I know, without a doubt, that this is just the beginning.

Axel leans in closer, his eyes searching mine, a question hanging in the air. He waits, his breath a warm whisper against my cheek, for my reaction. I lean back, my heart thrumming with nervousness and desire. This is the moment I've been wondering about, the moment that's been playing out in my dreams, the moment that feels both inevitable and impossible. And then, on the dance floor, just after my best friend married the man of her dreams, Axel and I connect, with a gentle, emotional, spectacular kiss. It's a kiss that's more perfect than I could have ever imagined, a kiss that's so much more than just a kiss. It's reveals the power of fate, the merging of souls. It's a kiss that's been years in the making, a kiss that was so very worth the wait.

As our lips break away, our foreheads still touch, a lingering fervor, a shared moment of wonder. We're both trying to comprehend the depth of what just happened, the emotions that have been unleashed.

And then, Reese, always the life of the party, starts whistling loudly, her eyes wide, her hands flashing thumbs-up signs in our direction. I can't help but laugh, a flood of pure joy washing over me. Sadie joins in, her whistle echoing Reese's, a chorus of support, a spectacle of love and laughter that fills this night.

But then, it's impossible to ignore the presence of Everett. He's a few feet away, dancing with Poppy, holding her up in his arms, swaying gently to the music. She leans in to him, her tiny hand pointing in our direction, her eyes filled with a seriousness that's both comical and endearing.

He looks up, catching our gaze, a classic Everett smirk spreading across his face, but then, he walks closer, bringing Poppy to eye level with Axel, and she looks him dead in the eyes.

"If you hurt her," she says, her voice surprisingly firm, a tone laced with a warning, "I'll punch your lights out."

A wave of laughter erupts. It's a moment of chaos and kinship, a testament to the loyalty that binds us all. The lights flicker with a sudden shift in the atmosphere, and then, a cascade of white feathers and balloons rains down on the dance floor, a magical spectacle that transforms the moment.

Whatever is ahead of us won't be easy. I know that. But I have survived the worst, the loss that had threatened to consume me. I have come out of the darkness, stronger, more resilient, more open to the possibility of hope. And if I could weather the storm of grief, I can face the challenges of love. I just have to believe in myself, to trust that I am worthy of love, of happiness, of a future that isn't defined by the pain of the past. And as Axel smiles, a warm, genuine smile that reaches his eyes, I know my soul has been stirred, awakened, and finally, truly, completely, found. Mission accomplished, wingman. Mission truly accomplished.

The End (actually, The Beginning)

ACKNOWLEDGEMENTS

To my husband Kenny, my biggest supporter. I am sure he will know he was mentioned in the dedication at the beginning of this book. However, I am more certain he will be unaware of this acknowledgement at the end. What can I say, this isn't *Hammer of the Gods.*

To my amazing beta readers, in no particular order: Calli, Jennifer, and Sheri: Thank you for your honesty and for accepting the fact that I'm about as educated in creative writing as a goldfish is in astrophysics. You are amazing!

To my parents, who gifted me a revolutionary piece of technology —a Apple IIc computer with The Print Shop floppy disk —in my youth. I have no doubt this book would have taken me another three years to finish and would have been written entirely in hieroglyphics if it weren't for your foresight. That computer taught me how to type and waste reams of paper.

To my incredible friends, especially Missy and Christal, for the countless nights over dinner and drinks, filled with laughter and endless encouragement. And we miss seeing you JG! You all keep me sane!

To Luke at Best Buy Geek Squad in Peoria. I thought I lost the entire kit and kaboodle. But you totally saved my ass and my file history. I promise I do daily backups now.

And finally, to everyone who took a chance to read this book: thank you for doing so. I hope you enjoyed it as much as I enjoyed writing it.

ABOUT THE AUTHOR

Photo Credit: Always Flourishing Photography

Tessa King is a fresh voice in contemporary women's fiction, blending her analytical skills as a medical laboratory scientist with a keen understanding of life's emotional journeys. As she embarks on her writing adventure, she explores themes of friendship, loss, and the exhilarating twists and turns of life's choices.

When she's not crafting stories, you'll find Tessa helping her husband at the drag strip, where the smell of burning rubber and racing fuel is almost as sweet as her freshly baked cookies with buttercream frosting. A devoted fan of Van Morrison's tunes, she enjoys a strong cup of coffee while spending quality time with their mischievous German Shepherd, Preacher, and a good book.

As a long-suffering Detroit Lions fan, Tessa knows that life—and writing—are full of surprises, heart, grit, and the occasional nail-biting moment. Join her on this exciting journey, where every story is a new triumph, and every character is a chance to explore the beauty of resilience and connection.

FOLLOW TESSA

https://www.tessa-king.com

https://www.facebook.com/tessakingwrites

Instagram: @tessakingwrites
Please follow me on Goodreads!
https://www.goodreads.com/tessaking

Also check out the *My Wingman* playlist on Spotify. A collection of songs that the characters share, as well as some that inspired the writing process.
My Wingman Playlist - Tessa King

https://open.spotify.com/playlist/6OMolYbNhy4pHmmwfzWJO
b?si=39f1c440e45a466a

www.ingramcontent.com/pod-product-compliance
Lightning Source LLC
Chambersburg PA
CBHW050522110726
47899CB00005B/1554